IBN  RABI'S SMALL DEATH

Modern Modern Middle East Literatures in Translation

Series Editor
Dena Afrasiabi

Other Titles in this Series Include
Poetic Justice: An Anthology of Contemporary Moroccan Poetry
The Fetishists
The Black Rose of Halfeti

Ibn Arabi's Small Death

— A NOVEL —

Mohammed Hasan Alwan

TRANSLATED BY

William Maynard Hutchins

CENTER FOR MIDDLE EASTERN STUDIES

The University of Texas at Austin

This English translation copyright ©2021 The Center for Middle Eastern Studies at The University of Texas at Austin Published in Arabic as *Mawtun Saghirun* (Beirut: Dar al-Saqi, 2016)

Translation of this novel was supported by a National Endowment for the Arts grant for literary translation for 2020.

The International Prize for Arabic Fiction (IPAF) also provided some initial funding for the translator as he began work and funded the author's literary agent.

Chapters 25-28 appeared in *Banipal 68* (Summer 2020) in an earlier version of this translation.

Cover Artwork by Samantha Strohmeyer
Book Design by Allen Griffith of Eye 4 Design

Library of Congress Control Number: 2021940173
ISBN: 978-1477324301

"*My God,*

I am not Your only lover;

But I have loved only You."

—**IBN ARABI**

CONTENTS

IBN ARABI'S SMALL DEATH

1 AZERBAIJAN 1212 CE/610 AH

This hut has a conical roof. When I lie down inside to sleep, I curl up, since the floor space is so cramped. When I stand, smoke from the fire chokes me, because it collects at the top, veiling the ceiling. When I walk outside, the sky before me resembles a fallen slice of itself rising straight from the earth. So I imagine I'll bump into the sky, if I walk toward it. The mountain peak reduces things on its slope until they're almost invisible. They look still and motionless—too insignificant to be of any interest. Grit has abraded the exterior of this hut and created countless cracks through which a cold wind whistles on winter days, rain seeps during storms, and bugs infiltrate on spring nights. When I leave the door open, an errant cloud may enter. The gusts of wind are frequently fierce enough to knock off a plank or two. Then, once the wind dies down, I spend an entire day searching for the boards. A stray nanny-goat may bleat at my door, and an ailing bird may land on the roof. Otherwise, not much happens here. Yet my heart's activities are multifarious, and the turbulence within me is dangerous.

The hut was like this the day I first took refuge here; all I've added are my belongings. These include a pallet of uncarded wool in a corner of the hut and a basin for ablutions with a comb in it. Next to the basin rest bundles of my papers, my lamp, and my threads and inkwell, in which the ink freezes during the winter. All these are on the one shelf attached to the hut's wall. Near the door is a flour bin with a water jug leaning against it. On the bin I keep a bag of salt and a basket of dates and dried figs.

Even these few possessions present many distractions to a person searching for *khalwa*, a spiritual retreat, and they pose far too many temptations for me. When I stay up late to watch the divine lights rise, the wool pallet tempts me to fall asleep. When I remain silent to hear the whisper of sacred secrets, my belly growls. So I feel hungry and grow distracted. When I light my lamp, bring out my papers, fill the inkwell, and place the paper just where I stopped the previous night, the ink as it touches the paper opens a window on the farms of Andalusia, the alleyways of Fez, the zawiyas of Tunis, the monasteries of Cairo, the trails of Mecca, the shops of Baghdad, Damascus's Ghouta, and Konya's lakes—what sort of isolation is this?

I have no idea where exactly I am on this earth, but that doesn't concern me, because God has buttressed my heart with His four Pillars. All I remember is heading east and leaving Malatya with a camel-hair bag of my belongings on my back. I walked till I felt tired, ate whatever I could find, and slept wherever I was when night fell. By the third day, the soles of my feet were callused and had turned such an odd color they no longer seemed part of my body. My beard grew increasingly shaggy, and my lips were so cracked that I couldn't open them to eat without a line of blood trickling down. Each part of my body groaned and complained as I journeyed on unceasingly. One road after another attracted me like a magnet. Hills raised me up, and valleys brought me low. I encountered people in villages and major cities and wild animals in the wastelands and deserts. The moon—crescent, waning, or full—accompanied me until mountains blocked my way.

Then I turned my face toward a peak and began my ascent. I climbed for many days only to find my way blocked. I had to descend and search for another route. I clambered higher only to find myself confronted by an abyss. I was forced to retrace my steps. So I scaled a third cliff face, looking for a passage that would bring me closer to the peak. The higher I climbed, the more acute my hunger became, because fewer plants grew there and the ground was rockier. My fingers developed sores, and my aches, which reduced me to tears at times, intensified. When I finally reached the mountain's summit, I slept out in the open the first night. The sky was clear the next morning, and I spotted this hut in the distance. I headed to it and discovered that it had been abandoned, apparently for a long time. Then I realized I had reached a retreat suitable for my calling as a *qutb*—a spiritual Pole—after fifty years on God's path, enduring seclusion, travel, hunger, exertion, and strife.

I was sleeping when the higher powers pledged support for me the night before I left Malatya. They elevated me till I rose above my bed and floated an inch in the air, lifted by the will of the Almighty, Omnipotent Lord. Levitation did not come as a surprise. I had actually been waiting for it to occur since I met the last of the earth's spiritual Pillars. This was something that had been destined before I was born. Each *jahba*, each divine attraction stuns me, though, and my heart becomes a dove in God's dominion. My speech is too ethereal, then, for ears to detect. My sight is dazzled by God's light, but my insight shines. Then God unveils to me His command for His impoverished worshipper, who is stripped of everything save Him. He orders me to write a book and disclose a science, to accompany a shaykh, to accept a disciple, to enter into seclusion when I need a spiritual retreat, and to reveal myself at the appropriate moment. Everything I do on my path toward God is what He has ordered and arranged: the easy tasks and the taxing ones, joyous and sorrowful moments, stays and departures, rational knowledge and ecstatic *shath* utterances, letters and numbers, and words and silences. So I have become the *qutb*, the Pole of divine concern, a succor for the temporal age, and a mirror of Truth. Almighty God's talisman is in my hand, as are the scales of *al-fayd*, the all-pervasive effusion, and. . . .

"Hey Man, are you here?"

The Azeri herdsman interrupted my train of thoughts—calling me from outside the hut in his foreign accent. I rose and immediately went to him, taking my container and jug. I greeted him, and he returned my greeting. He drew bread, grain, and radishes from his mule's saddlebag and placed them in my container. Then he took my jug, filled it with water from the water-skin dangling on his back, and returned it to me. Finally, he adjusted his water-skin, poked his mule, and said, "See you in a week."

I handed him two Seljuq dirhems, explaining, "I want ink and oil for the lamp."

He nodded and departed. I carried into the hut the supplies he had brought and went back outside to light a fire. I gazed at the eagles that soar around the summit at this time of day, every day, waiting for prey. I poured some water in a pot, added broad beans and a pinch of salt, and placed the pot between two burning logs. Then I sat warming myself by the fire and waited for the food to cook. I ate as the sun set and then prayed as a wolf's howl echoed from the distant mountain slope. The moon was concealed by lofty peaks, and night fell upon me like a dark box devoid of slits. Stars overhead assumed the same positions they had occupied the previous night. I eventually took shelter in my hut, lit the lamp, and sat down to write what only I can write and what only I will value. This is the life story of one of

God's friends—someone God chose, for whatever reason, and ordered to obey His command. I wrote this by the light of the lamp that never lies, even if people have different opinions about me and disagree with me on various matters.

In the name of God, the Merciful and Compassionate.

The wayfarer Muhyi al-Din Ibn Arabi said. . . .

TOME ONE

2

God granted me two *barzakhs*. The first liminal period preceded my birth, and the second followed my death. During the initial one, I witnessed my mother give birth to me. During the second I watched my son bury me. So I saw my father chortle with joy at his first-born son and my wife weep piteously on losing her aged husband. I observed the Almohads snuff out the wick of the Almoravid state in Murcia before I was born and the Tatars raze Baghdad after my death. I saw the friends of God delight in the birth of the Sultan of the Gnostics and the jurisprudents celebrate the death of the imam of the freethinkers. I witnessed all this thanks to God's universal unveiling and resplendent light during the few years of these two *barzakhs*. The speed of my passage and the need for my annihilation in this life, which is merely a line in His divine essay, the flash of a shooting star in His exalted sky, and a hoof-print on His wide earth, were all unveiled to me.

My first liminal period ended in Ramadan when I felt my mother endure the pains of labor. Her hands clutched the sides of the bed, and her mouth implored God that her newborn would be male and his birth easy. Fatima wiped the sweat of delivery from my mother's brow and the nagging fears from her heart. Once I was finally delivered, this genial midwife's face was the first I saw at the start of my life. I compared it to the thousands of faces I had seen during my *barzakh*: those of thousands of saints, thousands of pious people, and thousands of ascetics. Of all those, her face as it appeared to me then was the most compassionate. My mother blacked out when I was born, and Fatima could not place me on my mother's chest, as was customary. So she washed me, swaddled me, and began to stroke my face, like a mother. Thus my heart imprinted on her first.

She adopted me as her spiritual son the moment her eyes rested on my face, filling me with her overwhelming affection, which was my first consolation for quitting my *barzakh* and my sustenance at the beginning of my journey. It is extremely painful to leave a spiritual threshold, which consists of one unveiling after another, and enter the physical world, which consists of compound ignorance. My transition from the realm of certain truth to the world of dubious suspicions was performed by the good hand that drew me from my mother's womb: Fatima's. She richly deserved my devotion from that moment until she died in Seville, as a pious friend of God with superior charisms. By then she was an elderly woman, but her face was more beautiful and fresher than any other I have seen. She never ceased pointing to my heart and saying: "Purify this."

Once my mother regained consciousness, neighbor women and the midwife's assistants crowded around her. They kissed her and repeated: "Blessed emancipation!" Then more women entered our house one by one to congratulate my mother on having become a free woman by bearing her owner a son. Each woman looked down at me with her giant face, laughing and repeating pious sentiments: *Allahu Akbar, Subhan Allah,* and *La ilaha illallah.* That evening Fatima carried me to my father, who rejoiced wholeheartedly. When my gaze fell on his round face, I learned at once that my birth explained the mole that had rested beneath his left eye his entire life. Fatima interpreted it as good news for him and said: "Ali, the mole's location means you will sire a son who will increase your renown and preserve your status. Since it is beneath your eye, though, it means he won't follow in your footsteps."

My father had carried my destiny on his face since he was born, but only when his son slept soundly before him in the cradle was that prophecy made flesh. As I grew, I started reaching for that mole, wanting to fiddle with it. He would laugh, since he thought I was trying to move it. He didn't realize that I accessed pure faces and lofty voices through it. I recited Fatima's prophecy repeatedly so I wouldn't forget it, even though my father did. I have increased my father's renown—I know that—but have also deserted his path, shunning service in kings' courts. My face is round like his, though, and I have his brown eyes, prominent cheekbones, straight nose, and full head of hair. From my mother I inherited my delicate limbs, wide brow, neatly aligned teeth, and jutting chin. As a child, when I contracted my eyebrows for any reason, my mother would laugh because I looked so much like my father. I later added to my features a gash on my chin when the protruding branch of an almond tree plunged into it, leaving a gaping wound the length of my finger. The scar remained visible till my beard hid it when I matured.

That accident occurred when my father woke one morning to find I had risen before him and gone out to play in the garden. Redstart birds were fluttering between arching intertwined branches of the two orange trees on either side of the doorway. Red squirrels were scurrying around the almond tree, gnawing on nuts that had fallen from it. Thrushes swooped down to drink from the fountain and then rose to land on the tile roof of our house. My father had barely finished breakfast when he heard me bawling. He rushed to me and picked me up, soiling his thawb with the blood that spurted from the wound on my chin. He carried me to the home of the court physician, who lived in our neighborhood. He kicked on the man's door, since he was holding me, and shouted loudly to summon the doctor, who finally appeared.

"Will you take a look at this?"

"Good gracious! This will end well, God willing. What happened to you, boy?"

"The almond tree struck me."

He smiled and ushered us inside. I leaned my head against his thigh, and he wet a cloth to wipe away the blood so he could inspect the wound.

"Periosteum," he said, "but it didn't reach the bone."

"Will you stitch the wound?"

"Stitches won't help something this size. It will heal by itself."

"But it's bleeding."

"Bandage it with a sponge or piece of cloth, and the bleeding will soon end. The blow didn't strike a vein. I'll give you medicine to help it heal."

Heading to his medicine cabinet, he asked my father, "Would you prefer an ointment or a powder?"

"Whichever stings less."

"I'll give you some gallnut salve for you to apply to the wound today. It will smart but using litharge I'll prepare another ointment for you to use tomorrow to help the flesh grow back. I'll send that to your house."

"May God reward you!"

My father carried me home, deposited me with my mother, and went to wash and change before he departed for the palace—as his choice of garments revealed. If he wore his Tunisian vest, fastening it with a silk sash, and then donned a silk brocade jubbah and a turban, we knew that this was an ordinary day and that he was going off to work in King Muhammad ibn Mardanish's palace. If he placed a skullcap or shawl on his head, we knew he wasn't heading there but going out either to visit someone or to make a purchase in the market. If he wore a Berber burnous without a sash and a shawl without a skullcap, he was probably going to teach or discuss hadith at Murcia's mosque. Every pursuit had its own style of dress. Silk brocade was for attending the king. A *taylasan* shawl was for interacting with the general public. A burnous was for the mosque. My father's different occupations required him to be three men in one, without his ever noticing how harmful it is to lodge three hearts inside a single chest. There was a similar political division in those days in southern Andalusia, which was divided into three states: the Almoravid, Almohad, and Frankish.

The only person who dared to challenge my father about his internal contradictions was Abdallah al-Qattan. This happened the day I invited him to have supper at our house in Seville, many years after we left Murcia. I was sixteen then and spent a lot of time with al-Qattan, who didn't lecture in a mosque or madrasa but taught passersby and mendicants in the streets, without any remuneration. He discussed subjects they did and didn't understand, exhorting them to act in certain ways, not others. I asked him to dine in our house one day when rain was falling in torrents. He was soaking wet and sitting beneath the Haniya Arch in Seville. So he accepted. When my father, who was clad in short pants and a thin summer shirt, heard our din in the courtyard and that of the cook preparing our food, he called down to me from his balcony: "Muhyi, who's that with you?"

"Shaykh Abdallah al-Qattan."

"Our best visitor ever! Welcome and greetings to him. I'll join you."

My father came downstairs after pulling on his house burnous. Hastening to the shaykh, he kissed him between the eyes and greeted him cordially. "You honor my house and bless my dwelling, Shaykh. I hope you are well."

"I am fine, Ali. May God honor and bless you."

When the servant placed before us sweet and sour (*zirbaj*) pigeon casserole, a plate of figs, and a dish of cooked vegetables, my father urged al-Qattan, who looked quite severe, to begin eating. Al-Qattan stared down at the food, though, as if he didn't see it. Suddenly he raised his head, seized my father's chin, and yelled at him: "Ill-fated old age! Isn't it time that you feared God? How much longer will you keep company with these tyrants in their courts and palaces?"

Then he released my father's chin and pushed away the platter of food. Spreading his arms contemptuously, he shouted at my father: "Are you content to meet death in your pathetic state? Are you happy with that? What? Answer me!"

I stared at my father, whose head was bowed. He clearly looked embarrassed but, I thought, also vexed. The shaykh lowered his head to gaze into my father's eyes. In a slightly softer voice he asked, "Doesn't this son of yours provide you an example? He is young, with all that implies of youth's passions, but he has overcome his desires and rejected his demon. He has changed course to seek God the Exalted. He spends his time with God's people, while you, an iniquitous adult, stand at the brink of the pit of fire."

My father cast me a glance I couldn't decipher. Was he upset I listened to a shaykh who preferred me to him? Did he assume I had complained about him to al-Qattan and arranged this rude lesson? Then he sobbed, pretended to weep, and rubbed his eyes to cause a tear to fall. He began to declare that all power is God's alone and to ask God's forgiveness. Al-Qattan ended his sermon then, said *bismillah*, and reached for some food. His expression suddenly relaxed. He raised his eyebrows, and the angry look disappeared from his face.

As if he had not just been shouting at my father seconds earlier, he commented appreciatively, "What a plump pigeon, Ali! Would you believe that I first thought it was a little chicken?"

3

My father was too busy at court to offer any sacrifice for me on my seventh day, when my hair was cut, or on the fourteenth. On my twenty-first day, though, he took a sheep from the palace's livestock pen and led it to the butcher. Then he brought the meat home and instructed my mother to roast it in a single pan. So she did. Once the food was offered to people, my father's associates from the king's court ate the mutton. My paternal uncle Abdallah and his young children did too, along with the neighborhood's poor, who are invited to festivities for newborns. Qadi Ibn Urjun and Ibn Fatah, the preacher at the great mosque, however, ate only some of the vegetables and fruit spread around the platter's sides and avoided the meat.

A mendicant asked the two men, "Why aren't you eating the meat?"

Neither answered, so he left them alone. When my father went to fetch more food and my uncle rose to wash his hands, Ibn Fatah whispered to the man, "This sheep certainly comes from the king's pen."

"So? What's wrong with that?"

"Don't you know there are swine in his livestock pen?"

Without eating their fill, the judge and the preacher rose and went to the basin to wash their hands. They were pious and righteous men but also cowards. They didn't dare oppose the serious developments in Murcia, where conditions had deteriorated from bad to worse since Ibn Mardanish had exploited the power vacuum between the collapse of the Almoravid State and the rise of the Almohads to seize control of the city of Murcia and appoint himself its king. These two men's cowardice safeguarded their posts throughout those years. When a ruler is corrupt, corruption runs rampant through the community. When a land is besieged, fresh air cannot circulate through its stifling rooms. When career choices are limited and hope vanishes, people pleading hardship and necessity feel justified in perpetrating every type of evil.

Ibn Mardanish relied on Franks to prop up his rule, and Ibn Urjun issued the fatwa justifying that. Then the king concluded an alliance with the Frankish king Alfonso, who provided him hundreds of Christian mercenaries, who strutted everywhere in Murcia as if the city belonged to them. The king even built churches and taverns for them. If a Frank quarreled with a Muslim, their dispute was brought to the king, not to the qadi. That way Ibn Mardanish could guarantee the Christian received a verdict that wouldn't upset the mercenaries. Once the Almohads began besieging him, most Muslims enlisted under the banner of a caliph whose Islamic allegiance was clear rather than that of a king whose religion and true identity we no longer knew for certain.

Alfonso's mercenaries and Ibn Urjun's fatwas were useless during that punishing siege. Murcia's fruits, which had always been cheap and plentiful, became difficult for the general public to afford, and hardly anyone but the rich could eat meat. In the great carpet market, half of the workshops closed, due to the scarcity of wool, linen, and silk, which came from Valencia, Granada, and Tunis. Silversmiths bought more items than they sold. The streets were crowded with beggars, and boats disappeared from the Segura River after sailors stopped transporting people because the travelers could no longer pay. The one trade that flourished was teaching in the mosque, where the number of learning circles doubled because so many lawyers' practices had failed. Teaching was their only remaining source of income. People approached them searching for peace of mind and reassurance in a time of anxiety and siege.

Ibn Mardanish rarely left his palace. When he did walk through the streets, he surrounded himself with many soldiers and stalwart bodyguards, because he feared for his life. At noon on the fourth Eid al-Adha since the beginning of the siege, he was obliged to pray in public with the people, to offer a sacrificial sheep at the shepherds' fold near the river, and to announce that his sacrificial offering atoned for the transgressions of all his subjects. Therefore no citizen would be allowed to offer his own sacrificial victim, no matter how rich or poor he was. The herald summarized the king's declaration in this way: "Our great, triumphant warrior king Muhammad ibn Sa'd ibn Mardanish, out of affection for his subjects and to relieve their burdens, has sacrificed a plump ram on their behalf."

Following the Eid prayer, Ibn Mardanish delivered a speech that lasted only a few minutes, saying:

"My people, patience is the key to deliverance. As you see, God's enemies are besieging you and preventing you from earning a living. If they actually were your religious brethren, as they claim, they would not have done this. But God wants the best for you, and many an apparent harm proves beneficial. Have you not heard about the plague that has spread throughout Andalusia, carrying off the kids then their parents and leaving people without a single sheep or camel? Here you are, thanks to God, sheltered from it. This epidemic won't spread here or harm us while no one enters or leaves our city."

No one believed him. People were fed up, and their patience was exhausted. His alliance with the Franks had offended their pious hearts, and his raids against the Almohads had starved their empty bellies. Over and beyond all that, their own eyes saw Frankish soldiers swagger down the streets by day and behave wantonly by night. Their own ears heard how rude these foreigners were to Ibn Mardanish in his palace. Taxes were levied, in spite of the siege, on the pretext that new merchandise arrived now and then, whenever the Almohads temporarily lifted their siege because the Franks were skirmishing with them. The city's inhabitants hated him, and he knew it. He rarely left his palace for fear they would take vengeance on him. One day when he did venture from the palace on horseback, surrounded by his troops, he was accosted by a man who made people laugh with his dancing monkey: "Ibn Mardanish!"

The king ignored him. So the monkey handler cupped his hands to form a megaphone and shouted as loudly as he could: "Speak to me! Even God spoke to Moses."

Then Ibn Mardanish halted and summoned him. He demanded, "What did you say?"

"I said: Speak to me! Even God spoke to Moses."

Ibn Mardanish turned his steed's neck and yelled angrily at him: "That was Moses, but you're not Moses!"

As he rode off, the monkey keeper shouted after him, "That was God, but you're not God!"

The man received the beating of his life that day. A guardsman also drew his sword and struck the head of the poor monkey, which fell down dead. People gathered around the wounded man after the guards left, but he didn't say anything. Instead, he struggled to his feet, picked up his dead monkey, and disappeared from sight. No one ever saw him again. For his part, the king stopped leaving his palace and grew quite paranoid. He no longer visited his women's rooms by night. Instead, he chose a bed chamber of his own and summoned whichever wife or slave woman he fancied. Then he washed his hands of them and passed weeks without touching a woman. Eventually he grew so frightened that he had all of them evicted from his wing of the palace. Later he brought them back to his *iwan* but ordered a small tower built for him to sleep in. He stationed soldiers on the first floor, bodyguards on the second, and the loyal slaves he trusted most on the third. Then he slept on the top floor.

4

I walked before I was one. One evening, while crawling, I stood up without swaying or stumbling and walked like a child of two or three. Fatima laughed and predicted I would travel far, and I have. From the time God created me in Murcia till my death in Damascus, my life has been a continuous journey. I have seen diverse lands, met many people, associated with God's special friends, and lived under the rule of the Almohads, Ayyubids, Abbasids, and Seljuqs while I followed the path God ordained for me before He created me. Anyone born in a city under siege has an unruly desire to venture outside its walls. During excursions when my uncle took us and his kids near the river, I would stroke Murcia's stone walls and wonder what lay beyond them. *Another country like our own? Cities larger than ours? People like us—or different?* When I asked my uncle, he drew a small map in the dirt to show me the locations of nearby cities, as well as others farther away. The image of that dirt map was etched into my mind and allowed me to travel in my imagination south to Cartagena, north to Valencia, and west to Cordova, Seville, and Granada.

My uncle Abdallah was some years older than my father. They did not know exactly how many, but four babies had been delivered between them and died young. Our house lay on the way from my uncle's home to his shop. For this reason, he was always a familiar figure in our home, especially once my father was always at the palace and my mother gave birth to twin girls. Then no one in our house had time for me. My uncle noticed that and began to take me with him wherever he went—to his shop, where he sold oils, spices, herbs, and medicines, or to his house, which was enlivened by his three daughters and two sons. My father even performed the Friday prayer with the king at court. So my uncle felt obliged to take me with him when he went to pray at the mosque. Occasionally my uncle also ate lunch with my father and would take his siesta in our garden. During my mother's pregnancy, he brought her herbs and medicines. Because he took a keen interest in our household, he was troubled by my father's behavior.

Once, when they were dining in the courtyard, his criticism grew so heated that my mother opened her window to see why my father had raised his voice. He was asking, "Should I leave the court? Tell me, by your Lord, where I would go if I quit the palace, now that Murcia is besieged."

My uncle Abdallah spread his arms wide to show that he would welcome my father and then threw his head back as he offered, "Be my partner in my business. Sit with me in my shop."

"You barely make enough to feed your children. How could I share your profits?"

"Neither of us will die of hunger, but one of us may die by the sword!"

My uncle placed his hand on my father's knee and continued entreatingly: "Brother, I'm worried about you. What if the Almohads storm Murcia and arrest you along with the king because you're a member of his court? What if the people of Murcia rebel and don't distinguish between a vizier and a stable hand in the king's palace?"

My father was peeved by this discussion. Trying to change the subject, he said, "No one is going to rebel, man, and the Almohads lift their siege from time to time. They'll soon recognize us and make peace."

"That's court chatter. Would you like to know what the people are saying? Hear it from me: Everyone thinks the best thing that can happen is for Murcia to surrender to the Almohads. The people they rule—from Seville to Toledo—enjoy a good life in comfortable circumstances."

"Murcia's different."

"To the Maghribis, we're all Andalusians. The Almohads don't differentiate between eastern and western Andalusia."

My father sat up straight and retorted angrily: "Brother, suppose I listen to you. Do you think Ibn Mardanish will let me quit his court under these circumstances? By God, he will certainly throw me in prison."

My mother started sobbing when she heard the word "prison," and then my father yelled at her, "Close your window, Nur!"

My mother dropped the curtain over the window but left it open, and both my father and uncle lowered their voices. My father continued, "The king's circumstances don't allow him to tolerate any defections from his court. He's like a wounded lion."

Almost in a whisper, he added: "One of his slaves confided to me that some nights the king wakes up terrified. When he's jittery, he rouses everyone in the palace and orders them to keep him company."

My uncle sat up and stamped his foot lightly to show his annoyance. Then he replied, "Your king isn't a lion. He's a depraved wolf and will pay for his depravity. Where is his ally Alfonso, who used to pay him *jizya* to defend him against the Almohads? Where are his Christian pals who have filled our city with their churches? They've turned the backs of their shields on him now."

Resting his hands on his knees before he rose, he continued, "When the Almohad army attacks Murcia, they will certainly deal with him."

Her head in her hands, my mother wept at what she heard. Her anxiety had increased day by day, and what my uncle said only made her more fretful. How unlucky she was to have been emancipated only to find her city besieged. Even worse—she was the wife of a minister at the court of a besieged king who had bloodthirsty enemies outside and inside the city's walls. If things went from bad to worse, the Almohads might take her captive and enslave her again.

My father was aware of the grim prospects my uncle considered likely. His tongue denied them, but the rest of his body believed them. He lost weight, his beard turned gray, and his face lost its cheerful expression. At night he sat for long periods by the courtyard's fountain—till midnight occasionally—while he read court documents and received guests we didn't know. He imagined himself dying in any of a thousand hideous ways should someone dig a tunnel through which the Almohads infiltrated or if some fellow lit the fuse of insurrection for the hungry, barefoot people in the markets and alleys. Only God knew what the days would bring, but everyone was sure something would change.

The event that everyone anticipated, without knowing what it would be, so preoccupied people that everything ground to a halt. No one remembered the last time a new house had been built or a new shop had opened. No one placed confidence in the future. Each man kept a firm grip on his dinars and dirhems, selling and buying only basic necessities. As conditions worsened, the number of homeless and impoverished people wandering the streets and knocking on doors multiplied. They ate from rubbish bins and begged from passersby. Whenever soldiers weren't watching, they stole and looted. For this reason, Ibn Mardanish stationed his mercenaries throughout the city and charged them with patrolling it night and day. He positioned the fiercest of them at the wall to make sure citizens didn't allow the Almohads to slip in.

5

My mother spilled the pot of broth she was cooking for supper and scalded her toes and the side of her heel. She fell to the floor, and her hip swelled. She was weeping on the kitchen floor when my father came to help. So he decided to find someone to assist her. He brought home a short slave named Sallum, who was in his thirties, had curly hair, small ears, and a round face. My mother gave him a dark wool shirt and some old trousers that had belonged to my father. The next day she asked him, "What do you cook, Sallum?"

"My lady, your servant Sallum prepares Seville-style pickles, Fez-style meat casseroles, basted chicken, stews flavored with rose-water syrup, pot-roasted lamb, and all types of clotted milk and leavened foods, and sausages. . . ."

"Do you cook vegetable *marwaziya* stews or semolina and cheese dumplings? We don't have much meat."

"Yes, my lady. I fix those the way they do in Granada. I don't know how they're prepared in Murcia."

"With honey, figs, and almonds, when these are available, or with dates and plums."

My mother tested his cooking the first time my father hosted a banquet after he bought Sallum—inviting a number of guests without revealing their names. Sallum prepared many dishes, since my father had ordered him to go all out to honor these visitors. They handed around a letter that bore the seal of Ibrahim ibn Hamushk and spoke so loudly that they appeared to be quarreling. Addressed to the king, the message had been thrown over the wall and brought to my father by soldiers.

My father's guests departed, but he remained seated in the courtyard, clutching the letter in which Ibn Mardanish's last ally—Ibn Hamushk—announced that he was rebelling against him and had pledged allegiance to the Almohads. He reread it a number of times and then paced around the courtyard before sitting back down. He was so distraught that he threw the letter to the ground and shouted furiously: "You did it! You did it, you cropped-ear wonder!"

Then he called Sallum, who rushed to him. "Go to my brother Abdallah's house and ask him to come here now."

Sallum had barely opened the door to depart when my father called him back: "Never mind. Don't go now. You'll go tomorrow."

He continued circling the courtyard like a millstone. Finally, after moving the food aside, he brought his inkwell, its threads, and his paper and wrote:

From Muhammad ibn Sa'd ibn Mardanish, King of Eastern Andalusia, to Caliph Yusuf ibn Abd al-Mu'min, Caliph of the Muslims and Imam of the Almohads. . . .

At that point, he stopped writing and bowed his head. He was lost in thought, his mouth hung open, and his eyes gazed at an invisible object in the courtyard. Then he shoved aside the paper he had been writing on and brought out a fresh sheet. He wrote:

From Murcia's Judge, the Grand Mosque's Imam, and the Chief Scholar of Hadith
To the Caliph of the Muslims, the Imam of the Almohads . . . .

He set that sheet aside and took another piece of paper on which he wrote:

From Murcia's citizens, represented by Ali ibn Arabi,
To the Commander of the Caliph's army, Ibrahim ibn Hamushk. . . .

News of Ibrahim ibn Hamushk's revolt and of the Almohads' growing impatience riled the residents of Murcia. Rumors spread that the Almohad army possessed catapults that threw fire and flaming naphtha and that all the communities surrounding Murcia—in Lorca, Segura, and Almeria—had fallen to the Almohads, surrendering their fortresses and castles. Moreover, the Almohad army had established supply points all the way from Malaga to Murcia. Thus the current siege would not be intermittent, as previous ones had been. The mortal blow was delivered when Alfonso withdrew his small garrisons to the north of the city and moved them to reinforce his positions in the interior.

All these reports reached my mother's ear thanks to the beauticians who applied depilatories to her legs, seamstresses who made her clothes, wet nurses who helped feed her two infant daughters, women who sold fashion accessories, fortune tellers, perfume vendors, masseuses, and even the few neighbor women who had begun to visit her once she was emancipated and became the lady of the house. (Previously she hadn't been allowed to receive visitors.) As usual, these women mixed their reports together—while swearing to their reliability and accuracy. My mother believed each of them without the least hesitation. They told her the king had locked his mother in a room of the palace because he doubted her loyalty and had ordered that she be denied visitors. Food was handed to her through a hole in the door, as if she were a prisoner. The critical tone they used to relay this story revealed their intense disapproval.

"Disgraceful! . . . Just what you'd expect of Ibn Mardanish."

"His name's Ibn Martinez, not Mardanish, sister! He's a pure-blooded Frank!"

"This must be how Franks treat their mothers."

One day when my mother was flummoxed by all these rumors, my father returned home with a hauberk he propped against the fountain. Then he went up to his room. When my mother entered the courtyard and saw the armor, she began trembling with fright. She became nauseous and vomited in the fountain. Then she sat on the ground beside it with one leg extended and the other beneath her, the way keening women do at funerals, and began to wail. When he heard her, my father looked down from above and shouted, "What's wrong with you, Crazy Woman?"

She didn't turn to look at him or seem to hear him. She continued screaming: "War! War! Prisoners! Prisoners! Woe! Woe to you, Nur. You'll become a slave again after being freed."

"What war, woman? There won't be a war. Get up."

My mother was too weak to rise. She continued weeping softly and moaning. Her eyes resembled two waterwheels on the Segura River. She went on crying, even after my father told her that his hauberk was a messenger's armor, not a warrior's, and that he was going to take a letter from the King to the Almohad army the next day. "No one knows what it says, and God hasn't revealed that to me yet." Even so, she wailed some more and slapped her cheeks.

"Couldn't the king find some other messenger—not you?" she asked him. "People know you're his confidant and in charge of his palace. They will seize and kill you or use you as a bargaining chip."

"Woman, this isn't how war is waged. Messengers aren't killed."

I was the only one who heard my father's heart pound faster as he responded to my mother—with words that did not succeed in allaying his fears, let alone hers. He knew she might be right. The Almohads considered Ibn Mardanish and his whole court to be infidels because they had allied themselves with the Franks against the Muslims, and traitors because they had revolted against the Almohads and attacked them before the siege. They might decide it was too late for a truce or armistice and not grant amnesty to anyone for his previous treason or lies. There could be no more eloquent response to show Ibn Mardanish how angry they were than to kill his messenger.

But he had no alternative. None of the leading citizens of Murcia would agree to act as messenger. The mosque's preacher claimed to be ill, even though he was in the best of health. Ibn Urjun, the qadi, excused himself on the grounds that he had issued the fatwa legitimizing an alliance with the Franks and therefore might be crucified. The king's chamberlain claimed he couldn't leave Ibn Mardanish when he was so ill. The chief merchant had fled the city some months ago and traveled to North Africa, leaving the market without a leader. The king's two sons were busy with their own affairs and alleged that a king's sons weren't dispatched as messengers. Moreover, if the king sent someone who wasn't a leading citizen of

Murcia, that would be considered an affront to Ibn Hamushk and diminish any hope of a positive response.

So my father found he was the only person who could take the letter. He donned his armor and picked up the leather bag containing the king's seal and letter, along with other epistles from Murcia's leading citizens. Two horsemen and a woman in a howdah were waiting for him at our doorway. He joined her, and they all headed to the point in Murcia's wall nearest to the Almohad army. The soldiers raised a ladder for him. Then he climbed to the top of the wall and waved a courier's white flag toward the army. When he signaled to his companions, they assisted the woman out of the howdah and helped her climb the ladder. She had difficulty because she was plump. Once she reached the top, my father drew up the ladder and let it down the other side. When he descended, he found two Almohad cavalrymen heading toward him. He stood in front of the woman and proclaimed in a resolute voice: "I am Ali ibn Arabi, a messenger from King Muhammad ibn Mardanish to Caliph Yusuf ibn Abd al-Mu'min. This is Salma bint Hamushk. The king has ordered me to escort her, with all the respect due an honored, beloved spouse, to her brother Ibrahim ibn Hamushk. He has granted her a divorce; she is no longer his wife."

Meanwhile my mother, who was suffering from a terrible headache, had tied a yellow cloth around her head. My two sisters were playing with a dove they had found hobbling around the courtyard with a broken wing. Since late that morning my Uncle Abdallah had been sitting where my father normally sat, and one of his sons was with him. I went back and forth between them and my two sisters with the dove. The weather was clear, even though I sensed that God's descending decrees were casting shadows over Murcia. Since breezes gently rocked the branches of the two orange trees, I felt reassured that these were good decrees. The weather wasn't still, the way it was before the shout flattened Thamud, or violently windy as before Ad's punishment.[1]

Some hours later my father appeared at the top of the wall and climbed back down the ladder. The moment his feet touched ground in Murcia he mounted his horse and rode to the palace. When he arrived there, he yelled to the guards: "Where is Prince Ghanim?"

Before anyone could reply, Prince Ghanim ibn Mardanish, who had heard my father's voice, emerged from the palace. The two men entered the king's council chamber, where the king had not received anyone for months, and locked the door. They had a brief discussion, and my father left and came home. He entered the house while we were gathered around our meal. My mother rushed to him the moment she saw him but halted a few steps away. She was silent and didn't know what to do. She gazed at his face, conscious that what he said then would decide not only her fate and her children's but that of the entire city. His rigid features, however, revealed nothing and he headed to his room without uttering a word. My mother returned to sit with us. She reached for a bite of food but then set it back on the platter. She rose again and went upstairs to my father.

She asked, "What happened, Ali?"

"You'll learn in due time, Nur."

"Will we be all right?"

"Yes, have no fear."

My mother helped him remove his cloak and clothes, which she carried away. Then she brought him a basin of water for his ablutions. She washed him and spread out a prayer rug. Then he proclaimed God's supremacy and calmly recited with relief: "When God's victory and conquest come. . . ."[2]

6

The next morning, God granted victory and conquest—to the Almohads of course, not to Ibn Mardanish. People heard the royal herald in the streets and followed him to his customary spot at the entry to the souk. He stopped there, puffed out his chest, raised a hand as if to invoke the heavens, and declared:

> Our triumphant, most zealous king, Muhammad ibn Sa'd ibn Mardanish, manifesting his affection for the children of his subjects, to lighten the burden of the siege for them, since it has cost them dear, has received messengers from the Almohads. They have brought our king a portentous treaty in which they petition for hostilities to cease and the city gates to be opened; then the siege will be lifted. The king has consented to this peace treaty, with God as his witness, protecting those behind them.

That same day, when the gates opened at noon, the Almohads found droves of poor and homeless people waiting for them. Ibn Mardanish's soldiers had driven them there to greet the Almohads. If the advancing troops' intentions were good, their hearts would be moved by all these hungry folks dressed in dirty rags, with vacant gazes and matted hair. On the other hand, if their intentions were sinister and they ran their swords through these deplorable people, other citizens would be able to take steps to defend themselves or to turn tail and flee wherever they could.

Once the gate opened wide, minutes that seemed an eternity passed before anyone entered. Then a squad of infantrymen clad in chain mail and iron armor appeared in two parallel columns. Once they passed through the gate, these two columns separated, and each walked parallel to the wall beside it. Then another squad entered in the same formation. Next came groups of cavalrymen, four abreast. The men of each group stationed themselves in the plaza inside the gate: two to the right and two to the left. Behind them came columns of lancers brandishing their weapons. Finally came columns of infantrymen, who marched past the lancers and cavalry. They took the lead, proceeding slowly and cautiously, scanning windows and doors for any sign of an ambush.

In a matter of hours, half the Almohad army was inside the city walls, and the other half was stationed outside. Soldiers quickly took control of the city, staking out strategic points at entryways to the markets, mosques, and neighborhoods, with their units placed no farther than fifty meters apart, for fear they would be caught off guard and attacked. Weapons began to be collected in the plaza near the mosque, in separate heaps according to type. Swords went in one pile, daggers and knives in another, spears in a third, arrows in one stack, and bows in another. The army's heralds toured the streets to proclaim that anyone who turned in his weapon would be safe but that persons found with weapons would have their own blood on their hands.

In a few hours, the army felt confident that the city had surrendered completely, without any resistance worth mentioning. At that time, soldiers began to remove their helmets, and some entered the public baths to bathe. Others brought out their money and began to make purchases from shops. Soon passersby stopped to greet the Almohad soldiers, to chat with them, and to bring them food and drink. Local residents asked troops where they were from. Frankish mercenaries were permitted to leave Murcia unharmed and without a fight, provided they surrendered their swords, spears, and arrows. They were allowed to retain their horses and rations. Whenever I left our house, I saw Almohad flags, which resembled a chessboard, hanging over the city's gates, walls, and fortresses. In the mosque I occasionally stood beside a soldier wearing a breastplate and military gear. I shook hands with troops when the opportunity arose.

Life pulsed through the city's arteries once more as shuttered shops reopened, deserted markets thronged with customers, and vendors' voices filled Murcia's ears. Nomadic herdsmen returned to the city with many sheep and goats, and a caravan brought wool, linen, and silk from Cartagena. Mouths, bellies, and pockets filled, and contented hearts entertained Almohad troops till almost no house in Murcia failed to host a foot soldier, cavalryman, or commander at a banquet, as people tried to ingratiate themselves with these troops. For weeks my father continued heading to the court as if nothing had changed. Then one day he returned with news for my mother, who was thirsty for information: "King Ibn Mardanish has died."

My mother beat her chest and shouted: "My God!"

"And we're moving."

"Where?'

"Seville."

Four mounts were reserved for us in the caravan heading to Seville. My father discouraged us from taking many of our possessions, because most were worn out from use during the siege when no replacements had been available in the markets. The thought of travel made me giddy with delight. While our stuff was being carried from our house to the camels, I watched elatedly and toted as much myself as I could till we emptied the house and closed its doors. My mother then proceeded to sweep the courtyard, as if trying to console our dwelling, which we were leaving for the foreseeable future. Twenty years later, when I returned to Murcia to sell this house, I found my mother's broom still lying where she had left it beside the marble drain. Its straws had snapped and dried out, layers of dirt had settled on top of it, and grass was growing through the gaps. Both my parents had died by then, my beard had grown long, and I had been invested with two Sufi cloaks.

One camel carried two large bags containing all our family's clothes. My mother sat in a howdah with the two little girls on another camel. Sallum rode a mule, which also carried one bag of his possessions and a second filled with the pots and kettles he would use to cook for us en route. My father rode in front on a mare. His leather bag contained his papers, seals, an inkwell, and its threads. I began to switch from one mount to another and to walk when the ground was firm enough that animals wouldn't kick up dust. I got inside the howdah with my mother to sleep when I felt tired. I would also run forward about twenty camels to my Uncle Abdallah and his kids to play with them. Fatima bint al-Muthanna set out in the caravan with us, riding a she-mule. She intended to leave our caravan and head to Cordova. When we reached the intersection where the caravan split into two approximately equal halves, we all said goodbye to her.

When my turn came, Fatima said, "Come here, Son."

"Gladly, Mother."

"One of the four Pillars certainly lives in Seville."

"Who are these *awtad*?"

"They are the four perfect individuals who protect the earth from harm."

"How will I recognize them?"

"They will recognize you."

"How will I find them?"

"They will find you."

She hugged me for such a long time that I grew restless. Then she slipped her palm inside my shirt and held it against my chest while she closed her eyes and recited the Fatiha. Tapping her fingers precisely on the spot where my heart was, she said, "Purify this. Then follow it. Only at that time will your Pillar find you."

Because I was a child and cavalier about the pangs of separation, I remembered everything that happened but only felt the pain later, as an adult. The sufferings of God's friends are like debts that aren't collected from children but aren't excused either. Years later I was teaching a class, surrounded by students, when I remembered them. I suddenly began to weep for no apparent reason.

So they asked, "What's wrong, Master?"

I replied: "I just remembered a debt and have paid it."

"Who was the creditor?"

"God's decree."

"What did you owe?"

"An expression of pain at a separation that God imposed on me. I didn't pay my debt back then because I was young. It continued to hover between the heavens and the earth till the appointed time came and it descended."

My most perceptive student asked, "Why didn't God excuse your debt, since you were young?"

"If He had meant to excuse it, He wouldn't have decreed it for me at all. And He is omniscient. God's decree doesn't miss anyone. Each of you will pay your childhood debts when you mature. Anyone who starts feeling remorseful for no apparent cause and who experiences pain for no reason should realize that he is paying off a debt he forgot . . . even though the Creditor didn't."

For the first time in my life I saw Murcia from outside. My entire terrestrial world had been confined within those walls, and they had disappeared hours ago. When the sun set, we couched the camels, and people ate and drank. I sat on a pouf, near my father, who was surrounded by his colleagues. My father made me sit there for fear some harmful creature would bite me. I dangled my feet over its edge, but they didn't touch the ground. My ears and eyes were on the same level with those of the grownups. So I didn't feel I was any younger or less significant than the men around me.

"Travel not accompanied by some triumph is untrustworthy."

——IBN ARABI

7

An enchanting calm enveloped us that night—disturbed only by the camels' grumbling or the horses' whinnies. Shortly before dawn we began to hear the clatter of containers or the rustling movement of someone who had awakened early. Soon a man raised the call to prayer. Then everyone woke and made a ruckus, heading off in different directions to answer nature's call and perform their ablutions before offering the dawn prayer. Once that was concluded, we prepared to resume our travels. The caravan's grooms hitched all the camels to each other with a halter. People quickly ate whatever they had at hand and climbed onto their mounts after lifting women into their howdahs. Finally, from the front, the leader of the caravan shouted and his crew, who were distributed all along it, repeated his call to depart. So our trek resumed.

This route is pleasant in the spring. Our caravan walked beside rivers and canals. We were never more than a few hours away from a river or a small village. We walked parallel to the Guadalentín River as far as the city of Lorca. The river itself ended there, continuing only as rivulets, small canals, a string of lakes near the road, and other streams running south. When we approached Granada, we walked near the Genil River for a few days. We frequently couched our camels by the river so we could draw water for drinking and cooking. Whenever we had the camels kneel, the caravan's grooms came and unfastened the long halter that linked one to another. Then each group would sit between its own mounts. Sallum would rush to the river to fill his pots with water and prepare simple dishes from rabbits caught along the way or carp that servants speared from the river's shallows and sold to people. The caravan also carried bamboo cages filled with chickens and wild partridge as well as sacks full of Valencia rice and dried figs. Some animals carried wooden boxes that had vegetables growing in them, and people would pick greens to eat.

Occasionally a bunch of men would separate from the caravan as we approached a city. They would enter it and buy the supplies, fruit, and medicine that people in the caravan had ordered. My father once sent Sallum with them to buy Jaén grapes, but he returned empty-handed because vendors there wouldn't accept the Mardanish dinar, even though merchants in Lorca had. My father scolded him for not making it crystal clear that the Caliph hadn't banned the Mardanish dinar yet and that Murcia hadn't received any Almohad currency, which was minted in Morocco. It was hard for anyone witnessing this scene to understand how my father expected a slave to argue with market vendors about Almoravids, Almohads, dinars, caliphs, and kings. The poor fellow bowed his head and let my father vent his rage and reproach on him—serving as scapegoat for a man shamed by learning he didn't have enough money to buy grapes for his kids.

Following this incident, my father became anxious during the trip whenever anyone discussed currency. I heard him ask my uncle whether he thought merchants in Seville would exchange his Mardanish dinars for Almohad ones. He feared that if he were forced to melt them down, he would lose three-quarters of their value.

"You know Ibn Mardanish didn't mint his coins from pure gold or pure silver."

My uncle answered calmly and confidently: "Yes, and the Almohads know that too."

"What will I do with my dinars then?"

"The caliph will give you Almohad dinars."

My uncle had no clearer idea about this than my father did but worried less, because his wealth consisted of flasks, bags, and packets of medicine, spices, rare metals, and dry herbs. Two camels carried these and his family. He planned to open a shop quickly in Seville with these supplies. He frequently traded one herb for another without any money changing hands. At times he would give medicine free of charge to a person who couldn't afford it. He wasn't concerned about money or amassing wealth so long as he had enough to live on.

Later we passed other villages where people accepted the Mardanish dinar without any fuss. It seemed that some people hadn't heard yet that Murcia had fallen to the Almohads and that others simply didn't care. So my father was able to purchase fruit and other food for us now that our supplies were almost exhausted. That night Sallum grilled two chickens for us, and we gathered around the meal—me, my parents, and my two sisters. My mother and the twins were clearly exhausted, but my father seemed more anxious and nervous than tired. His uncertain future in Seville was evidently weighing heavily on his nerves. As for me—each day I spent traveling seemed as filled with joy, astonishment, and hope as my first.

When we finally reached the outskirts of Seville, at sunset, we couched our camels, planning to enter the city in the morning. The first trip of my life had almost ended. With every mile we traveled over God's earth, my heart seemed to expand by a spiritual mile. God extended my insight to horizons out of eyesight and filled my breast with air unlike any I had ever breathed. I was eager to see Seville because its renown had spread far and wide. Like me, some people in our caravan had never seen it before, and I listened carefully in the evening when they posed excited questions to seasoned travelers. My uncle was one of these knowledgeable people who had visited Seville many times on business.

"What is Seville like, Abdullah?"

"How much time have you spent there?"

"What's in their markets?"

My uncle interrupted their stream of childish questions impatiently: "Good news, ignorant folks! You will find a better house here than you had before. Stop pestering me with questions."

But they didn't. A silversmith asked him about the silver markets. A teacher asked him about teaching circles in the mosque. An oil presser asked him about olive orchards. The piper asked him if people in Seville danced. The barber asked if men let their hair grow long and trimmed their beards. The tailor asked what they wore. My uncle would answer one question and ignore another. People left him, because he was so parsimonious with his replies, and gathered around an aged herdsman, who was accompanied by his son. They had joined our caravan two days after it left Murcia. He spoke so softly that only people sitting beside him could hear. I sat where boys were allowed, right behind that aged man. So I was able to hear his low voice clearly. He spoke very elegant Arabic, free of any Berber or Muwallad terms.

"It is a populous city and contains fine villages, many settlements, noble fortresses, long-established markets, lucrative commerce, and large public baths. Its earth is a noble land, a generous soil, and always green. Nearby are orchards where olive trees with intertwining branches perpetually shade the ground."

People crowded around him until almost twenty men were listening to him with interest. I didn't know whether they were drawn by his knowledge of Seville or his eloquence. As he noticed that more people were gathering around him, his voice began to quaver. Lifting thick eyelids to reveal moist eyes like those of the elderly, he continued to speak as his voice acquired the mellifluous quality of a professional storyteller: "Its climate is temperate, its buildings are beautiful, its inhabitants are wealthy, but they are licentious and seize the opportunities of the age, hour by hour. They are tempted to this by their restful valley and happy park. A man who had seen Egypt and Syria was asked: 'Are Cairo and Damascus more beautiful or is Seville?' He replied, 'Seville, of course. It has fertile land like the Ghouta of Damascus but without the lions, and its river is another Egyptian Nile but without the crocodiles.'"

8 ALEPPO 1248 CE/ 646 AH

"Tahir. . . ."

. . . .

"Tahir, where are you?"

My son didn't answer. He must have left the house even though I can't move because my cough is so severe it breaks my rib. I want a sip of water to relieve the fire in my belly and the phlegm in my throat but don't feel capable of fetching it myself. The water jug is leaning against the wall near the window to keep cool. Beside it are the herbs, medicines, and oils that Tahir obtained after we arrived here from Jerusalem. It was that long trip and its cold nights that made me sick. But God is the Healer.

"Tahir! Where are you, Son?"

The only response I received was the echo of my words. I turned over with difficulty and tried to sit up. The moment I drew air into my lungs to help me sit, I was overwhelmed by a severe coughing fit. A thorny twig seemed to be scratching my throat and larynx, provoking this atrocious cough. Drops of blood fell on the floor and the edge of the bed. I felt angry at this son who had left me prostrate and gone off to do whatever he was doing.

The coughing subsided as I lay on my side; so I decided not to move for fear it would return. I closed my eyes and dozed off. In my sleep I saw a leafy basil plant sprouting from a large hand. I kissed and sniffed the plant repeatedly. It grew larger with each kiss and filled my lungs with its fragrance with every breath I took. From each finger of the hand another basil plant sprouted and grew till these were my height. I found myself walking across that hand, surrounded by a basil thicket, which became so dense I had to push basil branches aside to pass. In the distance I could hear the sound of the Qur'an being recited, a beautiful *dhikr*, Sufi hymns of praise for God, and a sublime prayer. Suddenly those intertwined basil branches turned into a thick, white beard with soft, silky hair, and I plunged into it like a bird entering its nest. Then I found him standing before me.

"Greetings, Sawdakin. Welcome!"

"Master?"

I raised my head. There he was! His face was as bright as the first hour after sunrise. His white beard resembled a pure cloud inseparable from his face. From his smile I harvested my daily bread and my *dhikr* by night.

Placing a hand on my face, he said, "I've been longing for you, Sawdakin."

"I've longed for you, Master."

"Join me, then. The station here is vast, and the Lord of the House is generous."

He spread his arms and rose into the air. I opened my eyes and saw Tahir's alarmed face. His fingers wiped away the line of blood that ran from my mouth. It had soiled my pillow and cheeks till half my face was a vermilion color that would have alarmed anyone who saw it.

"Father, Father. . . ."

"Tahir."

"At your service?"

"Carry me to the library."

"Father, tell me what you want, and I'll bring it to you."

"No, carry me there, Son."

He thrust one strong arm beneath my armpits and the other beneath my knees and picked me up easily. When I met the Supreme Shaykh in Cairo, I was as strong as my son. His entry into our khanqah was like spring's arrival to a parched garden. Blessings settled in our bosoms, bodies, and hearts till the *dhikr* we repeated each evening extended farther and made a profounder impact. Every lesson he taught us caused each of us to seek refuge in his own room in the khanqah feeling he had become lighter, more remote from the earth, and closer to the heavens. I sensed I had found my shaykh, the person I had sought for years as I frequented all of Cairo's Sufi masters. But wasn't he a foreigner and world traveler? What would I do if he resumed his travels and left? Nothing is worse for a novice than to be weaned prematurely from his master. He will never experience satisfaction afterwards. I couldn't stand the thought of the spiritual famine I would suffer if our master Muhyi al-Din ibn Arabi left me behind in Cairo.

The day he left, I sat as close to him as I could and rested my hands on his sandals. I waited till he said goodbye to his companions. When he was ready to depart, I helped him put on his sandals and accompanied him to the caravan depot.

On our way, I shared with him the thought stirring in my breast: "Master, I am a novice, and you're a world traveler."

"What do you want?"

"I want to accompany you, serve you, and learn from you."

"So, come with me. The station here is vast, and the Lord of the House is generous."

I was overjoyed and hugged him tight. He laughed because I was so strong and my arms so powerful. He patted my biceps and said, "The best man hires a strong, trustworthy person."

Now that strong man swayed in the arms of his son, who carried him like a sack of flour. Although my strength had departed with the passing years, my trust in my shaykh and master hadn't. The material manifestation of that trust rested inside the crates piled atop each other in the library. Tahir set me down on the writing pallet and brought a cushion to support my head. Then he rushed to fetch a basin of water to wash the blood off my face. I ran my eyes over the pile of books stacked beside the wall. Those were the ones I hadn't finished reading. The crates, which were piled atop each other, contained books I had read and wouldn't return to again.

"Tahir, what will you do with my books once I die?"

My sudden question left him speechless, and he didn't reply. This son had not followed my path and was not attracted by what attracted me. I had tried but failed to influence him. I had ordered him, but he had not obeyed. I had cajoled him, but that had proved futile as well. I complained about him to our master one day in Damascus. When he realized how concerned I was about my son, he asked, "Why do I see you so worried?"

"It's my son, Tahir. He hasn't followed my path or taken my road."

"The path is God's path, and He draws along it whomever He wishes."

"I hoped he would become a Sufi ascetic and find in his soul the same pleasure, relief, and contentment that I and my father before me found."

"If I had followed my father's path, I would have become a chamberlain in the Almohads' palace. That wasn't what I or you found. God chose a different path for me—not my father's. He has chosen a different path for Tahir—not his father's."

"It's upsetting to find he's interested in pleasures and commerce, not asceticism and worship."

"My uncle was preoccupied by commerce for seventy years. Then he died a saint with many charisms."

He placed his palms on either side of my face, as he did when he wanted his words to sink into my heart, so that not even vast stretches of time would erase them. He said, "Listen, Sawdakin, God's path is a public path; there are as many paths to God as there are creatures' souls."

"Is my son Tahir's path one of them?"

"Yes, commerce is one of the prophets' professions. Asceticism is internal, not external. We need not deny ourselves what we were created for."

Since then I haven't worried about Tahir. Although he's been busy with his business and with his worldly affairs, he has always been dutiful, especially since our Master died eight years ago. Weakness and ill health have afflicted me, but whenever I have felt any anxiety about him, I have remembered that his path is also God's path. If God has chosen this path for him, why should a devout person worry?

"Tell me, Son. What will you do with my books?"

"May God grant you a long life, Father. I'll do whatever you say."

"Take all of them to al-Firdaws Madrasa and establish them as a trust for students."

"As you wish."

"Now hand me that top box."

He rose, picked up the box easily, despite its weight, and placed it before me. I directed him to open it. He did and then took from it the manuscript that has never left me since my master died. This book has traveled with me wherever I have gone and settled with me wherever I have stayed. He handed me the book, and I clasped it to my breast briefly. Then I handed it back to him and said: "Son, this book is the one exception. Keep it with you and preserve it as if it were your eye in its socket. Pass it on as a bequest to your children after you."

Tahir's anxiety showed in his eyes as he touched the cover of the large book.

"Now, Son, open the book at random and read whatever looks easy."

I leaned my head back on the cushion, closed my eyes, repeated two *shahadas* to myself—silently, so he wouldn't fret about me and stop reading. I wanted to die while listening to the life story of my supreme shaykh, who was a bountiful sea of plentiful learning. I began to pass away slowly, in good spirits, listening to my shaykh's words read aloud by my son: "The wayfarer said: 'The station here is vast, and the Lord of the House is generous.'"

TOME TWO

9

When the muezzin launched the dawn call to prayer over Seville's doorsteps, we turned our backs to them and faced the *qibla* to pray. Once we concluded our prayers, I watched men embrace one another while tearful women shyly told each other goodbye. My father and Sallum readied our mounts and lifted my mother's howdah onto her camel. Mother handed me a leftover piece of bread and a prune for breakfast. My two sisters were so delighted to be entering Seville that they started singing kid songs. I had been as excited as they were since the previous day and had scarcely slept that night.

Guards stopped us the moment we entered the city's gate. Some officials who specialized in caravans were there, and the leader of our caravan started answering their questions.

"Where do you come from?"

"From Murcia and its outlying areas. A few of us hail from Jaén."

"Is there anyone who does not come from Andalusia or the Maghrib?"

"Just our slaves."

"Are you bringing any goods that belong to someone from Genoa or Sardinia?"

"We bring only our own possessions."

This expert stepped aside and gestured to the guards. Then the caravan started to move forward slowly, entering the city. The supervisor shouted to the caravan's leader, as he mounted his horse: "Untie the camels' halter and disband in the square that's straight ahead of you. Don't enter the streets of the city all together, because if you do, your animals will stir up too much dust."

The caravan's leader nodded, and the grooms hurriedly released the camels from the long halter rope. The supervisor kept on issuing orders, shouting louder when the din of the caravan increased as it started to enter the city.

"Don't enter our markets on your animals. Don't release them without a groom."

We entered Seville in a long line, and the market superintendent scanned people's faces and wares listlessly. He chose some to interrogate and to check their goods. My father's and my uncle's camels left the caravan when my father hired a boy to serve as our guide to show us the Guadalquivir River, where we saw large ships sailing a watercourse that looked like a sea. None of us had ever seen a boat larger than the skiffs that navigated the Segura River. My uncle's kids raised a hullabaloo, they were so excited to see such large ships, but my father and I exchanged silent looks of astonishment. The boy then led us away from the river as our group walked for some time—our four animals that carried me, my parents, my two sisters, and Sallum, as well as my uncle's five camels that bore him, his three daughters, and his two young sons. My aunt had died. She had contracted tuberculosis during the blockade and had been quarantined in a tent outside their house.

My father's elegy for her has stuck in my mind: "The poor woman was a victim of two sieges. The tent was quarantined, and she couldn't leave it, and the city was besieged, and that prevented her from seeking medical care."

There wasn't a physician of any standing in Murcia then, except for the court doctor, who was prohibited from caring for the general public. So my father claimed my aunt was his wife, not his brother's, and brought the palace physician to her tent.

He stood by the entrance and said, "Woman, stick your hand out from beneath the tent so I can see it."

When she did, he saw that her fingers had stiffened and resembled drumsticks. The doctor shook his head and told my father, "Once the fingers thicken, no cure is possible. Ask her to state her final wishes because she is at death's door."

She died a few days later, and my uncle never remarried. His oldest daughter looked after her siblings, and her marriage was postponed till all of them grew up. She started to tease me whenever she saw me, asking: "When will you come of age, cousin, and marry me?" This embarrassed me, especially since she kissed me when she said it. Then I saw the gap between her teeth and the wart on her nose and smelled her foul body odor—as if her father didn't sell perfume!

The young scout left us at a caravansary after he showed my father and us the large house they had leased on the west side of the river. It had four rooms and a large courtyard, where Sallum erected a tent for himself. My uncle and his two sons shared a room and his three daughters occupied a second. My father had a room to himself, while my mother, two sisters, and I were allocated the largest chamber. In a few days, though, my father and uncle moved into the largest room, and I was put in another one with my two male cousins. That left the two other rooms for the women, and my uncle's daughters wandered freely between those two chambers. Whenever I visited my mother, I would find one of them sitting with her. A few months after we reached Seville, my uncle's youngest daughter married a young Muwallad, and this infuriated my father, who objected: "He's not an Arab!"

My uncle laughed nonchalantly and retorted, "Where are you going to find a full-blooded Arab in Seville?"

They quarreled for months about this betrothal, but my uncle didn't change his mind. His oldest daughter's spinsterhood tormented him, and he feared that her two sisters wouldn't marry either. So he ignored my father and even mocked him within earshot of the rest of us: "A servant of the Berbers looks down on me for marrying my daughter to a Muwallad? Amazing?"

After the wedding took place and the couple moved from Seville to the nearby village of Shubarbul, my father and uncle quickly forgot their quarrel. When the governor eventually summoned him, my father found work at the palace. The governor told my father that the Caliph had resolved to come to Seville once he subdued some small villages near Cordova and that, as a result, the ministries would need to be reorganized before the Caliph arrived. My uncle, for his part, took advantage of the deflated price of shops near the Ibn Addis Mosque. Their value had decreased in response to construction of the new Grand Mosque; my uncle bought one and reopened his business there.

The quarrel between the two brothers flared up again one day when we were eating dinner. My father, as usual, was talking about the Caliph, the governor, some government ministers and secretaries, and the various ministries—praising all of them profusely. The governor had left the palace that day only to find that his steed wasn't waiting. So he had walked to the event.

"Seville is really blessed to have this ascetic, modest governor. The lack of a horse didn't keep him from seeing to the people's needs, on foot."

In a low voice, which we all heard, my uncle commented, "He might just as well have saddled you."

This barely audible comment, which struck us like a thunderbolt, was followed by total silence. The girls bowed their heads fearfully, and my father's veins swelled visibly as he tried to contain the raging volcano inside him. He rose and in a muffled scream told my uncle to his face: "Abdullah! There are children present!"

Then he threw down the morsel of food in his hand and went to his room. My mother urged the girls to continue eating but then got up and followed my father. The flare-up scared me, but I pretended to be in full control of myself and resumed eating with my uncle. When the two of us had finished, everyone rose to leave.

Just a few days later the Caliph finally arrived, and his new courtiers in Seville presented their gifts, which the governor had selected with my father's help before the Caliph's arrival. My father was awarded the use, albeit not the ownership, of a house in an elite neighborhood. So we moved there, and my uncle found a house near his shop.

10

A few days after the Caliph arrived in Seville, people were surprised by news that no one had anticipated: he planned to marry Safiya, the daughter of Muhammad ibn Mardanish.

When my father told my mother this, she gasped and covered her mouth. Then she asked: "Couldn't he find some other woman to marry besides his enemy's daughter? The child of someone he was just besieging?"

Removing his boots and plunging them in a tub of water, my father replied, "Caliphs are clever this way, Woman. Safiya is lodged in his dwelling, and her sister is in Ibrahim ibn Hamushk's residence. Two daughters of Ibn Mardanish, two sisters, are in the Almohads' lair!"

"Is he safe with her?"

"He will be safe around any of the offspring of Ibn Mardanish now that he has given them a taste of his determination and resolve. Each can be trusted while he holds all of them hostage."

"What if she poisons his food?"

My father laughed and responded: "Woman, do you think caliphs are like the rest of us? Do you think their wives prepare their food? Do you think they sleep next to these wives every night? A caliph's food is prepared by trustworthy chefs under the supervision of chamberlains. Loyal slaves watch every gesture and hesitation of these cooks. Each wife sees the caliph only once or twice a month."

To celebrate both his victory and his marriage, the Caliph hosted a festival that lasted for seven days. Squares in the city were filled with hucksters, snake charmers, and monkey handlers. People clustered around each one till he grew tired or they grew bored and moved on to the next performer. Day after day, we went out with my father—me and my two sisters. Occasionally my mother accompanied us, returning home at noon. At other times she complained of a headache. Storytellers lined up in front of the mosque's wall. Each had a boy who encouraged people to listen by striking the small drum fastened to his waist and crying out: "Listen to the amazing wonders of the East . . . Baghdad and Basra . . . Damascus and Cairo . . . We'll tell you about al-Zir Salim, Abu Layla al-Muhalhil, and the war sparked by the camel of al-Basus . . . Listen . . . Don't sneak off . . . Drive ennui from your heart . . . Have you heard about the Zanj Rebellion?"

I passed from one storyteller to the next, slipping my slim body through the crowd. If I couldn't find a path to get close to one, I would leave him for another. Eventually I reached a storyteller from Seville. He was someone I had seen repeatedly near my uncle's shop, but he hadn't been telling stories then. I sat facing him in a circle of twenty men, some women clad in Maghribi gallabiyas, soldiers still armed with swords, and boys of every age.

He was recounting: "And the pagans' boats entered Seville. They attacked the city's inhabitants with swords and axes. They seemed to have filled the sea with black birds and the hearts of citizens with grief and sorrow. They forced their way into mosques and houses, killing or capturing the city's inhabitants. They spent seven days in Seville meting out death to its people. . . ."

Describing the terror of this Norman raid, he deliberately made his voice quaver and his eyes bulge out so the little kids huddled together fearfully. "At that time, Seville lay fully exposed, because we had no wall. That made it easy for infidels and libertines to enter. They filled their warships with prisoners and captives and took all of them to the island of al-Qabtil in the Guadalquivir River. People fled in panic from Seville, thereby causing others to flee quickly too. Arabs shouted: 'Pagan Fetishists!' Franks shouted: 'Vikings! Vikings!' Neither man nor beast escaped their swords, and they plundered the entire city."

He concluded his tale with an ending fit for the Caliph's festival: "Then salvation arrived from Cordova and Carmona, and the Muslims mobilized support from Morón de la Frontera and Lisbon. They clashed on the outskirts of the city. They were the best descendants of the best ancestors. They erected catapults on both sides of the mighty river and used them to devastate the warships so the Pagans could not escape upstream or down. They killed the Slavs and the Barbarians among them. . . ."

People applauded and tossed copper coins on the storyteller's carpet. He collected their change while praising their generosity. Then his audience moved off in search of other entertainment.

During the final days of the festival, the streets filled with troops of every variety and complexion. The Maghribis wore crimson, chainmail hoods that hung to their shoulders over white, embroidered linen garments and carried red banners. Black soldiers with leather armor wore conical red caps, and their camels were decorated with bells. The Oghuz Turks had amazing beards, since they shaved both their cheeks and their throats, allowing only the hair of their jaw to grow long. Other soldiers were Berber, Arab, Slavonic, and different types of slaves. All these troops marched in an orderly way and did not utter a word or glance right or left. Each man had his eyes fixed on the nape of the neck of the fellow in front of him.

More than two thousand soldiers gathered in Seville's square opposite the mosque. Then groups of two hundred soldiers were commanded to form circles. Fifty men sat in the first circle, fifty in the next circle, fifty in the next, and so on. At the center of each circle stood a shaykh who addressed them, shouting: "Jihad is the peak of Islam's summit!"

Then all the men around the shaykh repeated in an awe-inspiring roar which made the walls of houses and shops lining the square tremble: "Jihad is the peak of Islam's summit!"

He remained silent while each soldier wrote on his slate the sentence they had just repeated. Eventually, the preacher shouted: "Jihad is a portal to paradise!"

So they all shouted this loudly and then copied it down. My father stood beside me, watching too, and we both heard the comments of passersby about this unprecedented scene.

My father turned toward me and asked proudly, "See this? I proposed this to the caliph. It was *my* idea. This is something I have accomplished."

"Why, Father?"

"Because the army consists of many different groups that lack any cohesion. I noticed that while recording their names in the army roster. There are Maghribis, Muwallads, Andalusians, former Almoravid soldiers, Christian mercenaries, and Slavic mamluks. I realized that they come from different sects, that their ambitions vary, and that their hearts are not united."

He urged me to continue walking as he finished his explanation. "I recommended for the Caliph's vizier to appoint ulema to teach the men slogans about jihad and the exigencies of our situation. He liked my suggestion and agreed to implement it."

Thanks to such ideas and suggestions, the governor grew increasingly interested in my father. He brought him into his administration but did not grant him a position higher than "secretary without portfolio". For this reason, my father did not spend the long hours at work that he had at the court of Ibn Mardanish. He blamed his marginalization to all the Maghribis at the caliph's court. When they wished to ostracize someone like my father, they would speak Masmudi Berber, which my father didn't know. So he came home following the afternoon prayer whenever he learned that the caliph wouldn't hold a public assembly. If there was one, my father stayed at court till sunset. That rarely happened, however, because the caliph typically felt more comfortable with his inner circle, which my father had not yet joined—and never would, because he wasn't a philosopher like Ibn Tufayl, a physician like Ibn Zuhr, or a chief justice like Ibn Rushd.

All the same, he showed no signs of discontent or frustration. He was grateful that the Caliph had found room for him at court in Seville, allotted him a monthly stipend, and granted him use of the house where we lived. This was a pleasant situation for a man who had passed wretched nights the previous year in Murcia, imagining himself being crucified alongside Ibn Mardanish in the city's citadel. Why would he complain? To serve as a secretary to a caliph who ruled the Maghrib and half of Andalusia was better than being the vizier of a king whose rule extended no farther than the walls of a single city. The palace comptroller had even accepted his Mardanishi dinars, on orders of the Caliph, and given him the same exact number of Almohad dinars.

My father devoted his free time to teaching me. He toured Seville's neighborhoods with me, one after the other. In each mosque he entered, he asked who its shaykhs and teachers were. He spent a long time in Qus al-Haniya when he heard that the city's top jurisprudent offered a course in the cramped mosque there. The next morning, he sent me back, after making sure I knew how to get there, but the shaykh turned me and the other new boys away.

He said, "My sons, go back to your families and tell them there is no room for more students in this circle. They can bring you during the month of Sha'ban when there may be space for you."

I went home and waited for my father to return from court. Then, while he was removing his turban, I told him what had happened. He immediately put the turban back on and took me to the shaykh's home. When he knocked on the door, the shaykh opened it, and his eyes gazed at us above a beard, which was dyed red with henna and below a broad forehead, which sported a large prayer callus exactly at the center.

My father said, "I beg your pardon, Shaykh, for coming during your leisure time, but it is very painful for a stranger in Seville like me to see his only son deprived of your instruction and barred from your light."

"All light is from God, my son. The circle is too crowded already. When there are too many boys, they create a hubbub, and the instruction's benefit is jeopardized. There are teaching circles in the other mosques."

"May God fulfill His blessing to you, Shaykh. I trust you, but there are some instructors in this city whose fluency in Arabic is inadequate. My son is an Arab, one hundred percent. Perhaps you will be able to find a place for him. In that eventuality, he will serve you and not disappoint you."

"Fine."

Then he turned to me and smiled. "Join me in the circle tomorrow, Son."

11

Our new house in Seville was less spacious than the one in Murcia but had been built more recently and was better ventilated. Since it was near the mountain, jackals' howls terrified the two little girls at night. My father calmed them by asking, "Why should a jackal's praise for the Lord of this world and the next frighten you?" Their fear subsided then, and I imagined predatory beasts attending God's pious friends who praise him night and day. My room was on the east, and that made it impossible to sleep once the sun rose. The window also offered the view of a small house in front of which an elderly demented woman sat all day long. Whenever I opened my window, she accosted me in a language I didn't understand. Occasionally she would scream and toss fruit pits at me. I feared her and rarely opened that window. My father had a chamber of his own, and my mother shared one with the two young girls. On the ground floor, most of the courtyard was taken up by a long, wide pool that had less than an inch of water in it. It was paved with thumb-sized red and blue tiles. I would count them and become agitated if I found more on one side than the other. There were no orange or olive trees, although many grew throughout the city. Seville's oranges were too bitter to eat, though, unlike those in Murcia. A grapevine climbed the wall. A quince tree grew on one side and on the other there rose a towering pine, which could be seen from near the beginning of our neighborhood. I used it as a landmark to find my way home during our first days in Seville. Sallum planted a kitchen garden with various vegetables to save himself the trouble of going to the market. We also harvested pomegranates, lemons, and quinces from our courtyard.

My father arranged a place for him to lounge beneath the grape vine and sat there most mild days of the year. He would write, read, receive visitors, and even eat there at times. His most frequent companion was a livestock broker named Abd al-Samad, who traded between Seville and cija and lived in his son-in-law's house at the end of our lane. He would knock on our door when he thought my father might be sitting in the garden. If my father was out, he would depart.

My father complained repeatedly to him about the Maghribis at the court: "I work on some project for two or three days without any of them noticing. When I'm almost done, though, they rush to the governor to tell him before I can."

Abd al-Samad would shake his head disapprovingly and remark: "Glory to Him who brought them to power after they were scattered throughout the desert where they were powerless and insignificant."

Then my father would change course, because such talk scared him. He would say: "No, no, in fact some of them are superb. They have made Islam triumphant and have established justice—especially the Caliph. Some, however, encroach on the rights of Andalusians and disrespect them."

"They think they saved us from destruction and spared us deprivation. Back in the days of the Andalusian caliphate, they would come to beg for work and a bite to eat."

My father would nod his head to show his total agreement but say nothing. Then he would ask: "Why do they speak that Masmudi language, as if they were still nomads in the heart of the desert? By God, I have frequently been with the Caliph but have never heard him speak this tongue, although he is proficient in it. He actually speaks such pure Arabic he might have been born in the Arabs' desert!"

"They don't want you to understand what they are saying and learn what they are plotting."

Abd al-Samad would leave once my father had vented his anger and felt better. Eventually my father's tasks increased till he no longer had time to sit in the garden. He began to eat lunch and supper at court and devoted his day to chores, which he might love or hate. These ranged from important ones like accompanying the Governor on his rounds of commercial establishments (to record what the governor commanded) to insignificant tasks like specifying how much fodder should be fed to animals used in construction projects. His workload increased once the Caliph's appetite for building grew, as tax collections increased and the poll tax on non-Muslims began to flow into the Almohad treasury—after their conquest of cities, forts, and castles in the eastern Maghrib and southern Andalusia. For his construction projects, the Caliph recruited builders, plasterers, and carpenters from Fez and Marrakech and hired dozens of accountants from Seville to keep track of these construction projects and to supervise the expenditures for them. The pace of work also increased to complete the Grand Mosque and to build the bridge across the river to link Seville and Triana. Then a famed expert known as Ibn Basa took charge of building the Buhaira Palace. He channeled water to it from Qala't Jabir and brought pomegranate and apple trees from Granada to plant at the palace. By combining the palace's various gardens, he created one vast plantation of mulberry trees to support silkworm cultivation.

All of Seville rang with the noise of construction and building. Even our quiet neighborhood awoke one morning to the clamor of dozens of construction workers carrying heavy, long tree trunks and heading to the shipyard, which the caliph had ordered them to enlarge. I saw that shipyard when we played near the river and swam in it on Fridays.

One summer my father decided he would teach me how to swim, shoot, and ride a horse. He started with swimming, which I had hated since I heard the tale about the Normans sailing up the river. Even so, I plunged into the water to swim, accompanied by Sallum, who obeyed my mother's command to cling to me like a bracelet. Unlike the Segura River, which was shallow and flowed slowly, Seville's river was cold and there were sharp rocks on the bottom.

My father shouted at me: "Jump in here and swim from here to there." Then he threw a metal floater in the river and commanded: "Retrieve that!"

These lessons continued fruitlessly. I hated swimming, and the frigid, filthy river disgusted me. My father didn't grasp that the real swimmer glides through God's spiritual dominion, the *malakut*, that genuine target practice is speaking truth in alarming circumstances, and that true horseback riding is travel in the pursuit of learning. My father embraced the exoteric meanings while God disclosed the esoteric ones to me. My father forced me to do stuff I didn't like and ordered me to do things I couldn't stand. One day he became so infuriated by my recalcitrance that he ordered me to stay in the river till I swam from one shore to the other. I wept and begged him not to make me, but he insisted. The current was strong, and the water was cold. My father stood frowning on the bank with his arms crossed, casting severe looks my way. I swam to the middle of the river, but my arms failed me there, and I struggled to keep my head above water. When I finally reached the other bank and climbed out, my father began yelling at me to swim back. He even threw rocks at me! Tired, afraid, and shivering from the cold, I slipped into the water and swam a short distance before I felt the current drag me downstream. Then I noticed that my father and Sallum were running along the bank to catch up with me. Finally, Sallum leapt into the water and pulled me to a place where we could both climb out.

On our way home, my father walked ahead of us and said nothing. My body was trembling because I felt cold and frightened. I pulled my shirt up to cover my head and continued walking, even though I couldn't see the road or feel my feet. The icy cramps I experienced down my back made my shoulder blades contract. Once I began to shake convulsively, Sallum took my arm. Then I lost control of my bladder and felt warm liquid run down my thighs. Finally, when my feet failed me, Sallum hoisted me onto his back. Entering our neighborhood, I glimpsed our pine tree and passed out.

"How wary I am of my wariness."

— **IBN ARABI**

12

I ran breathlessly down Seville's alleys. The gap between the paving stones seemed greater in each alley that I entered. So I would stumble, fight to maintain my balance, and keep on running till the gap between every two stones was the length of my foot. Then I started to place my feet in the unpaved intervals and avoid the stones. Next, the distance between them became so narrow that the stones trapped my feet. I could walk no farther because the whole road was nothing but fetters. Water started to rise through the gaps and eventually covered my ankles, calves, and knees. I tried to lean forward to swim, but water rushed into my mouth and nostrils. So I choked and could scarcely breathe. When I braced my feet and tried to break free of these rocky shackles, I noticed that a crocodile's tail was twisting around my leg. Norman ships with dragon figureheads appeared on the horizon, sailing toward me across a carpet of flame. The sailors on board brandished their cudgels at me from afar. I desperately pushed the water with my arms in hopes of extinguishing the fire beneath them. Then my fingers emerged from the water—locked together like a ball of yarn. I felt that I would surely perish and struggled to remember the words to recite before dying. A thick cloud of dust swirled through my head, creating small tornados on each corner of my withered mind's chessboard. Suddenly the water subsided, and I fell on my face. I heard their reverberating footsteps approach. I couldn't move. My cheeks were stuck in the mud, and my eyes could see no farther than my nose. Then I saw toes with ugly black nails and dirty tips. I realized that a Norman stood over me and was about to bash my head with his cudgel. I tucked my head between my shoulders, anticipating the blow, but it didn't come. What descended on me instead was a light but warm linen cloak. I wrapped it around me, while still on the ground. I saw the Normans race away, looking scared. Trying to scale the sides of their ships, they fell on top of each other. Then their legs were pelted by shots from the catapults on the shore. When these hit the Normans' legs, they broke the men's knees and shanks, causing the men to groan with pain. I turned and saw behind me the person who had covered me with the cloak. He was a commander but I couldn't make out his features. His shoulders were so broad that he might have been wearing armor beneath his cloak. He raised his sword toward the Normans, and catapults pelted them repeatedly. When he lowered his sword, the shots ceased. As he lifted his sword once more, blows rained down on the foe. In the throes of the battle he turned toward me and beamed. At the moment his lips parted in a smile, the sounds of battle diminished substantially and blended with the voices of boys reciting in a distant circle around a shaykh. Then that shaykh's voice drowned them all out as he recited: "We revive the dead and record what they have offered and achieved. We have enumerated everything in a clear standard."[3] I found myself standing on my own two feet, as if emerging from a tomb. Then I advanced toward the Normans, who lay crippled on the ground. I recited in unison with the shaykh: "If it develops, we will drown them. Then they will raise no shriek nor will they be saved."[4] As I approached them, they looked at me entreatingly, even as they continued to scream and groan. Their mouths opened so wide that some projectiles from the catapults entered them. I quickened my steps till I was virtually leaping as I recited: "Today We shall seal their mouths."[5] When I stopped beside one man's head, he grasped his leg and bit his lips because he was in such extreme pain. "And their legs will bear witness as to what they were acquiring."[6] Then he began to address me entreatingly with Teutonic words I didn't understand. I answered him with these words from the Qur'an: "Do not let their statement sadden you. We know what they conceal and what they proclaim."[7] Water flooded in and swept away the Normans and their ships. I watched the river carry them back to the sea, flushing them into it. I shouted after them: "Criminals, step aside this day. . . . Criminals, step aside this day."[8] Then the water dried up, the road leveled out, and the sky suddenly expanded as if to embrace the earth like a newborn child. I noticed that the commander stood beside me, gazing at the horizon. I asked him, "Who are you, Uncle?"

He turned toward me, opened his mouth, and seemed to reply: "Ya Sin, by the judicious Qur'an, you surely are one of the messengers."[9] I found that my father was chanting these verses when I forced my eyes open. He was seated cross-legged by my head, holding his hand on my forehead. I closed my eyes again so he would continue the recitation: "On the straight path, a revelation of the Compassionate Almighty, to warn people whose fathers were not admonished; so they were clueless."[10] I allowed my father to recite the entire chapter again and again, without letting him know I had regained consciousness.

My next few days were all devoted to the surah "Ya Sin": "Ya Sin" in the morning and "Ya Sin" at night; "Ya Sin" wherever I went. This chapter of the Qur'an established itself in my heart, as if I hadn't already recited it all seven different ways, as if I didn't already know each jot and tittle of it, as well as every voweling, doubled consonant, nasal pronunciation, and exoteric and esoteric meaning. This time, though, it wasn't merely a chapter of the Qur'an; it was a message from God straight to my heart and a luminous niche to guide me on the path. Every glad tiding in it was intended for me, as was each warning. For as long as I live, I will stand by the walls of this surah, asking God to disclose its secrets to me, to open its portals, to help me explore the beauty of its depths and fathom its heights. God grants the keys to the wall and opens the portals of the Qur'an only to God's friends, who truly know Him, truly love Him, and truly cling to Him. God was preparing me for what He had destined. The fever lifted from my bones, but "Ya Sin" lingered in my breast.

"The first take is never a mistake."

—IBN ARABI

13

People spread the rumor that the spirit of Archbishop Isidore of Seville haunted the Ibn Addis Mosque because stone from his sepulcher was used to build the mosque's minaret. That was alleged to be the reason that successive muezzins who offered the call to prayer from it died prematurely. Then, once the court ceased appointing a muezzin, a few men volunteered their throats for this task. This ancient mosque was so crowded with worshippers, week after week, that those who didn't arrive early were obliged to pray in the crypt. My uncle would wait till the rows of praying men reached the doorstep of his shop. Then he would spread his prayer rug beside them. So he prayed communally, without leaving his shop. He could not hear the sermon, but that didn't bother him. Often he could not hear the *takbir* either, especially if the winds were strong or rain was drumming on the sheets of metal that shaded the shop entrances. In these cases, someone in each successive row would take the initiative to repeat, "Allahu akbar!" At times, though, some men became confused, and the imam would rise from his prostration when they were just prostrating themselves. Then he would prostrate himself a second time, unbeknownst to them. Consequently, they would be surprised by the final benediction when they were still between the two prostrations and didn't prostrate themselves again or repeat the shahada.

I spent most of the day in this mosque, which was crowded with teaching circles. When I was hungry, I went to see my uncle, who fed me whatever bread, fruit, or cheese he had. He came to expect me late each morning and was delighted to see me, especially since his two sons had recently outgrown the circles and begun to act in ways he didn't appreciate. They did not work with him in his trade or sit with him in his store. Instead, they reveled in Seville's pleasures and spent most of their hours lounging by the Guadalquivir River, ogling Castilian women, who sashayed past, adorned with veils that barely concealed anything. Many of these women dreamt of marrying an Arab to guarantee themselves residence in Andalusia without fear of being enslaved or banished whenever Muslims and Castilians started fighting.

One such woman did actually catch my older cousin, and he decided to marry her. When my father learned about this he flew into a rage. That day he left the court and headed straight to my uncle's store, where I was, too.

"Brother, what are you doing to us? Do you want people to say we no longer know the difference between authentic and phony?"

My uncle, whose head was bowed, was overwhelmed by distress and didn't look up or reply. My father continued: "For your daughter to marry a Muslim Muwallad was tolerable although hideous, but for your eldest son to marry a Christian Castilian! What will people say about you?"

Brushing aside my father's hand, my uncle replied in a heavy, exhausted voice, "Leave me alone, Ali. I haven't blessed this marriage, but he's an adult, and his wedding does not require my consent. If he listened to me, you would find him here selling and buying medicine."

My father struck his hands together but asked in a calmer voice, "Won't you even lift a finger?"

My uncle rose from the cushion where he was sitting and started to fill his glass from the water jug. Without looking at my father, he replied, "You lift your fingers if you can. I delegate this matter to you."

There was nothing my father could do. The nuptials took place, and the newlyweds disappeared so completely that we didn't know whether they were still in Seville or had left town.

His oldest daughter, for her part, would return home running and shouting that someone was chasing her. The alley was deserted when neighbors searched it, finding no trace of a pursuer. Another day she prodded a fishmonger with a poker as he stood near the door of the house to sell fish, as he customarily did. He shrieked with pain, and she shouted at him. When people gathered, she complained, "This son of a bitch made eyes at me!" When whispered suspicions possessed her, she burned herself on the temple and made an abscess on the nape of her neck. Then she blocked the windows of the house with wooden boards and slept in a clothes chest for fear something would sting her. That hiding place offered no relief, and she began to rave.

My uncle's typical carefree expression disappeared beneath a gloomy mask of scowling distress. He grew so dependent on wine that he would close his store for most of the day while he drank inside till he fell asleep there, instead of returning home. I visited his shop in Seville frequently and knew that most of the pottery jugs lining the shelves held wine, not olive oil. He didn't realize I knew this till the day my mother experienced a splitting migraine and tried every known remedy to cure it. She rubbed her head with sugar syrup, soaked her feet in rose water, and inhaled the smoke of dozens of precious and ordinary types of fragrant wood. She bathed in salt water mixed with willow oil and anointed herself with a salve blended from oil and the ashes of a dead mole. She was cupped twice, but nothing helped. Then she sent me to my uncle during Ramadan, asking: "Some nigella seed, Muhyi, and oil."

When I reached my uncle's shop and entered without announcing myself, I found my uncle drinking from a camouflaged jug with his back to me. I retreated in alarm on finding him drinking, when everyone was fasting. I called to him from outside, as if I had just arrived, and he invited me to enter. I felt so disconcerted and shocked that I didn't know what to say. I blurted out: "My mother wants white nigella seed."

"What did you say?"

"White nigella seed."

My uncle stared at me, dumbfounded, and his expression remained frozen for a few seconds. Then he burst out laughing and guffawed for a long time. When he stopped, he threw one of the sponges lined up in front of him, and it hit my head.

"Why are you laughing?"

"I'm amused by your ignorance. Nigella seeds aren't white."

I was furious, and my blood began to boil. My mind fixated on the fact that someone who had committed the major offense of drinking *wine* during Ramadan's daylight hours would mock my knowledge of pharmaceuticals. Without meaning to, I shouted: "My ignorance of the color of nigella seeds won't hurt me with God, but your carousing and carelessness will hurt you!"

I ran out of his shop without waiting to see how he would react. My tears flowed as I raced home. By the time I reached our house, fatigue had dulled my rage, and my shock at my uncle's depravity was colored by my annoyance at looking stupid. I burst into my mother's room like a raging stallion and found her lying on her back with a cloth wound round her head and an arm over her eyes.

"Mother!"

Startled by my voice, she raised her head slightly and gazed at me with tired eyes. In a weak voice she asked, "What's wrong? Have you brought the nigella?"

"White nigella or what? How could you ask me to fetch something when I don't even know what color it is?"

"Nigella seeds, son. Nigella? It's a black seed. Don't you know 'black seed'? Could it be anything but black?"

My rage flared up again as my mother poured salt on my wound. No longer knowing what I was saying, I yelled at her: "How should I know? Do you want me to grow up to be a religious scholar who teaches at the mosque or a druggist who breaks his fast during the day in Ramadan?"

"What? Who is violating the Ramadan fast?"

"Uncle Abdallah! I saw him fill his belly from a wine jug!"

"My God!"

"Yes . . . yes . . . during the daylight hours of Ramadan."

She stroked her forehead with her palm and closed her eyes. Shaking her head, she remarked regretfully, "My God! Your mercy, my Lord. May God forgive him."

After that incident I stopped visiting my uncle's shop, and my mother started sending Sallum there instead. I took another route to the mosque to stay out of sight. This wasn't only from anger but partly from fear because I had no idea what impact my words had made on his heart. He might be waiting for me to appear so he could beat me. My uncle did not visit us often, and my rupture with him continued for many months. The longer our separation lasted, the more I dreaded seeing him again and the more my anguish about meeting him increased. I started to have nightmares in which I saw him give me a drubbing in the street as passersby tried to deter him.

Then my father traveled for a few days to Cordoba to carry letters from the Caliph to various religious scholars. As usual, he entrusted our affairs to my uncle, who came to see us several days after my father's departure. When I, myself, opened the door for him, I saw a man I barely recognized. In just a few months he had grown stooped and walked bent so far forward that his torso was almost horizontal. When he complained of feeling cold, I took him from the courtyard into a room. Then I brought him water and took a seat beside him.

After a period of silence, I asked, "Uncle, are you ill?"

At that, he started crying and looked up at me with tears in his eyes. "My boy, nothing ails me but my sins."

My uncle had repented. Once he closed his shop in the evening, he headed to the mosque, where he secluded himself in his devotions all night long. He slept briefly before dawn, when, after performing his ablutions, he would pray with the congregation and then head to his shop. He met no one, and his only companion was his neighbor Hasan al-Shakkaz, with whom he passed nights doing dhikr, reciting the Qur'an, and meditating. I harbored a suspicion that the angry sermon I had roared at my uncle after the nigella incident had been responsible for his transformation. When this thought occurred to me, I felt exultant and proud but didn't say anything for fear he would contradict me and dispute my claim. In the worst scenario, he would feel proud of his sin and revert to his previous conduct.

I began to visit the two men in al-Shakkaz's house. Whenever I entered, I found them doing spoken dhikr and continuously praising God. At times they recited passages from the Qur'an in unison, and one man's recitation would move the other to tears. Occasionally al-Shakkaz recounted hadiths about the Prophet, and we luxuriated in love of the Prophet during our uninterrupted spiritual retreat. At times I fell asleep in his house, and that was how I witnessed the first of my uncle's charismatic gifts—he woke at dawn one day and said, "Rise, dawn is here."

"How do you know?"

"I smelled it. Dawn's breaths have a special scent."

During just such a night my uncle's son knocked on the door, and I admitted him. He was staggering and looked drunk. "Where's my father?" he demanded.

I took him inside, and he headed straight to his father, scarcely noticing al-Shakkaz, who was seated there. He demanded, "Father, give me money. All the money you provided me is gone."

"I have no money. Scram!"

His son screamed at the top of his lungs: "I said: Give me money!"

"You can scream till you go hoarse. I have no money."

"I said: Give me money, you senile old coot! You just hoard it, and you'll die soon. Give me money!"

"If you don't leave, I'll beat you like a beast of burden with my cane."

My cousin suddenly leapt at his father, shoving him to the floor with both hands and straddling him. I caught sight of my uncle's eyes for a moment and saw in them both terror at the attack and extreme disappointment. Al-Shakkaz and I rushed to shove the son off his father. Before departing, my cousin broke a crockery jug and hurled a book that al-Shakkaz had been reading across the room. My uncle sat up. He was panting, and tears soon welled up in his eyes. His face quivered from those recent tears as he told himself: "You have wounded my heart. God has wounded your heart and brought your death closer."

Al-Shakkaz stroked my uncle's head and back while whispering to him, "Revise your statement and pray God will guide him. God guides men with their parents' prayers."

"This wasn't a prayer. It was an unveiling, a kashf."

Uncle Abdallah's tears flowed copiously as he said, "He will die before me. I will die forty days after him."

"Any place that is not feminine in gender is untrustworthy."

—IBN ARABI

14

Most learning and instruction circles moved to the Grand Mosque. The few that remained in the Ibn Addis Mosque had to compete with itinerant vendors who possessed permits to display their wares in its courtyard and others who intruded there unchallenged. I also moved to the Grand Mosque as a member of the circle of a shaykh with whom Seville's clear sky grew brighter one day. Yusuf al-Kumi arrived from Fez, preceded by his reputation for charismatic acts and majestic deeds. My father found a place for me in his circle straightaway and canceled all my other lessons. When I first sat in his presence, I felt I was sitting before a luminous niche. Most of the other boys fled from him, because his brow was furrowed and he was perpetually scowling. He might remain like that all day long, but if he saw a wretchedly poor man he would laugh and summon the pauper. He would seat the fellow next to him, share his food with him, and hand him all the money he had in his purse.

My father chose him as my shaykh and thus, without even realizing it, set me on my path. God in heaven had destined this, and my father on Earth had executed His will. So the novice finally met his novice master. I journeyed through his expressive features like a dove whose safest sky was this shaykh's face, and no spirit was more spacious than his. He chose me to sit next to him on his right. Then I would read aloud a text he would explain. He seated another boy named Ahmad al-Hariri on his left. I met him for the first time in that teaching circle, and we became lifelong friends. I offered him a place in my heart and never regretted it. We were the star students in the shaykh's orbit. One day he told us, "Starting tomorrow, you two will come daily to al-Mantiar."

"What will we do there, Shaykh?"

"We will read al-Qushayri's *Epistle*."

Even though I was happy to be chosen, I asked, "Why don't we wait till you return from your spiritual retreat? Then we can read for you in the mosque."

"You'll understand when we get there."

We three departed from the city's gate and arrived at al-Mantiar in time for the noon prayer, which we performed at the top of the mountain in an old hermitage where the shaykh slept. After we prayed, he pulled a copy of the epistle from his kit and handed it to me, saying, "Read this, Muhyi . . . if you can."

I took al-Qushayri's book from him, opened the book, and started to read. For no apparent reason I suddenly experienced a tremor. The epistle's first words stuck in my throat, and I couldn't utter them. Looking up at the shaykh, I found he had become a far more grandiose and majestic presence than I had seen before. I started to read again. Then my tremor increased and the pages shook in my hands till I almost loosened some from the binding. I tried repeatedly and failed each time. I seemed to have totally lost my voice. The book fell from my hand, and I looked up at the shaykh with my eyes wandering with fear and dread.

The shaykh picked up *al-Risala* with a slight smile and handed it to Ahmad, saying, "Read, Ahmad."

He accepted the book apprehensively and looked anxiously toward me. Then he recited the traditional phrases, taking refuge from accursed Satan and dedicating his reading to God. Once he opened *al-Risala* and started to read, his voice rang out clearly. He read easily till the shaykh stopped him and began to explain the text. We continued this way, with Ahmad reading a section and the shaykh explaining it, while I remained silent and didn't ask or answer any questions. My tremor had left me, but my perplexity continued about what had roiled my mind. When we performed the afternoon prayer, the shaykh said, "Muhyi, you'll stay here with me, and Ahmad will return home."

Looking at Ahmad, he said, "Go to Muhyi's family and tell them he is on a spiritual retreat with me till we finish *al-Risala*."

Ahmad departed, and, while the shaykh prayed, I scouted the little hermitage to pick a suitable corner to sleep in. When he finished his devotions, he pointed, without saying a word, to the place where I would sleep by the door. He went back outside, leaving me to wonder what I had gotten myself into. I had never been on a spiritual retreat before and didn't know what would be expected of me. The shaykh did not have a servant. *Should I wait on him?* I had not brought enough food with me. *What will we eat? Why did the shaykh choose me to finish reading* al-Risala *and send* al-Hariri *away?* I brooded about these questions till the shaykh came back inside the hermitage and headed to a corner I hadn't noticed before. When he returned, his hands were full of dates and dry figs, which he placed before me. He explained, "I know you didn't bring food with you. This is what you will eat."

"But that's really a lot, Shaykh. Five or six dates will be plenty for me."

"This is your food for the entire week, not just for today."

Pointing to a water jug, he said, "Bring that and follow me."

Leaving the hermitage, we walked toward the mountain's summit till we reached a spring from which warm water flowed. He told me to take a sip and fill the jug. The water had a foul taste. In any case, we performed our ablutions, and I followed him back to the hermitage. On our descent, I suggested: "Shaykh, reading the epistle was hard because I was tired from walking up the rugged path, and I. . . ."

"No, Muhyi. That wasn't it."

"We had walked without stopping since dawn; so I must have been tired."

"I told you that wasn't the reason, Muhyi."

Even though he spoke softly without turning to face me, his tone was decisive. I felt perplexed that he had rejected my explanation without saying why. He seemed to be censuring me for some unintended error. I said nothing more till we reached the hermitage and went inside. I deposited the water jug, and we sat down. He removed *al-Risala* from his belongings and handed it to me once more. "Read," he said.

Then I read from it, easily and fluently, without any hesitation or difficulty. My heart rate was regular, and I was breathing normally. When he finally stopped me, he observed, "Now you ought to be more tired than before, but you were able to read."

"Why, Shaykh?"

"The first time I clenched my fist as you read, and that made it almost impossible for you to read. Now that my fist isn't clenched, you can read."

"How can your clenched fist block me and your open palm set me free, Shaykh?"

"That's because I am your shaykh. God has destined me to be your novice master and for you to be my novice. By God's command I can clench you tight and spread you wide open. . . . Once you have set your feet on the beginning of the path, I will send you forth."

We passed a week on the mountain while I memorized al-Qushayri's epistle. I secluded myself for a lengthy time, begging God to guide me to the path He had chosen for me. Then the shaykh sent me away while he remained in his hermitage. One cold morning I headed back to Seville but did not feel the cold. I was determined to complete the long journey without tiring. When I reached the mountain's lower slope, I looked back up at the summit, where the hermitage was no longer visible. The tears in my eyes were caused by separation from my shaykh. Then I felt certain that I had become a true disciple who weeps when parted from his master. My shaykh inspired greater awe on al-Mantiar than in Seville. I could not grasp the secret reason for this, even though I brooded about it a lot and begged God to unveil its mystery for me. He did, but only many years later when I was in Mecca. As thoughts rushed copiously into my mind and cascaded down in cataracts accompanied by visions, I understood that this was an unveiling. Then I reached quickly for my pen and wrote:

On Mount al-Mantiar I attained the spiritual rank (the *makana*) of the Shaykh. *Makan*, "place," is masculine in Arabic. *Makana*, "spiritual rank," is feminine. Adam was male and was completed exclusively by Eve. Al-Mantiar was a mountain that was completed only by the shaykh. Adam without Eve would have been a single individual who lacked any offspring. The mountain without the shaykh is a worthless ridge. Place (*makan*) without a spiritual rank (*makana*) is insufficient. *Makan* must acquire the feminine ending "a" to perfect its rank, its *makana*.

15 **ALEPPO** 1259 CE/657 AH

I traded nineteen cows for one camel and felt I had made an incredible deal. When the enemies neared the city, the prices of riding animals soared and those of livestock plummeted. Merchants offered everything they had in their shops and storerooms for the cheapest imaginable prices, and people bought out all the provisions, foodstuffs, fodder, and dates offered for sale with all the dinars and dirhems they had in their pockets. One man sold off his merchandise so he could travel, and another stocked up on everything he needed for his trip. Anyone who could find a way was leaving. Procrastinators were out of luck. I saw people leave their home, stop by the market, and immediately quit Aleppo, without returning to their house first. Christians who chose to travel west toward Antioch, Adana, Sis, and Tartus assembled at the Antioch Gate on the western side of the city. There they removed the sashes that had marked them as Christians and some donned a small cross. When the goldsmiths heard the Christians had started buying gold and silver, they took their wares near that gate. Once people heard this, though, these refugees stopped buying jewelry, for fear thieves would ambush them on their way to Christian territories.

Most Muslims were heading south to Damascus or planning to travel beyond that city to the Hijaz or Egypt. For the entire past year, Friday sermons had filled worshippers' hearts with fear by focusing on one idea: the imminent fulfilment of the divine prophecy that as Judgment Day approaches, fire from the Hijaz will light up the necks of camels in Bosra, Syria. Preachers had continued, Friday after Friday, warning people that Judgment Day was drawing nigh and narrating the signs and events to expect. Once Baghdad fell to the Mongols, people spread the rumor that Hülegü was the Antichrist and a Muslim's only escape would be to seek refuge in the holy lands. Our preacher believed this fully and said:

People, he is called the Antichrist—al-Masih al-Dajjal (the Scoured and Anointed Cheat)—because he will scour the earth in almost no time at all. This Mongol commander Hülegü, may God curse him, has scoured the earth from Azerbaijan to Syria in just weeks. He also is an Antichrist who claims to be a Muslim, but Islam isn't responsible for him. Those of you who believe in the prophecy of our beloved prophet Muhammad, may God bless him and grant him peace, should obey his advice. He said the Antichrist will emerge from a fissure between Syria and Iraq and then wreak havoc to the south and north, flattening everything on Earth except Mecca and Medina.

People trembled fearfully in the mosque's courtyard and continued to discuss this threat in the squares, markets, houses, fields, and public baths. Such talk died down whenever Hülegü's siege of a city was prolonged but burgeoned whenever he sacked that city and moved closer to Aleppo. Even Mardin finally fell, leaving nothing to shield Aleppo from him. Then panic crept into people's hearts. I had never in an entire life spent in the market seen comparable anarchy. Goods were lined up by the doors of the stores, not inside them. Livestock were led straight to the center of the market, not restricted to its periphery, without any objection from the market's supervisors. Vendors' voices grew loud and strident as they attempted to drown each other out. Carpets were spread where they didn't belong. A saddler was in the apothecaries' market, and a textile merchant sold cloth in the blacksmiths' market. Scattered down the alleys were pans, flasks, broken jugs, and rubbish that people trod on when sellers dumped items for which they could find no buyer.

I led the camel quickly to our house, where I found my father standing impatiently at the door. The moment he saw me, he shouted: "What delayed you, Son? Hurry up. . . ."

I expected him to read me the riot act when he learned how little success I had had in bartering our livestock, but he didn't. We started lifting the boxes I had left for him and the slave, Yaqut, to fill and seal. Meanwhile I wondered how conscious he was of what was happening. Had he noticed that I had bartered twenty head of cattle for a single camel, or not? After he loaded eleven mules with boxes, sacks, and provisions, he stood there, panting. So, when I walked by him, I observed, as if to myself: "Twenty cows for one camel! How crazy!"

Without turning toward me, my father said, "The crazy man is the fellow who accepted your cows, which will perish in his care, one by one."

Then he gestured to the howdah, which sat closed on the ground, and urged me: "Let's go! Lift the howdah for your mother."

My mother finally emerged from the door, shaking dust off her hands to show that she had finished her work. "Tahir, nothing's left in the house."

"In that case, we'll depart before sunset."

My mother was astonished by his sudden decision. "By night? Shouldn't we wait till dawn?"

"No. Even if the Mongols don't arrive, chaos is quickly going to envelop the city, and being outside it will be safer than being inside."

"What about thieves and highwaymen?"

My father turned toward my mother and smiled for the first time since that morning. "Believe me," he assured her, "there will be no brigands between Aleppo and Damascus! Aleppo's going to be a deserted area in a few days."

A tear suddenly appeared in my mother's eye as she gazed down affectionately at the doorstep before her. "What about our house? Our family? Our neighbors?"

My father mimicked her tone and asked, "And my shop? My business? My wares?"

My mother's face was bathed in tears, and her voice resembled a death rattle when she exclaimed, "What a sorry state of affairs!"

"Umm Isma'il, right now we must keep our heads firmly planted on our necks. Mayafarqin, Mardin, and al-Ruha, which were more heavily fortified than Aleppo, have already fallen."

"I thought our walls were very high and our citadel impregnable."

"If they besiege us, we'll starve to death. I hear that when they entered Mayafarqin, after laying siege to it for a year, they found all its inhabitants dead!"

"Your grace, Lord. . . ."

While I sat listening to my parents' conversation, I was convulsed by both rage and fear. The Mongol armies were advancing toward us while those of al-Nasir Yusuf huddled in Damascus like a hen sitting on her eggs! He had not come to our aid or even tried to defend himself. For the first time since the dawn of Islam, Muslims lacked a caliph. Qutuz was in Egypt, al-Nasir in Syria, and al-Mughith in Kerak! Yes, by God, they're all chickens; each hen will sit on her eggs till Hülegü arrives and breaks them all!

My father entered the house and walked through all its rooms to check that they were empty. When he returned, he quietly began counting the boxes on the mules, pointing to each box in turn with a finger. Then he went into the house one final time, and brought back a tightly sealed, beautifully crafted wooden box decorated by an expert hand with handsome calligraphy. He placed this box inside the saddlebag of the first mule, the mule he himself would ride. Then he went to stand by the door till my mother emerged, tearful and pale-faced.

She asked my father, "Shouldn't we pass by Ruqiya's house? She may need our help."

"We will meet them at the Qinnasrin Gate."

"How about Sumayya?"

"All your daughters and their husbands will be there. Isma'il checked on each of them this morning."

My mother climbed inside her howdah and settled into it. I made the camel rise and handed his halter to Yaqut, who was already mounted on his mule. As we proceeded in our little caravan I brooded anxiously: *What kind of caravan is this for an Aleppine merchant: eleven mules and a single camel? No thief in this city or the outlying districts would be interested in it.*

My mother's voice reached us from inside the howdah as she reminded us to recite the traveler's prayer. Once we had left our neighborhood, I heard her recite to herself, in a shaky, mournful voice: "Conceal us, Concealer, and preserve us, Preserver."

When we reached the Qinnasrin Gate we found the rest of our family waiting for us. My father gestured to Sumayya's husband to ride one of our mules, since he didn't have a mount. Then we joined the throngs of people passing through the gate to escape the approaching Mongol inferno. The whole city was shedding its inhabitants like someone shaking snakes from her bedcovers. I saw our neighbors, friends, master craftsmen, and city officials. I even saw soldiers fleeing with their helmets and armor hanging from their camels. Some of us felt reassured to find that our caravan was protected by men who knew how to use weapons, even if they were fleeing from battle.

I had traveled this route between Aleppo and Damascus many times with my father when we conducted trade between these two cities. We had occasionally gone as far as Nablus and Kerak but had never seen the road so packed with travelers—not even in pilgrimage season. Once we reached Damascus, it too was more crowded than I had witnessed it. Fortunately, my father was held in high esteem by some merchants in the city; otherwise we wouldn't have found a place to sleep that night or shelter for our animals. Prior to our arrival, my father had sent someone to arrange lodging for us and a place for the mules and the camel. Most of the other migrants erected tents on the outskirts of the city, and there were hundreds of those shelters, in rambling lines. Drawn by curiosity, men, women, children, slaves, peddlers, and holy fools poked around these tents. Outstanding citizens also turned up to support these wayfarers.

The morning after we arrived, my father said, "I'm going to Our Master's Mausoleum. You all may come with me if you like."

My mother, Sumayya, and I went with him, but Ruqiya, who was pregnant, preferred to stay with her feverish husband, who had been bitten by a scorpion during the trip. We went on foot to Mount Qasioun, where the tombs of the Al al-Zaki are located. We entered the mausoleum together. Then, holding the beautiful box, my father stood before the tomb, which was covered with plaster, and saluted the Supreme Shaykh. My mother and Sumayya prayed in whispers too soft for me to hear. I also saluted the Shaykh, whom my grandfather Sawdakin had accompanied on his travels for many years. Then my father rose and greeted the Mausoleum's custodian, who was reciting Qur'an in a secluded corner.

After greeting this man, he sat down before him and said, "This is a book written by our Supreme Shaykh, in his own handwriting. On his deathbed, my father entrusted it to me and made me promise to safeguard it as carefully as my eye in its socket. I can think of no more secure place for it than in his Master's sepulcher. May I place it inside the tomb?"

The custodian's keen interest was obvious. Closing the Qur'an in his hands, he turned to ask my father, "Where is it?"

My father placed the book before him and opened it to reveal its handsomely bound pages with margins decorated by skillful scribes on glossy Aleppo paper treated with preservatives. The pages gleamed, and the handwriting was clear. As the custodian touched the book, a sigh escaped from his lips. He began to cry, and his eyes gleamed with repressed tears.

"Yes. You have upheld your trust. We shall return the trust to its owner."

TOME THREE

"Time is liquid space, and space is congealed time."

—— **IBN ARABI**

16

When the Caliph's brother died suddenly, my father was asked to travel to Marrakech. I begged to go with him, and he agreed. He told me to prepare for the trip but then had second thoughts. He explained that the group had decided to sail down the river to the Atlantic to save time and that there wouldn't be enough room on the ship for me.

He patted my shoulder affectionately and assured me, "If the trip was by caravan, that would be easy."

Bitterly disappointed, I felt sad and desperate. In my mind's eye, the walls of Seville were closing in on me to form a fearsome stone prison from which there could be no escape. I had turned fifteen, but Murcia and Seville were all I had seen of the world.

When my father caught me weeping, he was touched. "Don't lose heart, Son," he said. "When I return from my trip, I'll take you to Cordova."

He came back two months later with a large alum crystal box and explained that a merchant friend had entrusted it to him. I wondered how he had found space on the ship for a box twice my size, but not for me. He was obviously elated on his return. The Caliph was pleased to welcome the delegates and seeing them strengthened his fondness for Seville. So he ordered each one be offered a generous gift and wrote his governor a memo that said in part: ". . . since God has provided us bountiful amounts of *kharaj* land tax and many spoils of war, we order that the taxes owed by all citizens of Seville not be levied effective today. All praise belongs to God alone."

The Governor announced this decision to the people that same day and directed preachers to mention it in their Friday sermons. They were also instructed to pray that the Caliph would be granted victory and the power to subdue those who tried to elude his reign in Gafsa and the surrounding area.

The Caliph's gift included an Arabian mare for my father and jewelry from Marrakech for my mother. Her delight with the jewelry quickly evaporated when she learned the Caliph had also given my father a Castilian slave girl—one of a group that came to the Almohad palace as part of the *jizya* poll tax Alfonso was obliged to pay. My father didn't mention her to us till two weeks after the Governor received these orders. Durra (Pearl) arrived in a howdah, escorted by two soldiers. My father immediately led her to my sisters' room. Then he went to my mother and told her, "Listen, Nur. The Caliph has given me a slave girl. I don't want to have a child by her. So, don't you cause any problems and don't be rude to her."

My mother steeled her nerves and promised she had heard him and would obey. Once he was out of the room, though, she wept and wailed quietly, biting a pillow to dampen the sound. After getting all this weeping and moaning out of her system, she went to the girls' room, where she found Durra sitting silently off to the side while the two girls tried to edge closer and talk to her. My mother ordered her to stand up and follow her. She walked her through the house, going from room to room. Then she instructed her on how to care for my father—how to wash his clothes, make his bed, heat water for his ablutions, and clean his bath.

She told Durra: "From today forward, you will be responsible for everything that pertains to your master."

When my father returned that evening, my mother greeted him politely and said: "May God make your concubine a blessing for you. I outlined her responsibilities to her and explained how to serve you. As you can see, I have grown old and can no longer bear all the work. Moreover my migraine never leaves me. If you will allow me to live with my daughters in the two eastern rooms, you and Durra can have the two western ones. Muhyi will live in the room downstairs. This will be better for you, because you won't need to move from one bed to another every night."

After pretending to be annoyed and dissatisfied, even though he was secretly pleased, my father finally consented. I was the opposite; I pretended to be happy but actually felt miserable and sad. There was nothing in this household to inspire in me high aspirations or ambitions—not my submissive, tearful mother nor my father, who wavered indecisively between worldly and religious goals. My two sisters were adults and had started wearing veils but could scarcely distinguish between peas and beans. They were preoccupied by gossip, jewelry, and ballads. Even Sallum rarely spoke to anyone; he resembled an ox powering a waterwheel—just eating and working. I felt that my family obstructed my progress and prevented me from achieving my goals. Soon my parents would grow old, and I would be obliged to care for them. My sisters would marry and leave home.

A prisoner in my heart yearned to burst forth. A sun there waited to shine. A caravan was eager to depart. In our house, though, my father was busy with his concubine, and my mother with her daughters. Nothing new was happening outside the house either. Even the learning circles and dhikr sessions had fallen silent since the Caliph had departed and taken all the ulema, jurisprudents, philosophers, and physicians with him in his retinue. Seville lacked anyone who might spark thought or stir the intellect. The whole city contained not a single scholarly shaykh whose lessons I hadn't attended and whose books I hadn't read. There wasn't a single bookseller whose store I hadn't visited and whose manuscripts I hadn't examined. Even Yusuf al-Kumi had begun a spiritual retreat on al-Mantiar and canceled all his lessons. I was overwhelmed by boredom, which is a true demon that slays endeavor and saps resolve.

One afternoon I was walking aimlessly beside the river with al-Hariri, who was short enough to be my younger brother, even though he was two years older. We bought some sugared almonds and sat chatting on the riverbank. I told him: "I can't stand my family! My mother always has a headache, my two sisters are all wrapped up in their 'doings', and my father shuttles back and forth between 'his' palace and his concubine. The old woman who lives behind our house has escalated her abuse. Now, in addition to cursing us, she's begun throwing pebbles and sandals when we walk past her house."

Al-Hariri heard me out. Then he laughed and said that conditions at his house were no better. His mother was too old to care for herself; his older brother, a tailor, looked after her. Their father, who had been a soldier in the Almoravid army, had died the day the Almohads entered Andalusia.

"Why don't we run away?" al-Hariri asked with cheerful bitterness. I answered with a nod and a smile. He continued, "We'll go to Cairo or Damascus, or perhaps Baghdad."

I yearned intensely for all those cities and rejoiced at his suggestion, even though he was kidding. I let him continue spinning his dreams while he chewed sugared almonds and gazed at the horizon beyond the river.

"Have you heard about Ibn Jubayr al-Gharnati? The booksellers have one of his books."

"What's it about?"

"His trip to Mecca. People tell an amusing story about it."

"What do they say?"

He sat bolt upright, turned toward me, swallowed the last bit of an almond, and then replied gaily, "Fine. I read his book in the shop of a copyist who said that the Governor of Granada summoned Ibn Jubayr, wanting him to write an epistle. When Ibn Jubayr arrived, he found the Governor drinking wine. The Governor offered him a glass. Ibn Jubayr, a God-fearing man, declined it. The infuriated Governor then swore that Ibn Jubayr had to drink seven glasses of wine."

Al-Hariri laughed so hard he choked and had to stop speaking. My eyes were wide with astonishment.

Once he finished laughing, al-Hariri continued, "Imagine a man who has never drunk wine drinking seven glasses of it in quick succession!"

Al-Hariri guffawed and clutched his belly while chortling uproariously. His laughter proved contagious, and I laughed along with him till he stopped. Finally, with tears in his eyes, he continued, "The point is that the copyist says that once Ibn Jubayr drank seven glasses of wine, he stood up but immediately crumpled to the ground. Next he vomited everything in his belly and landed on his face. Feeling sorry for him, the Governor ordered his chamberlain to fill seven chalices with gold dinars for him."

"That's the least he owed Ibn Jubayr for tainting his piety!"

"Ibn Jubayr regained consciousness, returned home with all those dinars, and decided to spend them on performing the hajj pilgrimage to expiate his sin. So he traveled to Mecca, passing by Egypt, Iraq, and Sicily, and wrote a book, in which he certainly did not mention the reason he took the trip."

"Where can I find his book?"

"It's with a Tunisian copyist, and his shop is one of those between the mosque and the corridor that leads to the goldsmiths' market. You'll definitely recognize him because he has a squinty right eye and his shop slants like a triangle."

"How do you know all these stationers? I haven't ever seen this one."

"Most of them bring books they've copied to my brother, Muhammad, who sews the pages together. I've come to know all of them, and they let me read their manuscripts free of charge."

"We'll go there tomorrow."

"Never trust piety that comes with strings attached."

—**IBN ARABI**

17

Once al-Hariri introduced me to the book dealers he knew, their market became my second home. Still, I insisted on paying the fee for every book I read and each one I ordered. I wasn't going to read gratis. The more unusual a book was and the more curious I grew about it, the harder the search for it proved. I would go from one copyist to another, and each would take me to his storerooms to search for the book I wanted among their vintage manuscripts. I entered the lane that their shops lined dozens of times. The only two shops I never visited belonged to copyists for Castilian and Greek manuscripts, and I didn't know either of those languages. Translators who worked in those shops charged a tenth of the manuscript's weight in silver to translate it into Arabic and half that to translate it into Castilian. I brought a Greek book to one of them and hired him to translate it. He weighed the book, and I paid him half his fee in advance. Seated beside him was a short man in his sixties who looked Castilian. He had kind eyes and smiled at everyone who passed. He started looking at the book resting in the translator's scales. Then he glanced at me and nodded his head appreciatively. After greeting me, he said, "I'll pay half the cost of translation if you let me borrow it to have it copied."

"Of course. Sure. But I want to read it first."

"Certainly. Naturally. I'm in no hurry."

This was Frederick, and he proved to be God's answer to my prayer to remove boredom from my heart and to wipe lethargy from my mind. He did not have a shop in the stationers' market but, like me, was a constant visitor there. We engaged in deep conversations day after day, and he could answer any question I had about Greek or Frankish books. Moreover, I discovered that he knew a lot about Indian and Chinese books, scarcely any of which were available in Arabic translation. He invited me to visit his house, and I asked if I could bring al-Hariri. He agreed, and the two of us went there together. Frederick appeared, smiling, when we knocked on the door, and greeted us with his Castilian-accented Arabic.

There were nine men and two women at his gathering, where a man seated in the middle read from a book while everyone else listened. As I scanned their faces quickly, I discovered a range of complexions and eye color. Arabs, Muwallads, Franks, and Berbers were present. Frederick showed us to seats near the door, and we started listening to a discussion of Pythagoras. The seated man read a passage in Greek and then immediately translated it to Arabic. He continued reading aloud, translating, and discussing the text but eventually rose and sat down near us. Another man took a seat in the middle of the group and started to read from a different Greek book and translate it to Arabic. The man who had previously held the floor commented: "Only logic is eternal; everything else is transient."

So I whispered to al-Hariri, "By my life, that's what seduced Ibn Rushd!"

Al-Hariri and I became frequent visitors at Frederick's gatherings on Saturday and Sunday evenings, and he would make a fuss about us. Occasionally I arrived early and sat to talk with Frederick and his daughter before the others arrived.

One day I asked, "When did you come to Seville, Frederick?"

"I didn't move here. I was born in Seville."

"So when did your father move here?"

"No, my grandfather did. He was bishop of the church here before the Almohads conquered the city."

"So you've lived in Seville all your life?"

"No. When I was a child we migrated north and lived in a village near Toledo."

"What brought you back?"

"I returned on account of the war."

"The war between the Almoravids and the Almohads?"

"No, no. A war that flared up in Castile among the noblemen—about who would serve as guardian for Alfonso VIII, who ascended the throne as a child. I considered going to some paternal uncles in France but feared that the books I inherited from my grandfather might be seized and burned. The library I received from him was full of Greek and Latin manuscripts, some of which he himself translated into

Arabic and Castilian. While I was wondering where to move, we heard that the Almohads weren't as hostile to Christians as the Almoravids had been. By that time my wife had died, and my daughter Ghala was still fourteen. So we returned to Seville together."

As if in response to hearing her name, Ghala appeared, wearing a long gown that covered her entire body except for her neck, face, and luxuriant curly hair. Her eyes were almond-shaped and somewhat narrow. She looked at me in a way that clearly showed she felt uncomfortable in my presence. She started to shake the cushions and arrange them along the wall in preparation for the guests' arrival. That chore excused her from speaking or listening to me. So I ignored her too while Frederick continued telling me about his return to Seville.

"When I found that my grandfather's house was empty, I bought it. I also purchased a kermes oak plantation on a bluff outside Seville. I'll take you all there one day. It's lovely in the spring. You'll see the kermes scale insects from which we make a crimson dye that Goth women like a lot. I sell it to caravans that trade between Andalusia and France."

Someone knocked abruptly on the door, and Ghala hurried to open it, apparently delighted that the arrival of other guests would make her presence less problematic. Some men, whose names I did not yet know, entered and greeted us in different languages. I responded to the Arabic greetings and felt jealous of Frederick and Ghala, who answered all the greetings and conversed in Arabic and Castilian easily and fluently.

Frederick served us wine. I accepted a glass, but al-Hariri hesitated. Then he took one, following my example. When I had a sip, I noticed that he looked uncomfortable and perplexed. I drained my glass before al-Hariri had brought his to his lips. Finally I turned to him and asked, "Aren't you going to drink any?"

"I'm afraid."

"Of what?"

"That God will seize me while I'm sinning."

"You won't be sinning."

"How can that be? Isn't wine forbidden?"

"Of course it is, but you're a believer. Your belief is permanent, but your sin is momentary. Should God seize you, He will seize you by your belief. So all will end well for you."

"Really?"

"Yes."

Al-Hariri brought the glass to his lips and drank a little. He looked me straight in the eye, and I cheered him on. He smiled, and I smiled. His face relaxed, and he drained his glass. Frederick filled our glasses again. We drank some more.

"Who gave you this rule about permanent belief trumping momentary sin?" Al-Hariri asked.

"No one. God disclosed it to me as an unveiling, a *kashf*."

Al-Hariri drained his third glass. "Amazing!" he said. "God hasn't unveiled that to me, even though I've attended every circle and class you have."

"Spiritual unveilings are keyed to a person's gnostic ability to grasp them. A gnostic must already have taste, *dhawq*."

"Yes. You're right. Speaking of taste, I've never tasted any wine better than this."

"Liar! That's the first wine you've ever tasted."

"My God! Has God revealed that to you as well?"

I laughed at his mild sarcasm and responded, "No, your eyes revealed that, and now they tell me you're drunk."

"How much wine have we consumed?"

"Four glasses."

"Ibn Jubayr drank more than that. We'll need to drink seven if we want to travel like him."

Then he yelled to Frederick: "We need three more glasses, Frederick. We want to travel to the East!"

"A gnostic's consciousness colors reality the way a glass vessel colors water."

—IBN ARABI

18

Durra spent her first nights in my father's bed. Once his ardor calmed, he decided to honor his promise to me. So we left for Cordova in a long caravan of the Governor's messengers who carried letters, currency, and goods, petty merchants who didn't have their own caravans and thus availed themselves of the protection provided by the Governor's caravan, and servants and slaves hired to care for us during the trip. My father was in charge of the riders, and everyone obeyed his commands. During the first days of Ramadan we departed through the East Gate and headed north and then east. The route required no guide, astronomer, or scout, because the Guadalquivir River flows between the two cities, with only a few twists in some areas. Travelers walk parallel to the river till they arrive.

The next morning, men spotted a herd of wild donkeys, and a group set off to hunt them. I asked my father's permission to accompany the men, but he refused, insisting that we were on a trip, that he was responsible for the caravan, and that we didn't have time for any forays or hunting. He added, "Especially now that the Portuguese are ambushing our caravans!"

"Are we at war with them?"

"Definitely. Don't you keep up with current events? The Caliph's fleet destroyed half of their ships."

"Why didn't we polish them all off?"

"It's not that easy. The Portuguese are the toughest and most determined Franks."

"Are they a threat to our caravans?"

"They have actually plundered a number of them, killing the people in them."

"What will we do?"

"According to our intelligence, the Caliph in Marrakech has requested God's guidance for an attack on them."

We spotted Cordova's walls in the distance on the third day and entered the city during afternoon prayers. Then I experienced the series of slight surprises a young person meets when entering this city for the first time. Men do not cover their heads there and let their hair grow shoulder-length! Streets are illuminated by lamps that burn through the night and are extinguished at dawn. Buildings adjoin each other without alleys between them where trash can collect or beggars sleep. Ox carts pass through side streets to collect rubbish. People are so well dressed they seem to be wearing their holiday best.

We penetrated the city till we approached its market. Then boys sent by the city's merchants came to ask what merchandise we brought. Some petty merchants immediately began to bargain with them. Goods were exchanged and sales concluded. Before we reached the city's center, cavalrymen from the governor's castle appeared to escort us to the palace, where my father delivered the caravan's official shipments to the palace secretaries, who issued receipts for their delivery. Then the caravan disbanded. Soldiers went to the barracks, merchants to the caravanserai for merchants, and I went with my father and our hired slave to a hostel near the Grand Mosque, where the governor's guests lodged. Next we went to a bath house to wash away the filth and exhaustion of our trip. Once I had finished bathing, I donned a shirt, pants, and a cloak, leaving my head bare. A bath attendant had combed my hair till it felt soft and almost reached my shoulders. Then I joined my father, who was drinking hot mint tea in a room beyond the bath.

When he saw me bareheaded, he laughed. "Have you become a citizen of Cordova?"

"Haven't you heard what Ambrose the Frank said: 'When in Rome, do as the Romans do'?"

"Where did you learn this maxim? I didn't know you had Franks for friends in Seville."

"I heard that from a man named Frederick. In his gatherings he recounts information about the Romans and Greeks concerning their sciences and literature. His daughter Ghala mentioned this saying."

My father smiled apprehensively and asked, "What is this Ghala like?"

"She's beautiful, Father—like all the Frankish women."

He sat up straight and, turning toward me, said, "My son will never marry a Frank! Do you understand?"

"I didn't say I love her. I'll never marry, Father. Saints don't marry."

"Have you become a saint?"

"Not yet, but by the grace of God I will become a *wali*."

"Do you mean a *wali* like those men who wander the streets aimlessly?"

"No, Father, they are guided by their Lord. He illuminates their hearts, but that illumination is only visible to another initiate."

My father sighed and said, "Son, if you think I have devoted myself to service in the palace only for selfish reasons, you are mistaken. I have leveled a path for you so that your years may pass smoothly and your chores be light. I can put in a good word with the top people for you to serve as secretary to one of them. Perhaps later you may become one of the Caliph's secretaries."

"I don't want any of this, Father. My one wish is to become a *wali*."

"And how do you become a holy man?"

"God chooses his friends. I just need to ready myself for Him to choose me, to be prepared for His decrees.

"So you will wait, apathetically and unemployed, till God chooses you as a saint?"

"No, I will pursue learning, exert myself, and frequent the shaykhs. My heart loves this, Father, much more than the court and caliphs. So don't force me to do something I hate. My heart has attached itself to God. Don't pull me away from Him."

My father extended his leg, kicked me above my hip, and shouted: "God help me! Do you think I'm a demon who is trying to turn you away from God? Scram! May God never bless you! Get out of my sight!"

I didn't go near him all the rest of the day. Instead, I visited Fatima bint al-Muthanna. I reached her lodging after walking a long way. She lived in a small room on a small alley that led to the city dump, where rubbish was burning. Black smoke filled the alleyway, choking passersby. I knocked on the door, and a young girl I didn't know answered. She turned out to be the daughter of a neighbor, who left the girl with Fatima during the day while he worked. So each of them looked after the other. The girl let me in. Fatima sat in a corner covered with a thick blanket.

I kissed her hands and feet and sat down beside her. She lifted the edge of her blanket, wishing to cover me too. I agreed, even though I didn't feel cold. We sat, pressed together in that corner, covered by a single blanket. From up close, I gazed at her face, where each new wrinkle had made it even more beautiful. I asked her all the questions a son asks his mother after a separation, and she replied with all the answers a mother provides her returning son. She was weaker in every respect except for her voice, which remained as calm and melodious as if she were a young woman.

After a long conversation, I told her, "Mother, I haven't found my pillar yet, my *watad*."

"But he has found you."

"Why hasn't he declared himself yet?"

"When you're worthy, he will."

"You said that would happen once I purified my heart. Isn't it pure enough already?"

"How have you purified it?"

"I have filled it with virtues, a clear conscience, and good intentions and caused it to reject anything incompatible with all these."

"This is half of the requisite purification, son."

"How do I complete the second half?"

"By allowing it to receive every type of form."

19

Our arrival in Cordova proved to be an ill omen for the city's chief jurist Khalaf ibn Bashkuwal, who died while we were on the outskirts of Cordova. I attended his wake with my father and found everyone there dressed in white, as if it were a feast day.

Noticing my surprise, my father explained, "Residents of Cordova wear white as a sign of mourning."

"So when do they wear black?"

The longer I stayed in Cordova the more convinced I became that this city was the opposite of Seville in every respect. I thought this was just an idea that had flashed through my mind and was amazed when it resurfaced as a topic of conversation at the wake. Once Ibn Rushd entered, everyone rose and greeted him. His head was bowed, his expression sorrowful, and a tear could be seen lingering in his eye. From where I stood, I gazed at the man whose name had been repeated in every gathering I had attended in Seville since I set foot there. When I sat in teaching circles, I heard my shaykhs quote his words and reply to them. When I sat in my uncle's shop, I heard him cite Ibn Rushd's medical dicta and advocate his remedies. When I sat at home, I heard my father talk about him the way he discussed the Caliph's closest companions. Even my mother told me she had heard from a hairdresser who had heard from a Greek woman married to a merchant of Seville that Ibn Rushd had said there is no difference between a man and a woman and that women could rule as well as men and fight like them.

She asked me, "What do your shaykhs say about this, Muhyi?"

What could I tell my mother? Only two decades after she was emancipated from slavery she was thinking about ruling? Beauticians ought to muzzle their mouths before they enter a private residence—and even when they leave it. This happened the same week the Caliph ordered all the palace secretaries to set aside their work to devote themselves to making copies of Ibn Rushd's commentaries on Aristotle. Consequently, stationers started selling a copy for a quarter dirhem, since so many copies were on the market.

This deluge of copies reached our shaykh, Abd al-Qayum al-Randi, whose teaching circle for Shafiʿi jurisprudence I attended at the time. He arrived one morning and said, "What we've read so far suffices. Today we will start reading *Tahafut al-Falasifa: The Incoherence of the Philosophers*."

He ordered a student to run to his mule and fetch the book from her saddlebag. When the boy brought the book, our shaykh sat down, placed the book on his lap, and started to read aloud. We guessed he was reading it for the first time and had only just received the book:

I began to draft this book as a response to the ancient philosophers, to clarify the incoherence of their doctrine and the self-contradictory nature of their statements about metaphysics—the divine science—and to disclose the dangers of their sect as well as its defects, which on careful examination, are ridiculed by intelligent men.

It is also intended as a warning to the wise. I refer to what distinguishes them from the masses and the common people with reference to various beliefs and opinions. . . .[11]

Then he raised his head and immediately told us: "The chief justice of Cordova resembles them. Have you heard of him?"

I immediately replied, "That's Ibn Rushd."

The shaykh remarked: "May God thwart his efforts! In his assembly he says, 'Beauty is what the intellect judges beautiful. Ugliness is what the intellect deems ugly.' May God thwart his effort! What about God's judgment and law?"

I was thinking: *Woe to him! What of the heart's dictate and the Lord's unveiling?*

Now Ibn Rushd was here before me—sitting in front with the notables. I could hear him clearly. I listened carefully as if hoping he would say something to validate my opinion of him. The discussion centered on Ibn Bashkuwal. One man called him "Cordova's godly son," because he was born and died there.

Another agreed and added that the deceased had also served for some years as a judge in Seville.

A third man turned toward Ibn Rushd and asked, "Did you ever meet him in Seville?"

When Ibn Rushd shook his head, the conversation turned to a comparison between Seville and Cordova—just minutes after my private reflections on this subject. Ibn Rushd commented: "I just know we say that if a scholar dies in Seville, I would want his books brought to Cordova for sale, and if a musician dies in Cordova, I would want his instruments taken to Seville for sale."

Even though they were attending a wake, people laughed at his comment. I was annoyed that he had slandered my city, but my father laughed along with the others. When my father greeted Ibn Rushd, he showed profound respect for the scholar and kissed his head. My father felt that Ibn Rushd was an exemplary figure who had achieved every distinction: as a scholar, a judge, and a companion of caliphs. That represented my father's ultimate set of aspirations.

The following day I was surprised when my father told me Ibn Rushd wanted to see me.

"Me? Why?"

"To listen to what you have to say and for you to listen in turn to him."

"Who told him about me?"

"Skip these questions; they're none of your business. Go to his house following the afternoon prayer. He lives near the bridge. One of the governor's servants will show you the way."

As I said "Allahu Akbar" during the afternoon prayers I wondered whether this meeting with Ibn Rushd was part of some conspiracy to corrupt me. The prayer service, though, helped free me of some of my suspicions, and by its end I was able to look forward to this meeting as an ordinary interview, not an ambush I should dread. I had studied with dozens of shaykhs, read their works, asked them questions, responded to their queries, and debated who knew best. Why would meeting with Ibn Rushd differ from any of those encounters? When I left the mosque, I found a saddled mare waiting for me. The groom took her bridle, and we headed to the bridge.

His house was smaller than I expected, and there were more trees around it than usual. It was the first of a row of houses, which meant you couldn't walk around it.

Ibn Rushd's servant told me "the shaykh" was meeting with two of his students, who would leave soon. I entered, greeted them, and introduced myself. Ibn Rushd rose, welcomed me warmly, and asked me to sit next to him. Addressing his students again, he looked quite serious. He was pointing to some diagrams on a piece of paper, and I had no idea what they represented. Then he suddenly turned toward me and smiled again. "May God preserve and bless you. How have you found your stay in Cordova?"

Overwhelmed by his graciousness, I had no choice but to be polite. I remembered what he had said in praise of Cordova at the wake the previous day; so I replied, "This city is everything I could desire: its residents value knowledge, are of noble descent, and possess vast learning."

"May God be gracious to you! Have you met any of the city's Sufis?"

"I haven't met any of them but know the works of Yunus ibn al-Saffar, Abd al-Razzaq al-Ghaznawi, and some others."

"How about the philosophers? Have you studied any of their works?"

I realized then that God had meant for me and Ahmad al-Hariri to attend Frederick's reunions. I replied confidently, "I have learned about Empedocles, Pythagoras, and Plato."

He raised his eyebrows appreciatively and nodded his head slightly. Then he asked, "Have you found the natural laws that philosophers discover parallel the Sufis' unveilings?"

"Yes."

"That's beautiful . . . and . . . ."

Before he could finish, I interrupted: "And also no."

He drew his head back a little, contracted his eyebrows inquisitively, and asked, "What do you mean?"

"I mean yes and no."

"How can you answer both yes and no?"

"Yes, in that in our experience of this world, they correspond but do not coincide, because the world's condition changes."

"Son, explain your idea, for I have grown old and am no longer as sharp-witted as you."

"The philosophers provide positivist laws that explain what has happened but not what is to come; that's what *kashf*—unveiling—does."

"Yes, they do not offer prophecies about the unknown; but they do provide a law that whatever occurs will not violate."

"There is no such law."

"No such law?"

"Yes, there is no law. There exists only a creation totally dependent on the will of God the Exalted."

"Light that does not dissipate darkness is unreliable."

——**IBN ARABI**

20

We returned from Cordova to find that my uncle, Abdallah, was dying. His testicles had swollen tremendously, and he spread them before himself like a pillow. They caused him excruciating pain, for which he could find no medical relief. As was appropriate for a friend of God, he entrusted his fate to Him. When my father and I called on him, he was moaning softly, and we didn't know whether he was awake or asleep.

My father said: "I hope you feel better soon, Brother. Recover and heal, God willing."

My uncle opened his eyelids and looked at us. Then he replied, "Praise is due to God no matter what."

"How are you, Brother?"

"In God's hands. When He spreads them open, He is compassionate. When He clenches them, He is merciful."

We kissed the crown of his head and sat near him, saying nothing. Glancing around the room, my father murmured, "*La hawla wa-la quwa illa bi-llah*, all power and strength are God's."

Meanwhile I was gazing at my uncle's wrinkled forehead and his face, which seemed as dry as parched clay. When I noticed that his legs were spread wide beneath the covers, my heart was devastated by his distressing condition. Suddenly, without turning toward us, my uncle began to recite poetry:

Time passes, life passes.
An era returns with its burns.[12]

Commenting on this poem, my father responded sadly, "May God cure you and grant you happiness, Brother."

Tears were forming in my father's eyes, and he was almost sobbing. He squeezed my uncle's hand and kissed it. Then he rose and asked, "Can I get you anything?"

My uncle shook his head. Turning toward me, my father said, "Stay with your uncle. He has no servant here."

Al-Shakkaz and I did not stir from my uncle's house, and my father visited regularly. Sixteen days later my uncle's time came. Sensing it was near, my father decided to spend the night with us. Once we had completed the evening prayer, my uncle aligned his body with the qibla and prepared for sleep. In a faint voice he told us, "Relax. Lie down."

We chose sleeping spots around him and dozed off. When dawn arrived, I woke. I was the nearest to him and discovered that he wasn't breathing. I felt his brow, which was as cold as ice, and placed my hand on his chest to feel for a heartbeat, I found it warm, but there was no heartbeat. So I realized that his spirit had just departed. My sobs then were loud enough to wake my father and al-Shakkaz. Placing his forehead on my uncle's chest, my father began his lamentations. He repeated, "My brother, my beloved, my second father," as his tears soaked my uncle's shirt.

Al-Shakkaz decided to wash the body himself. A few days earlier my uncle had prepared the perfumed ointments for his body and his shroud. Al-Shakkaz brought them out and began to mix them. We all lifted him and placed him on a wooden plank that rested on two stones. We removed his clothes except his underpants. Al-Shakkaz washed my uncle's hands. Then he wrapped a cloth several times around his own hand, which he inserted under the sheet to wash my uncle's private parts. He stopped, looking astonished. He praised God and then raised the sheet covering my uncle's groin to show us that his testicles had shrunk back to their normal size, as if they had never been swollen.

We wept as al-Shakkaz commented: "This is a charism of a *wali*. This charismatic gift is a sermon. We can look at his genitals without embarrassment."

My father and al-Shakkaz sobbed as they washed my uncle's naked body and then covered him with the shroud. Since my uncle had unequivocally ruled out a wake, al-Shakkaz lay weeping over him, and my father teared up too. My eyes, however, were as dry as the vast desert from which the Almohads hailed.

We raised him to our shoulders and headed to the mosque. We placed my uncle's remains at the side of the mosque as worshippers began to arrive for the dawn prayer. As each man entered and saw the bier, he recited "All power and might are God's alone." After prayers, some worshippers assisted us in carrying him to the cemetery, and a small group remained to help us bury him. By the time the sun rose, Seville could no longer number my uncle among its residents.

Despite his grief over the loss of his brother, my father appeared composed. Within a few days, however, his profound sorrow became obvious. The last wall propping up his life had collapsed, leaving him even more anxious and rash. He vented his rage on us, and everything had to be meticulously double-checked. He wouldn't retire to bed without first securing his door and would not leave the house without first doing a complete walk-through. He limited his expenditures and ate sparingly. I was affected by all this and had to return home and leave at scheduled times. I felt increasingly confined in Seville. Whenever I mentioned travel to him, he warned about the dangers posed by the Portuguese. The fall of the fortress of Santafila to the Portuguese a few weeks earlier and the capture of hundreds of Muslims only made things worse. The preacher at the mosque goaded Seville's citizens to ransom their brethren, and my father gave me ten dinars to place on the huge cloth stretched out on the ground of the mosque. People dropped dinars and dirhems on it, as well as some jewelry. Enough money for the ransoms was collected in a few days because people competed to be more generous. Everyone seemed to fear he might meet a similar fate as those captives. I told my father this while we ate dinner, and my mother reacted as if my every word were a hammer blow to her head.

She asked, "How far away is this fortress of Santafila?"

"Several days' journey."

She began to recite "All power and might belong to God," while her hand trembled, her eyes teared up, and she rested her head on her palm.

My father asked tenderly, "What's the matter, Nur?"

"What's the matter? The infidels are capturing Muslims just a few days from here. Woe to me and my daughters!"

"No harm will befall you or your daughters! Ask God to protect you from Satan and stop this!"

My mother fell silent, but, sensing her fear, my father asked, "Do you think the Caliph won't respond to what they've done?"

"What's he waiting for?"

"He's waiting to raise a large army. Soon he'll come to Andalusia with those troops to teach these infidels a lesson!"

The Caliph finally did cross the Strait of Gibraltar and headed to Seville. My father shared this news with Abd al-Samad in the garden. Father was eating grapes while Abd al-Samad clutched his stick with both hands, leaning on it. He listened with great interest to what my father said.

"This is a much larger army than Andalusia has ever heard about! More than fifty thousand troops are already deployed on land, and twenty thousand are in ships at sea."

Abd al-Samad raised his eyebrows in amazement and left them halfway up. Drawing his words out, he proclaimed: "Praise God!"

Then my father continued precipitously: "This year and last, we forwarded the *kharaj* land tax to the Caliph in the form of armor, swords, and military supplies— instead of gold. Do you know why, Abd al-Samad?"

Abd al-Samad seemed to know but pretended he didn't so he wouldn't deprive my father of the joy of telling him. "Why, Abu Muhyi?"

"If we, together with Cordova, Granada, and Valencia, had sent him gold, gold's value would have dropped on account of a glut. That's why the caliph ordered each city to send him the *kharaj* in military supplies."

Abd al-Samad nodded to express his admiration and understanding and repeated, "Praise God!"

"Yes, indeed. We purchased every breastplate, sword, saddle, and bow offered for sale in the market and sent them to him in three caravans: the first to the land army the Caliph commands at Gibraltar, the second to the mouth of the Guadalquivir River, where Abu al-Abbas al-Siqili commands the fleet, and the third to the second fleet, which is commanded by 'The Raptor's' son, in the Guadiana."

"Ali, the son of the Raptor?"

"Yes.

"Son of the lame infidel?"

"Right."

"Praise God! A Christian commands the Muslim fleet."

"Man, he converted to Islam. Where have you been? Didn't you know?"

"I didn't. How would I?"

"Yes, he has converted to Islam. Moreover, his father once commanded the Greek army that served the Almoravids."

"Praise God!"

"What's important, Abd al-Samad, is that the Caliph seems determined to extirpate the Portuguese threat."

Abd al-Samad rose, supporting himself with his stick, and asked to be excused. "May God grant him success! I must go now."

"May good fortune accompany you, Abd al-Samad."

21

In the market, Seville's residents began stocking up for the war, each person according to his own assumptions. The blacksmiths' market was filled with Muslims getting their swords sharpened and buying body armor, helmets, and new shoes for their horses, fearful that if the Caliph summoned them to jihad, the army might not have enough armor or helmets for them. Christians started buying provisions they could store at home: grains, oil, and raisins, since they feared that the caravan trade might be halted by the war or a siege and that local farms might stop producing once Muslim farm workers were drafted into the army.

Abdallah al-Qattan, who had grasped my father's beard and delivered a futile sermon to him, left with the army, on foot, even though there were plenty of steeds. "My feet deserve God's recompense and reward more than horses do," he explained.

I avoided saying goodbye to him, even though I knew I could always find him in Qaws al-Haniya, preaching to passersby, keeping the roadway clear, providing water for dogs and cats, calling Christians to convert to Islam, and blocking tavern doors when people headed to them at night. He would surely ask me why I wasn't joining the jihad and make his question sound more like a reprimand than an inquiry. No excuse would satisfy him, and I wasn't going to join a jihad under a banner I didn't honor. I didn't hope the army would be defeated but I wanted it to win nothing more than a truce or a peace treaty. Don't people realize that living on God's path is more taxing and difficult than dying on His path?

The army finally departed; then Seville calmed down and grew even more boring. We read all of Frederick's Greek books and those of his Latin ones that contained philosophy. I contracted with a book dealer to bring us books from Cordova, but all he found there was a poorly copied book by the Indian author Shankara. We read that in two days and then were out of books again. So we reread books and adopted a different approach: we sat in two lines, facing each other. A person in the first line read a number of pages, and then someone in the second line would pick related passages from their books. Some nights our discussion lasted a very long time because we couldn't agree. On other occasions we would reach a conclusion that astonished Frederick. He wrote down these conclusions and eventually produced a charming book filled with Zeno's reply to Epicurus, Plato's objection to Socrates, and Ibn Sina's argument against Razi, Galen, and Ibn Masarra.

Some weeks later, Frederick told us that the kermes oak beetle harvest would take place soon and that he would spend the month at his country estate. He invited us to join him there. Seven of us erected tents at his farm beneath arbors for grapes used to make wine. He hired a lutenist, a drummer, and two female dancers. Shortly after sunset they would begin playing and dancing. We passed the time till sunset by conversing, walking, and reading. Wine flowed nonstop; whenever we emptied a jug, the servant filled it from a large jar located near the wine press. Once we grew tipsy, al-Hariri and I began dancing with some of the others. Ghala and Guido danced too. First the singer performed one Arabic muwashshah ballad after another and then a string of Castilian folk songs. Whenever I emptied my glass, I shook it as a sign for the servant to fill it. Eventually I began to rush to the wine jug myself to fill my glass. Then I volunteered to replenish the glasses of the other guests. Ghala danced barefoot on the smooth tile floor. If her feet felt cold, she climbed onto the table. When one of the dancing women joined her there, I feared the table would break and they would jump into our laps.

For the first time since I met her, Ghala smiled at me. I answered her smile with a smile and began to smile whenever our eyes met. Then I planned for our eyes to meet so we could smile, but she started frowning again. If I sat down near her, she would rise. When I offered her more wine, she would refuse it. I rose to dance with her, but she sat down. So I consoled myself with her father's wine for her brusqueness. Whenever she turned her face away from me, I drained my glass. Every time she left the room, I filled my glass again. Whenever I invited her to sit beside me and she refused, I asked the saqi to sit by me instead with his excellent flask. There would be no need for bartenders if maidens weren't so saucy. Why would we need wine, if women arrived when we felt lusty and slipped away once we were satisfied?

Finally Frederick stood in the center and gestured to the musicians to stop performing. Silence reigned, and we listened carefully.

He said, "Let's think about what Orpheus, whose lyre became a heavenly constellation, said: 'I am Orpheus. I have sung to storms till they fell asleep and to boulders to make them avoid our ship. I have journeyed to the end of the world and seen things more beautiful than you can imagine.'"

We shouted: "By God, this is beautiful!" and applauded loudly. We toasted Frederick and urged him to continue:

My God, you are the debtor who always pays your debt. We tarry on Earth briefly before returning to you and becoming yours forever. My beloved, though, went to you more quickly than she should have. She went to you before her flower had blossomed. I ask you only to lend her to me. You needn't give her to me eternally, because in a few years' time, we'll both return to you.

These words so touched al-Hariri's heart that he exclaimed: "God lives! He is the Rewarder!" Then he stood up to dance even though no music was being performed. He looked silly. So Frederick gestured to the musician to play. We all rose to dance in a circle around al-Hariri. We laughed exuberantly till dawn, when Frederick ordered the music to stop.

He said, "There are Muslims among us, and their time for prayer has come."

Al-Hariri and I left with three other Muslims. We performed our ablutions at the farm's brook and then found that Frederick's servant had spread a carpet for us and was preparing to pray with us.

Turning toward me, al-Hariri asked, "Does our prayer count if we're inebriated?"

"Do you understand what you're saying?"

"Yes."

"Then your prayer will count, because the verse says: 'Don't come to pray when you are too drunk to know what you are saying.'" [13]

They asked me to serve as imam, so I prayed with them and recited: "'I have given you Kawthar,' [14] for the first prostration. For the second, I recited the verse 'Mudahammatan.' [15] Then we finished praying and hurried back to the group.

While the army surrounded Santarém by land and sea, we surrounded Guido, and she read to us Shankara's prayer for mercy to his Lord: "I ask your forgiveness, Lord, for my three sins. I walked toward You, forgetting You are everywhere. I thought of You, forgetting You are deeper than any thought. I prayed to You, forgetting that you are higher than all prayers." Even as the water level rose and the wind raged, causing troops to fear that the river would sweep them away, I stood surrounded by my friends and said, "Consider God's compassion, which is demonstrated through His creation of us. Consider His love shown in drawing us from essential nonexistence to manifest existence." When soldiers struck their tents, thinking the Caliph had ordered them to withdraw, rather than to rally at the fortress, al-Hariri was asking the musicians to perform al-Qayrawani's song: "Night of love, when will its dawn come?" When swords clanged against each other by the walls of Santarém amid the rage and crush of battle, we were clinking glasses outside Seville and Ghala was turning into a twirling top. When the Caliph was stabbed beneath his navel, and his bodyguards carried him away—wounded and bleeding—Samh ibn Salih was reading to us what Shankara had said:

To emancipate yourself from servitude, you must first distinguish between what is and isn't your soul. Shed the belief that you are the hunk of flesh you call your body. Distinguish your true self, which you will find is outside of time, for it has no past, present, or future. Then you will achieve spiritual peace.

When the army was finally routed and returned carrying the Caliph's mortal remains, I stood at the center of the group, exclaiming: "Listen! Hear this!" So the musician stopped playing and the dancer sat down as everyone listened intently to me recite a poem that God had unveiled to me:

Love's true reality is that love is caused by love.
If our hearts were devoid of love, love would not exist.

Everyone liked my maxim and cheered. Then Frederick rose and said, "Pour us all a drink, Saqi, so we can toast this magnificent statement!"

22

I started staying for days at a time at Frederick's estate, and he fixed a room for me and al-Hariri to share. It overlooked a small rose garden. Frederick had imported the seeds for these plants from the land of the Goths. When I woke in the morning, my head would be so heavy it could have been a skin filled with buttermilk. Frederick's servant, who doubled as bartender by night, would bring us a bountiful breakfast, which helped restore our equilibrium and drive away our headaches. Then we would take an invigorating ride on horseback through adjacent pastures. We carried bows and pretended we were hunters but rarely hit anything. When we returned to Frederick, he would welcome us with a fire he had lit outdoors and a bucket of freshly picked mulberries from trees scattered around the farm. Whenever it was time for prayer, he would ask his servant to spread a prayer carpet and call us. Once night fell, tranquil and dark, those who hadn't stayed with us would return. When everyone was present, the drumming would begin, and it was soon joined by the sound of the lute. So we would embark on another night spent roaming the halls of altered consciousness as we soared free of our bodies and allowed our spirits a chance to cleanse themselves a bit from our normal clamor.

Twelve days passed without my setting foot in Seville. My family assumed I was sequestered with some shaykh on al-Mantiar. Al-Hariri would go to town and return—after conveying bogus news to my family, who gave him delicious food Sallum prepared for the pupils and shaykhs secluded on al-Mantiar. My drinking buddies and fellow dancers at Frederick's kermes oak plantation consumed it. Spring was splendid, the weather was fresh, the food was tasty, the conversation was diverting, the music was thrilling, and the wine was plentiful. I felt my heart expand and my chest grow more capacious while I was there. When I woke, the beauty of the place—the verdure, fields, water channels, and birds—intoxicated me. Once night concealed all this, I grew inebriated from the wine Frederick pressed and aged in barrels for his guests' consumption rather than for sale. With each passing day, I realized I was changing. I seemed to be ascending to celestial stations or traversing terrestrial stages. I felt that each passing day did not form part of my life and that I had, rather, borrowed it from someone who did not love happiness. I used my dinars to buy twenty plump sheep, which I led to Frederick's pen. Then I asked him to use them to serve us roast lamb every night. Frederick objected at first, pointing out that we were his guests, but I insisted.

Those days passed blissfully, until eventually al-Hariri returned from Seville looking troubled. We surrounded him and asked what the matter was.

He replied, "The Almohad army was defeated! The Portuguese are coming!"

Frederick's face turned pale, and he looked agitated. Guido clasped Ghala's hand, and she bowed her head in silence. Dumbstruck, Samh held his head. Everyone was quiet for a time until al-Hariri turned to me and asked, "What will happen now, Muhyi?"

They all gazed at me, as if they agreed I was the one who would know what was happening at court, because my father worked there. My knowledge of this war was limited to my father's comments on the massive quantity of the Caliph's war supplies and the might of his army. How could it have been defeated? How disastrous it would be if the Portuguese marched on Seville! Looking at all their faces, I said, "The Caliph recruited a mighty army. I doubt that the Portuguese were able to obliterate it. Perhaps they merely won a battle."

My words did not seem to convince anyone, and their eyes continued to look anxious, especially those of Ghala and Guido. Al-Hariri recited that all power and might are God's and started praying under his breath. I stood at the center of the group and exclaimed, "Friends! The Portuguese lack the capacity to attack us. They have merely expelled us from their lands. That doesn't mean they can assault us. They certainly have sustained some losses."

Frederick rose as if to adjourn the assembly debate and said, "May the Lord do as He wills. Muhyi will keep us informed of developments. Isn't that so, Muhyi?"

"Yes, of course."

"Now, I think it's not a good idea to remain outside the city walls. Let's return to Seville."

We all rushed back to Seville. The city appeared calm, as if the news hadn't reached every house yet and wouldn't till stragglers from the army started to arrive. Only Seville's native sons returned, for the army split up, and each battalion returned to its home base. The Maghribi one crossed the sea, carrying the Caliph's body home with them. Fear and dread settled on Seville. The Almohads were slow to announce who would be the new caliph. The four city governors who were also sons of the late Caliph departed to attend his funeral in Morocco, and Andalusia seemed at least temporarily abandoned, since it lacked a caliph, governors, and armies. The Almohads appeared to have deserted the region, leaving it exposed to perils. The court ministers were apprehensive about this power vacuum and ordered the guards to close the city's gates, as if a state of war existed. They were to be opened only two hours a day with the guards there on high alert. The number of incoming caravans decreased markedly with the exception of the regular caravans between Seville and Cordova. The construction boom came to a total halt without a caliph to support it, and the engineers, contractors, carpenters, and plaster workers all left for the Maghrib.

My father's mood was as mercurial as when the Almohads had besieged Murcia. It was a mixture of anxiety, anger, and ill humor. He ate alone and sat for many hours in the garden without speaking to anyone. Sallum received an angry slap on the nape of his neck because he forgot to buy firewood. My dad prevented a neighbor's daughter from visiting my sisters and sent her back to her family for no apparent reason. Durra appeared dumbfounded as she adjusted to my father's new mood, which she had never experienced before. My mother asked him nothing, since she realized that her panicky questions set him off more than anything else. Everyone in our household gradually learned to avoid my father. So he retreated into solitude, and we had no idea what he was brooding about.

The Almohads finally agreed on Ya'qub, a son of the late caliph. He reappointed his brother Abu Ishaq as governor of Seville. Once Abu Ishaq returned to Seville, the herald's call resounded throughout our streets:

People, wine is Satan's brew. Pour it out. Anyone caught in possession of wine will be executed. People: musicians, singers, and female vocalists are instruments of Satan. Any apprehended will be imprisoned. People, men are forbidden to wear silk and silk brocades embroidered with gold or silver thread. Any man caught wearing silk will have his clothes confiscated and will be whipped.

After this herald had made his rounds, policemen rushed out to execute the new orders. So much liquor was poured on the streets that its pungent odor filled the air for days near distilleries and bars. Singers of both genders deserted known music venues and hid in homes and on nearby estates. The cost of silk and brocades tumbled in the markets, especially that of ready-made clothes for men. These were sold at the lowest conceivable prices or ripped apart and altered to fit a woman. My father obediently brought out all the silk garments the previous caliph had given him and carried them to a tailor in the market to repurpose as shoulder sashes and veils for my sisters. He had his gold ring melted down and turned into a ring for my mother. In view of the new circumstances, he started heading to the palace with less finery, in more modest clothing.

One day my father summoned me to his favorite spot in the garden. He held a piece of paper he had half covered with ink. When he saw me, he said, "Sit down. Have a seat, Muhyi."

I did, wondering what he wanted from me. I glanced at the piece of paper and discovered it was a list of the names of many books. My father tapped his pen on each one as he counted them under his breath. When he had finished, he turned to me and said, "Dictate to me the names of all the books studied in the mosques."

"All of them? But there are hundreds!"

"Fine. Fine. Just tell me the names of Maliki books."

I dictated all the titles I knew. Whenever I mentioned one, he consulted his list. If he didn't find the book there, he would stop me and write down the name of the book along with the name of the shaykh who taught it in his circle. When I asked him what he planned to do, he replied, "We've received an order from the Caliph to terminate all instruction in Maliki jurisprudence."

"Why?"

"I don't know, Son. The Caliph's letter, which arrived a few days ago, ordered us to substitute Zahiri jurisprudence for Maliki and to ban debates between scholastic theologians. The Governor asked me to list the names of all the Maliki books taught in the mosques."

"To ban them?"

"Of course."

"We're talking about scholarship, Father. How can learning be banned?"

My father put his pen in the inkwell and started to blow on the page to dry the ink of what he had written. Without looking at me, he asked, "Do we have any say in the matter? They speak, and we listen. They order, and we obey."

"Scholars, people who receive unveilings, and Sufis who follow the path should advise this new Caliph. He is young and doesn't know any better."

My father laughed out loud at my comment. Then he nodded sarcastically and replied, "You think he's young? He's years older than you, Son."

He folded the paper and tied it with string. As he stood up, I asked, "What are you going to do with the list you just wrote down?"

Heading inside and limping a little because he had been seated so long, he replied, "We'll distribute the list to the police, who will make the rounds of the mosques to ensure that shaykhs observe this ban."

"No glimmer a man discerns is reliable, unless it affords him learning."

—**IBN ARABI**

23

I left the house at noon trying unsuccessfully to stifle my rage. Repression in our city had been bad enough even before these new commands and bans from the Caliph. What did we have to read now except Zahiri books, which stirred neither the heart nor the mind? Seville had really become insufferable. The markets were stagnant. People were scared. Souls were troubled. Christian and Muslim youths loitering on the riverbank clashed repeatedly. Beauticians spread strange rumors about Andalusia surrendering to the Franks. There were reports that Crusader fleets had called at Portugal's ports. A major rebellion in North Africa threatened the Almohads. Even winter was bitterly cold and brought strong winds that kept me from walking along the riverbank or roaming through the markets.

My two remaining sanctuaries were Frederick's house and his farm, but even these refuges were dreary now, because he had become cautious after the new ordinances. He only hosted a gathering a few days each month, and there was hardly anything to read at them, because he had packed all his books in leather-bound boxes and shipped them, with a caravan, to his brother in Marseilles, for fear they would be seized and burned. When he invited us to his estate one evening, half the habitués were absent, as well as one of the musicians. The only beverage in the flasks was rob—bitter date syrup—not real wine from grapes. I sat with al-Hariri, Frederick, Ghala, Guido, al-Samh, and Frederick's Slavic servant, whom he had leased. I don't even remember what they discussed; it meant nothing to me. I commandeered one bottle for myself and drank. I drank some more. And more. Then I asked them to quit chattering. I clasped Guido's hand to stop her. Everyone exchanged amazed glances and disapproving smirks. The musician performed a piece he could play without a drummer. Al-Hariri tried to take the bottle from me after the rob started to spill onto the floor when I started dancing. But I clung to it and pressed it to my lips. I drank till rob filled my mouth and this date wine became a tongue of flame inside me. I held the bottle to Guido's mouth, but she drew back and gently pushed the bottle away. Al-Samh and Ghala rose to dance and separated me from Guido. I emptied the bottle into my belly and went to fetch another. Frederick patted me on the shoulder, laughing, and said, "Relax. The night's still young."

I staggered, and al-Samh steadied me. I clutched another bottle and started to drink deeply from it. Then, as a line of wine ran down either side of my mouth, I began to dance. I embraced Guido and tried to lift Ghala from the ground, but they chose to stop dancing and sat down at the edge of the circle. Al-Samh and al-Hariri surrounded me and started to dance with me, exchanging meaningful glances and anxious smiles. They repeatedly attempted to snatch the bottle from my hands, but I clung to it as though rob were the elixir of life. Then, holding a drum, I mounted the table and began, in the absence of the drummer, to beat a ragged rhythm. I shouted to the musician: "Louder! Louder. . . ."

I started to twirl. I twirled, and twirled, and twirled. I raised my right hand, which held the bottle, and lowered the left. I felt I was as light as a feather or a queen bee ascending ever higher. Closing my eyes, I beheld an intense whiteness, which grew denser as I twirled faster and faster. I sensed that I had penetrated a fog and that my turban had changed into a cloud. I felt immersed in light as radiant as the Sun's. Stars and planets rotated around me. Then I plucked a star and kissed it. I halted a planet to embrace it. They all pulled off their cloaks, and I threw myself on all of them.

Suddenly a featureless man appeared from beyond the curtain of existence and shouted at me. He grabbed me forcefully, and I tumbled to the ground. The table I had been dancing on broke to pieces, and my date wine flowed across the floor as the contents of my belly mixed with it. When I opened my eyes, I saw frightened, frowning faces. An intense alarm unlike anything I had ever experienced swept over me. People sat me up. They splashed water on my face, loosened my turban, opened my shirt, and poured water down my chest. Every mouth repeated my name, and everyone was calling to each other. They picked me up, steadied me, and sat me down again. I immediately sat bolt upright and stared around me. I felt the room was suffocating and almost slaying me. Hard walls closed in on me. Gloomy faces threatened to bite my face. I rose, evaded them, and headed to the door. I raced away from the party, not knowing where I was heading, and left behind me a bewildered group of anxious drunkards, who had no idea what had happened to me.

I ran through the pitch-black night, making my way between the farms as the voices behind me grew softer and quieter till I could no longer hear them. I scampered over the hard ground, through mud, across grass, and then bare dirt. I ran upright, leaning forward, unable to see where my feet landed. I stumbled repeatedly, fell, rose, and then raced on, as if all of the earth's demons were after me. I wept as I ran, and tears spilled over my temples and ears. I finally discovered I had reached the city wall of Seville. So I paused and slowed my pace to a walk, panting and coughing. I heard sheep bleating and headed their way till I saw a shepherd clad in torn rags and dirty shorts. I went to him and placed my hand on his shoulders. I told him breathlessly, "Sir . . . give me your clothes for mine."

I didn't wait for his reply but started removing my garments as he watched apprehensively. I stripped off a shirt of soft cotton, a cloak, and my new pants, handing them to him. He felt them with his hands and found they were of the finest quality. I doubt he had ever worn garments like these. He looked up at me. Finding me buck naked, he immediately removed his clothes and handed them to me. I donned his filthy shirt and torn shorts and walked away, leaving him to wonder whether I was a jinni or a human being and whether he was dreaming or awake. I continued to skirt the city wall as a voice in my chest echoed endlessly. I finally found myself by the cemetery, which I entered. While greeting its residents, I wandered between the tombs, feeling God's serenity. Then I discovered a dilapidated tomb that had crumbled to become a small grotto. I crouched inside it and began to recite the Qur'an.

"No recurring state is trustworthy."

—IBN ARABI

24

Sallum found me the fifth morning. By then he was so desperate that he began talking even as his tears, which betrayed both his hope and exhaustion, coursed from his eyes. If I hadn't emerged from the cemetery determined to return to the city, my fugue might have lasted longer. The Governor had granted my father permission to dispatch ten soldiers to search for me in areas around Seville. Al-Hariri had reported he last saw me at Frederick's farm and had described my state when I left them. He had told my father everything . . . everything . . . even about our clinking glasses and the singer's performance.

I entered our house wearing the shepherd's clothes, which had become even filthier. The dirt that coated my face lightened my complexion, and my eyes had sunk into my face from my emaciation. My mother's heart broke when she saw me. As she usually did when she was overcome by a bout of weeping, she sank to the ground, with one leg folded beneath her and the other stretched out in front. She wailed like a mother whose child had just died. My father kept circling me. because he didn't know yet whether I had been taken prisoner and he should feel sorry for me, gotten lost and he should pity me, or become drunk and he should excoriate me. My two sisters stood at the door with the same look of astonished fear that had characterized them for the last four days.

I sat down beside my mother and answered all of my father's questions that I could. Then I heard him call Durra and order her to prepare his bath for me so I could bathe there. She set out soap, a bottle of rose water, and a new loofah. Then Sallum brought a tub filled to the brim with water, even though we normally used less. I washed as best I could and then dressed. My hair and feet were still wet when I retired to my room, where I slept till the midday prayer. When I woke, I discovered beside me a plate of fruit, cheese, and bread. My mother had placed it there while I was sleeping. I ate a pear and a few grapes. These got my digestion started; so I went to the latrine where I remained, squeezing my belly and experiencing severe pain in my gut. I complained to my mother, and she sent Sallum out to buy some cider vinegar, cinnamon, and sage.

She mixed the cinnamon with the vinegar, olive oil, and saffron and gave me that concoction to drink once I left the bathroom. Then she boiled sage leaves for me in water. She set that beside me and massaged my back and shoulders and rubbed my face. I rested my head on her chest and sobbed as hot tears flowed from my eyes.

When my father returned from court that evening he headed straight to my room and sat down on my bed. After reassuring himself about my health, he asked, "Where were you, Son? How did this happen to you?"

"I was in the cemetery, Father."

"Four days in a graveyard? We thought you had been kidnapped."

"By God, I didn't know I had been gone four days till I heard that from you just now."

"How can that be? What happened?"

I didn't answer and turned my face away. So my father repeated his question. I still didn't reply. Then he seized my chin, turned my face toward him, and repeated the question once more as he stared straight into my eyes.

"Son, tell me what happened to you. . . ." Then resolve replaced tenderness in his voice, and he concluded: "And don't you dare hide anything from me."

I took a deep breath, turned my face away again, and said, "It was *jadhba*, Father."

"*Jadhba*? What's that?"

"Sufi attraction or ecstasy."

My father was losing patience with my answers, which seemed murky to him. So, in a loud voice, he asked, "What is this 'Sufi attraction'?"

"It's an awareness of divine solicitude attracting a worshipper closer to the divine presence."

"How does this happen?"

"God perceived that I was in a state that wasn't the one He had chosen for me. So through His solicitude, he attracted me. God's attraction banishes rationality. Have you noticed that when a shaykh preaches to you in the best possible manner, your heart is perturbed and your soul feels troubled?"

"Yes."

"So how would you respond if God the Exalted and Almighty Himself preached to you?"

"Why does He preach to you and not to religious scholars?"

"Because I am one of his *walis*."

My father was silent for a moment. Then he turned his head to the right and left as if he were searching the room for something to calm his nerves. He sighed deeply and said, "Son, free yourself from whatever you're involved in and don't be blinded by error. What kind of twenty-two-year-old saint spends his nights getting drunk with courtesans and female entertainers?"

"God destined me to become intoxicated and mess around in preparation for releasing His *jadhba* on me and forcing me to repent."

"Just like that? It's that simple? We get drunk so we can become saints?"

I didn't answer my father's question, which blended sarcasm with pique, and continued silently to swallow his rebuke, which he repeated several times. Finally, at a loss for what to say, my father asked, "Why the cemetery? Why didn't you return home?"

"I attached myself to God in the cemetery and asked Him a million times to use me in ways pleasing to Him, not in ways that alienate me from Him."

"A million times?"

"Yes, Father, a thousand, thousand times, and once I finished doing that, I returned. Then you all said I'd been gone four days. According to the reckoning of my spiritual retreat, it lasted for a million prayers. That's how I keep time. Our systems for keeping track of time are really different!"

My father stood up, as if he had lost patience, and started to leave. Then he stopped at the door, turned back toward me, and said despairingly, "By God, son, I have seen pious and impious people, penitents and sinners, godly men and libertines, but I do not know what kind of person you are. I suspect that vanity has gotten the better of your intellect and prompted you to think you're a saint, when you aren't one, and claim to be God-fearing, when you're not that either. By my life, this has happened because you have too much free time and not enough to keep you busy."

"I stay busy remembering God, and my free time is filled with His light."

"By God, you're full of it! You busy yourself with singing girls and intoxicants and then fraternize with the dead in their tombs. You must have heard that Caliph Ya'qub has ordered that wine drinkers shall be whipped and that those who persevere in drinking shall be killed. By God, I fear you won't die a saint or a shaykh. So shape up!"

My father's despondent tone emboldened me to say, "Then let me travel, Father."

My request incensed him. Standing in the middle of the room, he raised his hands high and shouted: "You travel? I worry about your sanity here in Seville, where I can keep an eye on you. How could I trust you somewhere I can't monitor you? Shame on you!"

He walked out of the room but then suddenly returned to comment: "You should know that I'm going to have my people watch you. By God, if I hear anything I dislike about you, I'll make sure you regret it."

"You *are a cloud concealing your sun; so, know your* Self."

—IBN ARABI

25

During the next four years things happened that I never expected: I became a secretary for the Caliph and a husband for Maryam bint Abdun. God accomplished what He wished and brought to pass what He wanted, without any input from me. For all these pieces to fall into place, God first made Sancho I King of Portugal and my younger sister the mother of al-Sa'd. The former sought a peace treaty with the Caliph, who had crossed the Strait with an army to confront Sancho I at Silves. Then my sister conspired with my mother and other sister to find me a wife—to keep me from sitting in cemeteries. Instead, I ended up sitting with the Caliph by day and with my wife in the evening. No cemeteries. No Sufism. Still confined within Seville's walls, I now had two additional fetters.

After concluding the peace agreement near Silves, the Caliph decided to settle in Seville instead of returning to the Maghrib. Just as soon as he announced this intention, Seville's governor quickly left the army and headed back to Seville with three bodyguards. They rode the fastest horses they had, in hopes of returning in time to prepare for the Caliph's arrival. On his return, the Governor immediately convened Seville's market regulators, police supervisors, civic leaders, district heads, court secretaries, and judges to order them to work night and day to address all the citizens' concerns, in order that no one would have a complaint to raise with His Majesty the Caliph on his arrival.

At the meeting, he warned everyone: "In Marrakech, the Caliph made a point of visiting the markets, speaking to people himself, and asking what they need. Whenever he encountered an injustice, he took care of it, immediately. So be on guard!"

Then he ordered the mosque's beadle to replace all its carpets and rugs with new ones and to rub the sides of the pulpit and its private oratory with musk. He also commanded groundsmen to prune the trees and transplant flowers from nurseries to the sides of roads the Caliph would travel.

Since the Governor returned, my father had not slept a single night at home. The Governor kept him at his side every night to record all the judges' verdicts that had been executed and all the cases closed. This was because the Caliph, on assuming office, had ordered that no one should be subjected to Qur'anic *hadd* punishments unless all circumstances, arguments, testimony, and rulings were recorded. The Governor hadn't done this, because he thought his brother, the Caliph, wouldn't send anyone to check that his orders had been obeyed. Now his brother was approaching Seville in person and might ask for the court records at any moment. If he did, he would review them. If he reviewed them carefully, he would find that the ink for all the entries was the same thickness, color, and degree of saturation and that the handwriting was identical and lacked the normal degree of variation, since the scribe for all *hadd* cases heard over the years had been recorded in two nights by one man—my father.

The evening the Caliph arrived, he headed immediately to his palace after leaving the army in a military camp outside the walls. The next morning, people were surprised to find him walking through the market, trailed by two bodyguards. As soon as this was reported, the market supervisors and civic leaders rushed to join him. Then he started asking them about prices, goods, and food supplies. Groups of people arrived to greet him and to stroke his chest and garments.

He stopped two men and asked, "What do you think of your governor?"

One replied, "A fine man who is the brother of a fine man and the son of a fine man."

"Has either of you ever been before a judge?"

When both replied they had not, the Caliph raised his voice so everyone could hear and asked, "People, has any of you taken a case before a judge recently?"

One man affirmed that he had, and the Caliph ordered: "Approach me."

The man did, and the Caliph asked, "What was your complaint?"

"Scoundrels beat me in the market."

"Did the judge treat you fairly?"

"Yes, he ruled that one of the men should have his tooth broken and then set a price of five dinars on that tooth. So I accepted the money."

"Were you satisfied?"

He replied, "Yes."

The Caliph commented, "Remember that you will be held responsible for this testimony on Judgment Day."

"Your Majesty, everything I have said is true."

The next day my father ordered me to accompany him to the palace to greet the Caliph. When we arrived, we found ourselves surrounded by a swarm of people with the same intention. So we stood there waiting till he reached us. My father greeted him and introduced me to him: "This is my son, Muhyi al-Din ibn Arabi."

I held out my hand to greet him and prepared to pass by, but he kept my hand in his and studied my face. Then he remarked, "You're the one Ibn Rushd told me about."

I remained silent because I didn't know what to say as the Caliph scrutinized my features. Then, a moment later, he said, "Stay in the assembly till everyone else leaves."

While we sat waiting for the session to conclude, my heart was filled with stupefaction and astonishment, and my father looked wary and frightened. Neither of us thought that my brief encounter with Ibn Rushd in Cordova would have inspired him to mention me to the Caliph in some memorable way. I watched as the Caliph completed his statement greeting the people. He smiled modestly and wore the simple wool garments that ordinary people do. I wondered what conversation we might have once the others left.

Suddenly my father grasped my hand and whispered, "Son, put your best foot forward and be polite. Don't debate with him. If he asks you to do something, say: 'I hear and obey.'"

An hour later the chamberlain dismissed the assembly. Then he headed to us and said the Caliph wished to speak with us. We approached him, and he seated us beside him. Without preliminaries he turned to me and asked, "Did you really tell Ibn Rushd that philosophy doesn't unveil the Unknown?"

"Yes, because the condition of the world does not remain the same."

"Did you also say that the only law in existence is God's will?"

"Yes, I did."

The Caliph smiled and waved his hand happily as if I had just said something that agreed totally with his opinion. Then he remarked, "May God bless you. What's the use of doing philosophy then? Isn't it a waste of time?"

"Commander of the Believers, philosophy is the love of wisdom, and not every love is requited."

"God! Allah! What a beautiful statement!"

"But, also, we have no right to prevent a heart from fluttering or a soul from falling in love."

"Yes. You're right."

"May God do right by the Caliph!"

"You will attend my assemblies for as long as I remain in Seville."

"I hear and obey."

"The manifestation of reality reaches perfection in woman."

——**IBN ARABI**

26

For twenty-six days I attended the assembly of the Caliph, who enjoyed his stay in Seville. He received the public at each of these sessions and attended to their affairs and concerns, while I listened and observed. He opened each session with a recitation from the Qur'an and then listened as a few of the Prophet's Hadiths were read aloud together with glosses for some. Only then would he turn his attention to people's issues. Once they departed and the palace doors closed, he relaxed a little and granted me permission to leave and return home. After the evening prayer, I returned to the palace, where I would find him sitting with his ministers and chamberlains while he read the mail and dictated replies to his secretaries. I would ask permission to enter and then take a seat. Later we would dine at his table. The Caliph retired soon after dinner. He drank a hot mint infusion and went to bed early.

So I would leave his assembly and return home to find my father waiting for me cheerfully. He would ask what I had done with the Caliph that day, and I would tell him about a topic we had discussed and an issue we had decided.

Then my father would ask, "Is that all? What do you do all the time you're in his assembly?"

"He always seems to be preoccupied with providing supplies to the army, and nowadays most of those attending his assembly are merchants."

"Since he hasn't ordered the army disbanded yet, no doubt he's going to resume jihad, but no one knows where he will head this time. He has concluded a peace agreement with the Portuguese and an armistice with the Castilians, and the Tunisian rebellions have subsided."

"He'll head to Portugal, Father."

"Perhaps. Some say he will go east and sail to Majorca, which the Banu Ghaniya still control."

During this period, my sister Umm Sa'd came to my room one night while I was preparing for bed. She said, "You probably won't listen to me, but I want to tell you about Maryam bint Abdun."

"Who's that?"

"An urbane, educated, resourceful, and also beautiful woman."

"Why are you telling me about her?"

"So you will marry her! Why else would I discuss her with you?"

Her answer made me laugh, and I gently rebuffed her suggestion. "Let me sleep, Umm Sa'd. I'm not getting married."

She left my room, and I fell asleep. In a dream I saw Maryam. She was reading a book and smiling. Then, in my dream, I saw her with me, doing things I can't discuss. During the following days I found myself thinking about her incessantly. So I realized that this was clearly a sign that my heart would choose a woman by her name and that I would dream about her rather than any other woman. When I had that dream for several nights, I felt I couldn't sort things out for myself and needed advice. So I headed to Fatima bint al-Muthanna, who had moved to Seville.

I kissed her hands and asked, "Mother, what do you think of Maryam?"

"She resembles Maryam bint Imran, who was chaste and well viewed by her Lord. He raised her well, chose her, purified her, and exalted her over all the women of all the worlds. So she obeyed God, worshipped, and prostrated herself with other worshippers."[16]

"Do you know her, Mother?"

"No, my son, but I know she will be your wife."

I spoke to my father, and he immediately sent a letter to her father, who welcomed us into his home a few days later. The meal he offered us was lavish, his welcome for us was very hospitable, and his joy was obvious. My mother went to the market and bought combs, perfumes, silk and linen textiles, and wooden wedding clogs. Then I took all these things and a hundred dinars as a wedding gift for her. Only a few weeks later I married her. My father rented a four-room house for us near the Sharaf region. I chose one room as my study, allocated another to my wife, reserved a chamber for Fatima bint al-Muthanna, and the fourth was for a slave Maryam's father gave his daughter—a man named Addad.

I loved Maryam: her pointy chin, lively eyes, full body, and plump palms that I would stare at for too long and thus embarrass her. Then she would tuck them beneath her as she leaned back, and that would make me laugh. She offered me her heart, which resembled a tree that had just sprouted leaves. She fed me contentment, gave me peace to sip, and spread a bed of reassurance and relaxation for me. I would not have been able to stand Seville without her. I returned home after Seville's streets had become a strait jacket for me and its high walls a prison. Then I would lean against a wall she had lined with soft cotton pillows and beautiful fabrics. She would rest her head on my knee and look straight into my eyes, her face below mine, and ask, "Will you speak to me, Darling, or should I speak to you?" If I addressed her, she was as fragrant as Indian incense. When I spoke to her like a flame, she spoke to me like perfume. When she addressed me, she opened windows to the sky in the ceiling above us, and soon the stars and planets gazed down at us inquisitively, eager to hear her story.

The Caliph heard about my marriage and summoned me to his assembly room one night. He embraced and congratulated me, smiling happily. Then he called his chamberlain and told him, "Bring me *al-Musta'in*."[17]

The chamberlain left and returned with a book with large pages. He placed it in front of the Caliph, who asked me, "Do you know this book by Ibn Baklarish?"

I replied, "Yes, he was a Jewish pharmacist from Almería."

"Merciful heavens! You know everything."

I smiled and looked at the book, since I had never read it, as the Caliph thumbed through its pages. Finally the Caliph stopped at the page he was looking for and read aloud: "Drugs that increase sperm and arouse desire for intercourse and copulation: chickpeas, broad beans, pine nuts, figs, watercress, asparagus, salep, skink, European ash leaves, parsnips, and ginger."

My eyes opened wide with astonishment, and I pressed my lips together to hide my embarrassed smile while the Caliph guffawed mischievously. Then he continued reading: "Drugs that decrease sperm are the ordinary cucumber, the *qitha'* cucumber, Yemeni beans, purslane, sweet-amber, pumpkin, watermelon, mulberries, capers, palm core, ruby red wine, pepper, and cinquefoil."

"Chamberlain!" he cried, laughing merrily: "tell the cook to prepare for our supper all the foods you've heard mentioned, all the ones available. Then Ibn Arabi will eat dishes that increase his sex drive and I will eat those that diminish mine."

I observed that the Caliph was more relaxed with me than at any time in the past. He had removed his turban and skullcap and sat with me as if he were in his private chambers. He summoned the postal clerk to bring the mail that had arrived from all the cities and states, and the general public. The Caliph propped a foot on the chair in front of him and began to read a letter and then dictate a response to it to the secretary. Eventually a letter caught his attention and he read through it very carefully.

Setting it aside, he asked, "Muhyi, why can't jurists tolerate philosophers?"

"Citizens follow the religion of their kings."

"How is that? What are you saying?"

"See how they complain to you about Ibn Rushd in every set of letters. They didn't do that in your father's era."

"Praise the Lord! How did you know the letter I'm holding complains about Ibn Rushd?"

"God unveiled that to me."

The Caliph set aside the letter, rested his chin in his hand, and gazed at me suspiciously. He asked, "Really? He unveils the Unknown to you?"

I nodded but felt apprehensive about his abrupt reaction. I remained silent till he asked, "Why hasn't he 'unveiled' to you what will happen with Castile?"

"I have no knowledge about that."

"Why hasn't God unveiled that to you?"

"Commander of the Believers, God discloses to me what He wishes, not what I want. This is an unveiling, a *kashf*. It isn't astrology, intuition, divination, or sorcery. I don't eavesdrop or catch a fleeting insight. I simply remain in my state, my *hal*, and my mode or *minwal*, and then God may unveil something to me without my asking. This happens to *walis* and Sufis."

Leaning back in his chair, the Caliph said in a resigned voice, "I don't understand everything you say, Muhyi. Is a Sufi a philosopher or a jurist?"

"Neither, Commander of the Believers."

"How do they differ?"

"Philosophers are masters of thought and deduction. Jurists are masters of judging by precedent and reasoning by analogy."

"And Sufis?"

"Sufis are masters of taste and states, of *dhawq* and *ahwal*."

"How do you distinguish between them? They all attend my assembly, sit with me, write me letters, and lodge complaints, even though I don't know their cliques or coteries. Tell me, Muhyi: how do you tell them apart?"

"A jurist reads a text and then states what he understands from reading it. A philosopher thinks and says what he has inferred from his reasoning. A Sufi empties himself before his Lord and then says what God has unveiled for him."

"Why does God unveil matters to Sufis and not to the others?"

"God unveils matters only to those who truly trust Him, who truly empty themselves before Him in spiritual retreats, and who have a spiritual taste that enables them to understand unveilings and revelations."

"Fine. Don't drag me into these labyrinths. Just tell me which are most useful for a caliph."

"If you side with the jurists, you will silence your intellect. If you side with the philosophers, you will silence your heart. If you side with God's saints, they will furnish your heart and intellect with some of God's illuminating light."

"Do you side with the Sufis because you are one?"

"Commander of the Believers, I have grasped more about religion than the jurisprudents and more about philosophy than the philosophers. If you want me to be a jurist like Ibn Hazm, I will. If you want me to become a philosopher like Ibn Tufayl, I will. Or, I could become both at the same time, like Ibn Rushd. But God chose for me to follow the Sufi path. So, this is what I have become, just because He told me, 'Be!'"

"I tell you: Be in my assembly. Don't quit it. Then travel with us to Marrakech."

My heart was beating wildly when I replied, as if he had brought me glad tidings: "I hear and obey."

27

Maryam's fingers woke me the next morning as she gently caressed my cheeks and forehead. Opening my eyes I noticed a smile on her lips and tears in her eyes. She had suffered from insomnia for the last two weeks, as my trip to Marrakech neared, ever since she realized that I wouldn't take her with me. More than once she had mentioned that she had traveled repeatedly to Bejaïa and Tlemcen and had the stamina to endure the travails of the trip. She had pointed out that I needed someone to care for my needs and look after me, but all her attempts proved futile. I wanted her to look after Fatima bint al-Muthanna, who was bedridden. I also wanted to embark on my first long trip unencumbered by burdens and responsibilities, especially since I was duty-bound to attend the Caliph's assembly and did not know what that would entail.

I drew her closer to me and started kissing her neck and upper chest. Then she leaned over me, and we melded in profound love. Her hand investigated my entire body as if saying goodbye to every inch of it before my trip. Her thick black hair fell on my face as if night had suddenly returned to claim from me what the previous night had failed to obtain. Maryam's body was beautiful, soft, and pure, her round face was perfectly circular, and her languorous eyes always made her glances seem filled with entreaty, even when she was angry or critical. I admired her full-figured body, which was plump in a way I liked. Once love took hold of her and she submitted to it, she uttered words she would never dare speak in other circumstances. At such times she would strip me of my intellect and detonate my desires. Then I loved her with a passion greater than I had ever felt and would love her even more the next day.

She fell asleep on my chest, which was wet from her tears. At first I thought they were tears of sorrow, but then I realized they were the mix of sorrow and delight. Finally she revealed something God hadn't unveiled to me: that she had missed her period. Fatima al-Muthanna pressed her belly and confirmed that she was pregnant and in her third month. I hugged her to my chest after she shared these glad tidings with me. I wanted to press myself as close as I could to my Self, which was now in her belly. Then we started laughing together just like kids. This pregnancy calmed Maryam's mind, since now it—not her husband's gruffness— was keeping her in Seville. He, in turn, no longer knew whether he was more delighted by setting out on a voyage, which he had anticipated for a long time, or by the baby growing inside his wife's belly.

The bags containing my clothes and manuscripts had been piled at the side of our other room since we had packed them immediately after the Caliph announced his decision to return to Marrakech. Then he had fallen ill and had twice postponed his journey. Now it seemed the trip would start the next day, because he was feeling better, if not fully recovered. Just as I suspected, a messenger arrived from the palace that evening to inform me the Caliph had ordered that we depart after the dawn prayer. So I gave him my bags to load on my camel and went to my parents' house to say goodbye. My father frowned, my mother's face was flushed, and my two sisters wept. Before I left, to raise their spirits, I remarked, "Good news! Maryam's pregnant!"

Umm Sa'd and Umm Ala' shrieked with joy, but my mother put a hand over her mouth as if she had heard bad news. Then, lifting her hand, she repeated a prayer I couldn't hear. My father's expression changed several times after he heard the news, from astonishment to delight, followed by anxiety, acceptance, contentment, and happiness. I went from my family's house to al-Hariri's. He was elated about my trip and started telling me about all the shaykhs and saints in Marrakech. We had heard about them in Seville but had never seen them. When I finally returned home, I entered Fatima bint al-Muthanna's room. She was praying, and I waited till she finished. Then I kissed her hands, sat down at her feet, and asked for her guidance.

She said, "I recommend the Book's preamble, because whenever I have hoped for some boon and recited the Fatiha, I have always received it. I have never struggled against some evil by employing the Fatiha without finding it depart."

"If that's your advice for me, I have some words for you."

"What guidance do you offer me?"

"By the time I return from my voyage, you will stand upright, recover your health, and radiate light throughout this house, just like the sun."

Our caravan had barely reached Guadalete when the Caliph's health deteriorated. He became quite ill and even lost consciousness from time to time. His physicians thought he was dying. Too weak to mount his camel, he lay in a litter swung between two mules till we reached the ocean, where six large ships awaited us. I was delighted to see the ocean and didn't board till the last ship was preparing to set sail. Then I climbed aboard it and recited verses from the Qur'an till we finally docked a day and a half later in Ksar Al Majaz. I didn't sleep, not even for an hour during this voyage. Because of the rough seas, the Caliph was even weaker when he disembarked. The physicians advised him to lay over in Fez to recover his health before proceeding to Marrakech, and he agreed. We immediately made for Fez, but only the optimists among us thought he would arrive there alive. The secretaries wrote letters to the Caliph's brothers in Andalusia to inform them of his deteriorating health. Ships carried these letters back to Andalusia for delivery to Cordova, Seville, Granada, and Murcia.

We traveled rapidly to Fez, stopping only at sunset and then setting off again at dawn. The caravan was well supplied, and we didn't need to stop for provisions. On both sides of the road I saw familiar and unfamiliar trees. There were olive, gum, and cedar trees, which I recognized. I asked my Moroccan traveling companions in the caravan about the mastic trees, Artemisia, and esparto. I plucked some leaves to examine when I had time to rub and smell them, feeling astonished and happy.

Some days later we caught sight of potteries, oil pressing facilities, and sawmills on the outskirts of Fez. Then we saw a very long line of small shops. They accompanied the visitor all the way to the center of the city. All the types of goods I knew and many more I didn't were on sale in these stores in a city that had no walls.

The Caliph entered his palace, and the caravan started to disperse. One of the men in charge of the caravan took me to the lodgings where guests of the Caliph stayed. He told me that my room was already paid for but that I might want to give the manager some dirhems for a clean mat and fresh pillows. I woke early and ate the food that servants offered to guests in the courtyard. Then I set out on foot, feeling happy, delighted, and enchanted too. Ugly things looked beautiful to me, and cheap items seemed precious. I was fascinated by the canals that gushed with water from springs and creeks. They spread to every corner of the city, and the purling sound of the water satisfied the ear the way water satisfies the belly. The tilework on many exterior walls entranced me. In Andalusia such decorative tiles are found only inside palaces and mosques. Here houses were surrounded by gardens without any walls; they fascinated me since it seemed that private homes participated in the city's beautification. Alleys were occasionally so narrow that pack animals could barely negotiate them. In other locations the descent was so precipitous that I needed to keep a hand on the walls and walk slowly.

In the hostel I was briefed about the Caliph by men who worked for him. They also brought me food and provided me the daily allowance he had ordered for me. I learned from them that he wasn't receiving people and therefore I did not try to visit him. Physicians had advised him to stay in his room to avoid exposure to the cold air associated with autumn's arrival. During the seven months I spent in Fez, I went to the palace more than once to find—as I expected—that he wasn't holding an assembly. During that period, I made the rounds of the mosques and ribats of Fez, attended lectures, met pious *walis*, and read. While in this state—with my heart open to influences from all four directions—God granted me through effusion God-given knowledge, and I made intellectual ascents I had not before. I attained spiritual stations I had never reached and exalted levels that illuminated my path like a sun shining on all of existence. Soon *walis* and Sufis sensed my presence and sought me out at the hostel. When I met them, they smiled and I smiled back. They acknowledged my task or *sha'n*, and I recognized theirs. Nine of them took me to Ibn Hayyun's garden for a gathering of select *walis* who had attained a high station on the path. We conducted a spiritual retreat for weeks we didn't count. A sun other than the physical one rose over us, and a perfect full moon illuminated our nights throughout that month. Whenever one of us received a sacred secret through an unveiling, a brilliant meteor cleft the sky overhead. Whenever one of us discussed higher essences, one or two stars descended toward us. Whenever one of us experienced a *nafth*, a spiritual inhalation, we clasped his hands so what penetrated him would also penetrate our spirits. Each of us wore another participant's patched Sufi cloak as our hearts and spirits embraced, even before our bodies and physical manifestations did. When we returned to the sphere of the general public, each of us was at a new station, a higher *maqam* than he had ever reached before.

"Don't trust a dream that doesn't bring good news."

——IBN ARABI

28

Maryam's due date was approaching, and when, in a dream, I saw her belly open, like an oyster shell with a beautiful pearl inside, I knew she would deliver a girl. Then I asked the vizier to request permission from the Caliph for me to return to Seville to see my wife. He brought me not only the Caliph's permission but a grant and two camels. So I collected my belongings and set off for Seville. Within a month of my arrival, Maryam delivered a girl with a blessed face and a beautiful fortune; I named her Zaynab. When I held her, she would gaze into my eyes as if plunging through them, deep inside me, to search for our common link. Her face was just as round as her mother's and her hair just as coal black. I grew so fond of her that even when I was away from the house and attending to my affairs, I would imagine her laughing in my lap and immediately return home just to spend an hour playing with her. Maryam was happy I did and forgot the fear she had felt about giving birth to a girl.

I seemed to have been away from my father for years, not months, because in this interval he had aged and grown taciturn and gloomy. He did not speak unless spoken to and only left his house to go to court. He had little work to do there while the Caliph was ill; he wrote no one, and no one wrote him. My father spent his time reading the Qur'an, Hadith collections, and the many legal books he found either at my house or in the palace library. He did not hear well and therefore would not respond unless the speaker was within arm's length. As he sank into this condition, my sister Umm Sa'd became very close to him. She was his constant companion and fed and entertained him more than Durra did. My father welcomed her company, read books to her, and taught her some of the sciences of religion. In a few months she memorized the Qur'an and more hadith than she had learned in a lifetime. My mother told me that Umm Ala' was anxious that she wasn't married yet. When she sat with them, her eyes would fill with tears if they discussed a wedding in the neighborhood or a birth. She stayed awake nights brooding that she had reached a marriageable age without marrying.

Fatima bint al-Muthanna had not acted on the advice I offered her before I went to Fez. She had grown quite feeble and scarcely moved from where she lay. She slept longer, her voice was fainter, and her breathing labored. When she died, she was attended by me, my mother, and my wife. I spoke to her, but she did not reply. I bent over her hand and kissed it while I wept. Then she finally moved her head to face my mother and told her: "Nur, this is my son, and he is your father. So respect and obey him."

She eventually died as I expected she would. Then I gathered her possessions only to find that they were hardly worth two dinars. I donated them to charity as she had instructed me. At dawn, I buried her in the tomb—which I had refurbished for her—where I had spent four days asking God for forgiveness. We held a wake for her, but only al-Hariri and his brother, al-Khayyat, came.

There was another wake, at their house, some weeks later, and I was the one offering condolences. Their mother had died, and al-Hariri and I buried her while al-Khayyat wailed beside the grave—too distraught to climb down and help us. He dragged his feet as we walked back to his house. I began sleeping there so al-Hariri and I could take turns trying to cheer his brother, day after day, to no avail. They finally decided to sell the house where they lived and the brother's tailor shop. Then al-Hariri and al-Khayyat set off to perform the Hajj.

Feeling better, the Caliph started receiving people once more. I decided to visit him in Fez to honor our agreement, especially since I had become indebted to him by accepting his grant. I visited al-Kumi to pay my respects and to ask if he had any advice about Fez.

When I revealed my decision to him, he said, "Bide your time, my son. I think the Caliph won't welcome your company now."

"Why not?"

"I've heard he ordered Ibn Rushd imprisoned."

Troubled by this news, I returned home, regretting every present I had accepted from the Caliph and each of his assemblies I had attended. Just as soon as God had restored this Caliph's health, he had started putting people in prison. I felt that I would suffocate. Andalusia already felt like a prison, and now the Maghrib was becoming one too. I wished fervently to travel to a land beyond Almohad rule, a land where no one was subjected to their mercurial temperaments and cruel hearts. But where could I go—now that my parents were both elderly and my daughter was a baby? As the wars with the Franks continued, I felt certain the horizon would only grow darker, as one caliph succeeded another. Each victorious caliph would feel intoxicated by his victory and ruthlessly force people to adopt his views, and any defeated caliph would try to deflect blame from himself onto others. Then he would find fault with his citizens' corruption and deviation from "the truth."

With the passing days I became ever more disheartened and felt overwhelmed by worry. The grief that lodged in my breast seemed permanent. I was sure I had soiled my heart, which Fatima had ordered me to purify, by consorting with the Caliph and dining in palaces. I had also married Maryam and become addicted to the body's pleasures. I had accepted the grant and grown used to stuffing my pocket. No wonder, then, that heartbreak and gloom beset me. The only place I could flee now was the cemetery.

I returned there once more in hopes of reforming my spirit till it opened up to God's attraction, to His *jadhba*. I entered the graveyard at sunset every day like a dead man walking and sat there alone till just before dawn. Each night I asked God to bless me during my spiritual retreat, to afford me His presence, to purify my heart, and to grant me silence, hunger, and trust in Him. The dead gradually accepted me there, and we discussed death, the liminal *barzakh*, the stations, and the other world. Six months passed like six days because of the pleasure I found in my withdrawal and in the serenity of my spiritual retreat. I was thrilled to hear the call to prayer at sunset, because that announced my time to enter the cemetery, and was sad when I saw dawn's threads of light expel me from it.

One night, sensing the motion of another living person in the cemetery, I rose and found al-Kumi advancing toward me, leaning on his stick. Astonished, I greeted him, wondering how he had found me. I made room for him to sit down. Then he bowed his head in silence to savor the majesty and solace of the place. Eventually he said, "I congratulate you on spending time with those who live in this cemetery. People back on the streets are really dead but don't realize it. May I join you?"

"Of course. You will increase the blessings and guidance I receive, my shaykh."

Al-Kumi kept me company for seventy-six nights in the cemetery. We didn't miss a single hour between sunset and daybreak. We would praise God repeatedly for a time, then recite from the Qur'an, and engage in contemplative meditation. On the twenty-seventh night of Ramadan, the shaykh was late, arriving after midnight. He took a seat beside me with a severe expression I had never seen before.

We were silent for some time. Then looking straight at me, he asked, "Muhyi, tell me: when two gnostics come together in a single presence of witnessing with God, what is its property, its *hukm*?"

"This hypothetical case will never occur."

"Why not?"

"Because the Presence does not embrace two persons. In fact, the gnostic isn't conscious of himself in the presence of God. How could he witness another gnostic?"

"How can it be the subject of a hypothesis then?"

"This situation is hypothesized through disclosure, *tajalli*, because each gnostic has his own taste or *dhawq*, which is disclosed to him separately. Therefore it is possible for two gnostics to join in a witnessing presence, a *hadra shuhudiya*, because they are different naturally, spiritually, and spatially."[18]

"Tell me, Muhyi: who resides in the thirteenth grave from the wall?"

"The poet Ibn Zaydun."

"Then listen to me, my son."

"As you command, Shaykh."

"I am your first pillar. Your second *watad* is in North Africa. Seek him there so he may strengthen your heart."

29 DAMASCUS 1260 CE/658 AH

I finally made it down Darb al-Rihan but in the worst condition of my entire life. Since I was created eighty years ago, my hand had never touched a bottle of wine and my mouth had never tasted it, but now my garments reek of it. Its impure drops trickle from my hair, soak my beard, and wet my upper chest. This anarchy is unbearable. Christian hooligans have been wreaking havoc in the streets of Damascus since morning. It seems the Antichrist has rallied them from their neighborhood and provoked them to attack and hurt people in the streets and roadways. It is bedlam and anarchy. They hold crucifixes, and crosses dangle from their necks on chains. They shout in Arabic and Syriac. A group of ne'er-do-wells blocked the lane's exit and forced people leaving to bow beneath a wooden cross they had hung over the gate while they loitered nearby.

"Hey, graybeard!"

I glanced at the boy accosting me and thought he must still be a teenager. He was slender and red-haired, and his face reflected all the world's insolence. A brawny man with a broad chest and bushy mustache stood behind him, smiling idiotically as he delightedly watched the boy stop passersby, wave a brass cross in their faces, and poke weaker folks in their flanks. I saw what he was doing as soon as I set foot in the lane. When a man tried to pass through the gate without first ducking his head, the boy jumped him, along with a group of older youths. They slapped the nape of his neck to force him to bow. When the man tried to defend himself, a gang of men crowded around him. So he turned and fled.

"Hey, graybeard! Are you deaf? I said . . . hey . . . graaybeearddddd."

This made the other young fellows around him laugh. I stopped and glared at him but didn't reply. He held a small flask in his hand and jokingly asked, "Would you like some wine to gladden your heart?"

I turned away from him and continued walking while voices called out: "Venerable shaykh, don't leave without a sip that will rejuvenate you."

"And improve your sex life."

Their shameless laughter echoed behind me as I tried to quicken my steps as best I could to get away from them and to the gate before one of them tried to hurt me. I remembered what had happened to the other man and certainly didn't want one of them to beat me, not at my age. In any event I was walking bent forward, weighed down by my years. I passed through the gate, beneath the cross, while I repeated under my breath: "There is only one God . . . and 'they did not kill him or crucify him but they thought they did.'"[19] Just after I passed through it, a downpour of wine drenched my head, and they all laughed uproariously as if they were in a bar they had set up on the road. My stick fell as I attempted to shield my head with my hands from the ill-omened liquid pouring from a wineskin held by someone hiding over the gateway. When they signaled him, he released wine on the heads of people passing there.

I bent down to pick up my cane and to escape the deluge of wine. So he emptied a lot on my back, completely soaking my thawb. I finally escaped breathlessly from them, but my clothing reeked of wine. My tears started flowing without my being conscious of them. Then my face was drenched with two liquids that had never blended there before: tears of humiliation and Christian wine. I thought I had experienced everything, but now, in my eighties I was suffering this humiliation. *Lord, have mercy!*

I walked the rest of the way to the mosque of Ibn Abdan, repeating: "Living God, Sustainer . . . I seek refuge in Your mercy!" I didn't realize that my voice was becoming increasingly louder till I was almost shouting when I entered the mosque. After my first prayer prostration in the mosque, I broke down completely, sobbing in an unprecedented manner. Worshippers surrounded me and raised me to my feet. As soon as they smelled the wine that had soaked my clothes, they understood what had happened to me. They raised sorrowful cries of "All might and power are God's" and angry threats against the malefactors. When I finally regained control of myself, I turned to ask the person closest to me, "Has Yahya ibn al-Zaki come today?"

This man didn't know but repeated my whispered question in a louder voice. A boy, who seemed to work as a servant in the mosque, replied: "He's in his room behind the mosque."

I followed the boy to Yahya's room and waited while he knocked on the door. I was wondering how I could visit the Qadi of Damascus when my garments reeked of wine. Then the door opened, and Yahya's face peered out radiantly. I had known him since his earliest childhood when he had crawled before me, climbed on my shoulders, and slept in my lap when he was tired.

He smiled on seeing me and said, "Welcome, welcome, Uncle."

Before I could return his greeting, the boy blurted out: "The Christians clobbered him, Shaykh!"

"What?" Yahya shouted. "They beat you? Are you okay, Uncle?"

"No, Master. No one beat me. What they did was pour wine all over me and soak my clothes. So forgive me for my stench and soiled clothes."

Yahya took my arm, which the boy had been holding, and helped me enter his room. Before the boy could leave, he turned to tell him, "Prepare warm water for bathing and bring him some of my clean clothes."

"There's no need for that, Master. I'll clean up when I return home."

"Uncle, this is your home too. Have a seat and tell me what happened."

"Son, the town has been turned topsy-turvy. These Christians have suddenly gone stark raving mad. We can't begin to imagine what they intend to do."

Yahya released a long, heartbroken sigh and said, "I know. . . ."

"My son, what is going to happen? Do you have any news?"

"No one has certain news yet. The emir the Mongols installed in Damascus has emboldened these Christians and encouraged them to act this way. Ever since he took charge of the city, their priests and bishops are permanent fixtures of his assembly."

"But why? What does this Mongol want to achieve?"

"We don't know the secret motive for this, but clearly his love and preferential treatment for the Christians will continue."

"What about us? Won't these Mongols listen to us? Doesn't the Emir know that most of the inhabitants of Damascus are Muslims?"

"All of us judges went to him—not one of us was missing—together with eight jurisprudents, imams from the mosques, and Sufi shaykhs. We called on him in the palace and complained about our situation, but he ignored us."

"What did he say?"

"Whenever we raised a complaint with him, he turned to the priests and asked, 'Is their complaint well founded?' Then they would reply: 'They're exaggerating. Muslims are used to us being servile and obsequious. So they grumble and complain when we're not.' Then his face turned red with rage, and he exclaimed: 'This is not allowed in Möngke Khan's domain, where only Möngke Khan is mighty, and only his enemies are servile.' Then he ordered all of us expelled from his *majlis*."

"What? He expelled our judges and imams? All power and might are God's alone!"

"God is in charge, first and last. You've heard that the emperor's mother's a Christian?"

"I didn't know that."

"And his brother Hülegü returned to Khurasan, leaving the army under the command of Kitbuqa, a Christian."

"They've surrounded us on every side."

"God surrounds them, Uncle."

The boy returned and said, "The bath is ready, Shaykh."

Yahya rose to help me stand and walked me to the bath, where he left me in the care of the boy, who helped me wash, as thoughts tormented my mind and cares buffeted my emotions. I had decided to visit Judge Yahya to reassure myself that the current state of affairs was temporary, a transition after al-Malik al-Nasir fled from Damascus and the Mongols entered the city. But Yahya's news made me even more worried. The boy bathed me quickly and then helped me into a linen shirt, cotton trousers, and a turban that seemed brand-new. When I returned, Judge Yahya was still seated where I had left him, looking absentminded and not busy with any task.

"Master, I wish to ask your permission. . . ."

"Uncle, to do what?

"I have served in your family's sepulcher for more than forty years, and these two hands have buried both your grandfathers, your father, and six of your uncles there. I buried the Supreme Shaykh and his two sons there. I have communed with all of them in the mausoleum. Their benevolent spirits have sustained me, and I have been blessed by their noble graves. I have anointed myself with their gracious fragrances."

"You are part of our family, Uncle, not our servant."

"What I wish to say is that I have grown old and can no longer stand the pain. I have seen malefactors spill wine at the doors of mosques and vandalize shaykhs' graves. If these hooligans come to your mausoleum, I won't be strong enough to repel them or ward them off."

"God protects us, Uncle. No one will blame you"

"I plan to leave Damascus."

"You leave Damascus? Do you know any other land, Uncle? Where will you go?"

"To Kerak, my son. My cousins are there."

"Will they care for you?"

"God, who produced me from nothing, will care for me. I simply ask your permission to carry the mausoleum's books and epistles with me in hopes of finding a secure haven for them in Kerak. I worry that these wretches may storm the mausoleum and destroy its contents."

"You are in a better position to preserve them, Uncle, than I. I will give you a camel and a groom and try to arrange for two guards to accompany you to Kerak, because the road isn't safe."

He embraced me, and his trembling body revealed that he was trying not to weep. I left the mosque and detoured around Darb al-Rihan. I thought I heard a church bell ringing in the distance but wasn't sure. I may have been imagining that. What was certain was that I heard people shake the whole alley with the chant: "True religion has come. The Messiah's religion has won."

TOME FOUR

"Travel that doesn't enlighten is pointless."

—**IBN ARABI**

30

Since I could not go to Fez until Ibn Rushd's fraught situation was resolved and we had learned what the Caliph planned to do with him, I thought I would go to Bejaïa. I felt deep inside me that my second pillar was Abu Madyan al-Ghawth. Was any man in all the Maghrib better qualified to be a *watad*? If my pillar was in that region, I thought he must be it. My idea was to sail from Almería to Oran and then travel east till I reached him. I consulted the market supervisor, who told me a perfume caravan would leave the goldsmiths' suq in a week and would be guarded by some of the Governor's soldiers. I went to the supervisor of the goldsmiths' market and told him I would like to join the caravan. So he directed me to its leader, whom I paid to join. He promised to send me word when the departure time was definite.

We left a few days later, and the first half of the route awakened memories of my first trip from Murcia to Seville, back when I was a kid. I remembered the lay of the land, the watercourses, the smell of the forests, and the rivers as clearly as if I had been there the previous day. We reached Almería eight days later. I headed straight to the port to find a boat sailing to Oran and discovered one immediately. The cost of the voyage for me, my horse, and my luggage was five dinars. We set sail on a longer voyage than my first from Andalusia to Morocco. The wind was stronger, and the ship wasn't as sturdy or solid as the Caliph's ships that carried me the first time. The trip from Almería to Oran normally took two days, but our vessel took three and a half days. I felt nauseous and dizzy, and the only food I could keep down was dry bread and a few vegetables. My condition deteriorated till I could not stand upright without swaying. I spent most of the time lying on my side, wrapped in my blanket, praying that God would shorten the distance.

In this state, I thought I would throw up because my belly hurt so badly. I rose, while others on board were sleeping, and vomited over the boat's side. I gazed at the sea, which stretched turbulent and terrifying before me. Then, by the moon's light, I saw someone in the distance who appeared to be walking toward me on the surface of the water. I was too scared to speak and too weak to call anyone to see what I was witnessing. The man reached the side of the ship and raised his right foot so I could see that it wasn't even damp. Then he lifted his left foot, which was also dry. Before he turned to depart, on foot over the water, he greeted me. Then he left the way he had come, traversing each mile in only a step or two. I called to the sailors to tell them what I had seen, and they all exclaimed that all power and might are God's. Then one of them took my arm and helped me back to bed.[20]

We finally reached Oran, and in a few days I found a caravan heading to Jaza'ir Bani Mazghana[21] and joined it. Most of the travelers were Jewish. They wore free-flowing tunics with sleeves so long they almost reached their feet and the blue skullcaps the Caliph forced every Jew in his realm to wear, after forbidding them from wearing turbans. My caravan traveled along the coast to avoid falling prey to gangs from the Banu Ghaniya. These rebels would plunder and rob any caravan they encountered to raise funds to support their rebellion against the Almohads. The caravan left the coastal route, though, when we heard from other caravans that the Banu Ghaniya's fleet was lurking offshore, threatening ships. Seven days later we reached Algiers, where I joined a caravan bound for Bejaïa. When we arrived there, three days later, I booked a room in a hostel attached to the public bath. I spent only my first night there, because I learned there was a special residence for Sufis near the mosque where al-Ghawth taught. It was extremely calm there at night, dreamy even, and worshipful ascetics were provided mats plaited from camel hair and rush stalks as well as pillows made from hard, rough wool. When I slept on these, my body felt tired, but my spirit felt refreshed.

Two days later I walked to Abu Madyan al-Ghawth's house, where I waited for him to arrive or leave. I did not knock on the door, because I lacked the power, the *qudra*, to cause al-Ghawth to rise, walk to the door, and respond to the knock of a pitiful novice like me. Several hours later the door opened, and al-Ghawth emerged. His face shone so brightly it seemed to be part of a morning untouched by the night. His white beard only reached as far as his throat, and he had lost one of his arms doing jihad. He looked at me with an inquisitive smile. I greeted him, kissed his left hand, and what remained of his right shoulder.

Bowing to him, I said, "I am Muhyi al-Din ibn Arabi. I have come to you from Andalusia so you may assist me with your *ghawth*, extend to me your grace, and grant me your blessing, Shaykh."

I never missed one of Abu Madyan's lessons during the weeks I spent in Bejaïa. I answered whenever he asked a question. If some issue troubled me, I asked him about it. I walked him back to his house when the lesson concluded and then the next morning waited by the door to accompany him to the mosque. When he performed his ablutions, I brought his slippers, washed between his toes with my fingers, and wiped his elbow and brow with a cotton cloth, which I washed out myself every night before I fell asleep. Once he had finished praying, I brought his prayer beads and placed them in his left hand to count as he recited God's names. When he finished, I accepted them from him and hung the string around my neck where I kept it till his next prayer.

I waited a long time for him to reveal that he was one of the pillars and to hint where I should look for the third *watad*. I waited a long time for this. Toward the end of each evening, I remembered what Fatima had told me upon bidding me farewell in Murcia: "Purify your heart . . . then follow it." Had my heart become so besmirched that it would not be possible for me to find the second pillar? Fatima had pointed me to my first *watad* in Seville, but it had taken many years to find him, even though we were in the same city. I discovered him only after many spiritual retreats, attractions or *jadhabat*, presences or *hadarat*, and graveyards. Where would I find this second pillar, who might be anywhere in North Africa? How could I ever purify my heart sufficiently?

After a long wait, I began to despair and decided to broach the subject with Abu Madyan. I waited for him to finish the day's lesson and then told him I had something I would like to ask him privately. The shaykh bowed his head and replied, "My son, no disciple before you has ever asked me a question that my heart had not already anticipated, but I don't sense this now. I suspect you will ask me about some matter I do not understand and cannot handle. So spare me the embarrassment of asking me something beyond my ken and save yourself the embarrassment of asking me something beyond my powers."

I said nothing, but my eyes filled with tears. Then I asked his permission to travel, and he granted it. I returned to my residence, where I began to sob. Once I restrained my tears, I gathered my belongings together, preparing to leave the next morning, whether I found a caravan or not. Two weeks later I was in Seville again. Since I was bound to only one pillar, it seemed that I should circle round him like a pen tracing a circle. In all of the Maghrib, al-Ghawth was the only person I could picture as a pillar. Now I couldn't leave my family without a breadwinner while I journeyed through the central Maghrib, and Morocco was insecure. It would not matter, because Fatima had said, "He will find you." First I had to purify my heart, though. My God! Did Fatima realize that it would be easier for me to search all of North Africa for a pillar than to purify my heart?

On arriving in Seville I went immediately to my parents' house, where I found my father confined to his bed by ill health. My mother, Nur, had died in her sleep while I was away. My two sisters were heartbroken, nervous wrecks. When I embraced both of them at once, they began to weep on my breast, as if my return had reawakened their grief for our mother and their worries for our father. Their sobs made me weep too, and I experienced stinging regret for taking a trip that had only upset both my parents, who had fallen ill from sorrow over my departure.

I entered my father's room and found him very feeble. They had not dared to tell him Mother had died, for fear of the effect this news would have on him. Durra kept a vigil by his bedside all night long, and Umm Sa'd cared for him throughout the day. Neither knew when he might regain consciousness, during the night or the day. When he did, they would immediately need to help him to the toilet and then give him something to eat. I kissed his shoulders and head, but he wasn't aware of my presence. I called him, but he didn't respond. I asked Durra to leave us and sat near his head. With a hand on his brow, I began reciting the surah called "Ya Sin." After I had recited it many times, my father regained consciousness and looked at me with true recognition.

I said to him, "Father, I will be at the mosque till word of your death reaches me."[22] No sooner had I performed my prayers in the mosque than I found Sallum standing behind me, weeping.

"May God grant you a mighty reward, Sir. Your father has passed."

"Certainty colored by emotion is not reliable."

——**IBN ARABI**

31

The warning al-Kumi gave me when I proposed to travel to Fez was reinforced when a herald announced in the market that anyone who possessed a manuscript or book by Ibn Rushd about logic or philosophy should burn it. If he refused, the Governor would have him lashed. Exempt from this ban were books on medicine, math, and astronomy. Booksellers brought out all the banned books they had and tossed them in the market plaza, where they formed a huge pile. That showed how many of Ibn Rushd's books had been copied during the last few years. Then the Caliph ordered Ibn Rushd released from prison and banished to the Jewish village in Lucena. Andalusia was rife with rumors about the reasons for the punishment meted out to a foe who had once been a friend. I certainly felt my own burden of guilt. I suffered terribly about missing my mother's funeral and causing my father's illness. Now I felt remorse about Ibn Rushd. I had an inkling that I bore some responsibility for the Caliph's punishment. He had asked my opinion of philosophers and scholastic theologians. Had I perhaps exerted some influence in the assemblies of caliphs and heads of state? Had I slandered people and encouraged their persecution?

I brooded about many matters as I tried to cleanse my heart of feelings of guilt and painful self-blame. The Caliph had hated the philosophers since he first assumed power. Jurists had complained to him daily about Ibn Rushd in their letters. He would not have reached his decision solely on the basis of my opinion. But, why not? Hadn't I told him that I had received an unveiling, a *kashf*, from God? Perhaps he had believed me and accepted what I said. Perhaps the Caliph had been in a bad humor since recovering from his illness. He was reported to have executed his brother Abu Yahya, whose fealty he doubted. When the sword cuts the necks of brothers and other relatives, nothing will prevent it from reaching those of philosophers and Sufis. The jurists would increase their rumormongering now, after their success in getting Ibn Rushd banished. One day their letters would mention my name too.

Soon my feeling of guilt became a feeling of fear and alarm. What was I doing in Seville when my pillar was in North Africa? But what would I do for my sisters now that I was their only means of support? What would I do for my wife and for my daughter, who had started to walk and stumble? The city was tranquil, even though my heart wasn't. I moved out of my house, for which my father had been paying the rent, and settled my wife and daughter in my father's house. I moved into the two rooms he had occupied with Durra, whom I emancipated after Umm Sa'd told me that was my father's wish. She immediately departed for parts unknown. I worried that I had deviated from my goal and strayed from my path and that God was punishing me for my anxiety and alarm. My self-assurance, which I had acquired by frequenting shaykhs and attending their classes, deserted me, as did my tranquility, which I had sought in spiritual retreats and by brooding in cemeteries.

One day I opened my door to find a messenger from the palace of the Governor, who was inviting me to attend his assembly after the Friday prayer. So I headed to the palace after prayers at the mosque. On entering the assembly, I found a man I didn't know with the Governor. When I greeted them, the Governor told the man beside him, "This is Muhyi al-Din, the only son of Ali ibn Arabi, may God be merciful to him."

Then, turning toward me, he said, "Muhyi, this is Ahmad ibn Baqi, the Caliph's messenger to you."

The man rose and shook my hand. Then he said, "The Commander of the Believers has sent me to offer you his condolences on the passing of your parents."

"May God reward him with benefactions!"

"And he asks you to join him in Marrakech to serve as one of his private secretaries."

I bowed my head but replied immediately, "I don't need this."

The messenger seemed rattled; he had not expected me to reject the offer. Then the Governor intervened, "Abu Zaynab, the Caliph would not send for you if he did not value you. Your father was the best man to ever serve in this court. If you will heed my advice, you will accept the Caliph's offer."

"Governor, my rejection wasn't inspired by pride or ill will. But you know I'm not suited for this position. My father knew this work; I don't."

"I counsel you to consider this offer for a few days. If your opinion doesn't change, then don't make the messenger return to the Caliph with your refusal. Go yourself. This approach will be more pleasing to him and more likely to meet with his approval."

"I will reflect on what you say and return here soon."

Gesturing to Ahmad ibn Baqi, the Governor suggested, "Stay here as our guest until Ibn Arabi departs for the Maghrib, to avoid arriving there before he does. Don't send a message to the Caliph concerning this matter until Ibn Arabi arrives there himself."

"I hear and obey."

On my way home I realized that I had made a mistake. Here was an opportunity for me to travel back to the Maghrib, where my second pillar was waiting for me. Why had I refused? The Caliph would not have sent for me if he intended me harm. Had he wished that, he would have ordered the governor to dispatch me to him bound in chains. What reason did I have to remain in Seville, where I no longer had a family, anything to learn, or a pillar? I could take my sisters with me and wouldn't need to return to this city. There were shaykhs in Marrakech I hadn't met, books I hadn't read, and a pillar who might reveal his secret identity to me at any moment.

When I entered the house, I told Maryam we would be moving to Marrakech soon. She rushed to tell my two sisters. I soon found them standing at the door to my room with expressions that ran the gamut from anxious stupefaction to delight. They wanted me to explain what was happening. I told them the Caliph had sent a messenger to find me. They were so surprised that they proceeded to ask me meaningless questions: "Will we ride horses or camels? Go by land or by sea? Who will live in our house?"

I went back to the palace the next morning but discovered the Governor wasn't holding an assembly. So I asked the guards where the Caliph's messenger was staying, and they told me. I found him and communicated my acceptance of the Caliph's request. I said I would travel with my entire family to Marrakech. He was delighted and asked which caravan I had found in the market, because he wished to travel with us. A week later we set out on five camels that the Governor provided us, together with the howdahs. I departed with my wife, two sisters, and daughter, and we were accompanied by Sallum and Addad. It was summer when we arrived in Marrakech, where I leased a spacious house with five rooms, a courtyard, and a flower garden. Maryam and I lived upstairs, my two sisters occupied the lower floor, and the two slaves had the bonus room attached to the house.

Several days after our arrival in Marrakech, I headed to the Caliph's assembly. He smiled when he saw me there and patted me on the shoulder to express his satisfaction but didn't speak to me. This assembly was packed with architects and builders, who were presenting stacks of plans for the buildings he had ordered constructed to provide offices for an increased number of caliphal secretaries, who were to record the Caliph's decrees. I learned that in the near future the Caliph intended to build a long wall around the city of Rabat, with seventy-four towers and five gates, a large hospital in Marrakech with fresh water piped to every room, a huge tower for the Kutubiyya Mosque—comparable to the minaret they completed in the Grand Mosque in Seville—plus a defensive fortress on the river in Seville with domes and palaces, a new mosque in Salé, with a madrassa attached to it, a broad aqueduct to run from north to south through Marrarkech, and a few new palaces for the Almohad Caliph and princes in Marrakech, Fez, Ceuta, and Salé.

While I was at this assembly, one of the Caliph's secretaries took me aside. I followed him to the secretariat to the Caliph's palace. After sitting down at a writing table, he brought out a large book with ruled pages. He opened it and told me, "Your stipend from the Caliph is ten dinars a month plus a housing allowance, and remuneration for any lessons you give in the mosque."

"God bless you and the Caliph!"

32

While the Caliph's messenger waited in Seville for my reply, another of his messengers sat on Mount Guéliz outside Marrakech with al-Sabti.[23] I accepted the offer from the Caliph's messenger in a single night and headed to Marrakech, but the Caliph's other messenger had to spend thirty nights with al-Sabti, in his cave, before this saint finally consented to cut short his spiritual retreat and head into Marrakech. I stood with the others at Bab Agnaou to await his return from a forty-year retreat in the cave. Hours passed before his mule finally passed through this gate. People threw their prayer rugs down for the mule to tread on. Once she had, these men carried them farther down the road so she would step on them again. Her hooves did not touch the dirt till she reached a hostel the Caliph had ordered entirely vacated and reserved for al-Sabti, his students, and his classes. After dismounting, he brought out a purse embroidered with silver letters. It is in such purses that grants from the Caliph are usually awarded. Al-Sabti distributed the dinars from it to impoverished people around him until it was completely empty.

Despite the length of his spiritual retreat, he made a remarkable appearance with his long hair, pure smile, and enormous beard. His shoulders were broad—his abstemious diet notwithstanding—and his muscles were as clearly defined as the topography of the mountains where he had lived for so many years. People crowded into his lodgings, and I was able to introduce myself. I simply greeted him and kissed his hand, like all the other men, and left. The Caliph assigned me a hostel like al-Sabti's, but smaller, and I was told I could teach as many courses there as I wished. In the morning I offered jurisprudence and Qur'anic exegesis for younger students. I would increase the understanding of the pupils, whom I found showed promise. A few stayed for the exegesis circle, which lasted till after midnight. Among these students were two young men from Fez who caught my eye from their first days in my course. They were endowed with brilliant intellects and a love of learning. One day I kept them after class. Subsequently I took them to my home, where I discussed various subjects with them and tested their ideas about religious and worldly matters. I eventually decided to marry them to my two sisters. Both couples were so happy they almost soared into the air.

It was several weeks before I had an opportunity to meet with al-Sabti. I would walk to his class each day and wait till he had finished answering questions and attending to his students' needs. Then, pressed for time, I would excuse myself and leave. After doing this for many days, I started counting the number of students in his class. One day when many people were present, I realized he would not have time for me, and I retraced my steps. I decided to wait a month before I returned. By that time, the general public would have dropped out, leaving only the students he himself selected. I was occupied with the courses I was teaching and began to write a book, which absorbed all my time. At midnight, during an exegesis class, someone knocked on the door. One of my students answered and found al-Sabti standing there—looking hopeful and embarrassed. "Where's your shaykh?" he asked.

I raced to greet him and kissed his hand. Then he complained, "I haven't been able to sleep, it's so cold."

"But, Shaykh, it's summer!"

"Yes, and the chill I feel reveals that the patched cloak I wear, my *khirqa*, no longer belongs to me. My body will continue shivering from the cold till I surrender it to the person who actually deserves it, and he gives me his in return."

Chagrin hovered overhead and seemed ready to descend on me, but I made one final effort, thinking God might deflect this before it landed on me. So I asked, "Who is worthy of it, Shaykh?"

"You. No one but you!"

Then my disappointment was total. I had never imagined I would feel so chagrined and frustrated by an exchange of garments with an upright *wali*. But I had hoped he was my pillar. Since he had doffed his *khirqa* to honor me, he wasn't a *watad*. Who was left in Ifriqia, if neither Abu Madyan nor al-Sabti was a pillar? Where in this vast region should I go to search for a *watad*?

Standing before me, he removed his cloak, and I took off mine. He immediately departed, and I returned dumbfounded to my students, not knowing what to say. I requested their permission to cut short the lesson, with the understanding that we would conclude it the next day. I retreated to my room and attempted to continue writing where I had left off, but God did not grant me a single letter or numeral. I stretched out to sleep and reflected that it would have been better for me if Fatima hadn't told me about the four pillars. Waiting for them was slaying me, and the anticipation was bitter and lethal. Moreover the critical precondition—"Purify your heart!"—was obscure and open-ended. How should I purify it? What should I cleanse it of? How would I know if it was purified? How would I know when it was polluted? Here it was, beating inside my ribcage, with the same rhythm—whether pure or defiled. The sun continued to rise from the east whether I was righteous or dissolute, and night sheltered both God's servants and libertines.

I eventually fell asleep with a befuddled mind, covering myself with al-Sabti's cloak, which smelled of wood smoke. I woke in the morning feeling cranky but didn't know why. Perhaps I was annoyed by these three remaining pillars. What were they waiting for? Why did I need to purify my heart four times? Why didn't a single cleansing suffice to summon all of them?

I left my house for a walk, thinking my anger might dissipate; I couldn't imagine anything that had upset me in this city, no matter how apparently coincidental. In the market's main square, people were calling to each other in a way that suggested a herald was about to make an announcement for the Caliph. I walked along with them and stopped near the steps where the herald normally stood. He waited silently for people to gather. Then waving a folded paper, he declared in his loud voice: "People! This is a letter from Alfonso to the Commander of the Believers, who has ordered it read to the people to hear. Then you will decide what to do."

He unfolded the letter and read out:

. . . Caliph, I have heard you play for time year after year, putting one foot forward while pulling the other back. I do not know whether cowardice has slowed you or some renunciation of your revelation. Then I was told that you cannot wage war, because you fathom the discord and lack of reciprocal trust among Andalusia's leaders, whom I am humiliating by capturing their children, making an example of their elders, and slaying their young men. You lack any valid reason to delay coming to their aid, since destiny has proffered you a helping hand. . . .

The herald paused to allow people to raise their voices in condemnation. People could be heard shouting from various areas of the crowd: "Allahu akbar!" The herald allowed them time to express their anger before he raised a hand signaling them to let him continue. Then these protests died down.

He said: "People, you have heard what Alfonso the Infidel wrote to the Commander of the Believers. Now hear the response from the Commander of the Believers."

Silence reigned, and people listened attentively. To increase their interest, the herald delayed. Then he closed his eyes and recited part of the Qur'an's chapter entitled "The Ants":

"Return to them, because we will come to them with troops they cannot withstand and we will exile them in abject humiliation." [24]

The crowd sizzled like hot oil on a skillet. The Caliph's reply had awakened a ferocious excitement in them. They started loudly chanting his name as well as "Allahu akbar," while calling for jihad and cursing the Christians. The herald descended the steps, trying to conceal the smirk on his face, and left. A few days later heralds appeared in the residential districts, quarters, and mosques to recruit volunteers for the army. The Caliph adopted military dress and never appeared in his assembly without it. Alfonso's letter played a major role in whipping up a bellicose spirit among the people. Men who had never volunteered before did now, and fellows who didn't own a sword or spear set off on jihad. Hundreds of men in Marrakech formed a queue in front of the army's secretariat to request a place in temporary training camps. The blacksmiths' market was flooded with market regulators to ensure that the price for a sword wasn't inflated beyond the reach of the common man. Then the Caliph decided to buy out the merchants' entire stock of weapons for distribution to volunteers. His messengers hastened off to outlying regions of the Maghrib to encourage people to join the battle and to purchase stockpiles of weapons, trained horses, armor, and saddles. Some weeks later, the Caliph himself led two hundred thousand troops to Andalusia. These included Sudanese, Berbers, Arabs, Slavs, Muwallads, and Oghuz Turks.

"Don't rely on hunches."

—IBN ARABI

33

I was never so wrong about anyone as I was about an Ethiopian who had recently joined my classes. I thought he would never make it beyond the initial jurisprudence lessons, but he progressed to the exegesis circle in only a few months. I thought that the intimations, hints, explanations, and unveilings that I provided in class had sailed over his head, only to discover he had collected all of them in a book in which he had organized and explained them. I thought he frequented me because he wasn't used to life without a master to give him orders. I guessed he would stay at most a few days, but instead he spent twenty-five years with me. I thought no full moon would be black, but here was an Ethiopian moon that was one of the most perfect, luminous, reassuring, and delightful ones.

"Where do you come from?"

At first, Badr did not reply, as if he didn't know. Then he said, "I'm the emancipated slave of Abu al-Futuh al-Harrani. I've lived with him in Cairo, Damietta, Mecca, Bejaïa, Marrakech, and Fez. So I don't know precisely where I'm from."

"'From it were you created and to it will you return.'"[25]

He nodded his head in agreement and smiled with relief. I seemed to have offered him a solution to a major problem that had troubled him since his emancipation. He didn't know how old he was either but appeared to be in his early forties. He was distinguished, amiable, and helpful. When Abu al-Futuh grew elderly and feared he would die and that his children wouldn't emancipate his slave, he himself had emancipated Badr, who had been surprised and hadn't known what to do, since he had no occupation or savings. Then he headed to the mosque and started studying in the learning circles he found there, regardless of a shaykh's doctrinal affiliation. When he heard about me and saw how students flocked to me, he began to sit in my circle and listen to what I taught. Eventually he asked my permission to enroll, and I granted it. I felt sorry for him because I dealt with difficult topics that are hard to grasp.

Some weeks after enrolling in my circle he spoke to me after class: "Shaykh, I would be happy to follow and serve you. You do not seem to have an assistant."

"What do you hope to gain from this, Badr?"

"Your learning and your blessing."

So I agreed, and he began to follow me like my shadow, from my house to the hostel, from the hostel to the mosque, from the mosque to the market, and from the market to the palace. At night he slept in one of the rooms reserved for foreign students at the mosque, and shortly before dawn I would find him standing at the door of my house, waiting for me to appear. I grew fond of and accustomed to his company. I trusted him and delegated to him the job of organizing my lessons, distributing them to the students, and copying out of the book. Within a few months he became my right arm. I relied on him for everything, and he never disappointed me. I noticed from the beginning that he was an auspicious presence. God had endowed him with this attribute, and Badr's features and expression were good omens too. It was Badr who brought me the glad tidings of the Almohad Army's great victory in Andalusia. He also learned that the number of Andalusian caravans had increased rather than decreased. Each arriving traveler provided us with a different figure for Castilian casualties and the—seemingly endless—spoils. At first, travelers said twenty thousand had been killed; then others said fifty. I myself heard someone swear that more than a hundred thousand had been slain. Andalusian cities were so flooded with enslaved captives that ordinary people frequented the markets riding on litters carried by two or more slaves with blond hair and blue eyes. There was said to be so much booty that a lot was left behind, for want of pack animals to carry it. Alfonso was said to have deserted, fled from battle, and shaved off his beard and hair, which he resolved to keep shaved till he could avenge the huge defeat he had suffered.

When the spoils finally reached Marrakech, a prisoner was sold for one dirhem, a sword for half a dirhem, a mare for five dirhems, and a donkey for one. People often bought slaves wholesale, appraised their skills and abilities, and resold them in the market for higher prices, each according to his skillset. Most slaves were put to work at the construction sites of buildings the Caliph ordered erected, and their wages were paid to their owners. The markets and commerce were stimulated by the decreasing prices for slaves and pack animals. A sense of security and confidence in the future was widespread, and when the Caliph returned to Marrakech, people came out in droves to welcome him. He entered the city in a splendid procession, and citizens showered him with flowers and rubbed musk on the hooves of his steed. They spread carpets before it and kissed the tracks left by his horse all the way to his palace. Delegations from the cities of the Maghrib came in waves to congratulate the Caliph on his victory. Each time a delegation arrived, the Caliph's name was chanted in the streets. Storytellers created new tales about his victories, and drumbeats shook every neighborhood—even those farthest from the large squares. The Caliph ordered that all orphan boys should be assembled for circumcision near the palace and commanded that each lad be given a gold coin, a tunic, some bread, a pomegranate, and two silver dirhems. In celebration of the victory, merchants set up tables in every market with free goods for the poor. The chief seed merchant donated a hundred Almohad flags, which were flown at the entrances to markets and streets, and outside mosques. The palace hosted a large reception at which the Caliph sat on a dais overlooking the city's main plaza where people assembled below him. One poet after another recited either doggerel verses or portentous poems in praise of his victory.

In the days following his victory, the Caliph's assembly was held every day after the midday prayer. So I would finish my lesson and dismiss my students shortly before the call to prayer. Then I prayed and headed to the Caliph's palace. His assembly in Marrakech differed from the ones he had held in Seville. Here his ministers assigned people places to sit as they entered and directed each person to his assigned seat after he greeted the Caliph. In Seville, the assembly was smaller, and ministers were less concerned about where people sat. Thus I wasn't able to sit near the Caliph in Marrakech. All the same, whenever I greeted him, he never failed to welcome me by name, gesture to me, and smile; usually he didn't address people or know their names.

Once these celebrations concluded, entry to the Caliph's assembly was limited to men he invited. I was included as were dozens of army commanders, tribal shaykhs, preachers from the mosques, the city's judges, and Almohad princes. In these smaller assemblies, the Caliph presented new proposals for the realm and listened to opinions and responses. One time the Caliph complained about the Banu Ghaniya, who had, typically, exploited the army's deployment to Andalusia to renew their rebellion in Tunis. They had expanded their territories, occupying fortresses and cities that had previously been beyond their grasp. In his assembly, the Caliph said resentfully and indignantly: "We have fought them but have not intimidated them and pleaded with them but received no response from them."

The Caliph's minister, Abu Hafs observed, "But the Caliph has broken their might and quashed their forwardness. The remaining men are ignoramuses who agitate against the Caliph and mercenaries."

The Caliph replied to his minister with obvious exasperation: "I've heard this before, Abu Hafs. All you ministers say the rebels are weak and few in numbers. Yet when you engage them, they are better prepared and more numerous than we expected."

"May God grant our Caliph victory! Our army is still battle-ready and well-armed. We haven't disbanded it yet. If you want, we'll launch an offensive against them and uproot their tree."

The Caliph did not reply. He started fiddling thoughtfully with his beard. Before replying, he called on another man, whom I didn't recognize. Judging by his looks I assumed he was an army commander.

"If the Caliph will permit me, I would advise him against dispatching the army again immediately. The men are tired, and the hospital is full of sick and wounded troops. It is less than prudent to lead them from one battle to another while they are in this shape."

The Caliph gazed at the man's face for a long time—as if these words reflected his own thinking. But even so, he remained silent and did not comment.

Addressing the man, Abu Hafs said, "Yes. You are correct. But we needn't send the entire army against them, since they are far fewer in number than the Castilian troops."

The man bowed his head and did not reply. He apparently wanted to avoid a debate with the Caliph's prime minister and principal adviser. A man with a long beard stood up near me. He appeared to be a jurist. He approached the Caliph, assisted by a cane. Once he stood before the Caliph, he said, "May God empower the Caliph who has assembled the people beneath his banner and united everyone in his state. There are, though, still some disruptive, divisive elements. If the Caliph would allow me, I could name names, but I don't want to appear to be an informer."

The increasingly impatient Caliph remained expressionless, his brow furrowed, as he nodded to this jurist to speak.

Then the elderly man said, "Shu'ayb ibn al-Husayn has an adherent in every land and a disciple in every mosque. He does not adhere to our Zahiri doctrine and does not follow our praiseworthy path."

My heart skipped a beat when I heard this malicious reference to Ghawth Abu Madyan in the Caliph's assembly. I listened intently so I wouldn't miss a single word the Caliph uttered. He waved his hand dismissively, apparently unconvinced by what the elderly man said and sick and tired of backbiting. To prevent the Caliph from losing interest, the elderly man added, "People in Bejaïa say he resembles the Mahdi."

"Has he said he's the Mahdi?" the Caliph asked, staring directly at him.

"Not yet, but he will soon."

"How do you know he will? Are you a fortuneteller?"

"Where there's smoke there's fire, Master."

"When you see the smoke with your own eyes, tell me. I don't act on rumors. Fear God!"

"A free man possesses only what doesn't possess him."

——**IBN ARABI**

34

I entered the Caliph's assembly as usual the next week, in the afternoon, took my designated seat and watched a delegation from Sanhaja arrive. They acknowledged they were late in presenting their congratulations to the Caliph on his victories but explained that their chief had been ill. The Caliph welcomed them warmly and ordered a cloak of honor given to each of them. The next group were supervisors of Marrakech's markets. The Caliph asked them about their markets and the prices in them. Then he told them to lower the price of barley by selling grain from his warehouses. Next came emissaries from the Sudan. They complained that merchants from Marrakech bought ostrich eggs but did not pay for the ones that broke in transit. He ordered them remanded to a judge. Next he welcomed his military commanders. When they stood before him, he asked about their soldiers.

"May God strengthen the Caliph!" they replied. "We commanders present our soldiers' complaint to the Caliph."

The Caliph sat up straight. He looked interested. "What is their complaint?"

"They complain that their salaries are paid four times a year, but that the Oghuz Turks are paid monthly."

The Caliph gestured to his minister, who approached him, and they whispered together. Then the Caliph said, "May God forgive you. These foreign troops have no resources to rely on in this country, except their salaries. Explain this to your men and tell them they are on our mind and we shan't forget them."

Once the commanders left, the assembly was empty. I started to leave, but the chamberlain summoned me and asked me to approach the Caliph. So I did.

He leaned toward me and asked, "Do you know Shu'ayb ibn al-Husayn?"

"He's also known as al-Ghawth Abu Madyan; who doesn't know him?"

The Caliph sat back in his chair and gestured for me to sit down beside him. A man rose to offer me his seat. As I sat down, my heart began to beat faster. I remembered the previous slanders against Ibn Rushd and what had happened to him subsequently. Now the Caliph had asked for information about Abu Madyan, and his fate might be in my hands.

The Caliph dealt with some other matters and then gestured to the chamberlain to stop admitting people. As he rose, he said, "Come with me."

I followed him into the palace, trailed by the chamberlain. We entered a small conference room, which could only seat six. The Caliph told the chamberlain to summon Abu Hafs, al-Janfisi, and Ibn Baqi.

The Caliph made no further comment until these men arrived. Ibn Baqi, whom the Caliph had dispatched as a messenger to Seville, had been appointed a judge only a few weeks prior. Al-Janfisi served as the Caliph's governor of Bejaïa and its districts. I rose to greet all of them. Then the four of us sat down and waited for the Caliph to explain why he had summoned us.

He soon pointed to al-Janfisi and told him: "Repeat what you mentioned this morning."

Al-Janfisi cleared his throat and looked left and right in embarrassment. Then he said, "The Commander of the Believers, may God prolong his life, asked me about Shu'ayb ibn al-Husayn . . . and I told him what I know. He has a mosque that is frequented by many people and he teaches many subjects in it. . . ."

The Caliph interrupted to hurry him on: "From which schools?"

"A number of schools, including Hanafi and Maliki."

The Caliph turned to Abu Hafs and asked, "What did we order regarding the Maliki school, Abu Hafs? What?"

Abu Hafs replied quickly and calmly, "Your orders have been obeyed, Commander of the Believers. I informed all the governors in all the capitals that no Maliki jurisprudence should be taught in any assembly or mosque and that anyone found violating this ban would be considered in open rebellion and deserve punishment."

The Caliph then turned to al-Janfisi and asked him, "Did our order reach you?"

"Yes, indeed, Commander of the Believers. I began enforcing it at that time."

"What about this Shu'ayb, then?"

"Our agents informed him of this ban, and he heard them and heeded it."

"Why didn't you take him into custody when he violated our order?"

Al-Janfisi remained silent for a time as he collected his thoughts, but his expression showed how embarrassed and nervous he felt. Finally he replied, "Commander of the Believers, this Shu'ayb has countless followers in Bejaïa, Tlemcen, and Gafsa. Students come to him from Egypt, the Sudan, Syria, and Andalusia. He waged jihad against the Crusaders and lost an arm. That earned him enormous love from the citizenry. I fear that if I treat him roughly, civil strife may ensue. . . ."

The Caliph interrupted him, shouting furiously: "Then tell me! If you fear civil strife, tell me, so I can investigate the matter. Don't just let him defy my order flagrantly."

His head bowed, al-Janfisi nodded dramatically without adding another word while the Caliph excoriated him loudly, apparently without frightening or upsetting Abu Hafs. The Caliph continued yelling: "Now that his renown is widespread and his followers have increased in number, *now* you come to complain to me about him? You ignored him until he strengthened his hand and news of him has reached me from others—not from you, Wretched Governor."

During this whole spectacle, my brain raced like a gazelle fleeing a predatory beast. I had expected the Caliph would ask me what I thought of al-Ghawth and that I could shower praise and kudos on him. Now, though, it was clear such words would enrage and infuriate the Caliph. If he heard me praise Abu Madyan, he would suspect that his own assembly and court harbored supporters of al-Ghawth. I was still brooding about this when the Caliph did turn toward me and in an alarmed tone demanded: "Tell me what you know about this man, who is known to all my subjects, but not to me!"

"What I know about him parallels what the governor said. But, Commander of the Believers, I would like to explain that some religious scholars and shaykhs, like Abu Madyan, take one statement from a *madhhab* and one from another school of law in order to compare and contrast them, or to draw inferences. In this case, someone might hear him quote Malik or Abu Hanifa and assume he followed their legal schools instead of the Zahiri School. If you heard from him yourself, you could judge this."

The Caliph calmed down and seemed to be considering my words carefully. He leaned back in his chair and continued to gaze at my face as if I were still speaking.

Abu Hafs seized this moment to affirm: "Abu Zaynab is right. If you heard him yourself, you could ascertain the truth. What would the Commander of the Believers think about our inviting this man to come to Marrakech? Then you can judge for yourself."

The Caliph welcomed this suggestion and said in a soft voice, as though thinking aloud: "Yes, yes. This is good."

Al-Janfisi cleared his throat and said in a choked voice, "Whatever you say, Commander of the Believers. The only thing is that this man is quite old, and the trip may exhaust him."

The Caliph glared at al-Janfisi and remarked sarcastically, "You hid him from my ears and now you want to hide him from my eyes, al-Janfisi! What?"

"I take refuge with God, Master. I just wanted to be sure you understood his condition. Your command is all that matters, first and last."

"Only God's command counts. Write for him to come to me in Marrakech. . . ."

The Caliph rose, turning his back on us. But as he moved away, we heard him say: "And be quick!"

35

I didn't sleep properly for several nights. Maryam would doze off and wake to find me still brooding. She would clasp my hand and press it to her, hoping I would relax and calm down. If the Caliph harmed al-Ghawth, I would be the worst disciple on earth; God would never grant me *walaya*, *najaba*, or *qataba*, and my pillars would desert me like gazelles fleeing predatory beasts. I would be an enemy of God's pious saints, who were being shoved into prisons and sent into exile. Divine justice wouldn't delay its punishment for the evil manifest in me, whether that meant a cramped prison cell or distant exile. *My God, if no harm befalls al-Ghawth, I won't suffer; so have great mercy on me and on him.*

A week passed, and then another. The month ended, but al-Ghawth hadn't arrived. I didn't ask about him at the palace, didn't hear any mention of him, and God unveiled nothing to me. Unveiling? I didn't deserve an unveiling, a *kashf*, or a vision in a dream, a *ru'ya*. So let the people who deserved them receive unveilings—pious *wali*s who treated their shaykhs with due respect—God should be gracious to them. Fatima had instructed me to do something I had yet to achieve: "Purify your heart and follow it." But I hadn't purified or followed it. Here I was, slandering friends of God, fraternizing with caliphs, eating, drinking, and living comfortably like any other member of the general public and the masses. What sort of purity was this!

I couldn't stand it any longer. Al-Ghawth hadn't arrived yet. Either he had declined the Caliph's "invitation" (and thus confirmed the Caliph's suspicions that he was responsible for those repeated rebellions and successive revolts) or fled far away, beyond the sovereignty of the Almohads. I prayed to God to provide me a *kashf*, but He didn't. I passed every night in prayer and no longer slept with Maryam. I distributed half of my monthly stipend as alms and visited three sepulchers. When I prayed, I recited—with every prostration—the Qur'an verse: "Your Lord has not forsaken you nor is He displeased."[26] I slept two nights in the city's cemetery. A second month passed without God unveiling any message. I climbed to the roof terrace of my house to weep, so I wouldn't scare my daughter, and began to bawl.

The next morning, I went to the palace and sought out Abu Hafs, whom I hadn't seen for some time. Noticing the half circles around my eyelids and the sad look in my eyes, he studied my face for a time. Then he took my hand and asked sympathetically, "Are you sick, Abu Zaynab?"

Troubled by his sympathy, I looked at his face and replied, "I'm sick of my sins and ill from carelessness and conceit."

He laughed nervously and patted my back. "If you're sick of your sins," he said, "the rest of us should be dead, Abu Zaynab. Come sit here."

I sat facing him and wondered one last time if it would be appropriate to ask about al-Ghawth or not. Then I decided I would. Since two months had passed already without al-Ghawth arriving, the Caliph must have made some decision concerning him. In that case, my inquiry about al-Ghawth wouldn't harm *or* help him.

"Has al-Ghawth been delayed?"

The minister responded casually as he glanced over some documents: "Didn't you know? He's ill."

Relief flooded over me, the minister's words, like a pail of cold water, poured over my chest, which had been a blazing brazier for the last two months. Why hadn't I thought of this? Yes, nothing but ill health would have prevented him from coming. I was at fault for nourishing suspicions about my shaykh and imagining that he had launched a rebellion or fled. I hadn't given him the benefit of the doubt and guessed that he was ill. How wretched I had made myself.

"Really?" I asked the minister. "Does the Caliph know this?"

"Certainly he does. He sent two more messengers after the first to hurry the shaykh up when his arrival was delayed. The last one returned a few days ago and informed us that the shaykh had actually left Bejaïa, heading to Marrakech, but that ill health forced him to remain in Tlemcen."

"Did the messenger tell the Caliph when he might resume the trip?"

"He didn't. We think he hasn't much longer to live."

Now the bucket of cold water turned to steam scalding my chest as the conflagration started to engulf my ribs once more. Al-Ghawth was dying. The trip had exhausted him. I excused myself, left, and headed straight home, not stopping for any reason. Maryam was alarmed that I had returned early and scrutinized my face, trying to figure out what had happened. So I told her about al-Ghawth. When I noticed that Addad was feeding my mare, I decided on the spot to travel to Tlemcen to see the shaykh before his spirit ascended. I told Addad to prepare the horse for a trip and Maryam to gather what I would need.

Maryam protested, "You're going alone? Isn't there a caravan you can join?"

"I'm not going to wait on a caravan. I'm afraid he'll die before I can see him."

"It's dangerous to travel alone. Take Addad with you. I beg you."

"There's no horse for him to ride; if he walks, he'll delay me."

"He can ride the mule."

"The mule is slow."

Annoyed at my stubbornness, Maryam went off to prepare supplies for my journey. I heard her say something to Sallum, but I couldn't hear what. Then he left the house on some errand. Not much later someone knocked on the door; and, when I answered, I found Badr al-Habashi there, holding the bridle of a stallion. As soon as he saw me, he exclaimed, "I'm riding with you, Master. I have a stallion."

Glancing behind me, I saw Sallum there, and Maryam appeared, trying to find out what was happening. Then I realized that she had sent Sallum to ask Badr the Ethiopian to accompany me. There was no time to debate the subject. Since Badr had a stallion, everything was fine.

We mounted our horses and left the city. Badr showed me the route, which he had taken numerous times before. We rode all that day and most of the night. Five days later we arrived. We located the shaykh in a house next to the mosque. He could no longer speak or communicate with anyone, and one of his students was nursing him. I kissed his hands, beard, and forehead and sat next to his head. I asked the students there what had happened. They told me he had lost consciousness on the way to Marrakech. Tears flooded my eyes for this great shaykh, whom the Caliph had forced to embark on a trip that was too stressful and taxing for him, a trip that had pretty well killed him. I asked the owner of that house if I could stay at the shaykh's bedside, and he consented. I sent al-Habashi to the market to buy lots of food, so I wouldn't impose on this household, which seemed impoverished. I made a place for myself to sleep at the shaykh's feet, which almost touched my brow while I slept. When I woke, I sat by his head and recited the surah "Ya Sin" over and over again.

Some days passed without the shaykh's condition improving, and then our host brought out funeral perfumes and a shroud, which he placed at the side of the room.

I asked him, "What are you doing? Are you so sure he's dying that you've brought a shroud?"

The man's eyes filled with tears, and sobs interrupted his words as he replied, "I didn't provide them. The shaykh brought them from Bejaïa."

I choked up and asked, "Did he feel his end was nigh?"

"He didn't just feel that. He was sure of it. When the Caliph's messenger came to him in Bejaïa and ordered him to appear, people were concerned about the long trip's effect on him and begged him to write the Caliph that he was too ill to travel. He laughed at their suggestion and said, "If my demise isn't fated to be here, I must travel to the place where it is destined to occur.""

The man wept, and tears came to my eyes as well. Then he continued, "All the way from Bejaïa he repeated: 'I praise God Who has sent someone to take me to the place where I am destined to pass.' He kept repeating that till he lost consciousness."

Any hope I had that the shaykh would recover evaporated when I heard these words. I waited then for God to perform this charismatic act for his *wali* by harvesting his spirit, and He did. My shaykh died some hours later, and the news spread throughout Tlemcen. When we went to bury him, everyone came without any exceptions. There were too many mourners for the cemetery to accommodate. Groups of people took turns praying for him till sunset. At that time his grave was still surrounded by people weeping and paying their last respects.

Feeling troubled, I returned to Marrakech with Badr. I was furious with this Caliph, who harmed both God's special friends and scholars. Ibn Rushd was in exile and Abu Madyan was in the grave. I felt sure that the circle would eventually expand to include me—especially now that slanderous jurists had become the Caliph's cronies, arousing his ire against people even while he was drunk with victory and didn't know which spring he should draw water from—not while they served as his guides and witnesses.

"The bewilderment of bewildered people serves a purpose."

—IBN ARABI

36

Abu Madyan's death distressed the Caliph, who reprimanded Abu Hafs for recommending that he summon this shaykh. I asked myself whether al-Janfisi had told Abu Hafs that Abu Madyan was ill and wondered why the Caliph was blaming Abu Hafs. Some days later, when the Caliph assumed that this matter had been forgotten, a group from Bejaïa arrived to complain about the loss of their mighty shaykh, who had been alive when the Caliph ordered him to come but was now dead and buried in Tlemcen. They arrived as a delegation in Marrakech and asked to see the Caliph. Assuming they had come to offer condolences, Abu Hafs admitted them. When they marched up to the Caliph, they didn't greet him or offer condolences. Instead, a member of the delegation began to harangue him.

"Caliph, I hope you understand that you have harmed one of God's special friends. You made him leave his home and imposed on him a trip that was more than he could bear. So conduct yourself as you see fit in your assembly, but you will meet your Lord after opposing not just anybody but the Pole of the age, the Sovereign of the Prophet's heirs, and the Imam of the Righteous."

Another man declared: "God knows that al-Ghawth grew weak when he was still in his mosque and you were in your palace. He went to be with his Lord when there was barely enough food for two days, and you will go to your Lord after oppressing and exhausting him."

During these tirades, the Caliph bowed his head to appease them by feigning grief and contrition. They spoke at length

155

to express their surging anger and profound sorrow. I stood at the edge of the assembly, listening to what they said and hoping I would be able to tell the Caliph as much as they did and more. The barrage continued as one protester walked up to the Caliph's chair and pointed his finger at him, almost touching the edge of his tunic. "Did God squeeze the compassion from your heart?" he asked. "You ordered a shaykh in his eighties to ride to you on a mule while you sat on your butt in Marrakech?"

Another man shouted: "Tyrant, we are his students, disciples, and congregation. You have deprived us of our teacher, our shaykh, and our imam. By God, we will surely present our complaint to the One who does not neglect the rights of those deprived."

The Caliph eventually grew angry and impatient after many men had vented their wrath. So he began to argue with them and commanded them to be more polite, but they refused. They called him by his given name, omitting his titles. They started to demand the end of his reign and his immediate destruction. Then he ordered the guards to arrest the men who had raised their voices and infuriated him. There were more than twenty of them, and the guards swarmed around these militants, encircling them, and escorted them out of the assembly. As they were pushed outside, they raised their voices. One began to curse the Caliph, and others loudly endorsed this curse. No sooner had they reached the prison, than the Caliph sent someone to order the guards to release them.

For several days the Caliph skipped his assembly, not wanting to appear in public. He declined to attend to citizens' complaints that had been appealed to him and ordered all their cases remanded back to the judges. He summoned the sons of his brother Abu Yahya, whom he had executed, and awarded them incomes and houses. He ordered stockpiled grains removed from the warehouses to lower the price of bread, even though it hadn't risen. He released every prisoner who hadn't been convicted of a crime mentioned in the Qur'an. He stopped attending public prayer services and ordered that an imam chosen from the public should conduct them.

After that incident, I saw him twice by chance in the palace, and both times he only glanced at me. All the same, I sensed his intense regret and profound grief. Then, one morning, we were surprised to learn that the Caliph had pardoned Ibn Rushd and sent a guard unit to Lucena, where he had been exiled. He ordered them to treat him well and bring him back to Marrakech in a camel-borne litter. I was delighted by this news and sensed that a heavy weight had been lifted from my chest. Whether he was conscious of it or not, the Caliph wished to make up for the death of al-Ghawth by pardoning Ibn Rushd. But even if he had pardoned Ibn Rushd seventy times, that would not have made up for his sin, and God would do whatever He willed.

Two weeks after the pardon, Ibn Rushd reached Marrakech. He had aged visibly—as if he had spent thirty years in Lucena, not three. His beard had turned gray, his brow was furrowed, his eyelids drooped, and his back was bowed. I saw him from a distance as he entered the Caliph's assembly and avoided greeting him, since I was overwhelmed by a feeling that I should not. I feared a single look from him might induce a relapse in me to the massive sense of regret, which had been slowly lifting from me. I did not wish to risk such a relapse. I stood in the assembly with the others and watched him walk slowly forward as the Caliph rose to greet him. The Caliph seemed deeply affected to see him in this state. He obviously had not imagined Ibn Rushd's condition would have deteriorated so gravely. They stood together at the center of the assembly while the Caliph tried to look at the face of Ibn Rushd, who turned aside and bowed his head, focusing his gaze on the floor. The Caliph started to ask about his health, but Ibn Rushd nodded his head and repeated, "Praise to God in any case. Praise to God in any case."

The Caliph personally led him to a seat beside him and said, "Abu al-Walid, we have pardoned you and brought you back to our assembly. May God forgive what has happened."

Ibn Rushd remained silent long enough that we thought he wouldn't respond or hadn't heard. Then he suddenly said, "Even if you pardon me in this world, I will not pardon you in the world to come."

The Caliph frowned at this reply and shook his head sorrowfully and resentfully. He responded, "I know I have wronged you. If I had let people have their way, they would have killed you. I chose to exile you for your own safety and hid my true intention to pardon you once people's excitement had subsided."

Ibn Rushd raised his head and looked the Caliph in the face, smiling slightly. Then he said, "Exile didn't harm me. The whole world is a Believer's place of exile. Do you know what my heaviest burden was in Lucena?"

The Caliph shook his head inquisitively. Then Ibn Rushd continued, "I went to the only mosque there to pray with my son Abdallah. Then the deplorables, the common people you had incited against me, expelled me and prevented me from praying there."

The Caliph shook his head disapprovingly. In a louder voice, Ibn Rushd added, "I remained in Lucena for three years without ever entering a house of God. Do you know this? Do you?"

"By God, I didn't. I would never prevent a Muslim from entering one of God's mosques."

"It makes no difference now whether you knew or not. When a ruler follows the riffraff, injustices multiply and the earth is spoiled."

The Caliph reacted angrily and stamped his feet on the ground. He waved his hands and shouted at Ibn Rushd, "Don't be too harsh with your censure, Ibn Rushd! I'm not led by the riffraff, and you shouldn't criticize me for violating God's justice and His messenger's. Do you doubt their sovereignty?"

"Ya'qub, God will judge between us on Judgment Day."

Then, helping himself up with his cane, Ibn Rushd rose to leave, saying, "No doubt God's sovereignty will rule."

Turning his back on the Caliph, Ibn Rushd walked slowly toward the door, leaving the Caliph silent and bewildered, not knowing what to do. He bowed his head in silence as some of the men around him murmured as if to express displeasure for him. The chamberlain watched the Caliph closely, assuming he might issue some order, but he didn't. Ibn Rushd passed directly in front of me, and his cane almost brushed my tunic. Had he looked up, he would have caught me trying to hide my smile of approval for everything he had told the Caliph, since his words had helped heal my chest.

Once Ibn Rushd had declared that judgment rested in God's hands on Judgment Day, he advanced toward the court he had selected, and his spirit ascended to his Maker only a few weeks after his encounter with the Caliph. News of his demise struck the Caliph like a thunderbolt, even before he had recovered from al-Ghawth's death. Sensing that the world was closing in on him, he decided to retreat to his palace in the city of Salé and relax by the sea.

37

Ibn Rushd left instructions for burial in Cordova, and I decided to accompany his body there, not merely to see him off but to address my guilty feelings in hopes of burying with him the shears of regret that kept snipping at my heart. Accompanied by Badr, I walked to his house. We had barely turned the corner when we met a group of at least twenty men standing at the door with sorrowful expressions suggesting an everlasting love. Some had brought a camel, others held bundles, and still others had come without provisions or a camel. I sent Badr to the market to purchase provisions for people who had none. I stood with the others by the door, waiting for the body to be brought out. A young man wailed and fell to the ground, ripping his tunic, when he saw the coffin borne out of the house on the shoulders of Ibn Rushd's two sons and a servant, whose glum face was flooded with tears.

This small, mournful caravan set off in the morning. Ibn Rushd's camel was to my right, and I watched her from time to time. She carried everything this man had left behind on the earth: his body and his books. Some days later we reached the sea and set sail. The Mediterranean was calm and still, as if it too were seeing off Ibn Rushd. On the eleventh day of our trip we reached Cordova to find that news of this funeral had preceded us. Many of the city's residents came out to welcome us. People hugged men they knew and others they didn't. Tears flowed, wails resounded, and voices quavered. With trembling hands, people stroked the coffin while gazing at it with grieving, dejected faces.

The cortege passed through Cordova's streets as men called out from alleyways: "All power and might are God's" and women wailed from their balconies. The ranks of mourners swelled each time we passed through a neighborhood or market till there were hundreds of us. The cemetery welcomed us with open arms. We consigned him to a grave there and completed the burial as the sun was preparing to set. The crowd dispersed, and Badr and I found a hostel where we could shelter with our grief. I slept that first night in a bed, while Ibn Rushd lay in his grave. I wondered which of us had a more agreeable resting place and a calmer mind. I lay awake till midnight. So I brought out my papers, thinking that I might be able to write a little but found I couldn't. Instead I started to write Ibn Rushd's name on a blank page in my best calligraphy so I could contemplate it silently.

I passed a few days in Cordova, gathering some books I lacked in Marrakech. I toured the booksellers' shops and found that most of them carried Ibn Rushd's books. I was amazed to find they sold them, since the ban hadn't been lifted yet. I asked one dealer whether the market supervisors had seen these books. He did not reply directly but shouted to passersby: "Ibn Rushd's books: *Bidayat al-Mujtahid*, *Tahafut al-Tahafut*, *Sharh al-Arjuza*." They were obviously challenging the ban and resented the suppression of a man who had been a chief justice, a companion of caliphs, a physician, a philosopher, and a jurisprudent, but who had been denied access to mosques during the final days of his life. So they had dusted off all their copies of his books, which they had hidden the day that bonfires blazed in city plazas, burning them.

While many were expressing grief for Ibn Rushd, the Segura River crested its banks in Murcia. In Cordova we heard that it had flooded the lower portion of the city, destroying houses, mosques, markets, and shops. Properties, goods, books, and other possessions were lost, and people and livestock perished. Outlying regions were inundated, and field crops and fruit were destroyed. As a result, food was in short supply. The water level remained high, and people were forced to travel from one area of the city to another by boat. I thought of our house, which we hadn't checked on since we left, and decided to head there to see what the flood had done to it. I was motivated by a child's homesickness for Murcia, and I was that child.

The day Badr and I reached Murcia, the water had retreated from most of the city. The roads were still wet, and low-lying areas had become little swamps. Dead carp lined the streets together with red frogs, some of which were still trying to flee.

I traversed streets I had last trod when I was eight and reached our house as easily as if I had left it only the day before, without needing a guide. Water had swept away the garden wall and broken down the door. Because of this, miserable squatters were living there when I arrived. After one look at me, dressed like a Maghribi and riding my stallion, they quickly collected their belongings and departed fearfully and apologetically.

I walked through the house and discovered that restoring it would cost a lot. It was unrealistic for me to consider returning to any city in Andalusia now that it had become a sheep at which the Franks from the north, the Portuguese to the west, the Almohads on the south, and the Majorcans from the east were nipping. This would not be a good place to live while its condition was so unstable. My two sisters had married Maghribis, and I assumed they wouldn't have any use for this house. Thus I decided to sell it and went immediately to the market, where I visited various realtors and offered it to them. In less than two weeks, the sale closed. Then I accepted the money and, with my own hand, severed the first of my Andalusian roots.

I walked Murcia's streets with Badr al-Habashi. I felt depressed and didn't know where to head or what I could rely on. Badr tried to lift my spirits. He would ask me about everything he saw, and I would share my memories. We visited the house where Fatima bint al-Muthanna had lived, and I found that it had been incorporated into the adjoining house to enlarge it. I sat down on its stoop, thinking that some trace of her pure spirit might help me collect my shattered fragments and restore confidence and tranquility to my heart. A cold breeze whipped up, my vision went dark, and I wept copiously.

Badr didn't know what to do, so he began to weep with me. I found myself stretched out on the stoop, curled up like a baby, as my sobs echoed off the walls and became a wail. I pulled my turban over my face and closed my eyes, as if wishing to flee from this world. Al-Habashi placed my head on his thigh and covered me with his cloak. Then, feeling drowsy, I fell asleep. In a dream I beheld the divine throne before me, floating on a flame. While I was gazing at the throne, I saw a bird beautiful in both appearance and form. I had never seen a bird like it anywhere on earth. Its tail was longer than its body, and it was such a pure blue, it resembled a flying sapphire. My eyes followed him as he flew around the throne. Then he landed near me. When I approached, he told me: "Return to Marrakech. There you will find a man who will travel with you to Mecca." [27]

I woke and discovered I hadn't moved. I remained stretched out there, hoping to fall asleep again and complete my vision, but discovered I couldn't. I finally sat up and found that Badr had also been dozing. So I rose, and he did too. Then I sat back down, not knowing why I had stood up.

"Have you recovered, Master?"

"I think I have, Badr."

"Should we return to the hostel?"

"No, let's go to the market."

"The sunset prayer will be called soon; people will leave, and the markets will close."

"But the poor remain."

We hurried to the market. On the way, I brought out the purse that contained the money I had received for the house. I divided the money evenly and gave half to Badr. "This is my sisters' share from the house sale," I told him. "You hold on to it."

Badr fastened the pouch with its strap and then tied it a second time with a cord that hung from his pocket. He continued to grasp the purse in his hand, holding it near his chest. Once we reached the market, I took out my purse and gave every poor person I encountered a dinar till I emptied it. When we quit the market, we left behind poor people so happy that the world could scarcely contain them. Badr said nothing as we walked back to the hostel, but a smile as bright as the morning shone on his face.

"We'll leave tomorrow, Badr," I said.

"For where?"

"To Marrakech. I'm eager to see someone."

"Who?"

"A man's waiting for me there . . . but I don't know who."

38 **KERAK** 1309 CE/ 708 AH

The storm finally abated after I thought it wouldn't until after it had deposed kings and snatched off some heads. I can now sequester myself for a time in the castle's library after two days when I slept for only brief periods. Ever since I arrived here from Hama, I have been putting out one fire after another: one in the heart of al-Malik al-Nasir Muhammad, who has lived in this castle since he allowed himself to be deposed from the Sultanate of Egypt and retired into exile alone. Another fire in al-Zahir Baybars al-Jashnakir's letter, in which he ordered al-Malik al-Nasir to send him all the wealth of Kerak, leaving nothing for himself. A fire in the cursed mind of Baybars' messenger, Mughaltay, who treated the King contemptuously and began issuing orders to people in Kerak as if he had forgotten who he was. And finally, the fire in my heart, which was appalled to see al-Malik al-Nasir in this abased state, ordered around by men who were once his father's slaves!

They brought me honey, bread, and fruit for breakfast, and I ate alone in the small library, which no one seemed to have entered for years except the servants. I started to eat while I strolled past bookshelves where the books had been piled without being arranged in any order or system. I selected a book that caught my eye and placed it near me. I began to turn its pages while nibbling on a pear. My mind cleared gradually as I read, ate, and breathed in the gentle breeze wafting from the window. Once I finished eating, I summoned the servant, who collected the leftovers and disappeared. I stood contemplating the fields around the castle from the window and immediately recalled seeing sacks of barley piled in some areas. I had decided to discuss their premature harvest with the steward but hadn't had time. I called the servant back and asked him to summon the steward to the library.

He eventually appeared and asked permission to enter, "As you command, Abu al-Fida'."

"See here: why have you harvested the barley, now, before the grain has ripened, while the stalks are still firm?"

He spread his hands and shrugged his shoulders to show that he had no answer. I was furious that he wouldn't respond to my question. So I went to him, placed a hand on his shoulder, looked him straight in the eye, and said, "You are the king's steward and responsible for his estate and its crops. You know that harvesting barley prematurely harms the grain. Does the king know about this?"

The steward's blue eyes stared right back at me. Apparently not upset by my veiled threat, he replied, "Emir Mughaltay told us to do this."

"Mughaltay? When did he order that?"

"The day he arrived. He said he would take half the crop back to Cairo."

"Did you tell the king that?"

"Yes, we told him, and he didn't rescind the order."

That made me pity this poor king! He was a sultan with no sultanate and now a king without a kingdom. Even the barley harvest was beyond his control. I dismissed the steward and sat thinking about what he had said. Mughaltay wouldn't have acted so boorishly without first asking permission from Baybars, who obviously intended some mischief. I had reservations about the letters we had stayed up late writing yesterday and wondered whether they would save this king from the dangers that beset him on all sides. I thought I should revise the letters before I sent them off that afternoon. Once they were beyond the walls of this castle, there would be no opportunity to reconsider.

This idea of revising the letters had scarcely started to ferment in my mind before the library's doors opened suddenly, and the king entered, trailed by a servant who carried the box of letters. Startled, I rose to greet him, and gestured for him to have a seat. A glance at his face told me he hadn't slept at all the previous night. He had aged so much in a few days that no one who saw him would think he was only twenty-four. He had lost so much hair at the front of his head that only a few strands disguised his baldness. He sat down beside me, and the servant placed the box before us. Then he quickly brought the writing table and positioned it in front of us.

The king said, "I ordered them to release Mughaltay from confinement and plan to expel him from the castle today. He must take a letter with him to al-Zahir Baybars, and we need to revise it one last time."

"Whatever you say, Your Majesty."

I opened the box and took out the letter I had written yesterday on the red stationery reserved for the Sultanate. "Let me read it to you," I suggested to the king, "then you can tell me what I should change."

The king intertwined his fingers and rested his head on his hands. He placed his elbows on his knees and nodded his agreement.

So I read:

Praise to God in a manner that ameliorates temperament and obliterates distress. Our prayers and greetings for the Prophet who instituted compassion and ordered us to be merciful. To continue: The Mamluk al-Nasir Muhammad ibn Qala'un kisses the hand of His Excellency al-Malik al-Muzaffar and informs you of the arrival of your noble missive, which this Mamluk holds in high esteem. He placed the missive on his head and eyes, kissed the earth as if Your Excellency were present and this Mamluk was before him.

To continue: God Almighty and Exalted, through His previous care and the light of His guidance has shown this Mamluk the generosity of your merit and the grandeur of your significance. He therefore entrusted to you the Islamic Mamluk Sultanate, on land and on sea, in Syria and in Egypt, near and far, in valleys and highlands. Then this Mamluk retired to Kerak, intending to live here with no desire for anything save peace. It was our Master, the Sultan al-Zahir Baybars who raised me and who was the only father I have ever known. All I have comes from him and flows from him. His letter ordering me to send Kerak's wealth to him has reached me. As he knows, the proceeds I receive from Kerak serve to defray expenses and costs here. I have obeyed the noble missive and sent half the sum I have in hand out of obedience to our Master the Sultan's command. As regards the horses, some have died. I ride the only remaining steeds. With reference to the Mamluks, there are only those who have elected to stay with me, single men without a family or dependents. How would it be proper for me to expel them? May God Almighty guard our Master, whose charity is all I have left, and safeguard his precious soul, even when he turns on those who love him and discards those who serve him.

As I read this letter, which I had written, pain racked my heart for the sad king, who only two years earlier had been sultan while al-Zahir Baybars served as his deputy. Then their roles were reversed, and al-Zahir Baybars became Sultan and al-Nasir the "king" of Kerak. This king, however, seemed composed and content with the letter. He remained silent for a time, reflecting.

Then he asked, "What do you think, Abu al-Fida'?"

"I stand by my advice to you yesterday, Your Majesty. We should send him half the amount he requested while you keep the other half. Send this response immediately with Mughaltay and wait till he has left. Then send letters to the emirs of Syria."

"What if Baybars learns I am corresponding with them?"

"He won't learn that if we are circumspect and cautious."

"What if they tell him, themselves?"

"I think they won't. All the deputies and emirs of Syria were once your father's Mamluks and still feel great loyalty to him."

He looked up at me and stared me in the eye. Then he replied, "In that case, you will carry my letters to them. You're the only person I trust."

I wasn't surprised by his request. I had been almost certain he would choose me as his messenger to them because I know more than anyone else about Syria and its Mamluk emirs and would be the person best able to convince them to support al-Nasir, if al-Zahir Baybars turned against him and tried to harm him. I replied calmly and confidently, "I hear and obey, Master."

"After Mughaltay leaves, wait a day to make sure he is already far from Kerak. Then leave secretly for Damascus."

"I hear and obey, Your Majesty."

The king rose and prepared to leave but continued speaking: "Tell the steward to provide you a hunting horse so you will arrive as quickly as possible." Then he turned and began to leave.

I called to him before he left, "Your Majesty the King. . . ."

He looked back at me inquisitively, without speaking, and I pointed to the book that had been lying before me when he entered. I said, "If you don't need this book, I would like to take it with me to Hama, and if. . . ."

He interrupted me nervously and impatiently. Leaving the library, he waved his hand and said, "Is this the time, Abu al-Fida'? Take it. . . . Take anything you want."

TOME FIVE

"Possibility is a liminal state between existence and nonexistence."

——IBN ARABI

39

The Caliph has disappeared!

One morning in Salé, the Caliph's servant entered his bed chamber and found the room empty. He summoned his fellow servants and asked them where the Caliph was. None of them knew. They searched the palace's porticoes, the courtesans' rooms, the Caliph's oratory, and his library but found no trace of him. Guards spread out through the palace's gardens and courtyards, checking to see whether he had secluded himself somewhere—but to no avail. They headed to the coast to check whether he was strolling on the shore. They found nothing there save crows and seagulls. They dispatched messengers to the homes of the Caliph's ministers and boon companions, thinking that he might be visiting one of them, but no one had seen him. They sent a team of guards to the markets, assuming that he might be checking on them, as he was wont to do, but the markets were the same as ever, and they found no trace of the Caliph. Agents and soldiers spread throughout the city, the port, residential districts, and outlying areas, but returned empty-handed. The Caliph seemed to have evaporated. Finally, they sent a messenger urgently to Marrakech to take the news to the Caliph's son, Muhammad, who was the heir apparent.

This young man was stunned when they told him his father was missing and that no one knew where he was. Muhammad hastened to Salé at breakneck speed with a cavalry detachment. As soon as he arrived, he ordered a search of all houses within the city's walls and of the tents beyond them, without exception. Soldiers stormed every house, tent, room, and shack in the city of Salé and its environs without finding the Caliph. Every servant in the palace was summoned before the heir apparent for interrogation. Some wept anxiously, and all denied having any idea where he was. Then the heir apparent called a meeting of government ministers, the Caliph's associates, the eunuchs, and the courtiers. He threatened that if anyone had spirited the Caliph away, that person would be treated mercilessly. He also ordered them not to disclose the Caliph's disappearance to anyone outside the palace, on pain of beheading. In a display of anger, to demonstrate the force and seriousness of his threat, he drew his sword. A luckless palace slave who was bringing him water fell then, soaked with his own blood.

The heir apparent next convened an emergency meeting of his father's advisers and ministers. Every door was shut, and even the palace's servants were excluded. The crown prince paced around his father's assembly chamber like a wounded wolf that could not calm down or stay put. Glaring at his father's empty chair, he struck his hands together, as if he found the situation unbelievable and incredible. Had the Caliph been in Andalusia, he might have been abducted by the Castilians. If he had been in Tunis, perhaps the Banu Ghaniya would have taken him. But he had disappeared in Morocco, the center of his kingdom, from the palace where he was the safest! How could he disappear in Salé, which was isolated and surrounded on land by troops and in the ocean by the fleet?

He conferred with the assembled men, and they made some urgent decisions. They would send army units along the trade routes to check every caravan traveling in Almohad lands. A camel corps would be formed to head into the desert and search all the nomads' grazing lands and tents. These units were to storm each oasis, even if only two people lived there, and search it meticulously. Undercover agents were to patrol mosques and oratories, large and small, where the Caliph might have secluded himself for a spiritual retreat and met with some misfortune. Grave diggers, ship captains, caravan organizers, and the imams of mosques were to be interrogated to see whether any of them seemed suspect and deserved more careful scrutiny.

While all this was happening, people spread rumors, because they were startled by all these sudden deployments, intrusive searches, and the increased presence of troops on the streets and in the squares and residential districts. These initiatives eventually reached Marrakech. My house was searched during the early days, like all the other residences. Soldiers entered my bedroom and looked in every nook and cranny, leaving nothing where it belonged. They climbed onto the flat roof and rummaged around the courtyard and garden. They went from my house to my neighbor's. Throughout the neighborhood we heard pots and pans clanging together, children screaming, and old men reciting repeatedly that all power and might are God's alone. The soldiers could have cared less; they were under orders to enter every house in Marrakech before sunset.

A week passed without any trace of the Caliph being found. The clueless heir apparent returned from Salé to Marrakech. By this time his anger had abated and been supplanted by grief and fear. Finally a minister dared suggest that he might announce this disappearance in the hopes that a witness would come forward with some information or explanation, but the heir apparent objected vehemently and slapped the minister who had insisted on this—so hard that he fell to the floor. He shouted at this minister: "No one should say I lost my father!"

The ministers thought twice about offering him any more advice and abandoned the young man to his panic and anxiety. This matter weighed heavily on him, and the more he brooded, the more he realized that he would be the prime suspect in his father's disappearance, since people might suspect he had been too eager to ascend the throne. He stewed and reflected. Finally he decided to keep the matter secret and to direct the state's affairs as if his father had deputized him to do that while remaining in Salé. He ordered a contingent of horses and men sent into the desert to make it appear that the Caliph had set out on a hunting expedition. This situation dragged on for some time.

Finally the minister closest to the prince, accompanied by the chief justice, asked permission to speak with him. After greeting him, the chief justice remarked, "Prince, people will eventually realize the Caliph is missing—may God return him safe and sound! We are afraid that some will seize the opportunity afforded by his absence to incite people against the throne. . . ."

The vizier completed the chief justice's thought: "You yourself have witnessed how ambitious men scheme and attempt to seize power and become caliph. What will happen when people realize he is missing?"

With obvious nervousness, the heir apparent shouted: "What do you two want me to say if they ask about the Caliph?"

The vizier cleared his throat with obvious discomfort. Gaining control of himself, he offered advice that he had certainly mulled over thoroughly: "We can say he died in bed of a fever and left instructions that there should be no funeral and that no sepulcher should be built over his grave."

"What if they say his son killed him to ascend the throne?"

"What would prevent suspicious people from thinking that, even if the Caliph actually had died of natural causes?"

The heir apparent listened intently, and the minister's response seemed to have calmed his fears. Gazing thoughtfully into empty space, he asked in a low voice, "What if he is alive and actually appears?"

"In that case, he'll have to decide what to do. He will understand that we acted to safeguard the lives of Muslims and the welfare of the state."

They eventually convinced him. A messenger was sent on behalf of the Caliph to summon the Almohad princes, the state's leading citizens, judges, religious scholars, government ministers, and governors. Representatives were sent to the shaykhs of the Masmuda, Sanhaja, and Zanata tribes and to influential tribesmen. All these notables assembled in Marrakech a few days later, but the crown prince kept them waiting till Friday, when he appeared before them, surrounded by bodyguards armed with swords. He ascended the pulpit and delivered a brief sermon about the need to speak with a single voice and the ummah's unity. Next he descended from the pulpit to lead the prayer. When he ascended the pulpit again, he announced that Caliph Ya'qub ibn Yusuf had died in the city of Salé after a prolonged illness of many weeks. He announced that the Caliph had left instructions that—as a sign of humility and piety—he should be buried in an unmarked grave with other Muslims.

The moment he uttered the final word of his brief eulogy, a carefully choreographed routine unfolded. His chamberlain, who had been standing behind him, proclaimed in a loud, sonorous voice, which echoed through the mosque's porticos, where the crowds of people stood dumbstruck: "We pledge allegiance to the Commander of the Believers and Caliph of the Muslims, Muhammad ibn Ya'qub, may God grant him a long reign!"

The guards immediately formed two lines in front of the new Caliph to guide the congregation as they stepped forward to pledge their allegiance to the Caliph. Government ministers sitting in the front row hurried to be the first to pledge their allegiance, to forestall any other claimant to the title from stepping forward after he recovered from his initial shock. Members of the congregation jumped up and rushed to find places in the queue that grew so long it snaked out of the mosque. The new Caliph gave his uncles a warning look, and they rose, one after the other, to be among the first to pledge allegiance to him. I stood up, too, along with them, and pledged my allegiance.

"Trust anyone who befriends you for your essence."

—**IBN ARABI**

40

The specter of this stranger intimately linked to my destiny was never far from my mind. I pictured him in every possible manner: a student in one of my classes, a beggar in the mosque, a soldier on deployment, a merchant in the market, a Jew in a blue cloak, or a *wali* on a distant mountain. I began praying that God would hasten our reunion. As soon as we reached Marrakech, I sent for my two sisters and gave each one her share of the money from the sale of our father's house. They were delighted. Once they left the house, Maryam looked at me as if she expected me to give her an amount. When I did not satisfy her, she started talking about the furniture and carpets our house needed, thinking such talk might force me to speak.

I told her, "Maryam, we won't stay much longer in Marrakech."

"Where are we going?"

"East."

"When?"

"As soon as God grants us permission."

I realized that anticipation and waiting might upset me; so I chose to stay busy. I decided to start teaching again and to write a book. That way I would fill my days and nights till God decreed my next move. I went to the mosque, chose a corner for myself, placed my chair there, and asked Badr the Ethiopian to announce my class in the mosque. The next morning I found dozens of students waiting for me, but my chair wasn't where I had placed it the previous day. Badr told me that a man had removed it after the dawn prayer and that when the beadle had objected, the man had said he was from the Caliph's palace. This report gave me pause, but I sat on the ground. Then the students formed a circle around me, and I began class.

After the noon prayer, the beadle came to tell me that anyone who proposed to teach in the mosque had to request prior approval from the caliphal palace. I tried to extract more information from him, but he shook his head and didn't reply. He looked up at me plaintively to beg me not to press him on a matter like this. So I sent Badr to the Caliph's palace to ask the men there whether the beadle's account was accurate. I walked home as two contradictory emotions competed in my breast. One was annoyance about this new Caliph's interference in the mosque's affairs, and the other was relief that I had discovered yet another reason to travel, if that became necessary. Badr returned that evening with a wan face and lusterless eyes.

Before he could say anything, I commented: "So the report was accurate."

"There is more, Master."

"What?"

"You and four other instructors have been banned by the Caliph from teaching in any mosque in Marrakech."

"Why?"

"No one would say more than this."

When I woke the next day, I did not know what to do. I sent Badr to intercept my students and tell them that instruction was suspended. I sat in our courtyard, gazing at the garden, with a lot on my mind but unable to focus on anything. When Maryam asked if I would be going out, I told her I would not. Then she sat down beside me and began to stroke my back to comfort me.

"Darling," she said, "since you returned from Andalusia, you've seemed distracted and unlike your normal self. Did you see something there that upset you?"

"No, I saw something in Murcia that delighted me, Maryam."

"What was it?"

"A vision. A *ru'ya*."

"What did you see?"

"A bird that flew from God's throne ordered me to go to Mecca in the company of a man from Marrakech."

"Who is he?"

"I don't know. I am waiting for him to find me, God willing."

Maryam remained silent, reflecting on something for a time, while I gazed at the sky. Then she suddenly turned her head and looked me straight in the eye. Smiling reassuringly, she volunteered, "I know who he is, Darling."

I swiveled around. Her words had struck me like a thunderbolt. I gazed at her with an expression of both entreaty and censure and asked, "Who is he?"

"A man named al-Hassar."

"Al-Hassar? Do you mean Abu Bakr al-Hassar, the math teacher?"

"Yes."

"How do you know?"

"Some years ago, when we arrived in Marrakech, a boy knocked on the door when you were at the mosque. He asked, 'Auntie, are you all from Andalusia?' I replied, 'Yes.' Then he asked, 'Have you dreamt you would make the pilgrimage to God's holy house?' I said, 'No.' He said, 'Thank you, Auntie.' But I called out to him, 'Why do you ask?' He replied, 'Abu Bakr al-Hassar hired me and other boys to visit all the houses of Andalusians arriving in Marrakech and ask them this question.'"

I hastily donned my clothes and set out to find al-Hassar's house, even though I had never met him. I started to question passersby, one by one, until finally someone told me where he lived. Then I paused anxiously by his door, not knowing what to do. I had no unveiling, no *kashf*, to guide me and hadn't a clue what the fates might have concealed behind this door for me. I stepped away from the door, turned toward Mecca, prostrated myself and asked Almighty God that I would find something behind this door to delight my eye and comfort my soul, which had felt tormented for years. Then I knocked on the door. A woman responded without opening the door and said al-Hassar had gone out without telling her when he would return. I took several steps away from the house and sat down, deciding to wait for him. After performing the afternoon prayer near his doorway with some passersby, I sat back down.

The sun was setting when al-Hassar appeared at the end of the lane. He was tall, his beard was tapered, and his eyes were piercing. He noticed me sitting near the door of his house and stopped. I rose. We exchanged looks but no words of greeting. He approached me and placed his hands on my shoulders as he scrutinized my face. His expression became hopeful, and his lips quivered. A tear trickled from my eye, and tears flowed from his. He embraced me and started sobbing.

He said, "O my Andalusian! Oh! Four years. . . . I've been waiting for you for four years!"

"No form of knowledge that isn't multifaceted is reliable."

—IBN ARABI

41

I sold Sallum and Addad in the market. I divided the proceeds from Sallum's sale between my sisters, and with the money I received from selling Addad, bought two camels, supplies, and provisions for the journey. Then I still had more than half left. We left Marrakech in a caravan heading to Bejaïa. I took with me Maryam, Zaynab, and Badr. Al-Hassar set off alone on a chestnut stallion, and his supplies and provisions were loaded on a mule. He kept ahead of us all the time, so Maryam could leave her howdah when she wanted. Riding before us, he seemed to be surrounded by a halo only I could see. My delight at meeting him was superior to any other. Why not? He was an emissary of the divine throne. His own delight was multiplied by the four years he had waited for me since he'd experienced the same vision. When he narrated his vision to me, he described the same throne and the same sapphire bird with a long tail. Throughout the journey we continued to discuss everything, like lifelong friends who had merely been separated for a time—not strangers who had only just met. I don't know why, but each of us told the other his entire life story. I told him about Murcia, my father, Ibn Mardanish, Fatima bint al-Muthanna, Seville, al-Kumi, Ibn Rushd, and Frederick. He told me about his numerals, calculations, books, and writings and his understanding of geometry and algebra. When he discussed math, he used his hands to draw squares and circles in the air, showing me how they could meet and intersect. Then he explained fractions and how the half became a half, the third a third, and the fourth a fourth.

When we reached Bejaïa, we felt we had only traveled for a few hours—not a few days. We were all delighted; I because of al-Hassar's company, and Maryam because she would soon arrive where her family lived. I had heard her sing from homesickness for this city. She and Zaynab stayed with her relatives there, and we men took a room in a hostel near the sea until we could find a ship to take us to Alexandria. Within a few days, we heard that the Nile River in Egypt was low, and that the country was suffering from severe famine and inflated prices. The numerous Egyptians who arrived in Bejaïa by caravan painted an increasingly bleak picture of conditions there. We heard that people were eating cadavers, that free men sold themselves into slavery, and that every prayer service was followed by a funeral. Since al-Hassar was eager to visit Cairo before performing the pilgrimage, we decided to remain in Bejaïa till it was safe to travel there. Caravans continued to arrive frequently from Cairo, and each brought more news and information. I discovered two men from Seville among these Egyptians. They had curtailed their trip to flee from Egypt and its plague. They asked for our assistance, and we hosted them at the hostel till they found someone who would take them to Andalusia. They shared our food and sleeping quarters and told us about Andalusians in Cairo. I was astonished to hear them mention al-Hariri and al-Khayyat.

"They're my friends! I thought they were in Mecca!"

"They were heading there when the older brother took sick and ill health forced him to remain in Cairo."

"My God! Is his condition critical?"

"He seems to suffer from hemiplegia. He can eat and drink but cannot move."

"Your mercy, Lord!"

I now had my own reason for visiting Cairo, in addition to humoring al-Hassar.

Feeling ill at ease in Bejaïa, its beauty notwithstanding, I began to look for an opportunity to travel to Cairo as soon as possible. As news from Egypt, however, kept growing worse we didn't dare travel there. I spent most of my time with al-Hassar. I would read him passages from my books, and he would read to me from his. He taught me division on a slate tablet and about fractions, where the number for the part was written over the whole. If he wanted to write two-sixths in numerals, he wrote the number two, drew a line beneath it, and then wrote the number six beneath the line. He taught me how to add a fourth with a third and a sixth with a fifth, and how to subtract one from the other.

Once I had mastered this, he challenged me: "Now pay me my fee."

"What fee?"

"The fee for teaching you math and fractions."

"What payment do you desire?"

"Some of your knowledge. Abridge it for me. We mathematicians like to be concise."

I reflected briefly about what I could say. From our conversations I had discovered he had little interest in Sufi sciences or philosophy. When I had discussed such topics with him, he had listened only to humor me and be polite but hadn't asked any follow-up questions or requested a longer briefing.

After clearing my throat, I said, "Travelling Companion, you should know that there are three immaterial faculties in nature: revelation, intellect, and the heart."

He nodded his head and seemed interested. He listened carefully as I continued, trying to be as concise as I could: "A man primarily inclined toward revelation becomes an exoteric literalist and a Zahiri. If his bent is toward the intellect, he becomes a philosopher. If he favors only the heart, he becomes a Sufi."

"Can't he favor all three?"

"If he wants all of them, he must build bridges between them."

"How can he?"

"The bridge required between revelation and the intellect is exegesis, *tafsir*. Between revelation and the heart, the required bridge is commentary, *ta'wil*."

"How about between the intellect and the heart?"

"Love is the bridge between them."

I detected his interest from his expression. Then he looked down thoughtfully. Next he brought out his slate, which he had purchased from some Indian merchants, and sprinkled it with black. First he wrote something on the slate with white chalk but erased that. Then he drew three circles to represent revelation, intellect, and the heart and connected the three with the bridges I had mentioned. He gazed at them thoughtfully. Finally he looked toward me with a broad smile accented by his tapered beard, which made his face look like a handsome stallion's.

"You've paid me far more than the fee I requested."

"You're welcome to all you want; then return the balance to me with your useful knowledge."

This is how I learned arithmetic and geometry; he quizzed me repeatedly till I had mastered mathematics. By the time we left Bejaïa, I had learned most of this. If I had trouble sleeping, I would write fourths and thirds on the slate and recall how al-Hassar added and subtracted them so I wouldn't forget. Once we finished math, he began to teach me about medicinal herbs. We would hike to Mount Amsiyun[28] to the north of Bejaïa and look for plants he knew. From some, he prepared an infusion he asked me to administer to Zaynab, who was suffering from an intermittent fever, which would lift for a week and return the next.

Since we were staying in Bejaïa for months, we moved out of the hostel to a house with a single large room and a courtyard. Al-Hassar, Badr, and I slept there, and Maryam continued to live with her paternal uncle's daughters, who loved Zaynab a lot. They dressed her in adult clothes and taught her to dance and sing, caring for her like mothers. We decided to devote our time to writing. Badr got some paper for us from the market, and al-Hassar and I would sit opposite one another as each of us recorded his thoughts and knowledge. Whenever we finished a certain number of pages, Badr would fetch a tailor to sew them together as a book. After some months, God inspired al-Hassar to ask me to name his newly composed book, which I called *al-Bayan wa'l-Tadhkar fi Ilm Masa'il al-Ghubar* or *The Clarification and Reminder for the Science of Questions about Abstruse Subjects*. I was inspired to ask him to name my book, which he called *Insha' al-Dawa'ir wa-l-Jadawil* or *The Creation of Circles and Tables*. I didn't like his title for my book but wasn't about to second guess a name chosen by an emissary from the divine throne.

"Fear not attributable to the essential self can be discounted."

— **IBN ARABI**

42

Finally the reports reaching us from Egypt seemed less terrifying, and we began to look for an opportunity to travel there. Once I started to make my preparations, Maryam surprised me by saying she wanted to stay in Bejaïa. I had thought she wouldn't be able to bear separation from me. She offered many excuses: she wasn't strong enough to travel, she feared Zaynab would catch the plague in Egypt, she enjoyed life with her cousins and would join me once I settled somewhere. At first I was upset. Then, a few days later, I realized that her request made my life easier; I could travel unencumbered by worries about her and our child. So I was happy for her to stay.

We chose a fine-looking, well-built ship from Genoa and set sail in it. The weather was fine during the first hours, and the vessel sailed tranquilly east at a steady clip. Then the sea became so turbulent that I almost lost my mind. For three days the ship heaved and shook, and I thought each passing day would be my last. I saw an enormous wave the size of a mountain, and the ship's captain ordered the mainsail lowered to protect it and the smaller sails raised. Each time the sailors hoisted a sail, the ship swung in one direction and then the other. We passengers could no longer tell one direction from another and had no idea where the east, which we sought, was. The Genovese sailors began conversing in their language, and we could only grasp that they didn't agree with each other. We urged a Tunisian who spoke their language to tell us what they were saying.

After listening to them, he returned and said, "They plan to return to Bejaïa."

We urged him to go back and ask more questions after their discussion grew even more heated.

This time he reported: "We are closer to Alexandria now than to Bejaïa. We may sail through to Alexandria or stop in Tunis."

I grew so anxious that I urged him to eavesdrop on them a third time. Then he reported: "They are thinking of sailing north to Genoa; perhaps the sea will be calmer that way."

Each time this man returned, he brought worse news. I begged the fellows around me not to encourage him to listen to their discussion anymore. Instead, we should pray to God to carry us to dry land, to calm the waves, and to allow us to stand upright. But the sea did not calm down, neither by day nor at night. I didn't enjoy a single hour of sleep and couldn't keep solid food or liquids down. I couldn't think straight or even understand what was happening I was so hungry, nauseated, and sleep-deprived. I lay down in a corner between two boxes of equipment, hoping they would provide some shelter. Then one of them tipped over on me, almost amputating two of my fingers. I jumped up—so furious that I walked to the side of the ship and shouted at the sea: "Calm down, Watery Sea! A Sea of Knowledge sails over you!"

The vessel shook, and I almost fell. I staggered, my foot slipped, and I collapsed backwards onto the nape of my neck. I started shrieking in a voice weakened by exhaustion and fatigue. Some Genovese mariners took pity on me and fed me ginger to relieve my seasickness. Two of them helped me up and took me to the stern, where they brought me into their cabin and sat me on the floor so I could lean against a hay bale covered with a worn blanket. They were speaking Italian, which I didn't understand. They lit a fire in their little brazier and brewed an infusion for me with an herb I didn't recognize, although it resembled parsley, and had me drink that. I tried to lie down, but they stopped me. One of them gestured for me to sit and keep my neck vertical. I obeyed them as best I could and gradually felt better.

Badr finally entered that cabin after what had apparently been a long search. He was accompanied by the Tunisian who spoke Italian. The two of them took me back to our place on the ship now that I felt better. Someone placed a rag soaked in a fragrant liquid in my hand and told me to sniff it from time to time, and I did. Once I reached our place, I fell asleep for the first time since the ship had started to heave.

On the morning of the fifth day, the sun rose in a clear sky; the sea was calm, and the ship was stable. We began to hear clearly the creaking of the wood that the windstorm had broken. Sailors raised the mainsail again as they sang a vigorous sea chanty in Italian. The Muslims lifted their hands in thanks and praise to God and wiped off the salt that had dried on their faces. We finally reached Alexandria, after I had almost gone berserk and perished. I cursed the sea and swore I would never sail again unless I was forced to. I was true to my oath, and that voyage was my last experience with the sea.

The guide who spoke Italian came to say that the sailors were asking us to prepare to pay taxes on any cargo unloaded at the port. Al-Hassar laughed and, pointing to his head, explained: "All my cargo is here."

The guide turned to me skeptically, but I gestured to my heart and said, "And my cargo is here."

Thinking we were mocking him, the guide stalked back to the sailors. When the ship neared the harbor, men from the port began calling to the sailors. They gestured with their arms for us to stay on board and not try to land. Once we were docked, four agents from the port authority boarded our ship and spread through it. One man started counting the passengers. Another descended to the hold where the livestock were held. The third agent busily recorded all the merchandise, questioning sailors about each shipment's port of origin and contents. The fourth man supervised the others and kept a hand on his sword. He pointed to boxes their owner had stacked atop each other as he prepared to disembark and asked, "Whose are these?"

A Genovese merchant stepped forward and replied in pitiful Arabic: "Mine."

"What are you doing with them?"

"Commerce."

"Then you must pay zakat on them."

The Genovese merchant pointed to some boxes he had separated from the others and told the customs agent: "I will, but these are exempt personal items."

The agent nodded with apparent disinterest, and the merchant handed him a bag containing textiles and a purse of money. The agent searched it and handed it to an assistant. Al-Hassar turned to me and smiled knowingly, and I smiled too.

Once we had left the harbor, he laughed and commented, "It's amazing that the customs agent demanded the Muslim wealth tax, zakat, from someone who isn't Muslim!"

"It's also amazing that this Genovese knows the rule governing zakat!"

Once the customs agent and his men left the ship, the porters and their foreman boarded. The foreman started to bargain with the merchants about what it would cost to unload their cargo. They quickly reached an agreement, and the foreman started barking orders to his men, dividing the cargo among them. My ears began to detect instances of the Egyptian dialect in the words the foreman spoke and in his shouts to his men, who soon had unloaded, from the ship's hold, net bags filled with dried Tunisian pulse, jars full of tanning liquids, oils, and wine from Venice, as well as boxes filled with silk, ambergris, Andalusian carpets, pelts, wool, leather garments from Genoa, and bars of iron and tin from Gaul. After the slaves who had been working on the ship lined up, their hands were bound by a single rope, and they were led to the port. Once the ship was finally cleared, we were permitted to disembark, when each merchant had checked that his goods were safe and accounted for.

It felt sweet and refreshing to have dry land under my feet, and I sat on the ground, bowed my head, and looked up at the heavens, breathing deeply and regaining my equilibrium after having spent so many days standing, sleeping, or sitting on the deck of a ship that was heaving right and left. People laughed at me, but I ignored them.

Al-Hassar exclaimed: "Enough already! If God destines us to return to Morocco, we will travel by land."

We headed to a moneychanger, who sat behind a wide table that held weights, measures, and small, empty purses. Some people were lined up in front of him to exchange their currency. We placed our Almohad dinars and dirhems before him, and he began to weigh, sniff, taste, and tap them to hear their ring before exchanging them for their equivalent in local Adili dinars and dirhems. The exchange rate favored us, and we didn't attempt to negotiate. I put my new dinars in a purse as did al-Hassar. Then we saw boys who were distributing dates and fresh fruit to poor people at the port. So we asked one of them about hostels and caravansaries. Looking at my Maghribi clothing and appearance, the boy said, "If you're Maghribi, then go to the Maghribi House."

He gestured to indicate the direction. When we reached Dar al-Maghariba, we found many North Africans there. We entered a large room that held nine beds, which were lined up beside each other. Four were taken by other men who had strewn their clothes and gear on them, and five had only a clean bedspread on them.

We each chose a bed and placed our possessions on it. Then we washed, prayed, and slept. The next morning, we heard a boy outside the building shout: "Bread, you Maghribis! Bread!"

The steward of the house took a plaited palm-leaf basket out to him and said, "Seven."

The boy counted out fourteen loaves and tossed them into the basket. When the steward came back inside, he gave each of us two loaves.

I asked him, "Is this charity? I don't eat alms."

"It's bread for Maghribis."

"What's that?"

The steward shrugged his shoulders to indicate he didn't know. Then another traveler volunteered: "This matter goes back to the days of King Salah al-Din: two discs of bread for every adult Maghribi they find."

"Why North Africans in particular?"

The man laughed and walked away, muttering, "God endowed his heart with love for us. So eat your fill."

I returned and sat down beside al-Hassar, who had been listening to our conversation silently. He asked me, "Do you understand this?"

"I don't. But I'm eating charity."

Badr interjected: "Abu al-Ghana'im used to say that Salah al-Din liked having Maghribis in Egypt, because they're Sunnis and Sufis whom God used to cleanse Egypt of Shi'i Fatimid influence."

"Then this bread isn't *sadaqa* for travelers but hospitality for a guest?"

Al-Hassar replied, "Yes, that's right."

I sank my teeth into a loaf.

"You'll achieve nothing in religion unless you respect all creatures."

—**IBN ARABI**

43

We found a caravan that would depart for Cairo in two days. Waking up early, al-Hassar suggested we tour Alexandria before we left. We set out from the Maghribi House before sunrise and began walking along Alexandria's broad streets, which astonished al-Hassar. His comments contained mathematical references: "In a single street in Alexandria we could build a Fez-style house bordered on either side by an alley in which one cow could pass another without touching."

He stopped in the middle of a street and started to measure its width. He spread his arms wide and turned on his heel once and then a second time till he reached the other side. He recorded that distance on his slate, and we continued walking on level land, unlike Fez, where streets climb and fall. For this reason, I saw many donkey carts traversing the streets with ease. We reached the harbor where our ship anchored. Regarding it for the first time with a clear mind, I saw it was divided into two parts. The western half was for ships transporting passengers and commerce and the eastern for warships of the Ayyubid fleet. Soldiers were quartered in parallel lines of huts beside the warships, with each crew living nearest its own warship. Thus, if a herald raised an alarm, the fleet could set sail as quickly as possible. Beyond the soldiers' huts was a large area used as a shipyard, where vessels were built and repaired. Metal workers, sailmakers, and carpenters labored there. Beyond this shipyard was a large structure that was built— like most of the houses in this city—on huge columns sunk into the ground. This was the fleet's headquarters.

The sun rose, and its light spread everywhere. Then shops began to open, and the streets swarmed with pedestrians. We left the port behind us and headed to the center of the city. When we passed the Market for Franks, who were allowed to trade in Alexandria, we found it contained a hostel for each Frankish city. Its citizens could stay there and be waited on by people who spoke their language and cooked their cuisine. There was a Venetian hostel, a Tuscan hostel, a Danish hostel, a Saxon hostel, a Russian hostel, a Genovese hostel, and a Norman hostel.

Al-Hassar asked, "Don't you admire this?"

"What's to admire?"

"Al-Adil, the King, has dedicated an entire souk to Franks and uses the taxes he collects from them to equip armies to fight against them."

He had scarcely finished this comment when he sank to the ground. Alarmed, I leaned over him, having no idea what had hit his head and felled him. His temple was bleeding.

An adolescent boy raced up and, like me, bent over al-Hassar. He was saying, "Sorry! Sorry! Forgive me. . . . I didn't mean to."

Al-Hassar sat up and wiped the blood away with his hand as he praised God. Once I reassured myself that he was conscious, I looked at what had hit him. It was a curved piece of wood but didn't resemble anything I had ever seen before.

I picked it up, waved in the boy's face as I reprimanded him fiercely: "Boy, what is this?"

The lad, who looked afraid I would hit him with his curved stick, replied fearfully, pressing his hands to his sides, "This is a Pharaoh's Staff."

"Pharaoh's Staff?"

"Yes, a Pharaoh's Staff, which returns to the person who throws it. Don't you know about it?"

Al-Hassar was squatting on the ground, holding his temple. He looked up at us with interest and asked in a weak voice, "How can it return to the person who threw it?"

The boy took the stick from my hand and threw it. It began to circle far off into the sky and became so small we could scarcely see it. Then it returned to us, gradually growing larger, till it was over our heads. The boy leapt into the air and caught it. Then he handed it to me to try. Al-Hassar looked at me and smiled. I threw it the way the boy had. It flew into the air but didn't return to me. Instead it landed where I had thrown it. He raced to pick it up and returned this time to hand it to al-Hassar, who sat admiring it and turning it over in his hands. Then he spread his fingers at the bend in the stick as if to measure it.

Nodding his head appreciatively, he asked the boy, "How much do you want for this?"

"Uncle, you can buy five for a dirhem in the market."

"Really? How much does one cost then?"

"I told you: five for a dirhem."

"Yes, son. If they are five for a dirhem, one should cost a fifth of a dirhem. Do you know why?"

The boy shook his head apathetically and held out his hand to retrieve the stick, but al-Hassar handed him a dirhem, and said, "Let me have this one and buy yourself five others to ding the heads of Moroccans."

The teenager smiled and bowed his head in embarrassment. Al-Hassar stood up with difficulty, shaking his head with pain and smiling. As we walked off together he held the stick in his hand until we reached the Moroccan House. I ordered Badr al-Habashi to bring al-Hassar a clean thawb from his kit. Then I took his blood-stained one and gave it to the hostel servant to wash. The wound was small and the blood had dried around it so that it was almost healed by the time we reached our hostel. Al-Hassar took a short nap. Following the afternoon prayer, he rose and practiced throwing the stick till the sun set. He wrote an account of it and included its dimensions. Then, with great skill, he drew a picture of it on a wide piece of paper.

"Don't trust an affliction that isn't also a trial."

—IBN ARABI

44

When we finally departed, I felt an indescribable desire to meet al-Khayyat and al-Hariri. The road between these two cities was so frequently traversed by caravans that we could travel by night without any fear. People in the villages between these two cities cater to the caravans—selling them food and bringing them water. Some travelers didn't even bother to pack food but bought it en route. We reached Damanhur after a short trip and stretched our legs there for a time. We stocked up on fruit, water, and firewood. Then we continued traveling at a good pace, reaching Cairo by the end of the third day. We went to a hostel that Badr chose for us, had supper there, and slept. We headed out the following morning to search for the house of al-Khayyat and al-Hariri. In the hostel, Badr had made enquiries about it and learned which district it was in. Once we got there, residents directed us to their home, which wasn't actually a house but a small room attached to a Sufi khanqah. The doorway was so low that al-Hassar and I had to bow our heads when we entered. We greeted al-Hariri, and he gave me a long embrace. Then he hugged al-Hassar and al-Habashi, whom he didn't know—he was that delighted to see me. Al-Khayyat didn't embrace me nor I him. He was sleeping in a corner of the room, covered by many blankets, and a damp rag was draped across his brow.

"Ahmad, what's wrong with him?"

"He'll wake up, soon. He's been like this since the plague."

"Is it a fever?"

"It started that way. Then he became paralyzed; he can't sit or stand up."

When I approached him, my heart was broken—seeing him in such a shape. I kissed his forehead, but he wasn't conscious of it. I took his palm, placed it on mine, and squatted beside him. Then al-Hassar followed suit. Al-Hariri sat down near us, and we started to chat. After we had talked for an hour, al-Hariri asked me for news of Andalusia. I told him about the major flood, the devastation I had witnessed, and the drowning victims. He teared up and began to cry. My hand had scarcely touched his shoulder to pat him on the back when he broke down, sobbing bitterly.

"Don't take it so hard, Ahmad. Have pity on yourself."

"The world has closed in on me, Muhyi."

"Why?"

"Don't you see the state my brother and I are in? We're no longer in Seville but haven't reached Mecca. Since we arrived in Cairo, my brother has become an invalid, as you see. We have no one here in this land. My brother cannot travel. So I can't return with him to Andalusia and can't go to Mecca either."

Al-Khayyat woke up to the sound of al-Hariri sobbing. An incomprehensible mumble emerged from his mouth. Al-Hariri rose and sat his brother up. He said loudly, as if al-Khayyat were deaf, "This is Muhyi al-Din ibn Arabi and his companions."

Once his brother raised him up, al-Khayyat looked at us with blank eyes, as if he hadn't understood. Al-Hariri repeated what he had said. Then al-Khayyat spoke with a split face, since the left side didn't move, and his lip pulled back. The words emerged indistinctly from his mouth: "Welcome, welcome. . . welcome, welcome."

I pressed his palm to my chest and kissed his cheek and shoulder as he continued repeating: "Welcome, welcome . . . welcome, welcome."

Next he bowed his head in silence as if to collect his thoughts. Finally he asked me, "When . . . did you arrive. . .?

"Yesterday, Brother."

He said something I didn't understand. "What are you saying?" Al-Hariri asked him.

He repeated what he had said in an exhausted voice. Al-Hariri understood and explained: "He's asking you, 'How is Zaynab?'"

"Great! We left her with her mother in Bejaïa."

It seemed to me that his lips attempted to form a smile but failed. He turned toward al-Hassar, whom he hadn't set eyes on before. I quickly introduced him:

"This is my brother and companion Muhammad al-Hassar. He is a scholar and a generous person from Morocco. I had a vision in which I saw God order me to accompany him to Mecca."

Al-Khayyat raised his head with difficulty to study al-Hassar's face. Then he turned back, bowed his head, and repeated: "May God do as He wills. . . . May God do as He wills!"

We fell silent for a moment. Then al-Hariri began talking about their district and the Sufis who secluded themselves in the khanqah next door, while I looked back and forth between him and al-Khayyat, whose distracted glances lacked focus and attention. He stared into the void as a line of saliva occasionally dribbled from his mouth without his noticing. Al-Hariri would wipe it away and continue speaking. In a loud voice, al-Khayyat suddenly interrupted him and said, "I'm sick, Muhyi. . . . sick."

"May God heal and cure you."

Suddenly he began to weep and repeat, "I'm sick . . . I'm sick."

I rose and hugged him, allowing his head to settle on my chest as he wept; liquids flowed from his nose and mouth onto my clothes, without his noticing. Al-Hassar was moved by the sight and started declaring that all power and might are God's, while al-Hariri bowed his head in silence. Perplexed, al-Habashi stared at us sadly.

"Why don't you leave me alone with him?" I suggested.

They rose and went to sit on the stoop outside. I lay down beside al-Khayyat and hugged him, letting his head lie on my chest. I placed my hand on his forehead, pressed gently on his temples, and began to recite: "Ya Sin, by the wise Qur'an . . . ."[29]

"When the heart is bereaved of its spoils, only sorrow remains."

—IBN ARABI

45

Once I had seen my childhood friend al-Khayyat in this condition I couldn't sleep normally in Cairo. He was quite ill and paralyzed, unable to move his jaws to speak properly or to feed himself. I could not enjoy sightseeing in this great city while he was bedridden. So I asked al-Hariri's permission to stay in their room with them, and he agreed. Then I sent Badr to the market to buy new pallets, pans, a carpet, and food. I also asked him to inquire everywhere for a skilled physician. He brought al-Khayyat two doctors who gave him medicines and herb infusions to drink and rubbed him with various ointments and powders. They massaged his back, rump, and thighs, and in a few days his fever lifted, but he still couldn't move. Neither doctor expected him to walk again. I recited the surah "Ya Sin" to him day and night. He remained calm while I recited, and his soul was tranquil. Occasionally he fell asleep while I was reciting. I fed him myself the best and most wholesome food. I gave him a lot of water to drink and flavored it with mint, lemon, and orange blossoms. I turned him over on his bed when he wanted me to and entertained him if he was bored. When his mind was clear, I read him some of the books I had with me and recounted the blessed remarks, charisms, and histories of righteous *wali*s. Then his soul would be comforted. After a few weeks, he could speak clearly when he wanted to, understood when we spoke to him, smiled frequently, laughed occasionally, and could move where he wanted by rolling over or crawling. Some of the illness had lifted; but he still could not stand or sit up.

While I was enjoying al-Khayyat's improved health, al-Hassar died. The invalid who had escaped with his life from the plague that had claimed half of Cairo's residents recovered, but the healthy man who had traveled with me, over land and sea, from Fez to Cairo, died in a single day. He felt feverish in the morning and vomited the contents of his belly in the evening. As the night fell, he surrendered his spirit to his Creator. I was shocked! My divinely selected traveling companion had died before I completed my trip to Mecca. *My Lord, what do You want to disclose to me? Are you warning me against postponing my visit to Your sacred house? Are You teaching me how the dead live and the living die? Are You reminding me that Messengers die but the Message lives on? Have mercy on me, Lord! Your mercy."*

I buried al-Hassar in a cemetery, assisted by Badr, al-Hariri, and the gravediggers. We returned, stunned, dragging our feet, as the impact of this misfortune showed clearly on our faces. Badr could scarcely speak he was so shocked that al-Hassar had died this rapidly. He was spooked by Cairo's plague and feared he might be struck down by what had taken al-Hassar. Conscious of the boulder grinding my heart, Badr kept patting me on the shoulder as he guided me from one alley to another, without my knowing where he was leading me. Finally we ended up at a mosque, where crowds of people were lined up by the door, waiting to enter. So we stood there with them, biding our time. Only then did I rouse myself from my sorrow and recover from my gloom. Turning to Badr, I asked, "Where are we going?"

"We're going to pay our respects to a deceased person even more precious than your deceased friend."

When we went inside, I found it was the mausoleum of Husayn ibn Ali. The structure housing the tomb was covered with silk brocade and surrounded by columns. One of these was made of gold, and another of silver. Hanging over this sepulcher were lamps that shone night and day. Their light was refracted back by the sepulcher as glints of different colors. People touched the side of the sepulcher and stroked the grave to rub themselves with its dirt and humble themselves. When we stood before it, I found myself reciting—without having prepared the words in advance or remembering having used them at a tomb before: "I greet you Scion of my Beloved Prophet and his Cousin and also greet your brother, mother, and father." Then a breeze swayed the hanging lamps, and a golden light illuminated and warmed my forehead.

As we left, I asked Badr, "Did you see how the lamps signaled to me? Did you?"

Without looking at me, Badr replied, "Yes, yes. I saw that. Let's hurry back before the sun sets. You haven't eaten since morning."

Al-Husayn had touched my brow with the light suspended over his tomb as if to console me in the best possible way for the loss of my friend. That night I slept with a calm soul and a comforted spirit. The next morning, I decided to visit the tombs of all the members of the family of my beloved Messenger of God.

So I woke Badr and told him, "Get up and guide me to the Qarafa Cemetery."

He quickly washed his face and performed his ablutions. Then he set off with me, pleased to see that my expression was serene and that I had left behind yesterday's tears. We reached the Southern Cemetery, al-Qarafa, which was full of small mosques and sepulchers of various sizes. People crowded its narrow passageways, and some blocked an alley by sitting there. Others were ill and had chosen to die among these sacred tombs. Then passersby would step or—occasionally—jump over them. Badr knew this area stone by stone since he had once lived in Cairo. He took my hand to guide me from sepulcher to sepulcher, and by the end of the day I had paid my respects to Maryam bint Ali, Muhammad ibn al-Husayn, Zayn al-Abidin, Zaynab bint Yahya, Umm Kulthum bint Muhammad, Abdallah al-Qasim, Isa ibn Abdallah, and Ja'far ibn Muhammad. Once we had visited all the tombs of members of the Prophet's immediate family, Badr took me to another corner of the Southern Cemetery to visit al-Shafi'i's mausoleum, which was far grander than all the others.

When we returned home, we found al-Khayyat sitting up, reciting his praise for God and God's all-encompassing power and might. On seeing me, he said, "Brother . . . may God reward you mightily."

"May God reward you as well."

"Listen to me."

I sat down beside him and listened attentively. He said, "God has deprived you of your traveling companion but not of your path. Continue your journey without delay. God has prevented me from reaching Mecca with this illness and stymied al-Hassar with death; but He has preserved your health and life. So make your way to your Lord thankfully and mindfully. Don't delay."

"Praise to God for His edict and decree."

"Don't delay, Brother. Do not delay."

I started to rise, but he grasped me and drew my head to his mouth. Placing his lips by my ear, he said, "I know you have been waiting for a pillar in North Africa and that this wait has slowed your progress toward Mecca."

Tears came to my eyes, as if he had touched an open wound. Resting my forehead on his shoulder, I wept. The torment of waiting for years for the second pillar seemed to have lodged in my collarbone before now suddenly erupting in tears. Al-Khayyat held me with his one good hand. With his lips still by my ear, he said, "Your *watad* has died."

I felt that my four corner supports had suddenly disintegrated. A violent storm of sobs erupted from deep in my chest. I buried my mouth on the side of al-Khayyat's chest till I felt his skinny ribs press against it. Then I screamed mightily. I wept in a way I had never wept before, and al-Khayyat clasped his paralyzed hand with his good hand because he was so pained by my sobs and to show his grief at my grief. Woe to any *wali* whose *watad* dies before they meet. Woe to the wretch who hasn't purified his heart enough to prevent his pillar from shunning him. As my weeping degenerated into gasps, al-Khayyat continued to hug me to keep me from separating from him before my voice had calmed. My tears continued to flow as if the world were shaking me.

He said, "Don't punish yourself, Abu Zaynab. Relax."

How could I? How could I live with only one pillar? Winds would buffet me and adversities would blow my heart away. *My Lord, what did I do to make my watad desert me?*

Al-Khayyat whispered, "Relax. When a pillar dies, another person inherits his role."

I ignored his consolation. I was stupefied. A long dark road opened before my eyes. Every project seemed difficult, every hope impossible, and every goal problematic. My weeping turned into a faint wail as I hugged al-Khayyat.

Then, looking up at him with tear-filled eyes, I asked plaintively, "When did my pillar live? Why didn't he find me during all those years?"

"The *watad* does not conceal his role unless he finds some fault with his companion or believes he isn't ready."

I buried my face between his flank and his pallet and swallowed an astonishing lump of regret and humiliation. Al-Khayyat kept whispering in my ear, but I didn't hear or grasp what he was saying till he remarked, "Abu Zaynab, I am his heir."

I shot to my feet as if a sharp blade had poked into my abdomen. I shouted at him: "What?"

Al-Khayyat smiled with his whole mouth and said, "I am your second pillar."

46 SAMARQAND 1401 CE/ 804 AH

We hadn't sold this much paper since we opened our mill. Had slaves not been so cheap, we wouldn't have been able to produce the amount of paper scribes in Samarqand's madrasas and mosques ordered from us. I bought the third slave a few days ago. He's an Arab from Hama. I selected him from seventy men lined up in the market. The slave dealer was willing to sell them for any price, because he expected a new batch in the next caravan. I took an interpreter with me and asked each man what his craft was, but they were all soldiers or farmers. The craftsmen had been preselected by the Mighty Khan's agents before these slaves were offered for sale in the market. I don't know how this fellow escaped from their hands. He must have lied about his craft or grown tired of the slave driver's cold rations, which were meted out only once a day.

I asked him, "Do you make paper? Are you from Hama?"

"Yes."

"You make the finest types of paper there."

He smiled modestly as his eyes lit up with a gleam of pride rarely seen in this age of servitude. I didn't ask him anything more; he was obviously the best man there. I paid the slave driver, who removed the chain from the slave's ankle and released him to my custody, saying, "I'll send his title to you at your mill tomorrow evening."

The man walked behind me to the plant, looking at the city's buildings and mausoleums. We passed by a market where I bought him a tunic and sandals. Then I took him to the bath house for slaves, so they could wash and clean him and extract the lice and other bugs from his hair while I waited. Clad in his new *thawb*, he emerged with a radiant expression after bathing. Then we walked the rest of the way to the paper mill. Its doorway was almost hidden by sacks of hemp, bales of flax, and carts full to overflowing with carded cotton that suppliers had delivered in response to an order I submitted before heading to the market. The other two slaves were taking turns moving the raw materials into the mill under the supervision of my brother Kulabadh. One spoke Uzbek as a second language in addition to Turkish. The other was Greek and didn't know Arabic or Uzbek. He was muscular, though, and had a powerful body. Kulabadh had taught the Greek how to pound the hemp, flax, and cotton after they were soaked in lime water to remove the filaments. He had the other slave pour the pulp into the molds, cut sheets with scissors, and stick them on the wall. If my hunch about this new slave from Hama proved correct, I would give him the most challenging task: glazing the paper with powder, starching and polishing it. I hoped that his hands were skillful and delicate enough to perform these operations.

Kulabadh jumped off the pile of flax he was standing on while supervising and came to me laughing. Looking at the slave's face, he exclaimed, "God's will be done! Congratulations!"

"Kulabadh, from now on, you'll have no excuse. All orders must be delivered on time."

Placing a hand on the slave's shoulder, Kulabadh replied, "Whatever you want, Brother."

Then my brother and the slave disappeared inside the mill, and I went to the office, where I kept our books and received visitors. I wasn't surprised to find that two new orders had been added to the bottom of the list, in Kulabadh's handwriting, since I left that morning:

Seventy reams of glossy paper for copies of scriptures. Purchaser: Superintendent of Samarqand's Sufi Madrasa

Thirty reams of writing paper. Purchaser: Central Post Office

I took my pen, dipped it in the ink, and crossed out the order from the Sufi school.

Then I wrote it again, at the top of the list. I called Kulabadh, who rushed in, flaunting the smile that had become a permanent fixture since I took him off salary and made him my partner with a tenth share of the mill.

"When did the superintendent of the Sufi madrasa come?"

"He didn't come in person; he sent an employee with the order."

"Start work on his order before any of the others."

"But, Brother, Taqtinash, we have other orders that are behind schedule."

"All orders can be late, but not the Sufi madrasa's."

Kulabadh smiled and asked cheerfully, if naughtily, "Including those from the palace of the Mighty Khan Timur?"

"All orders rate the same except for those from the Sufi madrasa, which belongs to his noble sisters."

Kulabadh laughed, even though I hadn't said anything funny, and left with a parting shot: "They will all arrive on time, Brother. I'll deliver them myself."

"You get them ready and pack them in the wagon. I'll deliver them."

I was delighted that my brother was so involved with the work, after his earlier descent into a life of slackness, drinking, and hashish abuse. Even now his thinking was somewhat addled, and I couldn't rely on him one hundred percent for anything except the production skills I had taught him myself. As for commerce, sales, and contact with customers, I did not think he would be good at any of those. I was content for him to relieve me of the need to supervise the workers and slaves and to track our paper production. I had done all that myself for nineteen years, ever since I started my career. My fingers had learned only too well the sting of lime and the heft of the mortar and drying tube. I could tell precisely the paper's condition from the smell of the cooking slurry. I knew how thick it would be from its consistency, how durable it would be from its taste, and I knew its future color from the color it was when wet. Now I needed to turn a profit with my skills in selling and buying, not in boiling and coating, especially at this peak season. Samarqand was blooming—it was expanding and growing mightier under the guidance of our Mighty Khan Timur. The city's wall left horses panting by the time they raced all the way around it. Water was piped into our houses, to our hands. The domes of the mosques resembled the blue dome of the sky. Everything was being built and erected with materials imported from the entire world: stone from Sindh, silk from China, and jasper from Anatolia. All these raw materials were processed by us and by people the Emir brought to us from his conquests of Shiraz, Isfahan, and Syria.

Kulabadh entered again, without asking leave—one of his careless habits—and said, "I have fifty reams of paper ready now and can produce the other twenty in two days' time."

"Great! Load the fifty reams in the wagon, and I'll take them to the madrasa now."

"They're actually already loaded, Industrious Brother."

I climbed into the wagon, and the Greek slave prodded the mule's flank. So she set off. When we passed the Blue Palace, the headquarters of the Mighty Khan, the slave and I got out and kissed the ground by its entry. Then we continued on. Soon I stood at the madrasa's entrance. When I knocked, a student answered and pointed to the covered porch, where I found the superintendent seated with three of the older students. They were surrounded by books and manuscripts, some of which were piled on top of each other, all the way to the ceiling. Two students were each writing on the long sheet of paper in front of him while the third brought one book at a time from the piles and laid it before the superintendent. He would glance at the book's title and its first pages before handing it to one of the students to record on his list according to its type and language.

"Greetings, Professor Targhay."

The superintendent looked up with tired eyes and replied: "Greetings to you, Taqtanish. Welcome."

Then he seemed to have suddenly remembered the order for paper. He said with concern, "I submitted an order today for reams of paper and. . . ."

"I have brought them, Professor."

"Excellent, excellent! Please sit down. Won't you have some tea?"

I sat down near him, gazing at the astonishing piles of books. "God's will be done!" I exclaimed. "Your madrasa is well stocked with books and imprints, Professor."

"These aren't our books. The Mighty Khan's caravans brought them."

"God's will be done! What subjects do they include?"

"This is what I'm cataloguing now. Jalal here is recording books on religion, Shari'ah, and the denominations. Mirza is recording books on the sciences, medicine, and nature. Taghluq records books about history and geography."

"What will you do with the paper you ordered?"

"Taqtanish, we will copy these books, which are all written on paper of poor quality, except for those from Baghdad. Some were even written on hides or bast fiber. They will disintegrate in a few years."

Pointing to the heaps of books, I said, "I think you will need more than seventy reams then, Professor."

"Naturally. Of course."

"I am ready to provide you with as much as you want of the finest types of paper on the market at the cheapest prices, Professor."

He smiled wanly and said, "Yes, yes. I don't doubt this, Taqtanish. Have no fear. I will buy only from you."

"What I value above all else is serving scholarship and scholars, Professor. Now, if you will excuse me. . . ."

As I left, my mind started calculating the profits I could expect from sales to this madrasa alone. Kulabadh would die from happiness! Before I left, I heard the professor tell his student, "Jalal, add this book to your list. The author is Muhyi al-Din Muhammad Ibn Arabi al-Hatimi al-Andalusi. It comes to us from the Great Khan's conquest of Hama in the year 803 since the hegira of our noble Prophet."

TOME SIX

47

I, accompanied by Badr, joined a caravan crossing Sinai on our way to Mecca. Most of the others were soldiers whom al-Malik al-Adil was moving between Egypt and Syria to shore up the pillars of the state in its two most important hubs. I acknowledged Badr's merit in his selection of a caravan of soldiers to cross this challenging desert. I watched the camels slow their pace as their feet sank into the soft sand, and some of the mules died en-route. They were left where they sank up to their belly in the sand. Water was scarce, and there were only two watering holes on the entire trip, which took us sixteen whole days. We guided ourselves by stone posts, which were placed along the route in the Fatimid era to guide travelers, and by small garrisons the Ayyubids had stationed in the few oases we encountered.

We left the caravan at Ayla,[30] where caravans of Egyptian and Syrian pilgrims meet. We entered the town one cold morning and headed to the mosque, which has a roof covered with trellises. We prayed there and then found a soup kitchen, which was teeming with people. It had its own cook and baker, and waiters who distributed lentil soup, fruit, and olive oil to people, free of charge. We ate our fill there with pilgrims and travelers from everywhere. Badr learned from them where the hostelries of Ayla were located. So we all walked there only to find that all the rooms were booked and the stables were filled with beasts of burden. We erected our tent by the city's wall and spent the night in it. After we woke at dawn and prayed, Badr left me while he mounted the horse and went to search for lodgings. An hour later he returned with an apologetic expression. I tried to alleviate his great sense of failure by patting him on the back and telling him, "God wants us to make haste to please him. Search for a caravan for us, one leaving for Mecca at the first opportunity."

"But the pilgrimage caravan takes a month to reach Mecca, and that means we'll arrive a month early."

"I don't think we'll reach it in a single month, Badr."

"Yes, yes, we will. I went on pilgrimage once before with my master Abu al-Futuh, and. . . ."

Badr proceeded to enumerate all the places they had passed and the number of stages between one place and another. I allowed him to recount everything he knew about the route, confidently and happily, while I praised God privately that I was accompanied by this honorable man with gentle eyes and a brown face, which radiated contentment and sincerity. I gazed at him until he concluded by saying, "Then finally we reach Mecca in less than a month."

I placed my arms around his neck and told him, "But I plan to perform my pilgrimage by foot. I won't ride."

Badr praised and extolled God as he always did when he thought I had demonstrated my piety. After he readied the animals, we set off together to the market. When we reached it, he gave me a look indicating that he wanted me to give him money to purchase provisions for the trip. He then left me, and I sought out a portly cobbler near the mosque in which we had prayed when we first reached Ayla. He was still chanting his mellifluous call that had inspired me to perform my pilgrimage on foot:

Footwear for pilgrims:

Prepare for the scorching heat of Muzdalifa,

The ascent of Arafat,

The Tawaf circumambulation, and

The Sa'y run.

Footwear for pilgrims:

Maximize the emotion, and

Guard against Mecca's heat and

Medina's hardships.

Footwear for pilgrims!

I examined the shoes he made and discovered that they were sturdy and padded with cotton and bits of cloth, between two layers of goat skin. After turning them over in my hand, I asked if he could make shoes that were even sturdier and had thicker soles. He took the shoes I had been inspecting, scratched his head as his mouth hung open, and took a deep breath. He looked at my face, as if thinking what to charge me, and then said, "If you want, I can insert a strip of wood between the layers of the sole. I made a pair like that for an Egyptian merchant some weeks ago."

"How much?"

"Seven dirhems."

We left Ayla after I had fastened around my feet pieces of cotton and linen cloth and then slipped on the sturdy shoes, which the cobbler had reinforced with a strip of wood wrapped in two cubits of cloth. In my saddlebag, I had another pair I had bought for fear a shoe might wear out and I would then yield to the temptation of riding the rest of the way. I walked in the shadow of Badr's camel, which he rode, while another camel—tied to Badr's—walked behind us. We proceeded slowly and stopped frequently to rest. The first caravan left us behind, but then another caught up with us. There were so many Ayyubid garrisons on the route, we weren't afraid of getting lost on the way. Little markets, in which Bedouins and people from nearby villages sold their goods to pilgrims, had sprung up near these. They were protected by the soldiers, who appreciated their company in the desolation of the desert. Pilgrims benefited from all of this; we didn't go hungry, nor did our mounts, all the way to the designated pilgrimage stop at al-Juhfa.

We couched our camels on an extensive plain near this site, where we found several caravans that had already paused. Turbans were stripped from heads and veils from faces as people took off their heavier garments, which they stuffed into bags on their animals. Every man and boy donned the pilgrim's *ihram* toga, and we started to hear from one place and another "*Labaik Allah*," as pilgrims announced to God that they were heeding His call. We met pilgrims who had reached this designated *miqat* from other designated stopping points in directions and pitched their tents around it till this site became so fully populated that it seemed an instant, pop-up city. I donned *ihram* as did Badr, and we set up our tent. We fed our animals and then sat down to watch the sun set, surrounded by various sounds: the clatter of pans, plaintive whine of camels, and people calling to one another after darkness concealed them. Badr found cooks who were selling grilled poultry and bread. He obtained some for us, and we sat in front of our tent, eating while a moist, gentle breeze caressed us.

"What can be described but not comprehended is majestic."

—IBN ARABI

48

We awoke to find news spreading quickly among people—it was whispered by some and spoken publicly by others. One person would be amazed and believe it, but others disliked and denied it. We spent the whole morning in this state, lacking any confirmation. The sun disappeared, and we heard someone make the rounds of the caravans' tents, calling out: "People, Qatada ibn Idris is king. The king is Qatada ibn Idris." Some people praised God, and others pretended they hadn't heard. Badr was astonished by what he was hearing and told me, "I saw Ibn Musa during my first Hajj with my master, Abu al-Futuh, and we entered his house. I would never have thought that anyone but God would wrest his kingdom from him."

"God did wrest it from him, Badr."

The only rule that Mecca had known for two centuries was that of the Bani Musa, but this changed when we reached Mecca. These were all days God chose to allot to people. I paid no attention to this change of government—concerned instead by my feet, which were in a pitiful condition. I had lost sensation in them, and their outside skin was flayed. The entire length of the trip the pains in my back and pelvis had grown more excruciating. My steps were shorter because my knees hurt so much, and during the final days of the trip I walked quite slowly. Badr heard me speaking incoherently one noon and begged me to ride, but I refused. Then he couched both she-camels and spread a blanket between their humps so I could rest in its shade. He emptied an entire skin of water over my head. Badr told me that, while I slept in his arms, I talked a lot without knowing it. We walked for another hour before I collapsed once more. Badr informed me then, while I was lapsing in and out of consciousness, that we had entered the sanctuary's boundaries and that I had satisfied my vow. So I mounted the riding camel and collapsed onto her. Badr secured me to her with ropes to keep me from falling off. I don't know how long I remained in this condition.

I opened my eyes to find many men moving before me. My head was on Badr's thigh, and he was applying cloths dampened with water from the Zamzam well to my forehead, one after the other. Groups of people passed by me and disappeared; then others arrived. I finally noticed, through gaps between them, God's green Ka'ba. I sat up. Badr smiled, and I smiled with difficulty. I stood up, and he supported me. I walked to the Ka'ba and touched my cheek to it. I began to speak but couldn't hear what I was saying. My mouth moved and a sequence of words emerged from it, but I couldn't hear anything. I looked at Badr and saw that he was listening. So I was sure I was speaking. My mouth was open. My tongue was moving. My vocal cords were vibrating. But I couldn't hear what I was saying and wasn't conscious of it.

By the entrance to the Sa'y course, we sat down to eat and drink as I gradually recovered my health. Badr told me I had slept half a day and part of a night. As I leaned on him, we circumambulated the Ka'ba. Then we went to the hostel for pilgrims. While I dozed, Badr rented a room only a few steps from the Grand Mosque—close enough for me to hear the calls to prayer during my sleepless nights. He made my bed, helped me lie down in it, and stretched out near me. Again, I slept for a long time. Badr woke before me. It was Friday. He took me to the rest house's bath, washed the grime from our trip off me, oiled my body, and dressed me in a new *ihram* toga. Then he brought me bread, honey, and warm milk, and I ate while he went to bathe.

We set off for the Grand Mosque to perform the prayer. I sat near the place where they were erecting the pulpit for the preacher, who soon entered in a black tunic. Behind him came two men, each carrying a black flag. He proceeded to the Black Stone, which he kissed, and then climbed into the pulpit, where he invoked the Prophet, his entire family, his four caliphs, his wives, the Abbasid Caliph al-Nasir, the new Emir of Mecca, Qatada ibn Idris, and finally the Ayyubid king, al-Adil. Then he led us in the prayer ritual and departed. They removed the pulpit once he had left. I remained seated where I was, gazing at the doves of the sanctuary as they filled the sky, lifting my heart with them to land on the Ka'ba and fly away. I spent hours in this condition—until the call to the afternoon prayer resounded. Then I rose and walked to the space allotted to the Maliki imam to pray behind him.

During my first days in Mecca, as the pilgrimage month began, the city grew more crowded day by day. The markets that ran parallel to the course of the Sa'y ritual became very lively as the voices of vendors and buyers celebrated new merchandise that pilgrims had brought from all over the world. Sales lasted into the night, as the shops never closed. Two or three salesclerks would take turns, and some merchants slept in their shops, never leaving for their homes during the pilgrimage month. While we slept in our rooms in the hostel, we could hear their voices—speaking languages we understood and others we didn't. I sent Badr to purchase food with Egyptian Adili coins, and he returned with change in Yemeni, Nasiri, Artuqid, and Khwarazmi dirhems. Keeping track of all these coins exhausted me; I gave Badr all the money I had, to spend as he saw fit. I didn't retain a single dinar or dirhem.

For days in a row, I went to the Holy Sanctuary at dawn and didn't return till after the evening prayer. I worshipped, recited God's names, and prayed until my feet hurt. I wept until my eyes dried up. I clung to the curtain covering the Ka'ba till the muscles of my forearms were exhausted. When the sun was hot, I retreated to the shade of a wall or a column and began to recite the Qur'an. Badr would bring me food and something to drink from time to time. This routine lasted till the Hajj finally began, and we performed its rituals. Once it concluded, the markets calmed down, the pilgrims departed, the crowds went away, and calm prevailed. Then I did what I had intended to do for a long time. I sold the two camels, which the trip had exhausted, for an excellent price to pilgrims returning to their homes. Next I rented a camel for Badr in a Maghribi caravan, so he could return to Bejaïa and bring Maryam and Zaynab to Mecca. I bade him farewell and advised him: "Buy a strong slave and a riding camel in Bejaïa and have my wife and daughter ride in a howdah. Don't go near the Sea. I fear its effects on my little girl."

49

No sooner had Badr left me than I began to look for a house to rent, and I found one. It wasn't far from the Holy Mosque but had neither a courtyard nor a garden. When I opened the door of my room, I was on the street. When I retired to my bed, I heard the clatter of passersby's sandals outside my door. I began to attend Hanbali classes unlike any I had been able to find in Andalusia. In the evening, I sat with dozens of Sufis, whose faces looked Eastern, Western, Syrian, or Yemeni. Some were disciples, and some on the way to becoming disciples. I felt certain that others had no share of wisdom and no portion of the light. Some drew closer to me, and those who I thought would avoid me did.

I continued in this fashion for weeks until I noticed him sitting among my students one day. His forehead was so broad it resembled an open book. His beard was so white he resembled a vertical lamp. He was always smiling, as if he were the dawn. Even before speaking to him, I was conscious of his dignity. I embraced him like a lover even before I knew who he was. At the end of the class, we disagreed about which of us should host the other. We both ended up sitting on the doorstep, leaning against a wall. *Is he my pillar? Lord, let him be my pillar! I have waited so long, God. One watad isn't enough. I see Your light in this man's face, Your mercy in his forehead, Your blessing in his smile, and Your grace in his eyes. My God, let him be my watad, strengthen my heart with him, enlarge my breast with him, fulfill Your promise with him, since you promised me.*

Finally, he said, "Will you come to me or shall I go to you?"

"I'll come to you."

"Tomorrow, by Abraham's Maqam."

This was how I met Zaher al-Isfahani, the imam of Abraham's Maqam. I attended his lessons for an entire year, without missing a single day or night. He taught me everything he knew, and I tested everything I knew with him. Whenever I approached him in the morning, he placed his hand on my chest, over my heart, and asked God to protect me. Then we continued reading the text we were working on. When I asked his permission to leave that night, he would place his hand on my back, behind my heart and asked God to protect me. Then I would return home in the shade of a blessed cloud of contentment. He never failed to bless me in this way. One day when I left without informing him of my departure, he came to my house while I was preparing for bed and knocked loudly on the door. I rushed to open it. Then he blessed me on my doorstep and departed.

Zaher acted like a *watad*, but my standing with him dissuaded me from that hope. There was something I didn't know and can't explain. The two pillars I already had in my quiver may have provided me an ability to detect the two remaining ones! There was something about Zaher that made me anxious. To me, he seemed half human being and half an angel. Light illuminated half of his heart, and the other half was flesh and blood. He knew much, but not everything. There were things he could do and others he could not. He would almost produce a charismatic act but fail. He would be on target at times only to miss the mark at others. In any case, his status in Mecca was high. The Governor of Mecca honored him and would not have dared to withdraw the position of Imam of Abraham's Maqam from him. When pilgrims arrived from Iran in the month of Rajab or Dhu al-Hijja, they felt blessed by every thread in his clothes and by his every footprint. They would encircle him at the Mosque and sit by the doorstep of his house all night long. When it was the time of year for Persian pilgrims, he would speak to them in their language and delivered his lesson in Farsi.

During the year when he had tucked me under his wing, my wife Maryam arrived in a beautiful Maghribi howdah, accompanied by my daughter Zaynab in a sealed wooden coffin. When Badr, who had lost so much weight he seemed not to have eaten anything during the journey and whose hair had turned so white that it contrasted dramatically with his black skin, arrived he fell to his knees. He hugged my legs to him and began to weep like a child. This surprise did not stun me, because God had disclosed my daughter's death to me in a dream two days after they passed through Yanbuʻ. So I had prepared her shroud and aromatic ointments and waited for them. Once they arrived, we carried the coffin to the cemetery of al-Muʻalla and washed her body. We waited to perform the noon prayer, after which we prayed for her. Then I buried her with my hand, depositing with her in her little grave warm tears that I knew would float over her like a little jasmine blossom on the eternal stream of her father's grief.

When Zaher came to offer me his condolences, I dared to tell him, and only him, that my heart was pierced by a hole as vast as my love for Zaynab, whom I had deserted the day she was born, the day she grew up, and the day she died.

"What kind of father am I?"

He received my grief with a beaming face and hugged me to his broad chest. He bestowed on me a wave of compassion unlike any I had ever felt from a mother or a father.

He told me, "Abu Zaynab, God ups the ante and doesn't decrease it. What God takes from you with one hand, He repays with the other, till you have more than what you had to begin with. Won't that satisfy you?"

"Yes, by God?"

"Listen to your Lord's word then. . . ."

As he typically did when reciting the Qurʼan, he closed his eyes. I bowed my head and closed my eyes too. Then I heard him recite for me: "Do not despair over matters that escape you nor rejoice over those granted to you."[31]

Zaher left after offering me his brief condolences and told me as he departed, "Please allow my sister, Fakhr al-Nisaʼ, to offer her condolences to Umm Zaynab."

"If you want, I'll send Maryam to you to receive your sister's condolences, so she doesn't trouble herself to come."

"No, she will come to you this afternoon."

Fakhr al-Nisaʼ entered and greeted us while we were seated. This was the first time I had seen her, even though I had listened to the lessons she gave in her house. Many people attended, until she grew so old that she stopped teaching. She was years older than her brother Zaher, and he venerated her as if she were his mother.

She stood in the center of the room and asked in a raspy voice, "Which one of you is you Ibn Arabi?"

I stood up, out of the group of men. She addressed her words to me: "My son, may God magnify your reward and expand your breast."

"May God reward you, Aunt."

Then she entered the women's room to offer her condolences to Maryam.

I sat apart with my head bowed, while the other men remained silent, except for some brief murmurs and whispered praise of God. Once the wake ended, Maryam and I closed our door, sealing our pain within our breasts. I was finally alone with her and realized how much she had changed. She had gained weight—as if she hadn't traveled a long distance or lost a child. She laid out my bed and prepared hers, separate from it. She lay down by the wall, turning her back toward me. I asked her about her family in Bejaïa, and she replied as if I were a stranger. I asked her how she was, and she didn't answer. Then I heard her start weeping again. I decided to leave her alone until she calmed down. I fell asleep but doubt that she did. The next morning, she brought me food and sat down. Her expression suggested that she had prepared a long statement for me during the night and was about to deliver it.

She finally began: "I want to return to Bejaïa."

When I glanced at her, she looked away, far away.

I asked her, "You're in the best place in the whole world and you want to return to Bejaïa?"

She remained silent and didn't respond. She pursed her lips and continued to look in another direction, not toward me.

I said to her, "Listen, Maryam. Losing Zaynab has hurt both of us. Don't think you're the only one who has lost a child. Pray to God and cling to the curtains of the Ka'ba to remove your grief and console your heart."

"Let me go, Abu Zaynab. Don't ask me how I am. If God doesn't reveal that to you, it's better for you not to know."

A tear ran down her face. Then she started crying, rose, and moved away. I heard her weeping. I was amazed by her condition. I had thought she would be eager to see me; but losing her child had caused her to forget any longing for me. As I finished my breakfast, I pondered what I should do about her but didn't have a clue. I closed my eyes but received no unveiling. I went to look for her and found her seated in a corner of the room weeping.

Then I said, "Stay until you perform the mandatory Hajj ritual and then depart, if you wish."

"Love is a divine secret."

—— **IBN ARABI**

Ramadan arrived, and the people of Mecca welcomed it with barrel and goblet drums. All the reed mats in the Grand Mosque were replaced, and every imam selected a corner of the mosque to lead the special "Tarawih" Ramadan prayer ritual. The mosque was filled with candles and torches till some areas of it shone as bright as day. A lamp was placed in each minaret, and they were lit after the fast was broken each day and burned until they were snuffed out when fasting resumed. My lesson now started after the dawn prayer, and the number of students in it increased to almost a hundred. Zaher would occasionally sit with the students and absorb Western teachings, and I would sit in on his class, following the afternoon prayer, and absorb his Eastern teachings. Whenever some question perplexed him, he promised us that he would return with the answer the following day, after he had consulted his sister, Fakhr al-Nisa'. Then my mind became fixed on her, and I asked his permission to take lessons from her.

"She no longer offers public lessons. She's grown too old."

"I'll take private lessons with her then."

"Tomorrow I will ask her for you."

She finally granted me permission, and I started coming to her after sunset, when she had completed her household chores. She would seat me on the doorstep and read to me useful, coherent learning that was sweet and more digestible than any I had heard from men. I read one theological book after another with her and one biography after the other. Whenever we concluded one investigation, we began another. I never wearied of her discourse and even volunteered to perform some chores for her so she would continue speaking. Anyone entering her house would find me sweeping the courtyard while she spoke, washing clothes while she spoke, lighting the fire while she spoke, or feeding the domestic animals while she spoke—until it grew so dark that it was time for me to leave.

Each day I spent on the doorstep of Fakhr al-Nisa' benefited my intellect until God decreed one day that my heart would be the beneficiary. I was sitting on her stoop when a woman with the most beautiful eyes I had ever seen arrived. I scooted out of her way and then heard her say, "Greetings, Aunt."

Fakhr al-Nisa' replied, "Come in," and my heart did too. So, she entered the house and my heart at the same time. That was Nizam, "Source of the Sun and of Beauty," Shaykh Zaher's daughter. She was reading, with both her aunt and her father, books that I hadn't read as well as those I had but wished to read again. Her lesson with her aunt began when mine ended. When I was departing, I heard her aunt say, "Invoke God and begin, Daughter." Then I listened intently while I pretended to rewind my turban to prolong my stay long enough to hear her sweet, sparkling voice slip over my heart like a single drop of rain.

"Shaykha Fakhr al-Nisa', what was that girl reading to you?"

Before she replied, I added, "I would like to read it too. What if I stayed here on the stoop to read it with both of you?"

"God willing, we'll do that starting tomorrow."

This became a lesson for both the intellect and the heart, a lighthouse for sight and insight, and a torch illuminating the body and the spirit. When I asked a question, Fakhr al-Nisa' would have Nizam reply. When Nizam asked something, Fakhr al-Nisa' would ask me to answer. At no time during those lessons did Nizam ever address me directly, and I would only speak to her via her aunt. I had been thinking that Mecca was a spiritual key to which I had struggled from faraway Andalusia, but here she was knocking on the door to my heart in a way no one had knocked before. Nizam lit in my breast a lamp by the light of which I saw corners of this heart I had never seen before, desolate nooks, closed rooms, and secret passageways in which feelings lurked that had never been allowed to emerge in the life I had been living. She inhabited my imagination every moment of my day and night. In this way, her bright face revealed itself to me in every letter. Her eyes resembled the Arabic letter ha': ح to which a calligrapher had devoted half a day! How precise her nose was—like the Arabic letter dal: د —when the syllable ends with it! Her lips were as dignified as the letter tha': ث when she was silent and like ya' ي when she laughed! How like a hamza: ء that had escaped from its alif: ا was this scar on her temple! Her entire face resembled a book of light inscribed by angels' hands!

How intelligent she was! She made veiled allusions that escaped her venerable aunt. When her aunt asked her about some matter, she would respond with a lengthy answer that she concluded with a reference to the opening line of a poem. Then, once I looked up that poem, I would find that the rest of it was a beautiful love poem. If Fakhr al-Nisa' asked me about some matter, I would reply with an even lengthier response and cite a verse from a poem Nizam would understand contained messages directed to her from my heart, which was attached to her. From the first weeks, Nizam sat facing the door with her aunt behind her and me at the stoop. Thus I saw her throughout the lesson, but her aunt could not see that. Then she would lower her veil to reveal progressively her face, eyes, cheeks, lips, and then her throat, which resembled a pool of pearls.

With the passing days, I memorized from the lessons of Fakhr al-Nisa' twice what I had learned from Zaher's. The old lady spent so much time with me that I began to read books to her that I had already read with her previously, although she wasn't conscious of that, because she had forgotten. I would wink at Nizam, and she would wink back at me. Then we would begin another book we knew would take us a week to complete—a week I would spend soaring like an errant bird over Nizam's forehead, a week of contemplating her authentic Isfahani charm like a novice poet, a week of throwing kisses that would land on her mouth like an exhausted autumn leaf, a week of admiring the gestures of her charming hands, her wide eyes, her rosy lips, and a strand of her hair that saddened me when it covered the scar on her temple. I would gesture for her to brush that strand aside, and she would comply, laughing silently. Her scar grew deeper when she smiled and moved with her mouth when she spoke. It was a scar with a life of its own.

I silently directed her attention more than once to my chin where a scar from my distant childhood lay hidden beneath my beard—that old scar caused by the almond tree in Murcia. Nizam would frown inquisitively, and then I would try to separate the hairs of my beard so she could see it. When she still couldn't, I recklessly moved closer till my face was visible through the door. Then Fakhr al-Nisa' would see I had moved closer than I should have. I would move closer, and Nizam would move closer. With her eyes fixed on her aunt, who wasn't looking, she held out her hand and touched my face. I trembled like a child diving into the water for the first time.

I let her stroke my beard while she kept her eyes on her aunt. Her hand missed its target more than once as she stroked my nose, forehead, and eyebrows. When her hand approached my mouth, I could not restrain myself and kissed it. While her hand paused, I kissed it once, twice, and three times as I saw her face blush suddenly and quiver while she momentarily breathed faster. Then her hand squeezed my lip forcefully, and she drew it back beside her.

Nizam occupied all my time. I began to arrive early for the lesson so I could stand at the end of the street and watch her walk—modestly and sedately—from her father's house to her aunt's. She wore a silk wrap and hid part of her face with it. When she carried a book, a container, or food, she concealed herself inside her *jilbab* and walked more slowly. That only increased my enjoyment. When she departed, I stood in the same place and waited for her departure. I would trail after her, and she was certainly conscious of that, till her house concealed her. Then I headed home. Her figure rose before me in my imagination, and I would continue to converse with her passionately all night long, night after night, until I finally found myself purchasing a ream of paper that an Iraqi merchant had imported from Mosul because he said it preserved what was written on it in ink and the writing wouldn't seep through. I wrote down the poetry clamoring in my soul and exhausting the capacity of my heart. I called this poetry collection: "Tarjuman al-Ashawq," or "The Passions' Interpreter."

"Any love with a cause known to be transient is not trustworthy."

——**IBN ARABI**

51

I said goodbye to Maryam without any kisses; she turned her cheek away from me and merely shook my hand and kissed it. She climbed into the howdah I had booked for her in a caravan of North African pilgrims returning to their homes by first crossing the Red Sea from Jidda to Aydhab. I gave her more than enough money for the trip as well as what the slave whom Badr had purchased before they left Bejaïa, but I did not give her any advice. She left my heart, and I left hers without any farewell. That was what God willed. It was also what Mecca wanted; some loves flourish only in their homeland. Our love was a fountain that flowed only in Andalusia. The moment we left there, that fountain's waters diminished and then disappeared entirely in the scorching heat of Mecca.

The Maryam whom I had loved was being carried westward in this howdah on that camel, which stopped after a few strides. I thought then that Maryam would descend from the howdah and return; but she didn't. The camel soon resumed its trek and disappeared over the horizon. The only time I saw Maryam again was in my dreams. She returned to Bejaïa and spent sixteen years with her family, until she died. Many months after her death, when I was in Malatya, someone came to offer me condolences, but God had already revealed her death to me at the time it occurred, before the mourner arrived. I had felt pain in a rib while I was sleeping tranquilly and realized that she had died. I rose then, performed my ablutions, and prayed for a long time, asking that she be granted a noble station in paradise. Then I went back to sleep. The pain in my rib disappeared, and I knew she was in the care of God, Who knows how to reward women who have lost their children and how to console a deprived woman with His compassion.

When I returned to my house and did not find her there, I felt a hot fire ignite in my belly. Some months earlier I had been a husband and a father; now I was a single reed with neither wife nor offspring. How could I have said goodbye to her at this same door then without grieving only to find accumulated griefs waiting here for me now? I rushed to the Ka'ba and started circling it without counting the times. I sensed that an old person was dying in my heart and a child was being born. Drunken rages and screams. A grave and a cradle. One sun rising and another setting. Maryam retracting her love and traveling far away, and Nizam taking my feelings by surprise without stepping forward. *Between these two women, who am I? What has become of all my shaykhs, my lessons, and my remaining pillars? What shall I do? What shall I be?* The storms raging within me would not subside till I knew where I was heading. There was a storm in my spirit, another in my intellect, and now this third one in my heart. *Am I a Sufi or a lover? Or, both at the same time? A scholar or a gnostic? A shaykh or a disciple? A saint or a sinner? My Lord, I shan't stop these circumambulations till I can anchor in a harbor.*

I made circuit after circuit. Seven. Ten. A hundred and then two hundred. A thousand and then two thousand, pausing only to perform my ritual prayers before I continued circling round the Ka'ba. Midnight. Dawn. Morning. The shops opened. The mosque became crowded. The heat intensified. The light became more subdued. The day ended. The sun set. The vendors left. The mosque grew tranquil. I was exhausted, and my steps were slow. I felt dizzy. I leaned against the wall of the Ka'ba while I continued to drag my feet forward. I could no longer see what was before me or hear anyone near me. I crumpled to the ground and assume I slept on the sill of the Ka'ba. I awoke with the dawn call to prayer. I had spent two days circling the Ka'ba. . . . I performed the dawn prayer and then sat gazing at the Ka'ba. I planned to complete my circumambulations, even though my feet screamed with pain and fatigue.

I summoned my forces and rose. I completed one circuit and then another, while I was barely conscious. Under my breath I repeated: "I wish I knew whether they understood . . . what heart they possessed! I wish I knew whether they understood

. . . what heart they possessed! I wish I knew whether they understood . . . what heart they possessed!" I made multiple circuits, which I didn't count, in this state. I was walking aimlessly. Circumambulating incessantly. Raving meaninglessly. Until I felt a tap on my shoulder. I was startled. I turned around. She was behind me.

"Nizam!"

Her mouth was concealed by her veil, but her eyes revealed that she was laughing. I felt embarrassed about my condition and my exhaustion—by how dry my mouth was and how shabby my garments were. My confusion was obvious, and my tongue was blocked, unable to utter a word.

So, she said, "What are you doing here, Man?"

"Circling!"

"You're circumambulating the Ka'ba? Today?"

"Can't I circle it any day?"

Nizam was silent and stared at my face in astonishment. She seemed to have immediately grasped that I wasn't in a normal state of consciousness. She proceeded to inspect the face of the man who had completed thousands of circuits of the Ka'ba in two days, stopping only to perform the mandatory prayers. My face was covered with dust and revealed my exhaustion. I could not stand up straight. My voice was muffled.

Finally, she asked in a low, hushed voice, "Have you looked around you?"

I turned my head around slowly to see what she meant and was dumbfounded. There were many women. Only women. To my right and left. They were circling the Ka'ba and praying in the courtyard. This was an astonishing mass of women, and I was the only man among them. They were looking at me strangely, disapprovingly, critically, angrily, shooting me one critical glare after the other. I shouted in a strangled voice, which struggled to emerge from my throat: "My God! What's happening?"

Nizam answered me anxiously, "Today is the 29th of Rajab."

"Meaning what?"

"It's a day set aside for women's circumambulation! Do you see any other man in the mosque? Leave now!"

I moved away immediately, like a child whose mother had just scolded him. I walked unsteadily toward the door of the mosque, looking like a wayfarer who didn't know where he was. I tried to avoid the waves of women pouring in but bumped into one of them and stepped on the foot of a little boy whose mother was pulling him behind her; he began to cry. I heard clearly the curses aimed at me but didn't turn. I quickened my pace and struggled through the portal to find myself finally outside the mosque. I was relieved to see the faces of men like me walking in the street but discovered that one of my feet had lost its shoe. After removing my other shoe, which I tucked under my arm, I walked to my house.

52

We met the next day at the home of Fakhr al-Nisa'. I was so embarrassed I didn't exchange a single look with Nizam. We read what we were reading until we finished. When I started to leave, Nizam seized my wrist and signaled for me to wait outside. Then she closed the door behind me. I sat on the doorstep, feeling the place her hand had touched my wrist, sniffing it, and wondering what she wanted to tell me.

Nizam finally opened the door again and looked out. She wasn't wearing a veil, and her hair hung down over her shoulders like a cascade of almonds. Then I saw her whole face, unveiled, for the first time. Her eyes were much wider, her lips much fuller, and the scar on her temple was transformed into a nest from which a fledgling sparrow peeked.

"My aunt's asleep. Come in."

I entered and closed the door behind me. I sat down just inside it. Night fell, and no one passed by the door. She gestured to me to come closer, and I did. I was only an arm's length from her, near enough to catch the scent of roses and violets. A smile shimmered on her lips, revealing neatly aligned teeth. The one tooth slightly askew on the lower jaw was a beautiful novelty.

She said, "Fine. What's your story, Ibn Arabi?"

"My story?"

"Yes. Tell me what no one else will know."

I wasn't sure what she had in mind and repeated her statement to myself under my breath. Trying to gain time for further reflection, I asked, "What no other person knows are matters that God has concealed. Why would I reveal them?"

She didn't reply but shot me an encouraging look, as if to brush aside my response. After brooding a little, I said, "What no one else knows yet, Nizam, is that I love you."

I said that and bowed my head, waiting to hear her gasp, but she didn't. When I lifted my eyes toward her face again, I saw she was smiling calmly and broadly. She lowered her head a bit and raised her eyes to continue looking at me. Her meek appearance then would have ignited a mountain of ice.

My voice shook when I continued, "I love you very much, Nizam . . . with a love that accompanies me wherever I go and wakes me up whenever I fall asleep. It follows me during the day and into my bed at night."

A very gentle sigh escaped from her mouth, and she placed her hand on her heart. Her smile grew smaller till she pursed her lips as if they were preparing to receive a kiss. She bowed her head, and a lock of hair fell across her face. She brushed it aside with her hand, revealing her arm to the elbow. I felt a chill pervade my insides, as if a little cascade were spilling through my chest. We both trembled and remained silent. During that quiet moment we bowed our heads. She was looking at the empty floor, and I was looking at her hand, which sat on her knee. Then she moved her hand, rested her chin on it, and smiled broadly again. Looking straight into my eyes, she asked, "What were you saying while circling yesterday?"

"I don't remember!"

"You weren't praising God or begging for His forgiveness. You were reciting poetry!"

"Really? You heard me reciting poetry during my circumambulation?"

"Man. Every woman there heard you recite poetry as loudly as a muezzin."

"Really?"

Nizam laughed and hid her mouth with her hand while she tried to speak more softly. She glanced inside to make sure her aunt was asleep and hadn't heard her. I laughed with her, silently, and tried to remember the poetry she claimed I had repeated while circling the Ka'ba—but failed.

Finally she said, "You were saying, 'I wish I knew whether they understood . . . what heart they possessed!'"

"Yes, yes! That's right."

"Amazing! You're the leading gnostic of your age and you say something like this?"

"What's wrong with it?"

"You wonder aloud whether they knew what they possessed, even though you know that every enslaved person is known like an open book. Possession isn't real unless the possessed person is known. No one possesses what he doesn't know."

"You're right!"

"Is there more?"

"Yes."

"Recite it for me, then."

"And my heart if it knew . . . what path they followed."

"Amazing! You, the leading gnostic of your age, say something like this?"

"What's wrong with this too?"

"It implies that you aspire to know what path they followed, even though you know this path—which separates your passion from your heart and which your beloved follows into you—is what bars you from gnosis. Thus, if you knew the path, you would lose your spiritual insight. If you acquired spiritual knowledge, you would know the path. How can you wish for this instead of that?"

"You're right!"

"Is there more?"

"Yes."

"So, recite it for me."

"Are they safe? Have they perished?"

"Don't worry about them. You need to worry about your Self. Are you safe or have you perished?"

"You're right!"

"Is there more?"

"Yes. The last stanza."

"Recite it for me."

"The lords of love have become lost . . . in love and sinned."

Nizam nodded in amazement and then inclined her head a bit. She looked at me and protested: "Amazing! You're the gnostic of your age and you say this?"

"What's wrong with it?"

"It's just that you complain of bewilderment after love, whereas love drugs the senses, dulls intellects, and banishes thoughts. After achieving all that, what is left to perplex you?"

"You're right, by God. You're right!"

She lowered her voice then almost to a whisper and drew close enough to me that I could feel her breath as she spoke. She said, "Then, don't you know that the lover annihilates himself in his beloved as his tongue becomes his beloved's and his heart becomes his beloved's too?"

"That's true."

"How can your heart go astray when it has become your beloved's heart?"

I looked at her and smiled submissively. She smiled back in a way that eased my small defeat. She stretched her hand out, and I stretched out mine as our two hands met in a sweet embrace. Then she said, while drawing her eyebrows together in a significant way I didn't understand: "You must be passionately in love with Umm Zaynab for passion to have this effect on you."

I looked at Nizam and smiled my most confident smile since I had first met her. I remained silent for a moment, while she was too. Then I pressed her hand as if to chide her for her jealousy and said, "You claim that a person's heart is the heart of his beloved and that his tongue is the tongue of his beloved?"

"Yes."

"Then how can you not know that you are the only person to whom these verses are addressed?"

Nizam withdrew her hand with fleeting embarrassment. She pulled her veil over her head and said, "I need to leave, before my father becomes anxious."

"Your father fell asleep an hour ago, Nizam. He won't wake up till first light."

"How do you know that?"

"God grants me unveilings."

"What about my aunt?"

"Her eyes are closed, but her heart is open. She senses us and is happy for us."

"Really?"

"As truly as God Almighty is the Truth, and His unveilings are nothing but truth."

"Is this the extent of what God has unveiled to you?"

"He unveils to me what He wants—not what I want."

Nizam gazed at me anxiously and passionately. Then she raised my hand to her mouth, pressed it to her lips, closed her eyes, and kissed it slowly and repeatedly.

Next she cast me glances that seemed to implore my sympathy for the overwhelming passion that raged inside her. Not knowing what I dared do, I imitated her, drew her hand to my mouth, and proceeded to kiss one finger after the other. Then I imprinted a long, warm kiss precisely in the center of her palm. I heard her sigh as though she might weep and stopped. She withdrew her hand from mine and rose, and I did too. She covered her hair with her veil, tucking the fledging bird back in its nest, while my heart palpitated as if my life were at its end.

She said, "Since God has disclosed to you that my father won't wake till first light, I'll sleep over with my aunt."

"Sleep sweetly, Apple of my Eye."

She hid half of her face behind the door, which she was about to close, and said with a smile, "And you too . . . . Gnostic of your age!"[32]

"Nothing esoteric that does not show you its exoteric form is reliable."

—IBN ARABI

53

I was awakened by the Emir's herald's raspy voice, which penetrated the wall from outside. He was summoning people:
"Builders, carpenters, blacksmiths, artisans, come to the Emir's
palace." Then his voice gradually moved away till it was no
longer audible. I sat up in bed and felt the swollen wound at
the back of my head. The cupper had inflicted it two nights
earlier when he drew blood in hopes of ending the string of
nights during which I had suffered from a headache. The previous night had been a different headache, and I had slept for
only short stretches till I dozed off at dawn. I found bread and
sour-milk cheese beside the wall, where Badr had put them for
me to find when I woke. I ate and sat looking over the last of
what I had written the previous night. The distorted handwriting of the last lines showed clearly when the headache had
reached its worst. I looked at the stack of paper on the other
side of the room and wondered whether this headache would
allow me to fill all of them before I left Mecca.

I had spent two years in this "secure land" and didn't know
whether I would be able to remain here longer. Al-Khayyat had
inherited the status of being a pillar at the last moment, in time to
save me from losing out, but the brevity of time that had elapsed
between the death of the prior *watad* and his inheritance of the
role as the next pillar had not allowed him an opportunity to learn
where I would find my third pillar. All sites were equally possible:
India or China, Iran or Anatolia, Byzantium or Sudan. In fact, he
might be waiting for me where I hailed from—in Andalusia.

There was a knock on the door, and I rose to open it, without asking who was there. It was Shaykh Zaher, who was smiling as usual. I welcomed him, and he asked permission to enter. I invited him in.

"I have come to you without an appointment because I know your house contains neither a woman nor a child. . . ." He concluded his phrase with a chuckle: "Thus there is no problem about my coming whenever I want."

"My home is your home, my Shaykh. May your blessing always visit us."

"God bless you. I learned that you stopped teaching in the Grand Mosque some days ago but I only noticed your absence this morning. I hope something positive is responsible?"

I gestured to the open book, which I had been pondering when he entered. "I'm writing, my Shaykh," I said.

His face lit up with a pleased expression, and he smiled fondly. "Bravo, bravo! By God, this is excellent. What are you writing?"

"About everything God has revealed in Mecca to me of the gnostic sciences. I call the book *Al-Fath al-Makki* (The Meccan Opening or Revelation)."

As I made these last remarks, I offered the bread, cheese, and honey jar, which Badr had left, to the shaykh. The shaykh took a small piece of bread, dipped it in the honey, and satisfied himself with that. Wiping his palms, he said, as he finished chewing, "When do you think you will finish it?"

I sighed deeply as I prepared to share my complaint with my shaykh. I said, "I was determined to finish it in a few months, but I'm suffering from this headache. Whenever I sit down to write and complete a section of it, my head starts chattering. I lose the ability to think straight and make distinctions. That state persists till I am forced to stop."

The shaykh narrowed his eyes, and his face assumed a look of paternal affection. He said, "May God cure you, my son. How long have you been suffering?"

"Since I began writing this book."

"Did you ever suffer from a headache before that?"

"Never one this severe or persistent. No."

The shaykh was silent for a short time. Then he began to whisper a prayer that I couldn't hear. Next he pointed with his hand above his eyes, at the front of his forehead and asked, "Is it here?"

"Yes, Shaykh. The most intense pain is above my eyes, although I feel it in my eye sockets and temples as well."

He smiled and said, "I suffered the same way. You're forty now, my son, and your eyesight is becoming weaker."

I nodded regretfully as my mouth adopted a sarcastic smile for my age. The shaykh patted my back, stood up, and headed to the book. "Don't write on paper like this," he said. "You'll find sheets larger than this In the stationers' market. Write on them with larger letters and use very dark ink."

I indicated that I would.

He continued, "Don't write at night. If you absolutely must, put your lamp behind you—not in front of you. If you want, you could get two lamps and hang them from the ceiling. This will be better, and you won't exhaust your eyes with insufficient lighting."

"May God reward you, Shaykh."

Badr entered at that moment, kissed the shaykh's head, and looked around to assure himself that the room was clean. He gathered the crumbs of bread from the floor and stood back up to say to the shaykh, "My Master, give me a moment to fix you something to drink."

The shaykh declined his offer with a wave of his hand and said, "I'm leaving now. I came to reassure myself about Muhyi. I have found him growing older, like us before him."

His loud laughter concluded his statement, and he headed toward the door. Before he left, he turned toward me, having remembered something. He said, "The delegation of pilgrims from Konya has arrived early this year, and we will hold lessons with them. Join us if you want, God willing, tomorrow following the afternoon prayer."

"I will be delighted to attend your session, our Shaykh."

Before the shaykh left, the herald passed by again, though his raspy voice was slightly softer from fatigue: "Builders, carpenters, blacksmiths, artisans. . . ."

When I looked inquisitively at Zaher, he told me, "The Emir plans to build a wall around Mecca."

"A wall around Mecca? The One who protected it against Abraha still protects it. Why a wall?"

"I don't know, my son, but I fear a war is imminent, because the Emir of Medina hasn't conceded the emirate of Mecca to Qatada yet. Each man covets what the other rules, and hostile forces lie in wait for him."

54

Whether I was in my house or outside, Nizam's image never left me. When I wrote, I saw her in my books and papers and at the bottom of my inkwell. When I went out, I saw her on my route, when I circled the Ka'ba, and when I was running errands. Poems about her would descend on me—without any prior thought— like raindrops falling from a summer cloud. If I was at home, I would select the finest paper to record the poem, dip my pen first in the pouch of gum Arabic, and then dip it for a long time in the inkwell so the pen would soak up a lot of ink and keep writing. If I were away from home, I would feel upset and repeat the poem so I wouldn't forget and lose it. Finally, I procured a notebook to carry around with me. Then, whenever I felt like reciting a poem about her, I would step aside, take out my inkwell and pen, and write down whatever occurred to me. If people asked me what I was writing in this notebook, I was afraid to tell them and said, "I'm recording what happens to me today. Then, when I retire to bed, I can take myself to task for what I have done. If I need to ask forgiveness for something, I do. If I should be grateful, I am. If I need to repent something, I do that . . . until I finish with my entire day and go to sleep." As a matter of fact, none of that was a lie, because the entirety of what happened to me during the day was an effusion of my love for Nizam and my passion for her. I merely recorded all this as poetry. When night fell, I read it to myself and to her. Then, if I found I had written about her appropriately, I thanked God for making that possible and for inspiring me to write what was fitting for this entrancing beauty. If I found I had fallen short in describing her and failed to achieve what was due her, I asked God's forgiveness for my shortcomings and poor craftsmanship.

Fakhr al-Nisa' had exhausted her curriculum with me. I had memorized her entire repertoire and clearly demonstrated that, and so had Nizam. We exploited her weak memory, though, to continue studying with her so I could have an opportunity to spend two hours of my day with Nizam. Every time we finished a book, we asked Fakhr al-Nisa' to read another book with us.

She would ask, "Haven't we read that?"

Then Nizam would reply, "Yes, Aunt, but the subject matter is difficult, and there are many glosses."

"Then let us trust in God. Start reading, Daughter."

I began to sit inside the session, not on the doorstep, after Zaher interceded. During one lesson, he stopped by and found me sitting on the doorstep. "This isn't right," he said. "Come inside, my son. You're one of God's *walis*."

Turning toward Nizam, he said, "Lower your *jilbab* and sit on the far side of the room while he sits here. There is nothing sinful about this, because it is a scholarly session that is surrounded by angels."

Thus I began to sit on one side of the room, leaning against a comfortable cushion after sitting for many months on the dirt doorstep, leaning against a wall. The two women were beside each other on the far side, near a brazier and a water jug. At times Fakhr al-Nisa' might rise to do some chore, while Nizam and I continued reading the book, discussing it, and conducting a debate. Fakhr al-Nisa' might forget to return to us and retire to bed while we devoted our time to sweet talk. I might rebel against reading some word in a book; then Nizam would draw nearer to read it and demand as her fee a warm kiss from an impassioned mouth.

I recounted to Nizam everything that had happened in my life since I was born, and she told me all about her life. I told her about Andalusia, its rivers, bridges, and trees. She told me about Baghdad and the Tigris River, which had the Karkh neighborhood on one side and Rasafa on the other. Each of us reveled in recalling childhood memories from the two distant edges of God's land from which we hailed—I from the far west of the Muslims and she from their far east—to Mecca, where we fell in love. I would recite to her every poem I had composed the previous night. Then she would express her love for me in Farsi.

When I asked her to translate this to Arabic, she retorted, "Translation would smother my words."

"Why don't you compose in Arabic then?"

"Love must be expressed in one's native tongue, Muhyi."

"But you're proficient in both languages!"

"When I speak Farsi, there's no curtain between my words and my heart."

"How shall I understand them?"

"Listen with your heart—not with your ears."

"Recite, then . . . recite, my darling."

I noticed that with the passing days she grew even more beautiful. I didn't know whether I was growing fonder of her or whether she had started to adorn herself for me, especially as the eyesight of Fakhr al-Nisa' grew weaker and she could scarcely see where she set her feet. Nizam's bright part created two nights from the midnight of her black hair. I had never seen eyebrows so delicately arched and as intensely black as hers—beneath a luminous forehead the light of which was not diminished by any blemish. When she laughed, she modestly covered her mouth with her hand. Then I would not know whether I should delight in seeing her beautiful fingers or mourn the disappearance of her enchanting lips and sparkling teeth. To tell the truth, the major portion of our last lessons was unmitigated laughter. We would try to keep its volume down so Fakhr al-Nisa' wouldn't hear. If we did laugh out loud, she would ask, "What's so funny?"

Then Nizam would reply, "Muhyi's turban fell off."

Or, I would say, "I made a mistake citing this hadith's chain of authorities."

Things progressed in this manner while love for her gained such power over my heart that I could no longer think of any future she did not share with me. If Maryam had not been my wife and my responsibility, I would have sworn that Nizam was my first experience with women. She was the first woman for whom I felt total love, emotional passion, spiritual surrender, and complete trust. I had never seen anyone as beautiful and perfect as this girl. During a lesson when we were reading biographies of some expert on Hadith, while Fakhr al-Nisa' was in her room, Nizam closed the book and asked me, "Muhyi, if you write my biography one day, what will you say?"

I was silent for a time, reflecting deeply, and then replied slowly, "I will say that you, Nizam Qurrat al-Ayn, daughter of the Hadith expert Abu Shuja' Zaher ibn

Rostam al-Isfahani, were born and lived in the heart of Muhyi al-Din ibn Arabi and will never die there. A slender maiden who fetters observers and graces meetings, a scholar, a worshipper, and a pilgrim with an enchanting glance. When she darts ahead, she wears out everyone else. When she summarizes, she is concise; when she is eloquent, she is clear."

She laughed and leaned her chin on her hand, as if expecting me to say more. I contemplated her beauty, attempting to draw inspiration from it for words worthy of and appropriate for her. Then I said, "If you seek wisdom, speak to me and to her, because you will find that her wisdom is matched only by mine and mine equaled by hers. How could that not be so, when she is the foster child of the Two Sanctuaries and the product of the Secure Land?[33] She has read every book and mastered every science. Her only occupation is reading, and her only recreation is learning. Thus, she is a sun among scholars and a garden among authors. God has granted her a beauty He never granted any woman before her. She is a woman made from the nectar of flowers; her glances demolish caution, and her utterance softens stone."

Once I finished speaking, I looked up and found Nizam's eyes were washed with tears and her face sported a broad, loving smile. She squeezed my hand, and her fingers began to rub my palm as if wanting to retain some of my skin in her own palm. Then she raised my hand to her face, inhaled its scent deeply, and held her breath for a time. Next she closed her eyes and sighed deeply. Finally, she stood up, with her eyes filled with tears, and I knew it was time for me to leave.

55 AMASYA 1409 CE/811 AH

The chamberlain proclaimed: "His Majesty the Mighty Sultan and Magnificent Khaqan Mehmet Beyazid Bey!" Everyone stood up, including me and my brothers. Heads were bowed and backs bent, because no one was permitted to see the Sultan enter. We, however, kept our backs straight and our heads high, as was appropriate for sons of the mighty Khan Timur. The Ottoman Sultan strode between the two facing rows of men that lined his way to the throne. He was followed by his son, who was four or five and who had trouble walking straight due to the weight of his heavy Sultan's turban. The Sultan noticed the four heads that had not bowed and that were staring at his black beard, which had been carefully trimmed to frame his face like night framing the moon, and his mustache, which burst from beneath his nose at an acute angle, as well as his narrow eyebrows and his almond-shaped eyes, one of which stared sternly and rigidly at the world while the other emitted calm rays of mercy and nobility. When he finally reached his throne, he turned around, gathered his gown behind him, and sat down. My brother Aq started to sit down when the Sultan did but noticed that everyone else in the tent had remained standing. So he straightened himself again. The momentary silence then was dreadful before the Sultan gestured to the chamberlain, who shouted: "May God strengthen the Sultan!"

Everyone sat down and finally looked up. Necks swiveled so people could watch the Sultan's face, which seemed to stare at the assembled crowd without looking at any one person. His eyes hovered over the assembly. He looked but did not see. He contemplated but did not gaze. The chamberlain approached him with a list of the people who would present themselves that day. He did not look at it. Instead, he whispered something to the chamberlain. In a few minutes we noticed that the chamberlain had moved from behind the Sultan to behind our backs. He whispered to me and my brothers, "Which of you is the eldest?"

In a voice as low as his, I replied, "I am. Bashi."

"Have you brought presents?"

"Yes."

"I will summon you first to His Excellency the Sultan. Then you will introduce your brothers after you kiss his hands."

The chamberlain moved away, and my youngest brother Alp whispered to me, "Are we going to kiss his hand? I'll never kiss his hands."

Aq told him, "This is no time for stupid pranks!"

Alp grumbled, "It's no time for humiliations either!"

What my brother Alp said worried me, and I feared he might do something to sour the Sultan on us. We were sons of the mighty Khan in our land, but now we were in exile, and our fate rested in the hands of this Sultan. If he sent us back to Samarqand, our eldest brother Shah Rukh would hang us in the main square of that city. If the Sultan ignored us, we would continue to be pursued through the world and would never be safe from some ambitious, deadly, bounty hunter eager for the massive price placed on our heads.

Alp whispered in my ear, "I shan't kiss his hand. Don't forget that it was our father who appointed him Sultan."

I gritted my teeth in rage and told him, "Don't forget that our father is dead. You will surely follow him to the grave if you show your pride at the wrong time and in the wrong place!"

Alp started to say something, but the chamberlain's voice was raised to proclaim: "Bashi ibn Timur-i Lang ibn Aytmish ibn Kalingh."

I rose and passed between the rows of men, who craned their necks as they tried to make out my features. What a strange situation! I was walking toward the Ottoman Sultan and had almost reached him—only a few steps remained—but hadn't yet decided what to do about kissing his hand. What should I do? I, Bashi, son of Timur the Great? But what use was that, when I had been expelled with my brothers, when we were refugees in the custody of the Sultan, whose father was yesterday our prisoner?

I took the final step, to the place reserved for people to stand before the Sultan. On the ground was a small pillow embroidered with gold thread. The person presented to the Sultan would kneel on that as he bowed and kissed the Sultan's hands. I decided at that moment to kiss them. Circumstances had changed, and politics trumped pride. I placed my knee on the pillow and raised my hand to receive his soft one, on which he wore three huge rings of different colors. But he, instead of placing his hand in my palm, placed it on my shoulder.

I stood up, feeling slightly irritated. If he had intended to spare me the ritual of kissing his hand, why hadn't he done that before I tried to kiss it? He had not been generous to me—he had merely allowed everyone to see that he had decided to spare me that humiliation.

"Your Majesty the Sultan. Allow me to offer you a few presents that I hope you will honor me by accepting."

When the Sultan gestured to me, I looked toward my brothers, who in turn looked toward our slaves, who stood at the entrance. My slave came first, bearing the box with my present. The moment he reached the carpet, he bowed and continued, walking bent forward, carrying the small box, till he reached me and then placed the box before the Sultan. I opened it to show the ancient sandal inside its velvet lining. I said, "This is the sandal of our Master Muhammad, may God bless him and grant him peace."

The Sultan murmured a prayer and repeated his praise for the Prophet, raising his eyebrows, which met in the middle, with amazement. His expression changed to modest reverence, after having been haughty and self-important. I took the precious sandal from the box and lifted it toward the Sultan, who spread his palms next to each other so I could place the sandal upon them. He gazed at the sandal for a time; then he kissed it and touched it to his forehead. Meanwhile the servant had brought the box toward the Sultan; so, he returned the sandal to its place there. Then he whispered an order to the chamberlain.

When he looked back toward me, I said, "Allow me to present to you, Your Majesty the Sultan, my brother Jan ibn Timur ibn Aytmish ibn Kalingh."

Jan advanced quickly, approached the Sultan, and placed his knee on the pillow. Then the Sultan treated him the way he had treated me. Jan stood up and gestured to his slave, who brought his box to His Majesty the Sultan. He opened it to display a huge copy of the Qur'an inscribed on ancient parchment.

Jan finally said in his voice, which is always hoarse: "The Qur'an of our Master Uthman."

The Sultan took the Qur'an, kissed it, and touched it to his forehead. Then he turned its pages with extreme care. He read some surahs from it. Then he lifted it in his hands, kissed it again, and returned it, himself, to the box. He signaled to the chamberlain to care for it as respectfully as he had the sandal of the Prophet.

My brother Aq, the third of us, stepped forward not with one box but with three, each one bigger than ours. Slaves placed them next to each other, right by the Sultan's feet, and opened the boxes all at once. The Sultan's reverent look was replaced by a haughty expression of self-importance when he saw that the boxes were filled with agates, emeralds, and rubies.

Aq stammered, "The agates are from Yemen, the emeralds from Marv, and the rubies from India."

The Sultan nodded appreciatively and smiled. Then he looked toward my other brother as if to encourage him to make haste so he could leave his assembly. I introduced him quickly, and he approached, followed by four slaves who carried a huge box, which they deposited before the Sultan.

He said, "The works of the Grand Shaykh, the Red Sulphur, Muhyi al-Din Ibn Arabi the Andalusian, Your Majesty."

"You, Man:

You are the lamp, the wick, the niche, and the glass."

——**IBN ARABI**

The moment I saw the face of the man leading the delegation of pilgrims from Konya, love for him immediately flooded my heart. He shook my hand, nodded his head very respectfully, and smiled in an endearing way. My hand remained in his while he tilted his head to look at my face. I had trouble altering my expression, because of the effusion of the divine love that united us in those first moments. He did not give me time to collect my thoughts or plan my actions. I shook his hand just as hospitably but couldn't think what to say till, unconsciously, I adopted the Turkmen accent he used when speaking Arabic. I seated him beside me, retained his hand in mine, and offered him a date from the raceme Badr had placed before us.

I scrutinized his features to imprint them in my memory. Then they were enshrined in my heart: his broad brow and cubical head, his narrow eyes, which projected slightly, his short stature, his wide shoulders and powerful arms, the totally white hair on his temples and the salt-and-pepper hair elsewhere. When he smiled, parallel lines showed on his cheeks, and similar ones appeared on his forehead when he contracted his eyebrows thoughtfully. I don't know why I pictured him as a tree with a thick trunk, a few branches, and pointed leaves—a tree that the seasons didn't affect, that remained green in summer and winter, and that released a reassuring feeling of confidence and stability. Yes, these were the aspects I was exploring in his features and trying to pinpoint. Ishaq radiated comfort the way the sun radiates its warmth throughout existence.

Day after day it grew obvious to me what a beneficial and helpful friend he was for an anxious spirit like me. I loved him and stationed him in my heart with other friends of God. By the time we left Zaher's house, where we were guests, we had agreed to offer a two-person lesson at al-Hatim, the low, semicircular wall by the north side of the Ka'ba. I would provide him the luminous sciences I had gathered from the west, and he would share with me the sciences of the far north, from which he hailed. He brought a few books in a small basket, and I brought nothing. I recited, and he read. We kept that up for hours and repeated it for days. Finally, we stood facing each other, while I invested him with the light cloak I wore, and he invested me with the cotton-lined, fox-fur-trimmed, leather cloak he wore. We embraced, spirit to spirit. We fraternized in the divine love that gathers God's friends from the east and west. Then I suggested he live in my house, since he was single, having neither wife nor child, and he accepted. In this way I succeeded in moving him out of Zaher's house, which was admittedly cramped but was also where Nizam lived. Who said God's *walis* don't experience jealousy?

The Hajj ended, and the delegation from Konya removed their ihram garments. They donned their tall, cylindrical hats and spread throughout Mecca, buying and selling, attending classes, frequenting shaykhs, and practicing artisanal crafts in the markets. Every year the delegation delayed its departure from Mecca so they could imbibe Mecca's spiritual effusions to share in their distant, northern isolation. They were accompanied by translators and copyists who set right to work—just as soon as their Hajj was completed—translating and copying books of Hadith, jurisprudence, and exegesis into their language. Ishaq organized all their chores, assigned their duties, and expedited their activities. Everyone heeded his orders and obeyed him blindly.

In my house, he told me about a land I had never visited and roads I had never traveled. In the dark of the night, his longing for Anatolia would overcome him. He would tell me about a small garden he cultivated, a dry patch of land with an ancient pine tree in the center. One day when he was passing, he found the pine was almost speaking to him. So he bought the tract of land, built a low wall around it, and pledged to cultivate it himself—planting vegetation that would make the pine tree feel less lonesome. He surrounded that tree with lilies, hyacinths, saffron crocuses, snowdrops, and many other plants whose seeds he had brought back from his repeated trips throughout Syria, Iraq, Armenia, and Khurasan on behalf of the Seljuq Sultan Kaykhusraw.

He told me, "People thought what I was doing was strange. If this garden were at my home or if it produced fruit to sell, they would have understood. They didn't grasp that it provided a home for my spirit. The house where I live merely provides a roof for my body. It shelters me from the sun's heat, the night's chill, and gusty winds. When I retire to my house after a hard day of work in the Sultan's court in Konya, my spirit sleeps out in the open. This garden shelters my spirit, keeps it warm, and instills in it the comfort and stability of a house. When I go there and sit inside it, every blossom shelters with me, and every bough draws closer to me. They tell me what happened while I was gone: about the scent of the breeze, the taste of the pollen, the secrets of the night, the rustling of the leaves, the gnawing of squirrels, the sound of footsteps. . . ."

"Who cares for your garden while you're gone?"

He smiled and turned toward me. Staring me confidently in the eye, he said, "I do."

"How?"

"Today I raked the autumn leaves that had fallen, because I didn't want them to keep light from reaching the little crocuses that sprout in this season. I also thwarted a thief who wanted to pick lavender to sell to a perfumer with a bad reputation. During periods when there is no rain, I bring a cloud to my garden from the north."

I had stretched out, but now I sat up. "I understand how you can rake leaves and thwart a thief, but how can you propel clouds; isn't that up to God, alone?"

"God alone orders it, as you point out, and God forbid that I should attempt to usurp His will."

"Then how do you do it?"

"I merely entreat Him, and He humors me."

"Does He humor you every time you entreat Him?"

"Yes, but I don't entreat Him unless I already know He will humor me."

"How do you know that?"

He raised his eyes to the ceiling and stared at it as though wishing to pierce it with his gaze. Then he said in a dreamy voice, "I don't know. I just feel that. When God is pleased with you, the feeling is indescribable. A warm blanket surrounds your heart on a cold night, a glowing light pulses through your veins, or one of His angels slips into your spirit and embraces it like an old friend. It's indescribable, Muhyi, the feeling of God's satisfaction."

A tear slipped from my eye as I listened to him. He continued: "You imagine that God has not only been pleased with you but has allowed you to feel that satisfaction. Occasionally I am attending to some daily affair, seated while reading letters addressed to the court, walking to buy food from the market, or involved in a conversation with someone in an assembly, and then, suddenly, I will feel I've passed through a waterfall of light, walked beneath it for some seconds, and then have emerged on its far side. I feel as though I see before me the soul's sparkling clean corridors. It's as if I've just been created. I feel that every dream and hope I've ever had has emerged from my soul and ascended to the sky to be pruned, reordered, adjusted, and molded in a purer way before being returned to my chest again. Dreams, Brother, when they sit too long in your chest, spoil. If they remain in your soul year after year, they are distorted by stains, and dirty deposits of egotism, envy, ennui, and despair pile up on top of them. God's satisfaction creates you afresh with a new heart and pure dreams."

"Any love that doesn't cause a lover to prefer
his beloved's will to his own is phony."

— **IBN ARABI**

57

I felt that Zaher and Fakhr al-Nisa' wanted me for Nizam and wanted Nizam for me. So I decided to resolve the matter and offer myself as her suitor. I donned my best clothes and went to Ishaq, who was helping Badr fix the door latch, which we hadn't used since we settled in this house, but now Badr was concerned about raids from the Banu Thaqif.

Ishaq smiled when he saw me all dressed up and asked, "Where are you going, so finely attired?"

"I am visiting Shaykh Zaher."

He studied my face, his mouth half open, as if quickly reviewing some ideas in his mind. Then he said, "It seems I'll soon need to move out of this house!"

I laughed in response. Badr tried but failed to grasp what Ishaq was implying and then returned to his project. I went to the Grand Mosque and circled the Ka'ba while asking God to guide me to marry Nizam if that would be best for us. If the outcome would be evil, I asked Him to unite us, but only after warding off that evil. I took a sip of Zamzam water and held it in my mouth all the way to Zaher's house, not swallowing till I knocked on his door. He was expecting me, because I had told him the previous day that I would visit him at a time when I knew Nizam would be at her aunt's house. He welcomed me with his customary greeting and affectionate smile and then invited me to take a seat beside him. He held my hand in his for a long time.

I finally broached the subject and told him without being asked that Maryam would remain in Bejaïa, since I had no intention of bringing her back to Mecca. I proceeded to enumerate for him my reasons for asking to marry Nizam. I praised extensively her learning and her high character. He continued to listen to what I was saying with a calm smile that did not grow larger or smaller as I proceeded.

Once I finished, his smile grew wider and he scolded me, "Why have you waited so long, Muhyi? If I hadn't known who you are, I would have said you were naïve and didn't understand a hint or a nudge."

I bowed my head with a mixture of embarrassment and joy and, without looking at him, replied, "I was put off only by the dignity of your status, my shaykh."

He patted my shoulder and said, "We cannot find any better husband than you for Nizam, my son, but I will only bind her to what she herself wants. So be patient till I tell her and hear what she thinks."

I left his house soaring over people's heads with delight. I returned to the Grand Mosque and performed seven circuits to thank God. Then I headed to the market to purchase lots of sweets and fruit. Finally I returned home, savoring my rapturous joy and total delight. I considered where to place our bed in the room. I imagined us living in a different house. I visualized a child toddling back and forth between us. I imagined falling asleep and waking to find Nizam in my arms. Whether I stayed put or traveled, she would be my wife. I would write and compose while she read and revised. We would discuss this issue or that. We would differ about this doctrine or that. Love would mix with learning and gnosis with passions—what a fine life!

For two weeks I trod on this cloud of hope without receiving a reply from Nizam or her father. I met her father at Abraham's Maqam, and he spoke to me almost exclusively about lessons and instructional issues. I met Nizam at her aunt's, but her lips did not part to speak except when reading from the books she held. The signs, winks, and hints disappeared. I interpreted all this both optimistically— that she had begun to act as if she were a wife protecting her husband's prestige and status—and pessimistically, that she no longer loved me and rejected my offer. Her aunt's door closed just as soon as the lesson concluded. There was no farewell or goodbye, and I would leave for my house feeling anxious about my status. Was it conceivable that Nizam was having trouble deciding? What could dissuade her from marrying me? Had I neglected to do something before I asked to marry her so confidently?

At noon one day, the lesson ended, and I paused not too far from the door, waiting for her to come out. I followed her on her way to her house. Although she knew I was behind her, she didn't turn in my direction. She entered the last alley, where her house stood at the end. Since no one else was on the street, I moved beside her and observed, "I've been waiting a long time, Nizam."

She didn't turn toward me. She replied calmly and steadily, as if she had prepared for my question: "So what if it's taken a long time?"

"My heart's bubbling with passions, and my troubled spirit keeps me from standing still or sleeping."

"Deep affection purifies the spirit more efficiently than a marriage which is consummated."

"Your love isn't a goal to be obtained, and my love isn't a fire that should be extinguished."

"If your love has reached its perfection, what need do you have to marry me—if there is no room for further advancement?" She turned toward me and said, as she stared fiercely at me, "If it hasn't achieved its perfection, what need have I for an imperfect love."

Her sharp look frightened me, and my voice quavered till it sounded more like weeping than speaking when I replied, "Nizam. My love is older than you or I. It was destined before us and will persist after us. It didn't begin small and grow larger. It hasn't decreased after reaching its completion. It was created perfect and became embedded in my heart with its primordial nature."

When she stopped in front of her door and turned toward me, my heart pounded as our eyes met. Her tender lips moved as she started to say something but didn't. She pressed them together again and shoved the door open with her left hand. When it opened, she grasped my shirt with her left hand, and I entered with her. During a moment when time stopped, our lips met as silently as night meeting first light and dawn meeting morning. She embraced me as one cloud embraces another. She thrust her hand into my beard and up to my ear, which she took in her fingers. I thrust my hand to her neck and down her back between her braids. I felt I was imbibing, from her ruby lips, poetry, exposition, and languages I had never spoken before. I left on her tongue a book of passion I hadn't written yet. A celestial spring erupted from the point where our lips met and began to pour down on us, wetting us so we stuck together even more tightly, till we almost lost our balance more than once. Then she gently freed herself from my embrace, shoved me out of the house, and closed the door.

I returned home dazed, not knowing what I felt. Was it grief or delight? Was I enjoying her kisses or ruing their disappearance? What did she mean when she said that marriage merely fulfils a need and checks a box whereas affection purifies the heart? Did she wish to prolong our love till she was certain of it? Or did she hate becoming a second wife? Or was she put off by my striving to transform something fun into something serious and to turn love into marriage?

I removed my street clothes and sat down on one side of the room, staring at its emptiness like a crazed ecstatic. I lay down and tossed and turned in bed like a sick man. Then I rose and began to prowl through the house like a person stung by a scorpion. Ishaq came and looked at my face the way Abraham looked at the stars. Realizing that I was afflicted, he hugged me to his chest tenderly and rubbed my back as he asked, "What's wrong, Brother?"

My eyes filled with tears, and I told him how things stood with Nizam, without revealing any of her secrets. I communicated with him by means of whispers and touches. How she had winked at me, and I had winked at her. How I had flirted with her, and she had flirted with me. What had transpired between me and Zaher. What had happened a few short hours earlier by the door of her house. The anxiety and burning sensation I felt now. He listened to me intently till I finished and buried my face in my hands, unable to restrain my tears. He squeezed my shoulder with his powerful hand and said with firm tenderness, "May God grant you someone better than her, Muhyi."

"What are you saying, Ishaq? I haven't received her final reply yet."

Ishaq remained silent and did not reply. Suddenly I shook as some crazy fit afflicted me. I seized his shoulders and shook him forcefully as I shouted, "Tell me the truth, Ishaq! Have you seen Nizam and wanted her for yourself?"

"No, my brother."

"Yes, you have. You entreated God for her to reject my offer of marriage, and God has humored you."

"No, by God, Brother. I wouldn't abuse my honor by harming one of God's *walis*."

"Will you swear to that?"

"I swear it to you."

I collapsed to the floor, landing on my knees, and began crying like a little child. He leaned over me to allay my grief and affliction. He helped me to my bed, saying, "Sleep, a little, Muhyi. What you need is rest."

"Me, sleep? What kind of sleep will envelop me, Ishaq, when I'm in this state?"

He looked me straight in the eye and said in a calm voice, "Yes, you will sleep. I entreated God that you would."

"The measure of every man is his heart's discourse."

——**IBN ARABI**

58

Forty years had flowed through my veins like a long caravan that began in Murcia and ended at some murky horizon beyond my ken. On this day I felt they were a drummer whose approaching drumbeats I heard before he finally arrived at my forehead. I woke but didn't move or open my eyelids. I was haunted by this image of my life—one I had glimpsed in the last minutes as I awoke. A caravan! Each camel followed the one before her, bound together by time's halter. One scrawny riding camel and another powerful one. A camel sold and a camel purchased. A camel ridden and a camel left behind. A camel that would complete the journey to its end and a camel that would fall dead and be forgotten. A caravan looted of everything except its weakest beasts of burden and its cheapest merchandise. My caravan was on the verge of disbanding as each year of my life became a short tale without a beginning or an end, without a point or a moral. Devoid of wisdom or hope. Where did you squander your life, Ibn Arabi? Now that you've turned forty—without learning where your feet belong on the earth or where your route to the heavens lies, your chagrin is twofold: regret for a useless life and for a life proceeding aimlessly.

I sat up in bed, and my mind began to turn like penitents circling the Ka'ba, while my heart pounded like someone racing the Sa'y between the two hills. I recited my daily Qur'an passages, rubbed my eyes, and gazed at the floor. The caravan kept moving forward. The number of travelers was increasing, but the route was growing shorter. On the morrow, when there are more wayfarers than the route can accommodate, I will die. My caravan will become nothing but a story. The wind will blow away its traces and erase its tracks. People will say: a caravan passed this way. It will be related that it entered a city where people assembled and paid attention to it. It will be said that it then departed, and people returned to their houses. Some will contend it was lost en route. People who had entrusted cargo to it would express some regrets and then look for another caravan. It will be recounted that it reached its chosen destination but that its contents were plundered. This life, its trajectory, and its loot were obliterated.

I made the acquaintance of a wretched companion named anxiety. I didn't ask him to be my companion, nor did he request my permission. He leapt on my shoulders like a crazed monkey and has never left me since. Whenever I shove him off one shoulder, he leaps to the other. Whenever I push him off both at once, he clings to a tree trunk for a time only to throw himself on my neck again. If he allows me to slumber through a night, he turns the next morning as dark as the bottom of a well. Whenever I enjoy a morning's calm, he makes sunset arrive like a predatory monster that will feast on me all night long. To my eye, the world has shrunk so small that I no longer see anything in its true size. Every evil seems terrifying and frightening, and each blessing transitory and miniscule. In the calm of the night, I tremble at times from excessive anxiety like a feverish invalid without a fever. The morning arrives with me feeling as exhausted as if my eyes hadn't closed all night long.

Worldly affairs seemed of such miniscule importance to me that a day would pass with my doing nothing more than perform the mandatory prayer rituals. Weeks followed weeks while anxiety agitated every tranquil moment and sedated every active aspect of my life, which had turned dark and thorny. I would start on some project only to feel anxious about it and quit. Not having anything to do, I would feel anxious and start some task. I stopped writing *The Meccan Revelation* because I could find nothing to write that didn't repeat old topics. I would grow so restless when teaching students that I wanted to end the lesson as quickly as I could. The pupils would make mistakes I didn't correct. They would ask me questions that I answered tersely. I no longer saw Shaykh Zaher except infrequently between classes or by chance in the Grand Mosque. I informed Fakhr al-Nisa' that I had learned her curriculum and mastered her jurisprudence and would not be attending her private class any longer. She offered a long prayer for me and granted me permission to cite her as an authority.

With no writing I was keen to do to or lessons that excited me, my days became as empty as dry waterskins. I would leave the house only to return. I would pray in the mosque and take a nap. I would walk through the markets and buy something. I would teach in a teaching circle and dismiss the students. I would perform random, pointless tasks. I would write passages at night that made no sense to me the following morning. I would wander down alleys without knowing where I was heading. Something about the location where I found myself didn't agree with my condition. But where should I go? I didn't know where to head nor did I have any pillar to seek. If Mecca were the most likely place for my *watad*, because al-Khayyat had urged me to travel here, even though he hadn't said that in so many words, this was a puzzle! My pillar was but also wasn't in Mecca.

Ishaq stirred in his sleep and coughed. Then he woke. He saw me sitting up and smiled. In his Turkmen accent, he said, "May God make your morning a happy one, Master."

"Good morning to you, Ishaq. Have I disturbed you?"

Standing up and folding his bedding, he replied, "No, Master, but you seem upset."

"Perhaps, Ishaq. I won't hide that from you."

Ishaq went to the water jug and ladled some into a container, which he brought me so I could wash my face. Then he filled the container again and washed his own face. Badr heard us stirring and looked in on us. After greeting us, he began to fix breakfast. Ishaq sat on his folded bedding and looked me straight in the eye. He asked, "What's upsetting you, Muhyi?"

His question dumbfounded me. I said nothing. I started to reflect about something that was upsetting me so I could complain about it to him. I discovered that I hadn't prepared a list of such upsetting things yet. I appeared to be suffering from anxiety that had no cause. Or, I had yet to confront fully what was upsetting me. He didn't interrupt my train of thought, even though I devoted some minutes to it. Finally, I raised my head and told him, "The path."

"What about it?"

"Its directions seem jumbled, and I no longer know which way to head."

"What does your heart tell you?"

"It's not communicating with me."

"Oh yes, it is; it's talking to you. Didn't you awake feeling upset? No doubt your heart was communicating with you, but you haven't been able to interpret what it is saying."

"Who can interpret that?"

"You. Only you."

"Why don't I know how to explain it now?"

"Because there is a veil over your heart. Don't you see that if I muzzle my mouth with my hands and try to speak to you, you won't understand what I say? It's the same for your heart. It wants to speak to you but a coating over it prevents that."

"How can I remove this veil?"

"You've done that twice before, Muhyi. Have you forgotten?"

I looked at him, incredulous, and asked, "When?"

He smiled graciously and stood up. He sat down beside me and placed a hand on my shoulder. Then he said, "I see before me a *wali*, whom God has strengthened with two pillars. God won't send you another *watad* till you purify your heart."

A mixture of perplexity and awe fell over me. I rested my head on his shoulder and said, "You're right. My God, what a fool I am!"

Ishaq laughed and said, "There's some benefit to being foolish. If we weren't foolish occasionally, we would lose the intoxication of vigilance."

Badr served breakfast, and we all shared hot bread and fresh dates. We took turns drinking from a skin filled with milk. Then we all performed our ablutions and went out to perform the dawn prayer. Halfway through the prayer ritual, I felt a twinge. When we concluded the prayer, I looked at Ishaq and said, "Tell me the truth, Ishaq, in this Holy Sanctuary: Are you one of my pillars?"

"No, Master. What am I compared to the noble pillars!"

"But only the pillars recognize others like them."

"You're right. I don't know any pillars, but I know you have pillars. That's all."

Now that the other worshippers had left, there was room for me to sit down, and I did. Then I told him, "My second *watad* died before I found him. Then I met his heir. . . ."

Ishaq's interest showed clearly on his face while he listened to me. So I continued, "But the heir didn't tell me where to seek my third pillar."

"Does this make you anxious?"

"If this hasn't made me anxious, what would, Ishaq?"

"Muhyi, you don't find the pillar. He finds you."

"How can he?"

"Because his mission is to buttress you. Your pillar works harder to find you than you do to find him. He won't discover you till your heart has been purified as completely as possible."

Ishaq lit my path like a candelabra set in a tower to illuminate roads for strangers.

"Any passion that subsides when lovers meet is not reliable."

——**IBN ARABI**

59

Hajj season arrived, and Badr and I performed the pilgrimage, while I asked only that God would purify my heart and clarify my spirit. At the end of the pilgrimage, Ishaq informed me that he would be traveling. I embraced him for a long time in front of the tents of the delegation of pilgrims from Konya and returned to my house with a tear in my eye. This was the same tear I had wept when I said goodbye to al-Kumi and when I buried al-Hassar. I wept with it all the Red Sulphur that turns rusty hearts into lustrous gold. Ishaq had kept me company for almost a year and a half, and during that period he had read me like an open book. If I grieved, he consoled me. When I was bored, he entertained me. He did not miss the opportunity presented by his departure to invite me to go with him to Konya, promising me that I would enjoy a good status there and be a welcome guest. I smiled and said, "Who knows, Ishaq, where my next pillar will cast me."

"I pray to God it will be near us, so we may enjoy your proximity, Muhyi."

The Konyan caravan packed up and left Mecca. More pilgrims departed daily till the city was frighteningly empty. I was sitting with Badr, eating silently, when I suddenly realized I had become a branch from which the leaves had fallen never to sprout again. Only a few months earlier my sojourn in Mecca had seemed abundant and sociable. I had a shaykh, a companion, and a lover. Nizam had filled my heart with love, Ishaq had filled my spirit with hope, and Zaher had filled my intellect with learning. Now they had all deserted me. Nizam had disappeared through her painful breakup, and I no longer knew anything about her. Ishaq had left me for a very distant land where people did not speak my language, nor did I know theirs. Zaher had started treating me like a stranger—not visiting me, praying for me, or inviting me to attend his class.

I started walking Mecca's paths. Everything I encountered in its alleyways, regions, and precincts—a plain, a mountain, a wadi, a desert, plants, animals, the sky, cold or heat—reminded me of Nizam. Then I would write for her what my heart dictated about passion and conceal it in my notebook till I awoke to find that God had breathed a new spirit into her and that she had become a new creature who shared with me a settled life and travel, the search for the right word and finding it, and Nizam's love. As days passed, my poems and I constituted an army of passions that fought only for her love and belonged only to her. While this army formed in my heart, Qatada assembled another army. When my army was fully manned, I allowed Badr to copy it and entrust it to the stationery market. Once Qatada's army was fully staffed, he marched it to Medina to lay siege to that city. My army was full of passions, poems, sorrows, and heartbreak; his army was filled with Bedouin whose loyalty Qatada had purchased, mercenaries he had recruited from pilgrims who had stayed in Mecca after the pilgrimage, and Ayyubid troops who deserted from al-Adil's army after Qatada promised them higher salaries and posts. The drums of these two armies were beaten, and copies of *Tarjuman al-Ashwaq* spread through the stationery market like fire through chaff, while Qatada's army marched out of Mecca. Then a calm, which was redolent of war, settled over Mecca.

I awoke at dawn one day and sat frowning in my room—unable to think straight enough to summon a thought or to consider anything. Whatever I might do this day seemed dull and insipid—except my prayers and dhikr of course. I would have liked to sleep for a long time. I would sleep for centuries like the Sleepers of Ephesus, the people of the cave,[34] and wake to find myself in another world and a new era. I wondered whether I would experience culture shock. Why didn't I long for Andalusia and think of returning there? Did my forty years weigh that heavily on my enthusiasms and destroy my drive? How could that be, since the Prophet was the same age when he was granted the Message and reached his prime? Was my heart incapable of being purified? How could that be true, given that I had already met two pillars. That should show I could purify my heart—not just once or twice but three times. *What do you suppose has happened to you, Ibn Arabi? Why are you worried when there is nothing to worry about? Why are you sorrowful but lack any sorrows? You brood, but there's nothing in your mind to brood about? You're in pain, although every part of you is sound and healthy?*

What if I traveled a little to refresh myself? But wouldn't wandering around the world aimlessly be an indulgence? What if my travels sullied my heart and put more distance between me and my pillar? But is remaining in Mecca in my current state any better than that? What if love for Nizam overwhelmed and killed me? What if my unveilings dwindled and my charismatic gift vanished? This thought—and its opposite—overwhelmed me while I was still in bed, wrapped in my blanket. I thought to myself: *What if I call Badr now? If he answers, we'll travel. If he doesn't, that will be a sign from God to stay here.* I cleared my throat to prepare to call him, but he knocked on the door before I could. I laughed, and that surprised him.

"Why are you laughing, Master?"

I didn't answer and did not know how to respond. I sat up and gazed at his face, which still looked quizzical.

I finally told him, "I laughed because you have become part of my heart. You are my resolve, Badr."

"Your resolve?"

"Yes. And you have resolved that we should travel. What do you think?"

"Where?"

"You choose, and we'll head there."

Badr thought a little and then said, "Damascus."

"Any love that comes with a request is unreliable."

———IBN ARABI

60

We decided to leave in a Syrian caravan a week later. I visited Zaher in his house after the Friday prayer to say goodbye. I found he kept his head bowed most of the time and barely spoke. His broad smile had disappeared along with his jovial expression. These were replaced by a wrinkled brow and heavy eyelids, as a grimace of sorrow veiled his lovely face. I was sorry to see him like this and waited till the rest of his visitors left to approach him and sit at his feet.

Then I asked, "What ails you, my Shaykh?"

He sighed and was silent so long I thought he wouldn't reply. Then, without looking at my face, he said, "My time has come, my son."

He added softly, so no one else in the house would hear, "I fear for what will happen to Nizam, since she has no one but me."

I nodded sadly and offered no comment. For a moment I wanted to say that I would have been her family, her mainstay, and her husband, but that she had rejected me. He, however, spoke first in a quavering voice, as if he were about to start weeping: "I would have died with my mind at rest if I had conveyed her to your home and made her your wife. But she refused. When her mother died, leaving her as a little orphan girl, I vowed that I would never force her to do anything she disliked. It would be hard enough for a girl to grow up an orphan let alone have a stern, harsh father."

"Nizam will marry someone worthy of her and better than me, God willing!"

He struck his thighs with his hands and spoke in a louder voice, as if my statement had touched a nerve inside him, "When? Do you think you were the first man to ask for her hand? You were her tenth suitor, my boy! I don't know what this girl is thinking."

Suddenly Nizam's voice reached us from inside the house. She told her father, "Daddy, I have burdened this man with more than he can bear. I have weighed him down with things of no concern to him. . . ."

Then her father shouted at her: "No, it is his concern. Didn't he offer to marry you?"

I felt embarrassed by this situation. So I rose, preparing to leave. Nizam continued to address her father, but in Farsi, which I didn't understand, while her father kept his head bowed in silence. I kissed his head and said goodbye in a louder voice so Nizam would realize that I was about to depart. Then I asked the shaykh if he would offer me any parting advice before I set off on a voyage—so Nizam would know I was traveling. As I left their house, I felt an unforeseen solace inside me. Nizam was averse to marrying anyone. I wasn't the only man she had rejected. She was no doubt determined to pursue learning, and nothing else. But why then had she proclaimed her love to me and filled me with hope and expectation? My God, how difficult it is at times to understand women, especially those of such a rare caliber as Nizam!

We set off for Damascus in the Syrian caravan. When we reached Yanbu', we received news that Qatada had been defeated and repulsed from Medina, after that city's emir had routed him at its outskirts and counterattacked Qatada, laying siege to Mecca itself, before retreating. I did not favor either emir but grieved about their combat over these two holy cities, as if they weren't sacred sanctuary cities. Instead, blood had been spilled at their walls and they had been besieged, causing their residents to go hungry and blocking visitors and pilgrims from entering them. I gave thanks to God that I had left before I witnessed this myself. The image I preserved of Mecca, where I had spent my four previous years, remained pristine and untarnished. Safe and peaceful. God's city, which had filled my intellect with light, my heart with love, and my spirit with tranquility and gnosis. Then this city had sent me out through the world to spread my insights and my cares, my arts and my sorrows. Mecca had been necessary. There was no alternative to Mecca for me. Everything a person experiences in life is necessary for him. Every concern is essential. Every event is of pressing importance. Every matter we experience—joy or grief, peace or war, love or hatred—is one of our breaths, and we would have suffocated had we not gone through it. We would have vanished and returned to nonexistence.

"Pain disappears when its cause disappears . . . or lingers."

—— **IBN ARABI**

61

As our southern caravan approached Damascus, winds brought us breezes from its Ghouta—its agricultural zone—laden with the fragrance of peach, plum, and almond blossoms. The caravan's grooms reclaimed our two riding camels before we entered the city on foot, carrying our few belongings: a bag of books and two sacks of clothes. Porters and servants from the hostelries approached us, offering their services. We chose one, and he carried all our luggage in a large pack on his back, walking bent over. I proceeded like an invalid whose health was slowly returning to him. The city's smells, sounds, images, and people blended together like a compassionate hand that wiped fatigue from my forehead and touched my heart, calming it. Everything we passed once we entered the city gate—whether it was a market, a house, a garden, or a caravanseray—suggested a pledge Damascus made to be the best resort for tired foreigners whose hearts had been abraded by love once or twice.

The porter brought us to a hostelry with a beautiful entrance. Its rooms were furnished with wool carpets, which I was at first reluctant to step on. We left our belongings there and went out to look for a bath house. Every man we consulted pointed us in a different direction. We finally located one of the city's hundred public baths, and I washed thoroughly as if afraid I weren't worthy of Damascus. I asked the bath attendant to cut my hair, trim my beard, and clip my nails. Then I waited in one of the guestrooms attached to the baths while they washed my clothes and stretched my turban. By the time we left the bathhouse, the city had shaken the fatigue of the trip from us and swept the pains from my back and feet. We toured the neighborhoods closest to the city wall where the houses were larger, and each had a garden or orchard. Most had central courtyards with fountains into which water flowed from little cascades fed by the river. Set in the walls were finely carved alcoves. The mosques' minarets were carefully chiseled, and their wooden doors were decorated on both the outside and inside. They also had marble doorsteps, and their doorknobs were made of burnished metal.

After a little ramble, we ended up at the Great Mosque. We performed the afternoon prayer there and then toured its teaching circles. We would pause near each one and listen to the voices of the pupils to learn what book they were reading and which doctrine they were studying. When some of these circles finished for the day and the students dispersed, Badr spoke with some who told him about other mosques and religious establishments where Sufi circles met. Soon a few students from the Maghribi zawiya gathered around us, and some even started to stroke the sleeves of my tunic and ask whether I intended to begin giving lessons in Damascus. At sunset we were suddenly overcome with fatigue and returned to the khan, where we found its proprietors had spread out our bedding, covered it with a cotton blanket, and topped that with silk-covered pillows.

Badr ran his hand over his pillow in amazement and said, "I've never slept on a pillow this soft!"

"Damascus will spoil you, Badr."

Some days later, when we rose, we found a messenger from the Chief Justice at the door of the hostelry. When I went out to greet him, he asked, "Are you Shaykh Muhyi al-Din Ibn Arabi?"

"Yes."

"The Chief Justice, Zaki ibn al-Zaki, requests your permission to visit you this afternoon."

"He is most welcome."

I returned to Badr. We were both amazed that Ibn Zaki knew we were here.

"No doubt it was because of my discussion with the pupils in the Great Mosque," Badr suggested.

"How do they know me?"

"Know you? *The Interpreter of Desires* is on sale in the stationers' market, Master."

Zaki ibn al-Zaki arrived at the appointed time. He was my age and spoke with a beautiful eloquence. He dismounted and, as soon as he saw me, he kissed my head and took us both to his house. He summoned his young children and lined them up to greet me. One was a girl the age my daughter Zaynab would have been. I felt a pang of remorse in my heart when I reflected that I had turned forty and had no offspring. I picked her up, sat her on my lap, and began to run my fingers through her soft chestnut-colored hair. She remained silent and dubious, embarrassed and fearful. She looked at her father anxiously without moving. She soon stood up and disappeared inside the house, which reminded me of those in Seville. The vast courtyard contained a fountain, gleaming wooden seats, and shrubs among which you sat—as if they were members of the family.

As he brought platters of food to us, the Judge asked, "Which school will you illumine with your light and insight, Master?"

"I won't decide that till I tour some of them."

"I think the Taqawiya Madrasa is the largest and nearest. We'll provide you with lodging and living expenses from its trusts."

"I will visit it tomorrow. If I choose it, we'll live in its hostel, its khanqah. Don't provide us with a residence because we don't know when we will depart. We don't want to receive a gift we cannot repay."

The Taqawiya School was the most appropriate. Its courtyard was vast and large enough for all the pupils. It also contained large rooms that were suitable for instruction on cold days. The class began with many students. I recovered my desire to teach and resumed writing. My soul calmed down gradually, and I was as well regarded in Damascus as I had been in Fez. Both these cities make you feel at home as soon as you enter their gates. No one visits them without feeling they are his homeland. I passed my days with the tranquility and contentment I sorely needed. The sun beamed down day after day, and I felt hopeful and happy. I found in the khanqah good fellowship that nourished me. We spent nights in dhikr and mindful wakefulness, and mornings in lessons and learning. Books traveled from room to room, and our Sufi cloaks passed from back to back. The entire Sufi house was animated by divine love's effusions, which bathed our spirits, leaving nothing more to wish for.

"You are safe from everything when everything is safe from you."

—**IBN ARABI**

62

In such circumstances a year passed swiftly. Then the Syrian pilgrimage caravan returned from Mecca and entered Damascus. A traveler left that caravan and started searching for me in the city's Sufi khanqahs and schools. When he finally stood before me, he handed me a letter enclosed between two other sheets of paper. On opening it, I found it was from Zaher.

You should understand that I have already forgiven you even before blaming you and pardoned you before criticizing you. But I must share with you our circumstances after you left chaff ready to burst into flames. You bequeathed to us injury and harm, because in Mecca no one talks about anything besides your *Interpreter of Passions*. People have repeated statements—allegedly from you— that if you said them you would surely have spat them out and if you heard them you would have been incredulous. They have assaulted me with a pinch and my daughter with a wink. Remaining in Mecca has become unthinkable, because no place marred by accusations of a love affair and amatory verse is safe. We are forced to travel to a land where no one harms us and only the Unique One knows us. I assume, my son, since you are judicious and bright, that you weren't aware of the impact of what you were writing, especially since you mentioned her by name. As if that were not enough, you left a copy of your work in the stationers' market before you departed. By God, I ask Him to forgive you for what you have done and to protect us in our calamity.

I folded this letter and unconsciously placed my hand on my breast, assuming that my hand would be tinged with blood when I lifted it, because of this cruel thrust of fate, and that it would be singed around the edges by this fire, which I had no idea who had lit. Badr looked at me and saw my face lose its color and my lips start to tremble. He began asking questions I did not answer. He spoke, and I did not hear. He waved his hand before my eyes, but I did not see. Finally he took it upon himself to dismiss the students and announce the end of the lesson. He helped me stand up, and I walked with him to my room: drained of color and with a dry throat. An upset stomach. Trembling limbs. Unfocused eyes. He sat me down on my bed, removed my sandals and my turban, wrapped me in my mantle, and reached out his hand to grasp mine. Time stopped for a moment, and silence prevailed.

"What did the letter say, Master?"

"Read it."

Badr read it twice. Then he stood up and tossed the letter, which hit the wall and fell to the floor. He screamed loudly: "May God and all the angels curse them! May they suffer from His wrath, hatred, and scorn!"

Badr kept screaming while I trembled beneath my mantle. He finally fell to his knees, approached my face, and said in a thunderous voice, "Pay no attention to them, Master. They don't know any better."

"I have published love poems about Nizam!"

"No, by God. What your hand penned was nothing but chaste, virtuous poetry, Master."

"People wink knowingly at her on the streets, Badr!"

"People are ignorant rabble. They are responsible for how they construe what they read and how they interpret what they recite."

"The two of them will leave Mecca, fleeing from disgrace, and I'm to blame, Badr."

"Didn't you tell us, Master, that God is the Cause of all causes?"

The first tear fell from my eye, and Badr quickly wiped it away with his sturdy, dry fingers, as if forbidding me to weep. He shouted loudly by my ear: "Don't blame yourself, Master. You're not the first person to write poetry nor will you be the last. I beg you, Master, I beg you. Anyone with a mind understands what you wrote and is conscious of what you intended. The only people blaming you are riffraff and ignoramuses. They have never ceased to fault you a single day. Why should you heed them now?"

"Don't leave me, Badr. Give me your hand."

63 **ISTANBUL** 1617 CE / 1026 AH

I must ride from my house to the palace faster than it takes the Sultan to walk from his Divan to the Library. This is impossible. But the impossibility of this feat is not a reasonable excuse to use with sultans in their right minds, let alone crazy ones. I manage to avoid striking pedestrians in Istanbul's crowded streets as I ride, while clutching the brimless hat on my head to keep the wind from blowing it away and reflecting that this may be the last time I follow this route from my house to the palace. My fate will probably resemble that of my friends. Two months have passed since the Sultan ascended the throne, and during this time the man has considered any slip on the part of his employees a personal insult and a massive demonstration of contempt for his reign. For this reason, the punishments have been absurdly harsh and as crazy as the sultan who ordered them. Palace officials have been falling like autumn leaves tossed by heavy winds. Zadat Effendi, who was responsible for the Sultan's dinner table, received a tremendous slap, because the serving of soup was less than he desired. Yunus Effendi, who was responsible for the Sultan's signatures, lost his job because the signature he created for the new sultan was less grand than that of Sultan Ahmed, may God rest his soul. Oghlu Effendi—oh! How sorry I felt for you, my friend Oghlu! Thirty-two years in service of the palace did not spare him from being thrown out by the aghas, not because he neglected his work—Oghlu didn't know what "neglect" means—but because the Sultan remembered he hadn't included him at the royal iftar table. Did this

Sultan think Oghlu had the authority to remove him from imprisonment and seat him at the iftar table of the Sultan who had imprisoned him?

If I do not reach the palace in the next few minutes, I shall definitely join the list of those falling leaves. The truth of the matter, in fact, is that even if I arrive before the Sultan, that won't mean I'm safe. I have no idea what brings someone like him to the library. I wager he cannot read a single verse of the Qur'an without making mistakes. I bet he doesn't know how to write his full name, which includes those of his ancestors back to Ertuğrul the Great. What does he want then? Will he pretend to spend a long time in the library like his predecessor Sultan Ahmed? How different that brilliant, scholarly poet was from this deranged fellow, who can't walk in a straight line without swaying, while his hands make sudden nervous gestures that scare people!

I finally arrive. I push through the narrow gap without waiting for the gateman to open the door all the way. I sprint to the library and enter to find the space calm and empty; the librarians are performing their work as usual. I give thanks to God that the Sultan hasn't arrived yet. If my friends in the ministries through which he passed have been able to delay him, I will remain indebted to them for many days to come. I explore the library's galleries to make sure there is nothing to trigger his annoyance or upset him. Everything seems to be in order. The Turkish, Arabic, and Persian books are in the western section, and the Greek, Latin, Armenian, Hebrew, and Syriac ones in the eastern one. The wing containing sacred tomes is by the library entrance, and they are surrounded by guards. Everything is shipshape. Up till now, there has been nothing to worry about.

I sit in the chair to collect my breath and wipe drops of sweat from my brow. I straighten my brimless hat on my head and wrap my turban around it carefully. I start to crack my fingers nervously as if preparing for battle. Finally, the commotion becomes audible.

Looking out the window, I see the crowd approaching. I know now they will soon be here. I call to each of my library employees in turn and find that each is at his post. Then I take deep breaths to calm myself. One of the docents looks through the door and signals to me that the Sultan is about to enter. So I stand for a few moments that feel like an eternity till his lean, pale face appears, followed by aghas and bodyguards. I rush to kiss his hand with its thin fingers and long nails. It feels cold and dry to the touch. He begins to walk through the galleries of the library followed by the Grand Vizier, the Accountant General, and the Chief Sergeant. After only three minutes, he leaves!

I return to my chair, sit down, and inhale air redolent of the rose cologne his cloak diffused. I chide myself a little about my exaggerated dread of his reaction. He appeared calm and silent, even though his eyes kept swaying around in their sockets and didn't focus on anything. He did not comment during his brief tour of the library, while his Grand Vizier discussed matters unrelated to the library with the Sultan, who did not look at him. No one knew whether the Sultan was really listening or had sunken into his private speculations, because the Sultan offered no sign of consent or disagreement. He didn't murmur or grumble. He remained as silent as a statue walking on two feet.

I complete my day performing many of my customary tasks: sorting new acquisitions, following up on the restoration of manuscripts, having them copied, scheduling the translators' hours, arranging the entry of saintly men into the wing containing sacred tomes. Minutes pass quickly until it is time for me to leave. I take down my cane and head out. Before I pass through the portal, I meet Khalil Pasha the Chancellor, entering it. The moment he sees me he cries out: "Osman Effendi, thank God you haven't left yet! I was going to summon you from your house."

"At your disposal, Khalil Pasha."

"The Sultan has issued an order regarding this library."

"What is it?"

"The library must be vacated by the beginning of next month."

"What? Where will we take the library?"

"We'll move it somewhere else. The Sultan wants to add this area to the Vizier's Assembly Chamber."

"But there's no other space in the Palace large enough to hold the contents of this library!"

"Distribute them to several different locations then. Retain in the Palace only important books the Sultan might read!"

I want to say, "In that case, there's no need to keep even a single book here!" I realize, though, how painful impalement would be. Khalil Pasha leaves, and I hang my cane back where it had been, abandoning the idea of departing. I proceed to tour the place, feeling at a loss, not knowing what to do. Where will I take the thousands of books in two weeks? Suddenly I rush after him before he is out of sight and ask, "What about the sacred tomes, the bequests, Khalil Pasha?"

He thinks a little and scratches his forehead before he replies, "Put them all in one room. They don't need an entire wing!"

I return to the library angry and sad. Only walis and dervishes care about the sacred tomes! Bravo, by God! We'll cram the entire collection pertaining to the Prophet into one cramped room and vacate an entire wing for the Vizier's assemblies, which occur only once a month.

There's no time now for anger or grief. Time is short. I have just two weeks to remove thousands of books and manuscripts while searching for a new location for them. I summon the employees and inform them of the new orders. Some gaze at each other in disbelief. Then their expressions turn to irritation when I tell them that no one will leave the library before sunset. They became fearful when I informed them that anyone who isn't back here by sunrise might as well not come, because he will be fired!

The library gradually begins to empty out by the middle of the second week. I find a large storeroom in the cellar of the palace and stuff in it all the Latin, Greek, and Armenian books and the rest of those in languages the Sultan doesn't speak and therefore won't request. I divide the books in Arabic and Turkish—which fill half the library—according to their subject matter. Books about medicine and the natural sciences I transfer to Istanbul's secondary schools and hospitals. I send two carts full of history books and biographies of important figures to the Sultan Ahmed Mosque, which has just been completed and thus has a library but no books. I direct a librarian to start working immediately at the mosque every day and to check out books to scholars and students for their own use and to copy. I send all the Turkish, Arabic, and Persian poetry books, which the Sultan's wives request, to the Eunuch in charge of the harem, for him to divvy up among them. The geography books I divide between the Sultan's residences in Bursa and Edirne, where they are most in demand by the Grand Vizier's functionaries. For all the Sufi books I can think of no better place than the tomb of Maulana Jalal al-Din Rumi, may God sanctify him, in Konya.

I am so consumed by the library's affairs that I start sleeping here during the final days. I blot out everything happening outside and focus only on emptying it completely during the allotted time to keep myself from being terminated. Finally, the library is cleared of books and has become a vast open space waiting for new furniture. It is so empty that sounds reverberate sharply. Torn scraps of paper and strings littering the floor are swept around by winds infiltrating the windows. I contemplate the area where I have spent nine whole years and where I know the place every book belongs. Now it has been reduced to this state! Tears form in my eyes. I lock the doors and leave the place for the first time in six days. Then I find the palace's news waiting for me in the effendis' lounge.

"Bairam Pasha, what are you saying?"

"Amazing! Haven't you heard? Where have you been?"

"Don't ask about that now. Is this true?"

"Osman Effendi, the news is shouted in the streets: Shaykh al-Islam Zakariya Zadeh has issued a fatwa removing Sultan Mustafa from office."

"Who is our Sultan now?"

TOME EIGHT

"One can wander through a wilderness endlessly."

——IBN ARABI

64

Badr placed a ream of paper before me and started to untie its cords. I took the five reeds he had brought me the previous day and lined them up beside each other so I could judge how straight they were and pick the ones best suited for the text and those that would be more appropriate for marginal comments. I dipped each in turn in the inkwell and started trying them out on an old sheet of paper. I chose three and returned two to Badr, asking him to work on their side bevel.

Badr asked, "Are you finally going to finish writing *al-Fath al-Makkiy?*"

"No, this is a new book."

"May God open the way for you, Master. What will you write about?"

"*Tarjuman al-Ashwaq.*"

"What!"

"Yes, Badr. I am going to explain *The Interpreter of Desires.* People think the poems I wrote were merely love poetry written to court Nizam. They haven't understood the book consists of signs and metaphors for divine inrushes, spiritual descents, and lofty interrelationships."

"Do you think this will extinguish the conflagration or fuel it?"

"It will clarify my goal and clear my conscience."

"May God assist you, Master. What will you call it?"

"*Dhakha'ir al-A'laq fi Sharh Tarjuman al-Ashwaq*: 'Precious Treasures Explaining *The Interpreter of Desires.*'"

I finished writing this book in nine days during which I never left my room. I canceled my classes and devoted myself to writing. Once I had finished, I told Badr to hire a group of scribes who wrote in different scripts: Meccan, Maghribi, Egyptian, and Syrian. He brought four copyists to the khanqah, and I reserved a large room for them and placed in their hands reams of excellent paper and expensive inks. I commissioned each of them to produce five copies of the book. As soon as they had finished those, Badr put them in two saddle bags, conveyed them on his mule to the caravan depot, and chose some of my pupils to carry one copy each to Mecca, Aleppo, Baghdad, and Cairo. The person who traveled to Alexandria took two copies and was charged with finding someone there to take one of them to Fez and the other to Cordoba. In each copy I placed a certificate authorizing anyone who received a copy to have the book copied at no charge, in any style of calligraphy or language he wanted.

I don't know whether this sufficed to atone for my sin, but I had not stopped trembling like a blind cat till I had made this decision. Now, even as those copies have traveled all over the world, I don't know whether a copy will reach the hands of Zaher or Nizam. I don't know where they have gone. Whenever I close my eyes to sleep, what I see are the Great Shaykh and his daughter leaving Mecca in a sorry state, wandering the earth in search of a safe refuge where people won't harm them. I don't know what Nizam thinks even now, but she heard me recite some of the poems from that collection and knew I was turning them into a book. She never objected. As for Zaher, the blow came without any warning; he honored me, and I humiliated him. He treated me well, and I mistreated him. He opened his house and his sister's house to me, and then I flirted with his daughter and destroyed her reputation.

I felt ill at ease in Damascus and considered traveling. Nothing diverted me from my cares or lightened my sorrows like travel. I did not realize that my spontaneous decision to travel would open a wilderness before me in which I would wander for three years while Badr and I roamed aimlessly through God's land. We left Damascus for Aleppo, Hama, Mosul, Edessa, and Mardin and then returned to Damascus, only to leave it again. I would judge a city by my first weeks in it, for it would either extend a hand to settle my heart and calm my fear, so that I stayed there for months—or to make my heart apprehensive and fill my soul with dread, so I left it just as soon as we had recuperated from the fatigue of our travel. Whenever

I settled in a land, I hastened to meet God's friends there. If they did not already know me, I would introduce myself. Then I would either learn from them or they from me. Whenever one of them gazed at my face for a long time, my yearning heart palpitated in hopes that he was my pillar. But he wasn't. They would share my grief then without knowing why I grieved. The sorrows of God's friends are communicated by them, moving from one heart to the next, like water transported from the river by canals.

I felt anxious that Damascus might have expelled my *watad* from my heart and driven him from me. Badr helped me with everything till he seemed to be part of me. If I suffered some pain, he felt it without me complaining. When I was happy, he was happy with me, even before I shared the reason with him. I never wrote a book that he didn't seize from me like a drop of heavenly water landing on the surface of the earth. He would ask me what was in it, alerting me to what was hard to understand. Then I would provide more explanation according to his wishes. When I finished it, he would take it from me as if receiving a newborn baby from the hand of a midwife and rush to copyists to have three copies made. He would bring me a copy, keep one for himself, and the third he would leave with the copyists to produce more copies for anyone who wanted it. God uncannily decreed that we should be together. My love drew him nearer to God, and his love blessed me. Badr al-Habashi was my kith and a blessing. He never raised doubts throughout our many travels and never grumbled even once, although he was getting on in years.

I never counted the days I spent in any city, and I don't think Badr did, either. We started to reckon elapsed time by the number of different months of Ramadan. We fasted one Ramadan in Aleppo and another while visiting Jerusalem and Hebron. There was a third Ramadan in Mosul. We lived in Sufi houses when we found them, as we did in Mayyafaraqin (Silvan) and Mosul, or in mosques' hostels for students and shaykhs when they had room for us—as we did in Homs and Hama. At other times, news of our stay in a city quickly reached the ears of its governors and emirs. Those who loved God's friends would provide a house for us to live in and send us a stipend—as happened in Aleppo and Mardin.

With Badr I completed three circuits of the cities of Syria and Iraq. I was going to continue touring till God seized my spirit or I found my pillar, but God sent me a sign when I was in Aleppo. I went to the mosque only to find a gang of men blocking its door. I tried to slip around them, but they prevented me from entering, pushing me away with their chests without saying a word. I asked them why they were doing this, but no one replied. They just kept standing there, allowing anyone but me to enter the mosque. I sat down on the ground to watch them, as they watched me. Then I remembered Ibn Rushd and the day he told the Almohad Caliph in Marrakech about the mob that had prevented him from entering the mosque in his place of exile in Lucena. I felt alarmed. Was this to be my fate?

I returned to the house, where I found Badr surprised that I had returned so quickly. I told him what had happened and asked him to go to the mosque to investigate the reason. An hour later he returned with an angry look on his face and started to mutter curses under his breath.

"What's the matter, Badr?"

"It's *The Interpreter of Desires*, Master!"

"What about it?"

"They say: Down with a shaykh who writes love poems for courtesans."

"All power and strength are God's alone!"

"We're going to the governor tomorrow to complain about them."

"No, we're going to the market tomorrow to buy supplies for a trip."

"You're going to leave on account of dunces like them?"

"They're a sign that we should travel, Badr."

"Where will we go this time, Master?"

"I miss al-Hariri and al-Khayyat. We'll travel to Cairo."

"What fault of mine is it, if I said what I believe?
Let the ignoramus assume that truth is his enemy."

—IBN ARABI

65

When I left Aleppo to avoid a confrontation with the fools and their dreams I supposed that I had left them behind me; but I found them waiting for me. I had thought I would spend a spiritual time with al-Khayyat and al-Hariri in the Candelabra Khanqah, imbibing divine graces, higher learning, and sacred secrets—only to find myself combatting people who had neither a sword nor a banner. That was what happened. At al-Azhar, where my students invited me to teach, a genuinely hostile incident occurred. Students formed a circle around me, week after week, until the area could no longer accommodate all of them. So I moved with them to a larger one. Then we were forced to move again. Finally we ended up sitting in the shadow of the pulpit where the largest classes were conducted.

On a day determined by God I was sitting in my class when, from the outer rows, a man, who wore a dangling yellow turban and a shabby cloak and held a basket of dates beneath his arm, shouted: "Andalusian! You claim God unveils to you what He does not unveil to us, even though we pray and fast like you do!"

My students all turned to look at him at the same time. Then everyone looked at once in a different direction when a brown-complexioned man with a Nubian accent stood up and shouted: "Why do you think you're the only one from his Ummah to be an heir of the Prophet? You're not from the Quraysh tribe nor are you a descendant of the Prophet."

After a brief silence, pandemonium broke out. Once he had set his basket of dates on the ground, the first man shouted again, waving his finger at me: "Do you really say *wali*s are better than prophets?"

The students' necks swiveled again till they were looking at me. I could tell they were influenced by what they had heard. Some began to address each other, and their voices became louder. It seemed to me that the two men had agreed in advance about what each would say, even though they sat at a distance from each other. Badr looked at me as if to urge me to speak up and clarify what people found confusing before their ruckus became too loud. I felt slightly dizzy. I cleared my throat and the clamor died down a little. I raised my hand to invite the man with the basket to step forward. Students made way for him to pass, and I gestured for him to sit down in the front row, to my right. Then I signaled to the brown-complexioned man, and he sat down where he was—apparently not wishing to come any closer. Before I started speaking, a young man with a short beard and eyebrows that met in the middle popped up and turned his back to me. He began to address the congregation directly: "Brothers, God has blessed us in Cairo by making it a rich depository of scholars and a magnet for the inquisitive. From the time God illuminated this city with Islam's dazzling light until today, each of God's legitimate doctrines has had a shaykh among us."

Then, turning halfway toward me and pointing a finger, he said, "But God has also tested us with the vilest actors. Do you know who they are? The Qur'an gives you the answer, brothers: 'Those whose efforts in this physical world have gone awry while they reckon that they are doing good deeds.'"[35]

Some of my students grumbled to protest his insult, which was directed at me, and he raised his voice to drown out theirs, till he was almost shouting: "Whence have come the Companions of the Prophet, the scholars, and the descendants of the Prophet whose graves are in the City of the Dead? From the East, where the two Holy Shrines are located. Whence came the Fatimids who cursed the Companions of the Prophet and who claimed to be mahdis? From the West!"

Some students raised their voices to protest. Then others cried out: "Allahu Akbar" for no apparent reason. I glanced around at the faces and realized for the first time that I had never seen some of these fellows before. I felt that this confrontation had been planned in advance. Badr took my arm as the row grew louder and the commotion tenser.

A voice cried out from the rear, "This isn't a rule. There are true scholars and freethinkers in every area of the earth."

"No, he spoke the truth. We and our sons were fine until these Maghribis came to us."

Finally, Badr the Ethiopian decided to take control of the situation. He stood up and shouted at them, "Folks, listen to the Shaykh's responses to your questions. Listen. . . ."

After his appeal, some students rose and repeated what he had said. Some of them moved around shushing those who were speaking out of turn, one by one, until silence was quickly restored. The faces of all those I knew and didn't know turned toward me.

I said in a soft voice, "Our brother sitting here called me an Andalusian. I was born and raised in Andalusia, but as everyone knows I am a Hatimi and a Ta'iy, and Ta'y, as our brother who was there knows, is in the East."

I gestured with my hand toward the young man, who turned his face so our eyes would not meet. Then I continued, "My good people, I am a simple servant of God. I seek no advantage over other worshippers. To the contrary, I hope that every scholar will have the same footing at the highest levels. There are no spatial limits in the stages of learning and self-improvement. . . ."

The man with the basket interrupted: "But you say you are the Seal of God's *walis* and the heir of the prophets. What could be above that?"

I placed my hand on his hand to placate him and replied, "This is God's gift, which I will not reject. He granted me this to encourage me to help people."

The man knit his eyebrows and stuck his lip out aggressively. I directed my words to the crowd: "How did Moses become a prophet, brethren? Who will tell me?"

One of the boys in the front row responded, "When he saw fire beside Mount Sinai."

"May God bless you. What did he say after that?"

"He told his family: Wait; 'I perceived a fire, perhaps I'll bring you a firebrand from it.'"[36]

"He strove to help his family and returned a prophet. What about Khidir? Who can tell me about him?"

Silence prevailed, and no one responded. So I turned to Badr, whom I had taught this. He grasped my reference and answered: "He strove to find water for his people, and the 'water of life' came to him. Then he drank from it and God made him immortal."

"Bravo! My brethren, I bring you from Aleppo a statement I heard from its king, al-Zahir Ghazi. With God as my witness, I raised in one of his assemblies a hundred and eighteen requests from the people, and he granted all of them."

My attempt to shift the direction of the conversation failed. The young man with the conjoined eyebrows stood up again and addressed me this time: "Believer! Those were Moses and Khidir. They were prophets of God and companions of the angels. You're a Maliki jurisprudent from Andalusia and attend the assemblies of sultans. You draw your influence from their influence and your power from their power. Fear God!"

Then a man who had not spoken before stood up in the middle of the crowd. He grasped the sleeve of the young man with the conjoined eyebrows to get his attention and told him, "No, he's done something far more atrocious. He says that God and his creatures are one."

The youth listened to the man and then raised his hands high as if he had just won something precious. In a loud voice he said: "Did you all hear that? God is far more exalted than what they describe. What comparison is there between God Almighty on His majestic throne and us poor sinners?"

Then he softened his tone and lowered his voice to address the seated students: "Get up, Darlings, and leave this man before he spoils your religion. If you want to acquire beneficial knowledge you should go to madrasas, not to Sufi houses. You will reap benefits, lodgings, and useful knowledge there. Rise. . . ."

A group of students did rise, dragging their feet, and the crowd's eyes followed them. The basket-man picked up his basket, glanced at me askance, and left.

"When I focused on research and verification,
They left me without a human friend."

—IBN ARABI

66

During the next two days I resumed teaching without any fuss or commotion. Then on the third day, when I left the khanqah for the mosque, I found men wearing police uniforms waiting for me at the entrance to the mosque. I approached them, and they asked me to accompany them somewhere, without specifying where. I told them my class was about to begin, but they led me away. One of them pulled on my shoulder and another shoved me from behind. I stumbled when I was pushed and almost fell. Badr became excited and ran behind us yelling, "This is the Grand Shaykh! This is the Red Sulphur!" Hariri was much calmer and tried to speak politely and solicitously with the police, asking them to explain their reason for leading me away. He wondered aloud if they knew what they were doing. But none of them would grant him a satisfactory answer. I allowed those two policemen to lead me and finally found myself in a cramped stone cell in Cairo's prison.

I shared this cell with six other men, one of whom kept going from one prisoner to another to ask about everything. He was relieving his distress at being subjected to interrogation by hearing the stories of the others. As soon as I entered and sat down in an empty spot, he brought me a dirty cushion to sit on. Then he sat down beside me, gazing at my clean clothes and large turban.

He commented, "By God, you're not a typical prisoner. Who are you?"

"Now I have become one. What's the difference?"

"Your accent isn't Egyptian. Where are you from?"

"Andalusia."

The mention of Andalusia excited the interest of another prisoner who was playing with pebbles. In a hoarse voice he said, "Welcome, welcome, Cousin."

I turned toward him, but he did not raise his head and continued playing with the pebbles. "Are you from Andalusia?" I asked him.

"From Mallorca."

"What brought you to Cairo?"

The first prisoner laughed and replied for him: "He fled the swords of the Almohads."

The second prisoner threw a small stone at him, hitting him on the arm, and said, "If you don't keep quiet about such things, I'll draw my sword on you."

Two other prisoners laughed. I bowed my head, embarrassed by his words. Then he addressed me: "Which of Andalusia's cities do you come from?"

"Seville; but I left it years ago; so don't ask me about it."

"I've never visited it. I used to work on a boat that carried cargo to Valencia."

"What about you upset the Almohads?"

"They suspect all the Mallorcans of being linked to the Banu Ghaniya."

"That's not true. I was in Marrakech when the Almohads were at war with the Banu Ghaniya and associated with people from Mallorca who were safe and secure so long as they didn't raise their weapons."

The man laughed dismissively and said, "But I was armed! Anyone who joined the Banu Ghaniya received ten dirhems a day and a couple pounds of flour a month."

Then he returned to fooling around with his pebbles, as if he didn't wish to continue our conversation. The first prisoner seized the opportunity and began to introduce our cellmates to me: "This fellow is from Upper Egypt. Those two are from Cairo. That man is Greek and doesn't speak Arabic."

The Sa'idi waved his hand to greet me and smiled. The two Cairenes looked at me expressionlessly. Then the first prisoner asked: "Why are you in prison?"

"I don't know!"

He laughed loudly, exaggerating his laughter—as if he hadn't laughed for a long time—and then said, "You don't know? Who does know then?"

"God only knows. I think someone informed on me."

"Who ratted on you?"

"Someone who wasn't aware of what I was saying and didn't understand what I was writing."

He patted my back and said, "Never fear. The judge who oversees this prison is mild-mannered and goodhearted."

I spent a few days in prison before I stood before this mild-mannered, goodhearted judge. I had been allowed absolutely no visitors and neither a pen nor paper. Instead I entered a chain of unseen presences. Every time night fell, I sent my heart to anyone in whose presence it wished to be that night—whether he was alive or dead. I met with all of my shaykhs, whom I love to meet: al-Suhrawardi in Baghdad, al-Kumi in Saleh, al-Sabti in Marrakech, and al-Ghawth in Tlemcen, In fact, I also met with al-Khayyat and al-Hariri in the khanqah. My heart sat with them while my body was in the prison. I met with shaykhs who had died during my lifetime and others who had died before I was born. I listened, rejoiced, discussed, received, and learned till it seemed that in the few days I was in the Cairo prison I had visited the East and the West, meeting with dozens of shaykhs and reading dozens of books, and had ascended to the heavens and descended to the earth.

I was finally summoned to appear before his excellency the judge. I stood before him, the worse for wear, with filthy clothes and grimy face and hands. The guards positioned me before him. He remained silent for a time and then looked up and asked: "What were you teaching?"

I replied, "*The Holy Spirit in the Scrutiny of the Soul.*"

"What were people's objections to you?"

"Your Honor the Judge, this is the way people are. They wade into subjects they don't understand."

"Is everyone else wrong, and only you right?"

"Not everyone lodged a complaint with you, Judge. Some of them did."

"Do you really say that God is united with His creatures?"

"Only heretics believe in pantheism."

"Do you say that God indwells in his creation?"

"Anyone who says 'indwelling' misunderstands things."

"I have papers that contain accusations against you of making false, heretical statements. Do you deny making those statements?"

"What I say is: divert your mind from externals and look at the internal to discern what it really is."

"All we have is the external."

"That's what the masses say—not what qadis say."

"Mind your manners, or I'll order them to return you to the prison."

"I like prison better than what you're advising me to do."

"Return to prison till I investigate and render judgment on you."

"God alone judges. I, you, and everything He created are subject to His judgment and are judged by His command."

"What comes to you from an anonymous source isn't reliable."

—IBN ARABI

67

I felt sad when I returned to prison. I had thought my trial might last a long time as I defended myself and confronted my adversary. But the judge did not himself seem to have an opinion, and my adversary lacked a face. Consequently, my fate seemed uncertain. I was besieged by questions from the other prisoners, but I didn't reply. One of the two Egyptians had gone to his trial and not returned; we didn't know whether he was set free or hanged. His uncertain fate cast a shadow of anguished desperation over the rest of us, even though we only barely knew him. My Unseen Presence that night raised me to Ibn Rushd. When I told him what I was experiencing, he vanished into the fog. I tried to knock on the door of Abu Madyan al-Ghawth, but he wouldn't open the door for me. I searched for al-Kumi in the heavenly waystations. When I found him praying, he pointed to his mouth and said, "Your Lord has not forsaken you, nor does He despise you."[37]

It was some days before I was recalled for the trial. I left the cell intending to spend more time pleading my case and to insist that the qadi relate the charges lodged against me in succession so that I could rebut them one at a time. I went to him with this intention only to find him with an elderly man who looked familiar but whom I didn't recognize. I gazed at him for a long time without being able to place him. The judge addressed me, and I tried so hard to focus on both his words and the other man's features, that I could not think straight.

I asked the judge, "Is this my adversary?"

The judge smiled sarcastically and replied: "This man? He's not your foe. This is your advocate."

I was astonished that someone I didn't know had intervened on my behalf. I asked him pointblank who he was. The judge answered for him: "Stand beside your protégé, Abu al-Hasan."

Leaning on his stick, Abu al-Hasan took a few quick steps to stand beside me but avoided looking me in the face. Addressing Abu al-Hasan, the judge asked: "Do you, favored as you are by the Sultan and recommended by ranking religious scholars, swear that your protégé won't provoke the people's rancor or violate the principles of jurisprudence and legislation in the doctrine of the People of the Sunnah?"

For the first time since I entered the courtroom Abu al-Hasan spoke: "I so swear."

I remained silent while I heard him take an oath regarding my conduct—as if I weren't present—trusting my intuitive satisfaction with his appearance and my heart's warmth toward him, even before I remembered who he was.

The qadi continued: "Do you swear that your protégé will never again offer lessons in al-Azhar Mosque, which was created by the Fatimids and is an Isma'ili relic in Cairo?"

"I do so swear."

"And do you swear that if your protégé deviates from these restrictions, he shall be banished from the lands of Egypt or imprisoned?"

"There is no need for this. He will leave Egyptian territories just as soon as you are kind enough to release him."

I looked at him in astonishment, but he did not look at me; he kept his gaze focused on the judge's face, smiling calmly all the time.

Finally, in a louder voice, the judge ordered: "Take him away with you!"

Then he turned to his court clerk, on his right, and said: "Release him to the custody of Abu al-Hasan al-Bija'i on the conditions stipulated in the judgment."

I left the courtroom accompanied not by guards this time but by Abu al-Hasan, who preceded me. He was leaning on his walking stick, which I wondered whether he really needed, because he was walking so quickly. Looking carefully at his feet, I was astonished and squinted to make sure I wasn't emerging from a dream filled with phantasms. He did not seem to be walking. A delicate, invisible layer of air seemed to be transporting him over the ground while he moved his legs to make it appear that he was walking. Finally, once we were alone outside the courtroom, we stopped, and he looked at me for the first time since we had met. My face was one giant swirl of questions. He rested both his hands on his stick and continued to gaze at me silently as a pale smile crossed his face.

I asked the first question: "Why did they accept your intervention so easily?"

"I interceded first with al-Malik al-Adil, and he sent me to the judge."

"Why was the king annoyed with me?"

"He wasn't annoyed with you and didn't know who you were, but some people suggested to him that you are a heretical apostate, and he ordered you imprisoned."

"How did you get him to release me?"

While chortling, he managed to say, "I told him you're a Sufi, and that a Sufi in seclusion is far more dangerous than a Sufi out in public. Then he immediately ordered your release."

I bowed my head in silence, unsure whether I could ask who he was, for fear of insulting him. *Should I just thank him and say goodbye?*

"My son, you're leaving for Baghdad."

"Why Baghdad?"

"Because your third pillar is waiting for you there."

"My pillar? How do you know my pillar?"

"I am very well acquainted with him."

"Who are you?"

He smiled broadly and gazed at my face for a long time before replying: "I was your second pillar, Son."

"My second pillar? What are you saying! Al-Khayyat is my second pillar!"

"He only became your pillar on my death. Now one of us had to get you out of prison and send you toward your third pillar. Since al-Khayyat is paralyzed and confined to bed, I was forced to undertake this assignment."

Then he started to leave—as if he had not just cast a thunderbolt of anxiety and astonishment into my heart. "Please excuse me now," he said.

"Where are you going?"

"I'm returning to my grave."

He took a few steps on his hovering carpet of air before turning toward me one final time and saying, as he pointed to his chest: "Don't forget, my son: purify this . . . then follow it."

"Blessed is the Perplexed."

——**IBN ARABI**

68

I walked back to the khanqah as dumbfounded as if a heavy magic spell had just been cast on me. I reflected on everything that had happened, and those thoughts made me cry. I sat down in the middle of the road, selecting a spot that people wouldn't walk by, and burst into heavy sobs that drained all the fear that had accumulated in my breast about rotting in prison for years. My pillar had been delayed for so many years that I had almost succumbed to despair, but now God Almighty and Exalted had freed him from his grave to free me from my prison. What greater gift than this could the Lord grant a worshipper?

When I walked in on my companions they were seated around their meal. They fell on me, embracing me and weeping. I let them soak my shoulders and chest with their tears, and then Badr and a young man I didn't recognize prepared the place for me as quickly as if they had just been stung: shaking the dust from the bedsheets and opening the windows to air out the room. They shared with me the food they had been eating when I knocked on the door. I shared their arugula, goat cheese, and bread. I started kidding around with them to lift their spirits after this surprise, but that didn't help. Al-Khayyat's eyes were drenched with sad tears while Badr recounted to me all the news from the khanqah and the mosque since I had departed.

Al-Hariri, who hadn't been with them, returned and was mightily cheered to see me. He prostrated himself to God to give thanks before embracing me. He proceeded to gaze at my face as if wanting to learn what I had experienced even before I recounted it. Then he removed my turban and proceeded to pull on my feet to force me to extend my legs and rest. I told them about each night I had spent in the prison and the spiritual presences I had experienced. I did not tell the precise identity of my intercessor, because some of them didn't know the secret of the pillars.

The night became calmer after some hours of discussion. Badr spread the bedsheets we slept on and put two together for me. The young man I didn't recognize left the room then, and Badr said, "He came to look for you the day they imprisoned you and has stayed here since then."

"Have we met him before?"

"I saw him in your lesson several times, but he never argued in a debate or asked a question."

"What's his name?"

"Sawdakin."

I stretched out on my blanket and was able to extend my body fully for the first time since entering that cramped cell, where stretching out wasn't possible for me or for the other prisoners. I moaned from the pain in my bones. Badr was dismayed and started massaging my feet and legs without me asking. Al-Khayyat's voice could be heard from his bed asking weakly, "Brother, when will you depart?"

Al-Hariri lifted his head inquisitively, and Badr stopped massaging my legs while waiting for my answer. I would have liked to convey the news to al-Khayyat later, when we were alone, fearing that my departure would upset him, but he seemed to know all about this through some mysterious insight. I crawled over to him and squeezed his hand before I said, "Tomorrow or the next day."

"Good night, Brother."

He said nothing more, closed his eyes, and fell asleep. I returned to my bed and whispered to Badr and al-Hariri, who were still waiting inquisitively for news of this journey, "There's no place for me in Egypt. I'm heading to Baghdad."

Badr appeared relieved by this decision. My imprisonment had frightened him so much he had lost weight and looked paler. Al-Hariri bowed his head for a time and then said in jest: "Don't come back here again. Bidding you farewell is more painful than enduring your absence."

The next day, Badr departed at dawn to purchase provisions and to inquire about caravans. Sawdakin entered and began to clean the place. He brought us food—a little plate for each of us. These were prepared in the khanqah. I discussed routes and caravans with al-Hariri. When the young man heard us, he sat cross-legged beside me and asked with a mournful look, "Master, are you traveling?"

"Yes, my son. Tomorrow or the next day."

He looked so alarmed and disappointed that I patted his shoulder and hugged him to my chest. I had grown used to the sorrows of disciples whenever the time came for me to depart. I had experienced this and worse when I bade farewell to my shaykhs in Seville, Fez, Marrakech, Bejaïa, Mecca, and everywhere else I had met a shaykh and studied with him. I leaned over al-Khayyat and embraced him for a long time as our tears mixed. Then I embraced al-Hariri just as forcefully while he pressed on my back as though he wished to tuck me into his chest. When I walked out the door, I found Sawdakin there, holding my sandals. He immediately bent down to help me put them on. Then he picked up my belongings, and we walked off together to where Badr was waiting for us at the caravan depot.

On our way there, Sawdakin looked frightened, his steps were clumsy, and his expression was glum. I asked him about his family and kinfolk to raise his spirits. I learned that his father had lived in Sufi khanqahs since Salah al-Din established them in Cairo and had died in a pure Sufi state. I offered a prayer for him. After a short silence, when the caravan depot came into sight at the end of the lane, Sawdakin said, "Master. . . I'm a disciple and you're an inveterate traveler."

"What do you want?"

"I want to accompany you, serve you, and learn from you."

"Is there anyone left in your family?"

"Who would I have? I and my father were slaves of Nur al-Din Zangi, freed the day he died."

"Your father?"

"He died."

I gazed at his expression, which was a blend of anticipation and hope, and remembered that Badr was getting on in years. We would, sooner or later, need a strong young man to help us on the road. I placed my hand on Sawdakin's shoulder and smiled when I said, "Travel with us, then, if you want."

"I fear I will be a burden to both of you, Master. I have no money and no camel."

"The whole earth belongs to God. The station is wide, and the Master of the House is generous."

Once we saw Badr in the distance holding the halters of two camels, Sawdakin rushed to him and gave him the good news. Badr looked toward me, awaiting my confirmation, and I told him, "Hire another camel."

"Sorrow that doesn't haunt a person isn't trustworthy."

—— **IBN ARABI**

You enter few cities where you immediately feel their walls have been expecting you—cities where you at once encounter affection and desire and feel surrounded by contentment. Baghdad welcomed me this way, even though I was one of hundreds whom the caravan brought here. All the same, I felt the city was greeting me personally with the welcome that generous cities reserve for tired travelers. Ever since I entered the city, my expression was the dazed astonishment of a person being embraced by someone he doesn't know—someone who loves you but has never met you, who can describe you without ever having seen you. This astonishment lingers a long time—until the city teaches you its first lessons: how to walk beside the Tigris River without allowing your heart to be swept from your ribcage by this river, how to walk calmly through Rasafa without each palm tree stopping you with a new story it won't repeat the next day, how to stroll through the markets of Karkh without every pharmacist, textile merchant, and jeweler leaving you an earworm saying that will haunt you for the rest of the day with its eloquence, poignancy, and charm? Where can you find the willpower to close the door on Baghdad every night and fall asleep?

My delight in Baghdad became so great I couldn't hide it from Badr and Sawdakin. Something about the charm of this city wavered between revelation and secrecy. I had to listen a long time to learn what Baghdad whispered in the ear of each mindful person, and what I needed to hear. I entered this city a mess, and it organized me. I was a stranger, and it sheltered me. I was certain that I would not end up there the way I had in the other lands that had cast me out—places like Andalusia, Morocco, Mecca, Syria, and Egypt. The Almohads had told me: you can't teach. The Ayyubids had imprisoned me. The Aleppines hated my poetry collection. Mecca locked its portals to my heart at the height of its passion. God wishes to test the wayfarer till he finds his path and the mindful person till he tastes his faith. God has twisted me between His fingers, through space and time, till I tested the mettle of my soul and didn't flee from it. But from time to time, He has showered me with His mysterious gentle graces and His bountiful blisses—as happened this year in Baghdad. There was no anguish, no anxiety. On every street corner, a madrasa welcomed every discipline and accepted every doctrine. Down every road a house caught your eye and forced you to stop and admire its architecture and decorations. In every orchard there were trees I had never seen before and fruits I had never tasted. On every street, men carried water jugs decorated with bells that rang sweetly and provided water that was ice-cold. In every neighborhood, there was a market offering items not sold anywhere else.

I spent my first weeks in Baghdad as a tourist, exempt from lessons and books. I would leave the house to tour the city's regions, wishing only to read the sentences concealed beneath people's footsteps and God's words that history had compiled in this city, century after century. Feet would occasionally scan these as they walked and find more than eyes could inside books. Every day granted me a new excursion. When I entered al-Zaʿfaran Street, I found the fragrances of Persians, Arabs, Turks, and others, whether Byzantines, Indians, or Georgians—all created in Baghdad. When I approached the hospital, druggists' shops lined both sides of the street, and they, with their alembics and crucibles, were busily steeping an herb in a liquid, mixing aromatics with a poultice, distilling, blending, heating, and then setting out each medicine in a small flask by their doors. In the textile merchants' market, fabrics covered the ground and flew from it: cotton, linen, raw silk, and silk, and this market was surrounded by markets for carders, dyers, and spinners. When I entered the stationers' market, I needed more than a day to tour it, let alone to stand and read. Anyone who didn't know what he was looking for when he entered would get lost in its maze—as happened to me the first time I went there. You might encounter a lovely surprise like a little book called *Hasad al-Bahshiya* (Kermes Oak Harvest) in the shop of a man selling Andalusian books.

I picked up this book and investigated it but did not find the name of the author. I asked the dealer about it twice, speaking louder each time so he would hear me. The elderly bookseller nodded his head but didn't reply. Instead he gazed at the book I had picked out—as if seeing it for the first time. I paid him the price he wanted and sat down at the entry to his shop, flipping through the book's pages as if flipping the pages of my days, to go back in time twenty years. Here were Shankara, Pythagoras, Venus, and the Brethren of Purity between the two covers of a book compiled by the tipsy folks at Frederick's farm. Could this be one of his books? Whose else would it be? I placed the book in my basket, realizing that I hadn't stopped smiling since I first picked it up. The breezes of Seville wafted the scent of orange blossoms from every lane when I stood in the center of the stationers' market in Baghdad. Here was Frederick's greeting to me from an unseen world. I didn't know whether he was dead or alive. Had he stayed in Seville or traveled to his distant north?

I completed my expedition through the stationers' market. I wanted paper for a book that God hadn't inspired me to write yet, even though I had begun to feel it pulsing through the pages of my heart and intellect. Rows of paper shops near Bab al-Sharqi had reams of paper stacked in front of them. Each pile had a wooden placard on it with the price. Behind them were tubs of starch and hemp for making glossy paper and cotton and linen presses for Syrian paper. Sheets of paper were taken next by cutters and polishers who created different varieties of paper for every need. Large sheets were for letters and contracts, thick ones for copies of the Qur'an and of Hadith collections, the glossy ones for correspondence and agreements, and thin sheets for books and epitomes. The papermakers' shops were followed by the scribes' shops, which sold every type of writing equipment. These tempted me into discarding my old inkwell for another made of pure ebony. I bought a piece of every type of paper to try and then purchased oil-based ink for writing freehand, another type made of gallnuts from Syria for parchment, and a third made from ferrous sulphate (green vitriol) to use for the notebook I carry in my pocket. I bought a stick of Iraqi red ochre for the titles and covers of books.

70

My first year in Baghdad passed without that city's fascination ever fading for me. Whenever I thought I was growing accustomed to the city, it revealed new charms. I moved houses four times—not because I had grown tired of the previous neighborhood but because of my interest in the new one. I finally settled near the mosque of Bab al-Taq, where I taught for the longest time and where my classes had the largest attendance. The mosque's courtyard was spacious, and behind the mosque there were houses that lined the riverbank. Boats there were rented to people to use to cross the river or to embark on excursions. People sold fish they roasted alive on skewers. People ate these fish in buns while standing. Chairs were arranged the length of the mosque's exterior wall, and every Saturday Qur'an reciters took turns sitting in these. Their recitations from the Qur'an would cause passersby to stop and men who were standing to sit down, because their voices were so fine and their recitations so excellent. People hired them to recite at weddings, wakes, and circumcisions.

I rented a house nearby with money I had made, since I hadn't found a Sufi house with a large enough endowment to provide lodging for me and my two friends. I slept in one room, and Sawdakin and Badr slept in the other. The house's courtyard had a view of the river, and we cooked and hung our clothes to dry there. When I went to the mosque at dawn, I saw small flocks of ducks near the riverbank, and their quacks mixed with the sounds of waterwheels that drew water from the river to irrigate the gardens. If I stayed up late to witness the revelation of a new divine secret that my heart could almost taste, the sky would be so clear and the stars would shine so brightly that everything seemed to cooperate for Baghdadi revelations to descend to the heart of an Andalusian friend of God.

I devoted my days to teaching and my nights to writing. I had little impact in Baghdad's mosques, which were filled with shaykhs teaching people every sect and every Sufi path. Only a student whose heart my path affected made his way to me. Such a student wanted to learn from me and no one else. When I had time to spare, I walked to Dar al-Hikma—Baghdad's Grand Library—where I found every precious and valuable book, whether in Arabic, Farsi, Greek, Syriac, or Sanskrit. The collection was shelved in long rows that were meticulously arranged. If the book I wanted wasn't available in Arabic, I took the book to the translation area and returned a month later to find it translated into my language, free of charge, except for the tip I happily gave the translator.

Since we had arrived in Baghdad, Sawdakin had worked hard to serve both me and Badr. He wasn't upset about accompanying us without material or financial compensation, and he was never happier than when working. He cooked food for us every day till I ordered him to stop cooking so much—so we wouldn't be denied some meritorious hunger. If he noticed a tear in my clothing or a break in my sandals, he would mend the tunic and spend the night fixing the sandal so that when I woke the next morning, I would find them in the best possible shape. Whenever I stretched out a leg to relax, he would bend down to massage it. When I entered the bath to bathe, he would stand by the door with water for ablutions and my comb. When my nails grew long, he would clip and file them. Over and beyond all this, he was eager to learn. He attended the lessons I taught, read the books, and memorized the texts, despite all the work and service he voluntarily performed. Badr enjoyed his company and the help he provided him; the two of them were rarely ever apart.

I received a letter from my sister Umm Sa'd; it was brought by an Iraqi pilgrim who had just returned from pilgrimage. He, for his part, had received it from a Moroccan pilgrim. I had tears in my eyes when I read her words—written in the Maghribi script, which I had not read for many years. When I reached the section in which she lamented the death of her son, I broke down and sobbed for her child, whom I had never seen a day in his life. I sensed that she was both elegizing him and chastising me. I set aside her letter, on which the ink had dried many months before it reached me, and started walking with no destination in mind. I entered Sulayman Lane, where judges, merchants, and court officials lived, and sat down at its end by the river, where I could not be seen from any of the nearby houses. I wept a little and then continued walking till I left those neighborhoods for poorer ones, where all the houses were built of mudbrick and did not last very long. They seemed to die when their owners did, not enduring long enough for anyone to inherit them. I walked on until I was outside the city's wall and continued hiking through its suburbs. I reached livestock lots filled with mangy animals, which were banned from the city. Approaching them, I gazed at the mournful, bleary eyes of camels that complained of sorrows they could not avert. Their skins were coated with tar to treat their mange, and some of the tar had mixed with purulent blood. I stretched out my hand to them, and some came to sniff it slowly and despairingly. I found a break in the fence and entered. Some animals were wary of me and joined others at the far end of the lot. I sat down and exchanged silent looks with them for a long time, till I felt tired. Then I removed my turban to use as a pillow and fell asleep.

"Only someone who has opposed his own caprices wins His satisfaction."

——**IBN ARABI**

71

I awoke at dawn with a clear mind. The beasts were moving around their pen and appeared more energetic, despite their maladies. Dawn seemed to provide them temporary health. I wound my turban again, opened the gate of the feedlot and left to return to the city with a lighter spirit and a calmer heartbeat. The lines I would write in my letter to my sister were arranged in my head, and I did write her before I performed the noon prayer that day. I kept that letter with me for a few weeks till I found someone who would carry it to Egypt. I entrusted it to this man without knowing when it might reach her. It might take a year, or perhaps a little less. Perhaps it would never arrive. I returned then to my teaching, my house, and my books, after exhausting my entire share of bewilderment. Habit ruled my heart, and Baghdad's pleasures and charms lost their allure for me. I no longer spent time in the market, by the river, or in a garden. I focused on what I had been accustomed to doing my entire life. I would leave the house for the mosque and return by the same route every day. At night I would light two lamps in my room and write down the thoughts that had been sparked in my mind during the class by the pupils' questions. I would leave what I had written open for God to bless. When I awoke, I would find that one word had become two, and one line two lines. Then I was unable to reject any of these additions. When the heavens are generous, the earth does not protest.

As months passed, I began to feel increasingly isolated. Anxiety started to course through my veins again and to plant its prickly weeds in my heart. When I closed the door to my room to sleep, I wished someone was there to keep me company and entertain me. Badr and Sawdakin slept in the other room. I would hear them talking at times. Badr was teaching Sawdakin what I had previously taught him, and Sawdakin was telling Badr what he thought about me. I, whose sciences and learning they recounted to each other, was meanwhile languishing in another room, unable to sleep and not knowing what to write. When insomnia got the better of me, I would leave my room and enter theirs. Then we would sit together to do dhikr chanting and have *samar* conversations till midnight. I would pretend to doze off then, so I could sleep in their room, where I was comforted by Badr's snoring, which grew louder the older he became. I contemplated my arms one night before going to sleep and noticed that they resembled two limbs of a dead tree. I felt the bald spot on the top of my head and the folds of skin below my chin and realized that I would soon turn fifty.

One morning in those days, while I was in the mosque, clamorous voices were heard outside, and the heads of those in front of me turned to look. I realized that I didn't control their minds at that moment. So I ended the class at that point, and we all went outside to see what was happening. There was drumming and whistling as boys ran here and there and a crowd of men lined up in front of their shops. Then a donkey passed with a man seated backward on it. There was a chain attached to each of his legs and their ends were held by soldiers of the Caliph. I proclaimed the almighty power of God and sought refuge with Him from this scene. I went back inside the mosque while my students continued watching Sanjar, who had been the Caliph's governor of Khuzestan but was now disgraced, till he disappeared at the end of the street. Then they returned and sat back in their places. I decided to take advantage of what they had just seen to tell them about God's cunning, His *makr*, against which no man can guard himself no matter how profound his faith, righteousness, learning, and insight are.

Sanjar was imprisoned then, and we heard nothing more about him, but the image of him being driven through Baghdad's streets remained etched in my mind. When I retired to bed, my heart raced as if I were a stallion on the nearby racecourse. My imprisonment in Cairo still haunted me, brought me nightmares, and kept me awake some nights. I would recite the Qur'an surah called "Joseph" in hopes that its reference to prison would alleviate my suffering while I continued to feel afraid. What kind of *wali* was I who felt anxious every night and lacked belief or tranquility? If those pupils knew how fearful my heart was, they would desert me, and I would start wandering the alleys of Baghdad like those holy fools[38] who are oblivious to everything. I no longer knew whether, when I settled in a new city, I should approach its princes and prominent citizens to solicit their support in case common people disagreed about me—or—approach people in the neighborhood mosques, larger Friday mosques, and Sufi houses, to solicit the support of the masses should the sultans turn against me? My faith instructed me to seek strength from God alone, but the matter wasn't that simple, even for "friends of God," because I was incapable, by myself, of knowing what He thought of me. When God granted me worldly favors, I feared His cunning. When He afflicted me, I feared He had deserted me. What a situation! I would dream occasionally that I was in seclusion and that no one could see me, nor could I see anyone. At other times I dreamt that I had been too quick to publish my gnosis and the perfection of my knowledge before I grew old and was no longer good for anything. Days passed while I remained awake after deciding to write at home and go to the mosque only to pray. Then, by noon, I would chastise my soul for its cowardice and negligence of my disciples and students and fear that what we imprison in our breast might punish us in our graves; then I would go out to meet with them.

72

I began my third year in Baghdad in this anxious state, which raised and dropped me when I was surprised by something I hadn't reckoned on. Glory to Him Who changes states and Whom states never change. One day Badr interrupted my lesson, which was quite unusual for him. He lifted his tunic and began to pass through the sea of students' necks on his way toward me. They moved aside for him after he stumbled and almost fell. When he finally reached me, he whispered something to me that shook my being and caused my heart to quake. I was astonished and surprised, but God is to be praised in every situation.

"A funeral procession that *you must join* has left the Shaykh's mosque."

I looked him straight in the eyes, trying to understand, and detected in them a determination that said there was no room for quibbling. So I dismissed the students and asked God to be gracious to me. During their noisy departure, Badr grasped my arm and said: "Shaykh Zaher al-Isfahani."

"What did you say?"

"Yes. The funeral procession of Zaher al-Isfahani left a short time ago from the Shaykh's Mosque."

"Are you sure? Could you be confused about the name?"

"No, I uncovered his face and looked at him. God reward you mightily, Master."

Badr pulled on my tunic to hurry me along and said no more. Sawdakin caught up with us, and we hastened our steps till we were almost running at times. My turban slipped, and I held it on with one hand and held up the hem of my tunic with the other. The tears running down my cheeks blew far away with the wind.

When did you come to Baghdad, Master? How long have you been here near me without me seeing you? Why have God's unveilings deserted me to the point that I don't even know who lives here with me in this land and who dies here? What sin have I committed that I treat my shaykhs disrespectfully? Reduced to walking in their funerals like a member of the general public? Without kissing their lofty foreheads or washing their pure bodies?

We entered the cemetery, where people were gathered around two graves. We headed to the first of them, but it wasn't the shaykh's. So we rushed to the other one, where we found them scattering dirt on his body. I saw only the edge of his shroud, only for a few moments, before dirt hid it from me. I prostrated myself by the side of the grave with al-Habashi and Sawdakin and wept as I had wept for my father and my uncle. The other mourners left, and I asked my two companions to depart as well. They did, anxiously. I strained my memory and proceeded to recite over Zaher's grave all the hadith he had recited and the lives of Companions of the Prophet he had recounted—everything I had learned from him—and the views I had gained from him. I narrated over his grave his fatwas, the opinions of scholars he favored, and the doctrines of jurisprudents. God inspired me with what to say as I recited over his silent grave everything I had previously recited while I sat with him, enlightened by his beautiful face and friendly smile.

If Zaher was spending the night buried in Baghdad's soil, where was Nizam? I went alone to the mosque from which Zaher's funeral procession had come and began to ask everyone I encountered there. The fifth person I asked directed me to the house where he had been living, and I headed there immediately, nourishing the hope of seeing Nizam, whom I had desired with a yearning I could no longer describe. I also feared seeing her so strongly that my very ribs quivered. *But my yearning has overwhelmed my fear, and that's why I am standing before her door now.* I found two boys playing with hajaf, leather discs, in front of the house. My heart almost sank from my chest. *My God! Are these two her sons? Has Nizam, that luminous sun, finally been eclipsed by some other planet—not me? Has she accepted some man—not me? Did your father force you to accept what you disliked—or did you not dislike it?*

I stopped at the end of the street, barely able to stand on my two feet. I would take a step forward and then retreat—my eyes fixed on the two boys—as my heart pressed me forward, to see Nizam, and then drew me back to shield itself, from news that might dash its few remaining hopes. Finally, I decided to knock on the door, come what may. The two boys stopped playing when they saw me knocking. I kept myself from looking at them for fear I would detect some resemblance to Nizam in their faces. No one answered my first knock. I knocked a second time. My hand was trembling, and I had trouble breathing. Finally the two boys entered the house, as though they intended to tell the residents someone was knocking on the door, and left the door ajar. Immediately a third child looked out. *My God! How many children does Nizam have?*

The child looked up at me with wide-open eyes and did not move. He stared at me, and I stared at him. He had a round face, a double chin, and rosy cheeks. A line of saliva dripped from his open mouth and hit the ground as he continued to stare at me. I smiled at him, and he retreated. I leaned over to draw closer to him, but he crawled quickly back inside the house. I felt hurt. When you are feeling very hopeful, hostility from a child you don't know can be hard on your heart and feel like your eternal destiny.

I knocked on the door loudly and shouted my greetings, hoping that someone would hear. I finally overheard, briefly but not clearly, a conversation between two women. Then one of the two boys came and slammed the door shut. I had already knocked on the door three times, and that was once too often. So I sat down on the stoop, at a loss for what to do next. *There are obviously women and children in the house, but what are the odds that Nizam is on the other side of the wall against which I'm leaning?*

"Everything in existence falls into one of two categories: lover or beloved."

—— **IBN ARABI**

73

I languished there for almost an hour, my head bowed, not moving a muscle. Then God ordered the door to open. A short, feeble, elderly woman emerged with her face concealed beneath a tattered shawl with large holes in it. She closed the door behind her and set off down the street.

I caught up with her and said, "Aunt. A good day to you."

"Who are you?"

"I am Muhyi al-Din ibn Arabi."

"What do you want?"

"I wish to ask you whether the funeral procession of Shaykh Zaher, may God be compassionate to him, came from this house."

When the old woman sighed sorrowfully, I knew even before she replied that it was. "Yes, it is his house."

"Is his daughter Nizam in it?"

"No, Son. Do you know Nizam?"

"Zaher is my shaykh, as was Fakhr al-Nisa', in Mecca."

"May God be merciful to both of them, my son."

I was shocked that I had not thought of Fakhr al-Nisa' until this woman lamented her. A tear fell from my eye, and I didn't know whether I was weeping for my professors or for my own sorry state. The old woman surprised me by wiping the tear from my face, but then another tear and yet another fell. I sat down on the ground and wept fervently.

"May God shelter you, Son. Enough. That's enough."

I did not reply till I had finished weeping while she stood over me, praising God's might and power and invoking God for me with many prayers. Finally, my tears ceased, and I stood up again. Gazing at her plaintively, I asked, "Where is Nizam?"

"Nizam, my son, has lived in a house of women religious since they came to Baghdad."

I sighed deeply, as the hand that had been squeezing my heart released its grasp. The elderly woman informed me that she was Nizam's aunt, and that Zaher had lived in her house since he fell ill and could no longer move. I thanked her and walked away. My pulse rate returned to normal, and I could breathe normally again. Since Nizam was living in a convent, she certainly had not married. Convents house pious women who dedicate themselves to worship and the care of orphans.

I headed to the area of the city where Muslim monasteries are located and began to ask for convents. Only one religious establishment for women was mentioned, and I went straight to it. I stopped at the door. My hand did not obey me till I ordered it to rise and strike the door. I surrendered my heart to God and trusted Him to treat my heart as He saw fit.

The door opened immediately once I knocked, but no one was visible. "Peace to you," I said. "I am looking for Nizam bint Zaher al-Isfahani."

The door opened wider, and she looked out. She had opened the door, as if she had been expecting me to knock. I gazed at her face which was haloed by a black shawl that made her complexion look even whiter and brighter. She gazed at my face where she saw the effect of years of yearning, fear, and dread, and of the love that had been postponed till now. For some moments we exchanged baffled looks. Then she smiled at me, and I cried out: "Nizam!"

"Welcome, Traveler."

"Welcome to you."

I was silent for a time as many words rushed to emerge from my mouth only to find their way blocked. I could not utter one of them. Finally, an anxious, pathetic sentence emerged from my mouth: "Shaykh Zaher! I only learned of his death from your aunt!"

"How could you have known."

"May God reward you mightily."

"Us and you."

Nizam continued to stand at the door with me outside it. There had always been a door and doorstep in the way of our love. At the door of Fakhr al-Nisa'. At the door of Nizam's house in Mecca. Now the door of the convent in Baghdad. These doors opened for me to enter but also remained open so I could leave. Good doors and tyrannical doors. Generous doors and stingy ones. But they fully expressed the nature of my relationship with her: a love with doors. *If you knock and she answers, that does not mean you will enter. If you enter, this does not mean you will remain. If you leave, that does not mean you will return.*

I sensed that I had stood there too long without saying anything. I summoned my courage and said, "Listen, Nizam. . . . ."

She leaned her head on the door frame shyly, smiled, and said, "Speak, Muhyi."

"You know my heart is filled with love for you. . . ."

Her smile became even broader and purer; "Yes, I know that, and I shan't forget it," she said as calmly as if lulling a baby to sleep.

"I know the love you have in your heart for me."

"No, you know part of it. If you knew all of it, you would be incredulous."

The Tigris River crested and poured into my veins when I heard her say that. I responded immediately, without noticing that I was speaking louder, though we were on the street: "Then why do you rebuff me when I declare my love for you and commit myself to you?"

She drew her head away from the door, stood up straighter, and sighed deeply. Then the reassuring smile returned to her rosy lips before she asked, "How much do you love me, Muhyi?"

"By God, the sun has never risen or set on a person I love more than you."

"By God, the moon has never risen nor set on a person I love more than you."

"Then why do you refuse to marry me?"

She held out her hand. Yes! She extended her hand—while we were on a street and people were passing—and touched my collarbone. Her smile narrowed while her eyes grew wider. Looking at the area her hand was traversing on my neck, she said, "Because I can't, dearest."

"Why not?"

"Because I am your third pillar. . . ."

". . . ."

"Pillars marry the earth, Darling."

The Tigris, which had been rushing through my veins, dried up with amazing speed, as if it were flowing over a massive sand angel. I stood there like a statue incapable of locomotion. I looked at Nizam's face with eyes that could not focus, I was so astonished. She stroked my face with her palm and plunged her fingers into my beard and continued, "Your fourth and final pillar is in Malatya. Go to him and strengthen your heart."

74   **DAMASCUS** 1873 CE/1290 AH

I swore an oath to wait for him at the door of the religious house where I said goodbye to him seventy-three days ago. Since then I have counted them as carefully as I count my prayer prostrations and the beads of my rosary. That day, I placed the horse's reins and the purse of money in his hand and squeezed his arm, needing reassurance more than he did. I told him, "I envy you for being able to lay eyes on the words of the Shaykh before I do."[39]

"In less than two months, Emir, they will be in your hands."

Since that day, I have sat on this chair, which has a view of the entire ribat. I have replaced the cushion beneath me every two days when it grows so hard that my back hurts. Students have quickly grown accustomed to my presence here and form a circle around me. In the morning I explain the works of the Supreme Shaykh in my house to a limited number of students. The students at noon are those to whom I explain the Qur'an in the Jaqmaqiya Madrasa. The evening students read al-Bukhari's Hadith anthology in al-Ashrafiya. The night students copy down passages I have shared from my book *al-Mawaqif al-Ruhiya* and revise them with me every week. Along with these, there are others who seek a fatwa from me, and each of them tells me about his concerns. Other men ask me to intercede on their behalf with our governor Subhi Pasha. There are those who ask my blessing and wipe the sleeves of my gown with the swaddling clothes of their newborns and the bandages of their invalids. Algerians who stream into Damascus head to me their first day here to ask me to intercede for them to find work or lodging or to exempt them from Ottoman taxation. Employees of the municipal council have started bringing me their papers to stamp with my seal after I stopped visiting the council. Christians still, thirteen years after the civil unrest during which their district, monastery, and churches were violated, come regularly to me every week, led by their priest, to listen to my lesson. Even children are not deterred by the crowds from slipping past the adults to make their way to me, realizing that I favor children over adults. They repeatedly ask me, "What is Paris like, Emir Abdelkader? How did you resist the French, Emir Abdelkader? Describe the Sublime Porte to us, Emir Abdelkader. Have you ridden on a steamship, Emir Abdelkader?" I tell them stories that shake the dust of sixty years from my memory and open veins that had dried up in my heart. When night falls and the night watchmen start their patrols, my student al-Qamqashnawi accompanies me to the house, insisting that I return to my customary sessions at home, in the tekkiyeh, and inside the mosque instead of sitting by the road like some wayfarer.

Then I tell him, "Not until Tantawi returns."

"But when he returns, he'll come to you wherever you are, Emir."

"My boy, I know that. But Tantawi will, God willing, return with a copy of the works of the Supreme Shaykh. I'm concerned about the message not the messenger."

"What would you think about our positioning someone at the gates of the city to watch for him?"

"Yes, that's a good idea."

"Who do you want me to send on this mission?"

"Me."

The poor fellow was disarmed, and I started offering my dawn prayers and then quickly proceeded to the Bawabijiya Gate, on the north of the city, where caravans arrive from Anatolia. I found a place among the cobblers, whose hammer strokes blended with the clamor of my lessons. Those who knew me stopped hammering, retreated into their shops, or perhaps closed their shops and came to sit with those listening to my class. Every day one of them would give me a new pair of shoes until I stopped accepting them. They then started offering me leather bookbags, which I distributed to the students.

On another night, al-Qamqashnawi asked me, "What is taking Tantawi so long, Emir? The trip between Damascus and Konya takes fifteen days going and another fifteen returning. He said it would take him a month to copy the book. This means he is twelve days late in returning."

"Actually thirteen and a half days, Qamqash."

"Do you think something has happened to him?"

"If he had suffered some misfortune, I would have heard about it. No doubt copying the manuscript has taken him longer than he expected."

Despite the optimism I expressed to al-Qamqashnawi that night, the anxiety he expressed wormed itself into my heart. I twisted and turned so much that night that I woke Khayriya. My sleep continued to be restless till the final third of the night. Then I woke, rose early, and stretched to nap on my prayer rug while waiting to perform the dawn prayer. During a dream, I saw a pearl the size of a fist. It was rolling along the road between al-Suwayqa and al-Salihiya, illuminating the route. Once the dawn call to prayer resounded, I quickly performed it and praised God for al-Tantawi's arrival. The moment I had finished the dawn prayer, I found him before me, embracing me even as I sat there.

"What took you so long, my boy? Didn't I tell you to copy *The Meccan Revelations* and return at once?"

"Yes, Emir. But I found another book in the mausoleum of Mawlana Jalal al-Din al-Rumi. Then I consulted God and decided to copy it too. I knew you would never forgive me if I didn't."

I thrust my hand into his bag, which hung from his neck, and brought out the book. I shouted at him, "Tantawi! This isn't your handwriting!"

His eyes shone with a childish gleam as he squatted before me and said, "Yes, Emir. It isn't my handwriting!"

"Whose handwriting is it then?"

He did not reply, but his ever-wider smile provided the best answer. I gazed at the handwritten lines till my tears prevented me from seeing the page. I asked him in a feeble voice, "But . . . how could this be, my son? How could they give it to you?"

"It's your fragrant life story, Emir. They agreed to allow me to copy the book, and I did. When I finished transcribing two copies of it, I wrote on the cover of each one: 'Library of Emir Abdelkader ibn Muhyi al-Din al-Hasani al-Jaza'iri.' The mausoleum's custodian read this when I was preparing to depart and understood that it referred to you. Then he kept the two copies I had made and decided to give me the original, since it would be in your safekeeping."

I rose without help and walked without anyone lending me a hand. I headed to my office, followed by Tantawi, who was still dressed in his travelling clothes. I entered the library and searched for a place fit to hold a book written by the hand of the Supreme Shaykh himself. I immediately headed to the corner reserved for presents. I set aside the French Legion of Honor medal, the Russian White Eagle medallion, the cross given me by Pope Pius IX, the Ottoman Order of the Medjidie medal, the two American pistols, and the English rifle. All these presents had piled up in my closet since the end of the civil unrest. They would almost have stepped aside, themselves, if I hadn't moved them to replace them with this book.

Al-Tantawi left my office as I sat in the middle of it, checking its corners, windows, entrances, ventilation ducts, and water pipes for anything that might harm the book. My eyes finally settled on the box containing my testament. I opened this box and took out my last will and testament, which I had written during my exile in France, twenty years ago, and have never altered since. I placed the book where my testament had been. Then I took out my pen, opened my will, and added an addendum to it: "Dated Damascus, 1290 since the Hegira of the Noble Prophet: This miserable pauper Abdelkader directs that he should be buried near the Supreme Shaykh, the Elixir of the Gnostics, the Imam of the Verifiers, in his blessed tomb in al-Salihiya. May the blessing of the Muhammadan Inheritor reach him and may the curtain of eternal Qutb—the Absolute Pole—drape over his sinful spirit."

TOME NINE

75

All morning long I kept my face looking north to smell my way. It had been three years and nine months since I last traveled through wild desert lands. I sensed that Baghdad had cast its nets over me till I was no longer able to aspire to a further goal or voyage. Today I sent Sawdakin and Badr to the market to buy supplies for the trip to Malatya and to inquire about caravans. So they left me alone in the house. For the first time I was torn between opposing desires to stay and to travel. Whenever it had been time to travel before, my spirit had preceded my body to my destination. Baghdad, the City of Peace, though, really had blessed my spirit with peace. Here I hadn't contacted any sultan to inquire about his interests and hadn't dedicated myself to any work that would not provide a beneficial return.

Badr returned with the supplies I had requested but with news I had not expected. The King of Mosul was assembling an army for an inevitable war with the Georgians; therefore, travel by that route wasn't recommended. I gazed at his eyes, which had grown narrower as he aged, even as his eyebrows became bushier and whiter. I asked him, "What are the caravans doing?"

"They are all going to Anatolia by way of Aleppo."

I shook imaginary dust off my hand and said, "We'll go with them, then."

Our caravan, which combined three separate caravans, flew the banner of the Abbasid Caliphate and contained hundreds of camels fastened together with more than one halter. We made our way to Aleppo in twenty-seven days, during which two component caravans left to head in different directions. We received news of the Mosul army, which we were avoiding, from caravans we met at crossroads and rest stops. It had barely set forth before the war ended in a unique way: the Georgian king became intoxicated and rode off on his steed alone. They plunged into a pit. Agents of the King of Mosul dragged him out and ransomed him for the freedom of their entire city. Then the siege was lifted, and that whole story, which had made us head west instead of north, ended.

Everyone rejoiced at this news while we were on the outskirts of Aleppo, although I couldn't get the matter out of my mind. Why had God wanted me to head west instead of north? *It's not Your way, Lord, to act in vain, and my life is not expansive enough for me to ignore heavenly allusions.* This concern kept me awake my first six nights in Aleppo. Eid al-Adha found us there that year, but I didn't know whence sleep would return to my wakeful eyelids. I finally entrusted my concerns to God, for Him to lead me wherever He would. *I am his wali and can only turn where He sends me. My sole path is the one He leads me down.* I woke up Badr and Sawdakin, who were sound asleep.

Once they were fully awake, I looked at them and said decisively, "We'll stay in Aleppo . . . for the time being."

Badr rubbed his face vertically and horizontally, as is his wont when he wakes, and then said with his increasingly acerbic tone: "Why didn't you tell us this in the morning, Master?"

Sawdakin gazed at me as if waiting for a reply; I then said in a tone that quavered and almost betrayed me: "So I could get some sleep!"

I returned to my bed and fell into such a deep sleep that Badr had to pat me on my shoulders and face several times to wake me for the dawn prayer. Previously he would only have needed to whisper. In a dream, I saw a clay oven in which a fire was blazing. I approached it till I stood on it. Then its mouth opened wider till I found myself inside, but the flames didn't burn me. Next I saw my breast split open. Two large pieces of ice, each the size of a pear, emerged from it and immediately melted. Then I left the oven, felt my chest, and found that my shirt was punctured over my heart. People around me were amazed by this perforation and pointed at it. Some made fun of it and laughed, forcing me to run home and change my shirt. When I removed this torn shirt, tossing it on the floor, it suddenly rose and became a woman who embraced me.

I woke and remained in bed, trying to find an explanation for my dream, but failed, and God did not unveil any interpretation. *A lost heart; a beautiful woman. What does God want from His impoverished worshipper?* I called Sawdakin and asked him to make the rounds at Aleppo's mosques, asking for anyone who interpreted dreams. He was gone the whole day, returning after sunset.

He sat down before me and said, "I consulted five. Two told me the oven is the punishment for adulterers in the Next World and that the person who had the dream should repent and turn to God. The third said that ice emerging from the heart signifies that the heart is empty, cold, and distant from the truth. The fourth said the person who had the dream is hovering around the flames, about to commit a major sin."

"What about the fifth?"

"The fifth did not explain the dream but instead said succinctly: the person who had this dream should marry."

I retired to bed that night, plunged as deep into the waves of thought as a ship in the Atlantic Ocean. In the middle of the night, I anchored by land. I woke Sawdakin who rushed to me in alarm, thinking some harm had befallen me. I said to him, "God unveiled to me the exegesis of my dream. God removed Maryam and Nizam from my cold, healthy heart, leaving it empty. God will send me a woman who will emerge from my tunic—in other words she will follow my path and take my direction. She will embrace me—in other words, I will marry her."

Sawdakin rubbed the sleep from his eyes and said anxiously, "This is all good news, Master."

"Yes, it's all good. You can go back to sleep."

Sawdakin did go back to sleep, but I got a basin of water, performed my ablutions, and began to pray. During my prayer I asked God to guide me and to bring me the woman quickly to plug the hole in my heart, the one I had seen in my dream. I prayed until dawn, when we all went to the mosque. The sun rose, and I went to the market to buy paper. I found pavilions and tents had been erected all along the road, as if a grand occasion was about to be celebrated. Al-Malik al-Zahir, however, wasn't starting a jihad and hadn't won a war. When we asked, we learned that he had a new son.

Aleppo continued to be decorated in honor of this birth for almost a month, and al-Malik al-Zahir commanded that tables be set out every day so people could eat free of charge. During the baby's third week a huge circumcision party was held. All the leading citizens brought their sons to be circumcised together with the newborn prince. It was obvious to everyone that the king was in the best possible spirits, thanks to the birth of his son. Before all these festivities concluded, he ordered a bunch of new building projects: three new city gates, a defensive wall, and renovation of a mosque that had burned. After all this—my dream vision and the beautification of the city—I knew exactly what to wish for: *My God, choose a bride for me.*

76

During the few days following my dream, the image of this prospective wife never left my imagination, and I fell deeply in love with her, even though I hadn't seen or met her. I began to ask God in personal, prostrate prayer to draw me closer to her and her to me so that my heart would be compatible with her and my spirit find comfort in her company. God quickly answered my prayer.

There was a man at the door of my house when I returned from the mosque. He was sitting with Sawdakin on the doorstep awaiting my return. When they saw me approaching, they rose, and the man kissed my head as I tried to get a peek at his face, which looked familiar.

"God's peace to you, Master."

"Welcome."

"I am your devoted servant, Yunus ibn Yusuf."

I turned toward Sawdakin and asked critically: "Why is our guest sitting on the doorstep, Sawdakin?"

Sawdakin bowed his head in shame and said, "I pleaded with him to enter, but he wouldn't. . . ."

Yunus interrupted him: "It's true, he invited me inside, but I preferred to wait here to welcome you, Master."

Directing my words to Sawdakin, I pointed a finger at him threateningly, "No guest of mine will sit on the doorstep, so long as I am a Hatimi and a Ta'i tribesman."

"I hear and obey, Master."

We entered the house together, and Sawdakin quickly prepared food to offer our guest, who declined to sit beside me and squatted before me instead. He said, "God bless you for your learning and your good deeds, Master. I attended your lessons and quenched my thirst from the sea of your learning."

"Which course did you take?"

"That was a few years ago, in Mecca, before you left there, breaking our hearts with your departure."

"That's why your face looks familiar, even though I could not place you."

"But you remain present in my heart, spirit, and memory, Master."

"May God bring you the best and fill your heart and spirit with His contentment and blessings."

Sawdakin brought us fruit and bread and sat down near us in his customary way: pressing his knees to his chest and resting his chin on them. We consumed what he had brought, and I asked the man where he was from.

"From Mardin, Master, but I visit Aleppo every summer."

"What brings you here?"

"My daughter married an Aleppine man, but he has died."

"May God be compassionate to him. Does she have children?"

"No."

"What do you do in Mardin?"

"I teach young Turks there Qur'an and the Arabic language. When I come to Aleppo, I interpret dreams."

I glanced at Sawdakin, who smiled in a knowing way. Then I looked again at Yunus, who seemed to understand that I would like some further clarification. He quickly added, "Sawdakin came to me a few days ago to ask me to interpret your dream. And I did. Before I returned home that night, someone came to summon me urgently to my daughter's house. I rushed there and discovered that a messenger from the Bureau of the Army had informed her that her husband had died as a martyr."

"Martyred? I didn't know we were at war!"

"It wasn't a war, Master. He was in an army unit the king dispatched from Aleppo to ward off the harm the Franks are causing to Tarsus, but the Franks ambushed the unit, killing all of them."

"All might and power are God's!"

"God decreed this, and what He wishes, happens. My soul told me that perhaps God's plan may have been for my daughter to be widowed the same day I interpreted your dream and that I would not be able to find a more suitable husband for her than you. So if you want her, she will be your wife, without any dowry."

"God bless you, Yunus, but you are giving me what is not yours to give. I will come to see her, once her prescribed mourning period ends. If God draws our hearts together, I will ask to marry her, and the decision will be hers alone."

"As you think best."

When Fatima's requisite waiting period ended, I married her. Then I discovered that she was exactly as my heart had wished. Perhaps my empty heart would have been content with any woman and my weary body would have welcomed any boon, after many years of travel and spiritual retreats. The important point was that she brought serenity to my spirit and solace to my soul. She soon blossomed in my breast like a jasmine garden, and her father returned to Mardin, feeling reassured about his daughter. I grew accustomed to her love, and my age seemed to reassure her. The only anxious one in the household was Badr.

I entered his room one evening and found him lying down, before it was bedtime. He sat up with difficulty as soon as he discovered that I had entered and began to complain of chronic back pain.

In a voice interrupted by groans, he said, "I sent Sawdakin to fetch water."

"You did the right thing."

I sat down beside him, and he wrapped a cloth around his foot. We remained silent for some time till he asked, "And now . . . why don't we head to Malatya?"

"Divine will caused us to head west, Badr."

"But 'west' encompasses a huge area. Why should we remain in Aleppo?"

"What's behind this?"

Badr looked at my face in amazement. Then he shook his head regretfully and asked, "What is there in Aleppo? Nothing but the jurists who love you and the preachers who are your disciples . . ." His sarcasm caught me off guard. Even though his expression was glum, I burst into laughter. Ignoring my laughter, he continued: "They don't merely swing wide the doors of the mosques for you, they open the doors of their homes and sit before you to absorb your erudition."

I laughed even louder. Badr paused, but his expression hadn't softened at all. Instead, he stared at my face and asked critically, "Have you forgotten what they did to you years ago when we were forced to flee from them to Cairo? Even if you've forgotten that, I don't think they have forgotten you."

I didn't answer him; I was laughing too hard. Even as I hid my face in my hand, Badr's rigid expression was visible to my mind and his sarcastic words echoed in my ears, even as I continued laughing. For the first time since he had become my companion, he had addressed me sarcastically, as if he could no longer tolerate me or put up with my ecstatic dicta and leaps. I glanced at him to find that he was still frowning and looked sleepy and exhausted. He started brushing dust from his tunic and avoided my eyes.

I told him, "I don't remember the last time I laughed so hard, Badr."

He shot right back while still fussing with his garment, "But this is nothing to laugh about. I think it's not in your best interest to remain in Aleppo."

Then he looked up at me and said, "If your divine allusion directed you westward, then let's go west. God's west is expansive, and let's distance ourselves as much as possible from the bastions of the Ayyubids and their kings, whose only opinion is that of the masses and whose only preoccupation is politics."

I bowed my head in silence and did not respond. He stroked my shoulders and then raised my chin with his hand till I was looking at his face. He said in an admonitory tone: "Master, the gallows on which al-Suhrawardi was hanged still stand in Baghdad, and the Ayyubid who strung him up was the greatest and wisest of all of them: Salah al-Din. So what's your opinion of the fools who are his offspring and the children of his brothers? They kill each other. Do you think they will preserve the blood of a Sufi *wali* from Andalusia?"

"God safeguards me, Badr."

"God also forbids you from endangering your life."

I fell silent, as did he. Sawdakin arrived to find us both sunk in silence. He placed food before us without a word. We ate, hearing only the sounds of our jaws crunching the food. I was reflecting deeply on what Badr had said and trying to weigh it on the intellect's scales, divorced from unsubstantiated fears. *I know that he's getting on in years and that anxiety has become his companion. How can we distance ourselves from the Ayyubids when they control Egypt, Syria, and Yemen? Indeed, how can we escape from our enemies when they are everywhere?*

We finished eating, and Badr turned his back toward Sawdakin for him to massage. Then he renounced that when his pain only increased. I felt sorry for him, for what he was suffering. He had been my inseparable companion all these years.

He had never disobeyed an order or rejected a request. He had grown old, keeping me company, without me giving him a thought.

"Listen, Badr."

Both he and Sawdakin turned toward me. I looked Badr straight in the eye and said, "All the west indicated to me by that allusion is ruled by the Ayyubids. . . ."

Badr interrupted me in mid-sentence and said: "Let's go to Damascus then. At least Chief Justice Ibn al-Zaki will protect you there."

I smiled broadly. This was what I was thinking and had intended to suggest, but I didn't admit it. I nodded to express my agreement and said, "That's what we'll do, Badr. I hear and obey. We'll travel to Damascus as soon as your back grants us permission!"

"No volition that makes no difference should be trusted."

—IBN ARABI

77

I sent Fatima to her father in Mardin, and we set off for Damascus. But we didn't reach it or arrive there. How many a traveler does not reach his destination or attain his goal! Glory to the One Who brought me out of Baghdad heading to Malatya only to land me in Aleppo. Then He brought me out of Aleppo heading to Damascus and I ended up in the Bekaa Valley. This happened when we were only a day or two from the city of Damascus, and my mount headed west. She gripped her halter with her teeth and bit through it. When I dismounted to lead her, she dragged me some distance before I was able to stop her. Sawdakin and Badr dismounted from their mounts and started to groom this rebellious she-mule, but she would have none of this and began to bray noisily. We wondered aloud whether she was tired or hungry. We offered her some hay, but she refused to eat it. We tied her to a tree and sat down near her, thinking she would rest.

Badr told Sawdakin, "You shouldn't have bought a Greek mule. She's strong but stubborn."

I defended Sawdakin, asking, "How can you tell an obedient mule from a stubborn one, Badr?"

"All those Byzantine mules are stubborn. If he had purchased an Egyptian mule, we would already be there now."

I teased him jocularly, "You really love Egypt, Badr!"

He turned his head away and didn't reply. Then he said suddenly, "That's the only homeland I know. That's where I was raised and grew up."

I walked a short distance from them and lay down in a tree's shade, hoping to take a nap. Then I heard the voice of an elderly man praying and invoking God poignantly. I stood up to try to hear better and asked my two companions, "Do you hear what I do?"

They looked at each other and didn't reply. Then Sawdakin asked, "What do you hear, Master?"

I closed my eyes and started to turn in a circle, raising my arms high and letting my two heels set my circuit. I felt dizzy but didn't stop twirling. The dizzier I became, the clearer the elderly man's voice grew, till he seemed to be beside me. I whirled and whirled and whirled and felt I was rising from the earth's surface and swimming in the heavenly realms. In the darkness of my eyes, which were closed, a wave of light shone: the man was seated in the witnessing pose of a worshipper proclaiming the oneness of God. Then he proceeded with the prayer ritual, offering the first and second prostrations. Next he looked straight at me and said: "Exile, Brother!"

As I fell, Sawdakin's two arms caught me. He had evidently been hovering around me ever since I started whirling, afraid I would fall. We sat down together on the ground, and I rested my head on his chest. I tried to open my eyes in the glare of the sunshine, succeeding for a moment only to fail the next. Badr sprinkled water on my face and then wiped my forehead. He bared my chest and began to explore it with his wet hand. I finally felt my body return to the earth, after having left it for some seconds, and my spirit return to my body, after preceding it to the Bekaa Valley.

I had lost my equilibrium when I was twirling but had found my way and learned my destination. I stood up, headed to my mule, and kissed her broad forehead. I untied her and mounted. Then we headed west.

Badr and Sawdakin followed me without uttering a word. We traveled for an hour before Badr finally asked, "Where are we going, Master?"

"To the Bekaa Valley, Badr al-Tamam, my full moon."

"What is our destination there?"

I pointed to my mule, which was advancing energetically and said, "Ask her!"

Badr fell back and grumbled something I couldn't hear. I knew he was tired and that his back occasionally hurt him. But I wasn't mocking him. Since I had been riding this mule, she had led me. I wasn't guiding her. I didn't know why I was heading to the Bekaa Valley. I had heard a voice and seen a shaykh but didn't know who he was or what he wanted. All I knew was that I would reach him mounted on this mule. I would stay on her till she we arrived, even if that meant traversing the entire earth. Allusions aren't random, and unveilings don't descend in vain.

"Any exile that does not benefit a person isn't trustworthy."

——IBN ARABI

78

We rode for hours and hours, and Badr began to moan loudly. He lay on the she-mule to relieve the pain in his back while clinging to her neck. He finally shouted, "I can't bear this anymore!"

He dismounted from his mule, lay down on his back, gasped, and then screamed, "My Lord, be benevolent! I can't take any more."

Sawdakin and I got on either side of him and carried him to the shade of a tree and left him stretched out there. His forehead was sweaty, and his back pain was obvious from the expression of his face. I felt sorry for him—that he was feeling such pain when he was so old. At times a disciple's patience is exhausted, and God tests his willpower. He may grow old, his back may hurt, and his joints may creak. He may yearn for a quiet, tranquil life in a secure monastery, for a residence only steps away from the mosque, for easy lessons, a limited number of books, warm rooms, and predictable events. But all this was not his to command—nor mine. We had to travel to obtain insights. A Believer is on an endless voyage. All of existence is itself a voyage within a voyage. Had I not been Badr's close friend who could not bear to part with him, I would have allowed him to settle wherever he wished. But I wanted him to have a deeper life, one more grounded in experience. I wanted him to achieve the level of Sufism that matched the purity of his heart and the virtue of his spirit. Didn't he realize that quitting the journey meant quiescence, which itself meant fading into nonexistence?

"Badr. . . ."

"Yes, Master."

"Give me your hand."

He extended his hand. I gripped it and asked him, "Do you know who the disciple is?"

Badr cleared his throat as if the question had surprised him. He took his time to reply, sensing that my question harbored criticism for him. After a brief silence, he replied, "The disciple, Master, is the student of your learning and the pupil of your understanding."

"No, Badr. By saying this, you have equated all disciples, regardless of their spiritual aspirations, as students of learning."

"Instruct me, Master."

"The disciple, Badr, is the person who renounces his own volition in favor of God's. Do you know who the object of the disciple's volition is?"

"He is the shaykh to whom God has granted wisdom to dispense to disciples like me."

"No, Badr. By saying this you have made even schoolteachers and grooms in stables objects of volition!"

"Instruct me, Master."

"The object of the disciple's volition is the one who has no volition."

Badr remained silent and didn't comment. I knew he was waiting for some clarification from me, and that forced me to review with him the Sufi principles—after he had been my companion for all these years! He may have suspected that there was some implied rebuke.

I said to him, "Badr. You are a disciple who has voluntarily renounced your own volition, but I am an involuntary object of volition. No personal choice played a part in my abandonment of my volition."

Badr listened intently to my words: "This is why at times the matter is so hard on you: you are wrestling with your ego and its caprices. I do not suffer a similar struggle in my soul, because my volition was extracted from me when God attracted me into His orbit."

"May God increase all your stations and your states, Master."

"But this means that your wages will be greater than mine, since your effort to control your ego is greater than mine."

Badr was visibly moved and wept. His voice quavered when he said apologetically, "Forgive me. I've grown old, and my body has grown heavy. My soul hankers after rest and ease."

"It's not your fault, Badr. Do you recall al-Bistami's statement that I cited repeatedly in my lessons?"

"Which one, Master?"

I tapped him on the shoulder and replied jovially, "You've become forgetful too, Old Man. Do you know who I am?"

He smiled with embarrassment and replied, "You are my shaykh and my master."

"My shaykh and your shaykh, al-Bistami said, 'I kept leading my weeping soul to God . . . until I could lead it there laughing.'"

Badr's tears flowed down his wrinkled face and mixed with the sweat flowing from his temples to his cheeks, even as he continued to smile with embarrassment. I gazed at him in that tearful, smiling condition and hoped I had succeeded in calming his soul and soothing his mind. Feeling an overwhelming love for him, I put my arm around his neck and began to wipe his forehead. I said, "We still have a long day before us. So, let me tell you a story to entertain you Badr, my Full Moon."

"I'm all ears."

"One day in Seville, I felt upset and depressed, because that city had almost lost its spirit and was closing in on its residents. My father was also forbidding me to travel the way an adult keeps a young child away from fire. Most of the shaykhs had quit the city for Fez, Salé, and Marrakech, and the stationers' market was so stagnant that there wasn't a useful book left there that I hadn't read. My mother's migraines had grown so severe she couldn't see straight. On this day I left our house, heading nowhere in particular, and ended up walking along the bank of the great river, thinking I might find relief from my despairs and mitigation of my cares there. Instead I found the youth of Seville fooling around in disreputable ways. They were talking trash and doing nasty stuff. They had lost any sense of shame, and their manly virtues had been lost, till you no longer knew what these kids feared or hoped for. Then I felt even more worried and upset. My feet led me to the house of my shaykh al-Uraybi,[40] with whom I sought refuge from every bit of bad luck and to whom I complained of my every sorrow. I knocked on his door and entered to find him in his oratory, as usual. The moment he saw me with such a pale face and furrowed brow, he asked, 'What ails you, my boy?' I replied, 'The world is closing in on me, and my worries keep piling up, Shaykh.' He didn't ask me why I was upset or what concerns I had. He merely said this one thing: 'Focus on God!' Then he returned to his oratory as if I weren't there. I left his house and walked off aimlessly until my feet eventually led me to the house of my other shaykh, Musa al-Mirtuli. I found him, as I often did, in his spiritual retreat braiding palm leaves and making baskets. I approached, sat down beside him, and began handing him fronds, one at a time, to weave into a basket. He asked me, 'What's the matter with you today, Ibn Arabi?' I told him, 'A concern I can't remove from my chest and a crisis from which I find no relief.' Without ceasing his work, he replied: 'You should focus on your soul!' I was outraged! I felt I was becoming lost in a wilderness of anxiety, between this shaykh and that one. I threw down the frond in my hand and stood up, preparing to leave. He asked, 'What's the matter?' I told him, 'Master, I am in a quandary, torn between you and al-Uraybi. He says: focus on God, but you say: focus on your soul. You are both my imams and my guides to the truth.' Then he told me, 'Return to him and tell him what I have told you.' So I returned to al-Uraybi's house and told him what al-Mirtuli had said. He declared, 'He was right.' I protested, 'Shaykh, but he said the opposite of what you said!' He explained: 'He showed you the path . . . and I have shown you the Traveling Companion.'"

"Glory to God!"

I squeezed his biceps and told him, "Badr, if God is our Traveling Companion, what is there for us to complain about?"

"Avoid people, so they are saved by you instead of vice versa."

—— **IBN ARABI**

79

The mule finally reached her goal after two days of travel along the Bekaa Valley. She paused by a small hill, which she would partially circle only to turn back again. I contemplated the area around me and found no one there. This broad plain was lined by low hills with few trees. As far as the horizon, no building, tent, or other sign of man was visible. We had left the road that travelers use many hours earlier, because the mule had wanted to. Sawdakin had tried to warn me about that, after Badr stopped offering objections. I had considered the danger of leaving the road that travelers use and penetrating deep into a land that we didn't know and that bordered on the Franks' territory. But I had placed my faith in God and decided to plunge wherever the mule did. So we had proceeded together. She knew her route. She climbed no mountains with us and descended into no valleys. Instead she continued to walk along the widest part of the valley till she reached this place.

Badr and Sawdakin looked my way, as if awaiting some decision. We would not be able to camp in this location where there was no water, nothing to eat, and no sign of a human being. Once the sun set, wild animals and beasts of prey would emerge and find three tired, unarmed Sufis. I reflected. I dismounted and started to walk. When I kept thinking for a long time, Badr dismounted from the animal he was riding, removed the goat hide from her, tossed it on the ground, and stretched out on it to rest his back as he groaned softly. Sawdakin squatted near him and rested his head on his knees. His long legs resembled tent poles

319

as they protruded from his tunic. I stared at the eyes of the mule and realized they looked the way they had when we were heading from Aleppo to Damascus. She had performed her mission and that was that. I now needed to decide what we should do or wait for some further sign. I tried whirling about, but that accomplished nothing. I grew tired and sat down where I was, not feeling giddy or even dizzy. I was conscious of no allusion, no voices, no fog.

I finally decided: "Sawdakin and I will climb this hill. Perhaps we'll find some houses. You stay here, Badr, with the animals."

Sawdakin stood up to accompany me and tied the halters of the three animals together. Badr remained flat on his back while I headed to the hill and started climbing. Sawdakin followed me, carrying a water skin. It didn't take us long to reach the top of the hill. Then we waved down to Badr, but he didn't wave back. The other side of the hill was just as desolate as the side we had climbed; God seemed to have destroyed whoever had once been there. A cold breeze blew, announcing that the sun would soon set and warning that this wouldn't be a cozy place to remain. We would have to return to the route travelers used and spend the night somewhere that people frequented, and predatory animals avoided. On the morrow, God would accomplish what He willed.

I told Sawdakin this, and he obediently nodded his head in agreement. We started to descend, but then Sawdakin cried out: "There!"

I looked in the direction his long finger pointed but saw only more hills in the distance, like the one we stood on. Sawdakin wagged his finger, as if that would make the view clearer, and described the surroundings: "That boulder. . . that slope. . . . Do you see, Master?"

"What do you see, Sawdakin?"

"Something like a cave! Something like a house!"

"Are you sure?"

"Yes. Stay here, Master. I'll go check it out."

"No, let's both go."

We walked down the other side of the hill and could no longer see Badr. After a short walk, I was able to discern what Sawdakin had seen and I hadn't. There was a cleft in the hill, and half was covered by a boulder. The other half had a manmade roof composed of crossed planks and branches. We headed straight there and then heard a dog bark.

Sawdakin observed, "It's got our scent. It must be a shepherd's dog."

We finally stopped at the door of this house and heard the clatter of vessels from inside and the light rustle of a person walking. I stood near the entrance and called out: "Peace to you."

He emerged wearing a jacket with torn-off sleeves. Bareheaded, he had a furrowed forehead, bushy eyebrows, and a round face. His beard covered his entire chest, and his shoulders were broad, even though his back was bent. In one hand he held a small empty basin and in the other a walking stick. He approached us, trying to discern our features, and said, "*Wa alaykum as-salam*."

He moved even closer and studied my face. I also moved nearer to him to scrutinize his. Each of us continued to contemplate the other for some seconds without saying a word. I finally asked, "Are you who I think you are?"

He didn't answer me. Instead he gestured with his hands, which held the basin and the stick—as if he had seen something amazing. Then, as his mouth flashed a broad smile, he approached me and exclaimed: "Muhyi!"

We embraced each other, while Sawdakin stood there dumbfounded—as if watching shadow puppets. The man's copious tears washed his face. Then he released me and prostrated himself in prayer to God. After that, he hugged me again, for a longer time. He continued to grasp my upper arm as he gazed at my face with a tearful smile. Meanwhile I soaked in his features and tried to detect the trajectory that time had taken traversing them. Tucking my hand beneath his arm, he led me inside the cave, which was scarcely large enough to hold two men. He didn't seem to have noticed Sawdakin at all—or, perhaps the surprise had made him forget to look. I turned to Sawdakin and asked him to go to Badr and bring him. So he darted off while I sat before the man, whose eyes were still wet with tears, which flowed down the folds of his wrinkled face and into his thick beard.

"What are you doing here? Do you live alone?"

"Alone? No, I was alone when I was surrounded by all of you. Now God is with me."

He said this while looking around him nervously, as if searching for something he had lost. He soon collected some sticks of firewood from a corner of the cave and carried them to a circle of ashes that had piled up from successive fires that had been lit there repeatedly and died out. Then he entered a hut and brought out a radish, which he placed before me. He went back and fetched some flour. He placed it in a bowl, poured water over it from a jug with a worn mouth, and began to knead it.

I asked him, "Didn't you find God when you were among us?"

"God is everywhere, but you all hid him from me."

"How long have you lived in isolation?"

He laughed, extended a hand to seize the tip of my beard gently, and replied, "Since your beard was entirely black, Muhyi."

I unconsciously grasped my short beard, smiled with embarrassment, and said, "Your kinsfolk think that you're dead."

"And you? What did you think?"

"I could see you praying and entreating God but didn't recognize you."

"I have also seen you approach on your mule without being able to recognize you."

He made a spark, and eventually a fire caught. He started blowing on the dry grass and twigs till the firewood began to burn. He sat there silently, not looking at me, with an expression of earnest humility. Then he said, "Stand up so I can show you."

I rose with him, and we entered the cave. Once inside, we turned and I saw a small wooden door with a latch, which he turned. When the door opened, I saw that the rock-carved room inside was tall enough for a person to stand, long enough for prostration in prayer, and wide enough to sit down. It lacked any slit, porthole, or window through which light could enter. Even though it was still day, it was totally dark. When I was inside this cell, I found there was another latch on the inside of the door.

He told me, "This is where I retreat spiritually with my Lord."

"But this isn't required for a spiritual retreat."

"I know. But cutting all ties with people requires this."

"Cutting ties with people isn't necessary either! God's friends retreat into His presence in their homes, markets, shops, and mosques."

He smiled at me as we returned to our flaming fire outside. He replied, "Those are God's *walis*—not me! My soul became so polluted that only this isolation would purify it. Just so you'll know: I have remained in this cave for nine years, struggling and contending with my soul, and have only actualized my spiritual retreat in the last few months. Before that all I did was discipline my soul."

"What have you learned from your spiritual retreat? Instruct me."

He returned to his dough and replied, as the fire cast its light and shadows on his face with the evening's approach, "For a few years I continued to avoid people—to ward off their evil, blame, and censure—but didn't achieve my goal. I thought that if I would just avoid them to spare them dealing with me and my evil, my soul would find some relief. Once I focused on my soul, my solitude ended and my spiritual retreat commenced. Brother, spiritual retreat is the most refined degree of exile. Spiritual retreat is a retreat from solitude."

Tears came to my eyes without my realizing it when he spoke about spiritual retreat and his delight in it. "Tell me more," I said.

He lifted his hand from the dough, which he left in the bowl, sat cross-legged on the ground, and replied as he gazed at the fire: "I lived my entire life ruled by fantasy. I was never able to control my fantasy till I entered a spiritual retreat with God in this cave."

The ensuing silence was interrupted only by the crackling of the fire. Then we heard the hooves of the mules approaching. Soon Badr and Sawdakin were with us. When he saw the dough in the bowl, Sawdakin immediately approached the fire to arrange its embers. Badr approached and offered his greetings. He had only just taken the man's hand when he stared at his face and Badr's words became trapped in his throat. His features were so frozen for a time we feared he had stopped breathing. His expression suggested that he might start weeping, he was so astonished, and we started laughing. He finally took a seat on the ground, stretched out a leg, and looked back and forth between us without saying a word.

"Loss is inevitable. Grief is inevitable!"

—IBN ARABI

The sun had scarcely reached the middle of the sky and our shadows had hidden themselves beneath our feet when we reached the first caravanseray on the road to Baalbek. We had traveled the few hours since sunrise, following the few landmarks that Caliph Ya'qub ibn Yusuf described for us with great accuracy after he led us in the dawn prayer and bade us farewell with tears in his eyes and sorrow in his heart. This was the first hostelry we had encountered in many days. Just as soon as he saw it, Badr tied his animal by its portal and entered before me, even though he had always waited for me to enter a door first. He sat down before the attendant at the foot-washing basin, and the man started removing the thorns from his feet. We all bathed and oiled our bodies. Sawdakin collected our clothes and took them to the clothes-washing basin. Next he took my mule to the blacksmiths, whose shops were in a row near the khans for travelers, to have her shoes fixed. After the sun had set, we finally sat down—at a long dining table with all the other travelers—to consume soup, bread, and some meat.

We decided to stay there at least two nights after we learned from the proprietor of the caravanserai that the next lodgings were nine or ten full days farther on the road to the city of Homs. It was for this reason that this hostelry was jampacked with travelers. Four other men shared our room. From their appearance we assumed they were Muslim until they began to speak and we realized they were Christians. They explained to

324

us in broken Arabic that they had come from Antioch and were heading to Tripoli. The following morning, they changed out of their Arab clothes, removed their turbans, and donned tight-fitting trousers and leather shoes. Hanging down the back of one man was a shawl with a large cross embroidered on it. When the portly innkeeper entered, his cheeks were red from pulling bread for us from the fiery bread oven. Sawdakin asked why the Christians changed clothes. He immediately replied: "They're all like that. They disguise themselves with Muslim attire along the way for fear of being killed."

The word "killed" upset Badr, who asked in a loud voice betraying his anxiety: "Who would kill them?"

Sawdakin, catching fear's contagion, answered: "Highwaymen, among others."

After the innkeeper placed the last disc of bread near me and picked up his empty basket to leave, he said: "There are no highwaymen here. Just Isma'ilis. They're the ones who target Christians."

Badr calmed down a bit and began to eat his breakfast lethargically. I glanced at his feet and found they had open wounds—some of which were still oozing blood. I touched them and found that they were hard and swollen and that the skin had been worn away at their ends. I lifted his legs and placed his feet in my lap. He was embarrassed and attempted to draw them away, but I held them tight. I started to feel them with my fingers while reciting the surah "Ya Sin." Then his mood improved, and he started to eat his breakfast calmly and tranquilly. I completed my recitation from the Qur'an and began to wipe some of the blood from his feet. I noticed that he didn't wince with pain when I touched the open wounds. I pinched him near his heel, and he didn't feel it. I was dismayed by this and surmised something I did not wish to believe. But it was true. A month and a week later, when we reached Malatya, his right foot had turned into a black, bloodless lump he dragged behind him. Badr refused to allow the physician to amputate his foot, and so his leg died. Finally, when he was stretched out on a plank of wood from which he had first fled, the doctor amputated his leg from the knee down with a knife and a saw. Then he cauterized the wound with hot iron. Badr was unconscious for many hours while I wondered how I would survive if he died. But he regained consciousness—raving and weeping. We brought him back to our house, and he was silent and gazed into the void as if resentful about something— we didn't know what—or angry at something he would not elucidate.

"Patience can't be trusted if you haven't complained to God about it."

—IBN ARABI

81

I spent the days after Badr's foot was amputated nursing him. I would wake before he did, prepare his food, carry it to him, feed him, lift him, and sit him up. Sawdakin measured him and ordered a crutch for him from a carpenter in the neighborhood. His wound healed, and he mastered walking with his crutch, but he never regained his original form. His anger gradually turned to grief, and he remained still most of the time. He was silent and would only speak if I spoke to him. He hardly ever went out with us, except to the Friday prayer. He gathered cushions in a corner of the room, placing one behind his back, another under his remaining leg, and a third behind him to lean on. In front of him there was a small table. Transferring the power of his lost leg to his hands, he began weaving wool to make bedspreads and shirts. Next he started hammering on the table's wood and carving it. Then he focused on copying manuscripts. We would bring him paper, and he would huddle in the house, making a copy of this book or that, till he got his hands all black.

I rented a house with a room that had a baked-brick ceiling. At the center of this room were wooden columns. The door opened on narrow interior corridors, and it had one small window, which admitted the sun's rays. We turned the courtyard at one end of the house into a garden. Winter arrived two months after we did, and I put Badr in the warmest room. I placed a brass stove near him and vented the exhaust into the courtyard. On bitterly cold nights we would all sleep in his room after covering the floor with two layers of carpeting. We also spread blankets and covers throughout the house. We fell asleep to the sound of Badr's moans, inspired by his pain, which the cold exacerbated.

Ishaq knocked on the door on one of those cold nights. Even before he said hello, he remarked critically, "You sneak into my country and you don't even tell me, Muhyi?"

Embracing him, I laughed and replied, "We entered through the city's gate in broad daylight. We didn't sneak in. We had no way to contact you, because you're insulated by chamberlains and government ministers."

Ishaq entered, and we all sat down around Badr. Ishaq was shocked to find him crippled and fought back tears while sitting next to him. He tried to appear jocular and cheerful to avoid adding to Badr's sorrows.

I asked Ishaq: "How are you?"

He replied, "I'm a traveler who rarely sets down his walking stick."

"Where do you go?"

"At times to His Majesty the Caliph in Baghdad, at times to His Majesty the Emperor of Nicea, at times to His Excellency the King of Aleppo, and other times to Her Excellency the Queen of Georgia. Then I return to our Sultan in Konya with letters and news. His mind remains unsettled till he is reassured about his relations with all of them."

"That's far better than wars without a flag or a reason."

Ishaq sighed, and stretching his feet out before him, said, "Wars are inevitable. The Sultan is currently mobilizing against Antalya and will lead the army himself."

"Will you accompany him?"

"No. I'm on my way to Baghdad. The Sultan wants the Caliph to send him jihadis to establish a center for like-minded youths in Konya."

"What does he want them for?"

Ishaq laughed sarcastically and answered: "You ask about this, Muhyi? Have you gone into Malatya's markets and seen the types of people here? Anatolians are a mixed bunch who know neither their lineage nor their path."

"What do jihadis have to do with this?"

Ishaq shrugged his shoulders, as if the answer were self-evident, and replied, "With them, people gain a battalion in the Sultan's army and mujahidi ghazis for the frontiers."

I looked at Ishaq, smiled, and said, "The Army's Central Command can mobilize people for jihad and enlist them in the army. Ghazis aren't troops or soldiers. They're a group of people who believe in God and to whom God has granted guidance."

"The Sultan wants to recruit them for their faith and their guidance."

I looked straight at him and inquired, "Do you think faith and guidance are obtained by drinking salty water and wearing jihadi trousers like they do in Baghdad?"

Ishaq bowed his head and didn't reply. I leaned back against the wall once more to await his response. After some moments he said, "You're right, Muhyi. But I am a messenger, and all a messenger does is deliver the message. The Sultan wants to have mujahidin in Konya like the ones in Baghdad. He assembles young men for jihad and combat instead of letting them loiter in the streets, where they cause mayhem and disturb the citizens."

Then he raised his eyes, which looked regretful, and said, "To tell you the truth: these are some of the Sultanate's secrets. Raising an army is no longer easy, no matter how generously the Sultan remunerates the troops and allows his soldiers a share of the booty. All his enemies offer them what he does. They may transfer their loyalties in an hour, and then a charge becomes a flight. People are mingled together in the armed forces to the point that you will find, in a single army brigade, Arabs, Bulgars, Armenians, Greeks, and Georgians, some of whom have fought on more than one side and under more than one banner. Who would trust an army like this?"

Ishaq didn't wait for me to comment. Instead, he stood up suddenly and said, "I must go. I have precious gifts from the Sultan for the Caliph in my baggage and must deliver them to the governor's palace before nightfall."

He turned toward Badr, who had been listening to our conversation with a sad, fixed smile, embraced him, and kissed his forehead. Then he gave me a farewell hug and said, "I'll pass by Malatya on my return trip."

"Stay safe, Brother."

Sawdakin saw him to the door. When he returned, I asked him, "Bring me paper and an inkwell."

Sawdakin did as I requested, and then I sat down to write. After asking for God's help, I wrote, "In the name of the powerful and steadfast God Who sent the young men to the cave when He was nearer to them than their jugular vein. To continue: This is a chapter concerning what is known about chivalry, jihadi knights, their centers, their classes, and the secrets of their poles."[41]

82

It seemed to me one morning that the time had come for a solution. Travel was no longer easy now that my companion had only one foot, my wife had arrived from Mardin, and my fifty years had accumulated like rust on my joints. My last pillar was waiting for me somewhere here, and my longing to travel had grown subdued compared to my longing to write. Everything in Malatya suggested we should stay put. Its cold winter forced me to stay in the house and concentrate on writing, and its long nights made me want to pray and engage in spiritual retreats. It also had an Arab minority distinguished by their huge turbans and brown complexions, and finally Fatima's belly had grown round and was slowly swelling.

I loved her; I don't know whether she loved me or not. Something in her eyes suggested that she was still fond of her deceased martyr. He had been a young man in the prime of life. Since he was a soldier in the Army's Special Forces, whom the King sent on important assignments, he must have had a handsome body and bulging biceps. Now she was married to a skinny man with a pot belly, male-pattern baldness, a gray line in his forelocks and in the beard on his cheeks. She hadn't turned thirty yet, and her long hair was as black as a lover's night. Her complexion was wheat-colored like that of women in Mecca. Her limbs were delicate, as if they had not matured with the rest of her.

Discovering whether my love was reciprocated probably would not have changed our relationship in any way. Everything proceeded normally, as if life were pointing toward my chest with her hand and then to Malatya's green earth. Fatima grew most of what we ate—cucumbers, peas, celery—in the courtyard, which had become a garden. During the last six years the apricot tree had grown tall and begun to provide us shade and even more fruit than we needed. Sawdakin carried our surplus apricots to the mosque to feed the poor and the pious fools there.

Ishaq returned some months after his departure. He had succeeded with his assignment and brought back young jihadis to instruct boys and old men and to teach them to read in the mosques. He was having a meal at my house when he said he was staying in Malatya because the Sultan was on his way here to launch a jihad against Armenia. A few weeks later, little Malatya was teeming with the Sultan's courtiers and army. Sawdakin told me the Sultan rode around town on a Greek horse with a massive back and rump. People began to toss rose petals beneath the horse's hooves to celebrate the Sultan as he proceeded to his residence in the Governor's palace. Ishaq left my house that morning to join the Sultan's entourage, and I missed our daytime lessons and our evening talks.

Even so, our separation did not last long. The fourth day after the Sultan's arrival had scarcely ended when Ishaq knocked on my door. He was accompanied by the Sultan's chancellor, who stood before me like a soldier at attention. He drew a letter from his cincture, opened it, and read it to me: "Our Master, Mawlana Muhyi al-Din—Sultan Izz al-Din Kayka'us asks you to honor his assembly today."

Ishaq smiled as if he understood how unusual this invitation was. I informed the chancellor that I accepted the invitation, and he departed. Ishaq stayed behind, and I asked his permission to wash and put on fresh clothes. I went inside to urge Fatima to prepare an outfit for me. She took my shirt, cloak, and sash from the clothes chest and began to shake them out quickly. Then she fetched a clean turban—one of the two I wore for the Friday prayer service. I hastily adorned myself with the best clothing I had and applied some of the rose and violet cologne that people of Anatolia love. Then I went back out to Ishaq, who seemed to have been smiling nonstop while I was in my bedroom.

We stepped outside my house to find a horse-drawn palanquin that nearly blocked the narrow alley on which my house was located. We both climbed into it, and the two horses took us to the Governor's Palace as people peered inside, trying to make out who we were. A group of boys chased behind the palanquin till we approached the Governor's Palace and then disbanded. We entered a palace with narrow corridors. Vents in its walls blew warm air from a furnace set atop the palace to warm its corridors and rooms. We soon found ourselves in a large chamber that contained at its center a single chair, which was reserved for the Sultan. People sat around him on thick wool and cotton rugs lined up around the sides. We sat on the ones closest to the chair and listened to the hubbub presaging the Sultan's arrival. Once he entered—with a smooth, clean-shaven chin and a bushy mustache—he ignored the people addressing him and hurried to us. He hugged me fondly and then kissed my cheeks. I kissed his. Then he said in an eloquent Arabic with a Turkmen accent: "Welcome to the Sea of Realities, our Shaykh, Ibn Arabi. Malatya is blessed by your presence. All of Anatolia is blessed by your presence."

"The blessing is from God, Whom I ask to bless you and your realm."

"We hope you will remain with us so we may be enlightened by you and benefit from your learning."

"May God prolong the Sultan's continued enjoyment of what he loves."

Then the Sultan turned toward Ishaq and spoke to him in Turkmen, which I did not understand. Once they had finished, Ishaq turned toward me and said to the Sultan in Arabic, "Mawlana, you are well aware that this is the mightiest guest to alight in Malatya."

The Sultan also switched to Arabic, and said affably, "No doubt. . . . No doubt."

The Sultan remained affectionate and turned toward me from time to time to repeat his welcome. When the time came for the afternoon prayer, he ordered prayer rugs brought in and insisted that I serve as imam and lead the prayer. So I accepted, and he and Ishaq lined up behind me. When we finished performing the prayer, he ordered up some food. They brought in a roast lamb with the spit on which it had been roasted still inside. They placed it in front of the three of us. The Sultan descended from his chair and sat with us on the ground. He didn't touch the food till the taster responsible for testing his food had eaten a morsel, chewed and swallowed it, before retreating to the side of the room. Then the Sultan began to eat. He carved the meat and placed meat before me with his own hand.

We ate our fill and then drank cold milk. After the servants cleared the food, they brought censers, from which heavy incense wafted, and circled us. Next they brought us water to wash our hands. Last of all, they brought a platter of chestnuts with a brazier containing a single coal. The Sultan began popping chestnuts on the hot coal till they cracked open. Then he would pull them out with his hand, shuck them, and eat them with gusto. We followed his example. The Sultan discussed whatever came to his mind: preparations for his army, his plans for waging jihad against Armenia, and a series of letters from Levon II of Armenia petitioning for a truce. After he shook the bits of chestnut husks from his hands, he looked very serious, contracted his eyebrows, and said, "I would like to ask your advice about something, Master."

"What's that?"

"You know what happened in Antalya: Franks attacked and occupied it, after killing a large number of Muslims."

"Yes, I know about this."

"Perhaps you also know that they wouldn't have won had the Christians of Antioch not offered them assistance and supplies, thus betraying the treaty of protection we had granted them."

"Right."

"Do you think I was wrong to guarantee their security? Do you see how in Malatya, Konya, and the countryside there are many Christians, whom I no longer trust?"

The Sultan was silent, waiting for my response, while Ishaq focused his eyes on my face, as if he weren't sure what I would say. I bowed my head briefly in silence and then said, "Sultan. . . ."

The King, who had been leaning on his right hand shifted to his left and listened intently.

"Have you heard the news from Madrid?" I asked him.

"What news do you have in mind, Master?"

"How could you not have heard that the Muslims were defeated by the Franks, who killed countless men who recite the Muslim creed that there is no God but God? I know they are in a country far from your own and are in a realm different from yours. But the conquerors were Christians and those who were defeated were Muslims."

The Sultan grew restless—as if he had not expected a sermon. Waving his hand in the air he said, "God grants His religion and His army victory everywhere."

"You complain about the Christians, but the fault does not lie with them. It lies with you; the problem is instances of disbelief in your land. Your treatment of them reminds me of what Ibn Mardanish did in Murcia when he allowed Christians to gain the upper hand in his land. Then he lost his faith and his kingdom."

"What should I do, Master?"

"Do what Umar ibn al-Khattab did and follow his advice regarding the People of the Book."

The Sultan raised his eyebrows in astonishment. Then his expression suggested that he disagreed. He retorted, "Master, times have changed. How can you want me to order the Christians to shave the front of their heads and fasten girdles around their waists when we share borders with them and most of our subjects are of their religion?"

"Every time is God's time, King: past, present, and future are His to command."

The Sultan raised his voice and turned his neck so that he wasn't looking at me when he objected, "That's difficult, Master. Difficult."

"You're right, Sultan. It is a difficult matter."

I left the Sultan's assembly after the sunset prayer. Before I climbed into the palanquin, his chamberlain caught up with me and handed me a folded piece of paper. He explained, "This is our Master the Sultan's present for you, Shaykh. A new house in the palaces area."

He ordered a court employee to show me my new house. I thanked him and tucked the piece of paper in my belt without opening it. The two horses moved off as I listened to the rhythm of their hoofbeats on the stone pavement. I felt awful about this huge gift—not delighted. I had feared he would give me something that would knock me off course. For a moment I felt immensely angry and regretful that I had accepted his present, but it would have been unthinkable to return and hand it back to him, because I would then seem like someone who was originally convinced but had had second thoughts. I closed my eyes and prayed that God would relieve me of this disgrace before I reached home. Minutes later, God granted me relief in the form of a beggar who started racing along beside the palanquin, yelling as loudly as he could: "Alms, Master! My children are hungry, and I'm sick."

I shouted to the driver of the palanquin, and he stopped the two horses. The supplicant approached, his eyes filled with entreaty and hope. He started to repeat his plea in a softer voice as he moved his head entreatingly and rubbed his fingers together to arouse my sympathy.

"I am poor and hungry, Master. Give me something, and may God repay you."

I pulled the paper from my belt and handed it to him. "All I have is this house," I said. "It's yours."

83

The Sultan left Malatya heading toward Sinop, where he would try to launch his first attack against his foe, Levon. Before he departed, Ishaq visited me and brought his wife and their two-year-old son Muhammad. He picked his son up the moment they entered and placed him in my arms. I pressed the child to my breast, and he laughed. Then his little hands began to explore my beard, stroke my brow, and try to remove my turban. I sat down with Ishaq, together with Sawdakin and Badr, on a small rug in the garden, while our wives were in the inner room. Muhammad started to wobble between the plant beds and then felt the soft jasmine blossoms with his finger. Next he picked up an apricot from the ground, gazed at it, and threw it toward his father, hitting his chest.

Ishaq laughed at this and exclaimed, "Good shot! Just what you would expect from the youngest warrior in the Sultan's army."

I gazed at the young child and remembered a recent unveiling from God, Who had shown me what had befallen the defeated Muslims in Madrid. Columns of prisoners had been led to the market by Franks for sale as slaves. Alfonso had raided the remaining fortresses and castles that the Almohads had fled, collecting children in mule carts, each of which contained ten to twenty children. They were being taken to a distant fate beyond the ken of their family, who would never see them again. I don't know why I imagined little Muhammad among them as he played in my garden. This flight of my imagination scared me, and I immediately turned to Ishaq and said, "Don't you have concerns about taking this little guy with you to a war?"

Ishaq smiled and immediately replied, "I don't believe it will be a bloody war. Levon's letters keep coming to the Sultan asking for a truce, but the Sultan ignores them, hoping Levon will capitulate even further. Once the Sultan achieves what he wants, we'll return to Konya."

"Will you pass by Malatya or Sivas on your return?"

"Malatya, definitely."

"Listen then: let the boy remain in my house, and Fatima will look after him. You can take your wife with you, or she can remain here with her child."

"But I'd miss him. I scarcely get to spend any time with him now because I'm always traveling. And I wouldn't want to burden you."

"I beg you to spare him the risk."

Ishaq finally consented and called his wife Safiya to ask her opinion. She told him within earshot of me, "If my son stays, I'll stay with him."

I replied, before Ishaq could, "Then you'll stay. I'll give you my companions' room."

I turned to Sawdakin and ordered him, "Take the household funds you have and rent a room in this neighborhood. Make sure it will be easy for Badr to enter."

Ishaq prepared to depart. He stood at the door hugging his son and playing with him. Picking him up, he asked me whether the boy resembled him. I inquired whether he had given the boy an honorific nickname like his own, and he said he hadn't. I pondered the boy's deep eyes and remembered my daughter Zaynab, whom I had buried with my own hands when she was about this boy's age. If she hadn't died, she would now be a bride to be escorted to her new home. Tears came to my eyes at this thought. I opened my arms and called to the child, who came and clung to me. I picked him up and told Ishaq, "He is Sadr al-Din, God willing. Do you agree with me?"

"You have chosen an excellent sobriquet for him."

"If God extends my life span, I will teach him my path, take him along my way, and ask God to open for him His heavenly knowledge and sacred secrets."

Ishaq said amen to my words and embraced me and the child in my arms. Then he said goodbye to his wife and departed.

For many weeks this handsome child enlivened this house, filling it with joy and delight. Every time he saw me sit down to write, he would come and walk over the pages, getting ink on his bare feet and leaving footprints on the page. If I stopped him from doing that, he would walk around me, climb on my back, take off my turban, and place it on his own head, where it would slide down, covering it. He would raise it to see the light and then lower it again. The alternation of light and dark before his eyes amused him and made me laugh along with him. Sawdakin got him a nanny goat and her kid from the market, and little Muhammad would follow the kid around the garden all day long till it grew tired. Then he would try to pick it up, and they would both fall. The little goat's hooves would scratch him, and he would cry and complain to me.

Then Fatima went into labor. I awoke in the first watch of the night to hear her screaming loudly. I left my room to find Safiya was already standing by Fatima's bed and holding Sadr al-Din, whom Fatima's screams had terrified. We quickly exchanged roles. I took Sadr al-Din from her and carried him back to the guest room to calm his fear while she rushed to fetch the accoutrements of childbirth, which Fatima had prepared in advance. Then she entered Fatima's room and closed the door. Sadr al-Din didn't fall asleep again, nor did I.

From time to time Fatima released a scream so loud I thought it was her last. Then I would call to Safiya through the door, and she would reply, "Not yet, Master. Not yet. . . ."

Dawn arrived, and I went out to pray, taking Sadr al-Din with me. When we had finished the prayer ritual, men asked me how my wife was, because they had heard her screams. I told them she was in labor. I had barely returned to the house and shut its door behind me when there erupted a loud knocking on it. I opened it to find three neighborhood women who had come to assist Fatima with her delivery. They entered her room, one at a time, and shut the door. I went to the goat in the garden with a milk pail to milk her so I could give it to Sadr al-Din. The pail was almost filled with warm milk when the newborn's cries and the women's shouts reached my ears. I sat down in the garden and wept at what God had willed for me, without the goat or her kid understanding why.

Safiya placed my son in my arms and said with great joy: "A boy, Master. . . . A boy."

I looked at his closed eyes, little mouth, and damp hair, and for some seconds the earth spread out before me. A son when I was over fifty? *My thanks and blessings to You, Lord, for blessing me the way you blessed Zakariya when both of us had grown frail and our heads were flaming with gray hair.* The newborn screamed and I pressed him to my breast, brought my lips down to his ears and recited the call to prayer sincerely, as if saying its words for the first time in my life. Safiya asked whether I wanted to perform my son's ritual first symbolic feeding with soft date pulp or would rather have the experienced woman next door do this. I chose the latter option. I returned my son to her and felt my first pangs of separation from him. I didn't know what to do. I stood by the door of my room, waiting for my son to return to my arms.

Safiya soon brought him back and told me, "Fatima asks you what you will name him."

I went to the door of my wife's room and called to Fatima. She responded in a feeble voice. I said, "Fatima, I ask your permission to name him Imad al-Din, after your martyred first husband."

For some moments Fatima didn't respond. Eventually I heard her gasp and then begin to weep.

84 DAMASCUS 1925 CE/ 1344 AH

I sat up and patted her shoulder while she slept beside me. I said, "Lutfiya, get up!"

"Abu Hatim, it's not dawn yet!"

"As you like. You sleep a lot!"

I lifted my round clock from the bedside table, stood up, and, while heading to the bathroom, remarked, "The bombardment will start in fifteen minutes in any case. Only bombs wake you up!"

I washed and performed my ablutions. I spread out my prayer rug in the corner where I had prayed since I hadn't been able to go to the mosque, because of these circumstances. Halfway through my prayers, the house was rocked by the first bomb's reverberations. As usual Lutfiya was scared out of bed by the start of the bombardment and wailed, as if this hadn't occurred at four every morning for the past three days. These Frenchmen are punctilious and elegant even in their destruction of our city.

I finished praying and leaned against the wall to complete my expressions glorifying God while Lutfiya checked that all the windows of the house were shut—as if bombs would slip through windows instead of falling on roofs. The bombardment hadn't left us a single window that wasn't damaged. The glass in all of them had broken in succession—like the rest of the windows in our neighborhood. They were now covered with heavy fabric in some houses and had been boarded up in others. There was nothing left to dampen sound, so all the quotidian conversations, stories, quarrels, and guffaws were shared by every resident of the neighborhood—as if we were living in one large house through which words traveled unimpeded. Some days earlier I had laughed when I heard our neighbor Abd al-Hamid scold his son sarcastically.

He heard me laugh and then laughed in turn and shouted: "You laugh too much, Abu Hatim!"

"May God protect you from that, Abu Shukri."

The first week passed in this manner. In the beginning we grumbled about the influx of sounds and the lack of privacy. Then we took comfort in our shared auditory realm, which the bombardment had left behind as a communal consolation for us while we didn't know when the advancing Frenchmen would target us. When the bombardment ended at nine p.m., women would ululate. Abd al-Hayy would occasionally shout from his window: "*Takbir!*" Then calls of "Allahu Akbar!" would rise from men and boys and echo throughout the neighborhood. At times, Abbas al-Shobaki would bring out his Arab lute and sing a ballad or a song for us. Youngsters would amuse themselves by calling to each other through skylights. Men would exchange news: "Today they bombarded Sidi Amoud, Souk Tawil, the Shaghour neighborhood, and al-Sanjakdar district." Any family with relatives in those unlucky areas would respond: women wailed and men exclaimed, "All power and might are God's alone!" Everyone else would add their condolences and consolations.

Lutfiya placed olives and zaatar bread in front of me and donned her prayer shawl. I ate breakfast quickly, dressed, and left the house as morning slowly split night's cloak. The Sheikh Mahdeen neighborhood was still undamaged except for the smashed windows. The French planes and artillery hadn't targeted it the way they had other areas, where the revolutionaries had fortified themselves. Bombs had flattened those and set them ablaze. I don't know what their condition really is and don't dare walk there, because I might not return. It's bad enough just hearing the bombardment. From hearing bombs explode in distant regions and watching smoke rise, I could estimate the scale of the disaster. If I climbed the minaret of the Khankar Mosque, I could see the roofs of demolished houses in the distance, count their number, and estimate the force of the strike. When I was obliged to leave Mahdeen, as had happened two days ago when I delivered my father's rusty rifle to a revolutionary on the off chance that he might be able to use it, what I saw broke my heart. The dome of the Sinan Pasha mosque had been punctured by a shell. Sanjakdar's warehouses had become a pile of rubble. In the midst of all this, the city's thieves and mercenaries also deemed everything fair game and had begun to plunder anything they could set hands on. My heart felt sad for the residents of those devastated neighborhoods, even though I didn't know any of them. Every day we exchanged condolences for a martyr, and we had started to go to the cemetery, even before we met someone lamenting a loved one whom we would find being buried at the cemetery. What I saw filled my heart with sorrow and contentment. A person requires aerial and land bombardments to level an entire city in order to praise God that his wife is barren and will never conceive. What would I have felt had I had children in such a devastated city?

Before advancing down the alley to the mosque, I passed Faruq al-Safadi's house and found its door open. He was backing out, trying to carry a heavy box. I rushed to assist him, and we finally removed it from his house and lined it up beside some leather valises and two other boxes.

"Where are you going, Faruq?" I asked him.

"To Hama, Abu Hatim."

"The city is under siege! How will you leave?"

Faruq went back into his house and emerged with a rifle. He replied, "With this!"

I shook my head sadly and told him, "Faruq, you're old and have children. You're not cut out for fighting!"

"Who said I'm going to fight?"

"What are you planning to do with the rifle then?"

"The French are collecting rifles. Anyone who delivers his rifle will be allowed to leave the city."

"So that's the plan. Have a safe trip."

I embraced him and proceeded to the mosque, where I started by performing two units of the prayer to greet the mosque. Then I went to wipe down the bars of the mausoleum and its base, which I then dusted. I probably should have held onto my father's rifle instead of donating it to the revolutionaries. I may be forced to quit Damascus if the shelling continues in this manner or reaches our neighborhood. The timber frames of our houses would burn easily, and the river isn't nearby. But where would I go? The only place I know is Damascus, and I was born here. My only employment has been serving this blessed mausoleum. If they shell our neighborhood, the roof will fall on my head and I will die in the presence of my Shaykh. Lutfiya herself hasn't considered fleeing, not even now, when I'm brooding about it, although I'm a man!

I made the rounds at the mosque, which had been deserted by most of those who normally worship here. I noticed the personal effects left by homeless people who had lost their houses and started sleeping nights in the mosque, leaving it during the day. I moved these aside and opened the doors wide to welcome participants for the "Presence" or *hadra* ceremony. They filtered in, one after the other, until there were nine of us. I stood among them and we began our *dhikr* together:

He truly is the Reviver of the Religion: Muhyi al-Din,

The succor of all the gnostics,

A servant of the pure way,

My Master, the Supreme Shaykh.

Glory to Him Who granted him a locus of manifestation

Shared by all scholars.

During our *hadra*, Faruq haunted my mind. I closed my eyes trying to immerse myself in our repetitive mentions of God's names and chanting. I moved my head rhythmically right and left to expel worldly concerns and to seek the Divine Presence.

His portal is the Worshipper of the Independent One:

The *Wali* and son of the *Wali*;

A sea of prophetic wisdom,

Shaykh of the Lords of Certainty.

But Faruq squatted in the middle of my imagination, and people don't appear during God's *hadra* for no reason. *Faruq is departing, and travelers carry letters. They are depositories of trusts. They deliver allusions. Faruq wants something.*

Clear insight: The hadra has succeeded.

The good news has arrived. My Dear One. For God's people.

We had even thought: a person who is not one of us.

I've lost my mind, My Dear One, by remembering God.

He who did not find, let him invite ecstasy.

Purposefully manifesting, My Dear One,

By God's grace.

The *hadra* ceremony ended quickly. We saluted each other, asking leave to depart. I rushed to the sacred room. I slipped the key in the lock, turned it twice, opened the door, and then locked it behind me. I cast my eyes around the printed books and manuscripts and picked out four. I pulled out a musk-scented piece of fabric I used to perfume the tomb for the feasts and wrapped it around those four books. Then

I bound the parcel securely. I left the room, locked it carefully, and headed to the outer door. To Faruq's house. He had finished moving all his belongings outside and had placed them in a donkey-cart.

"Faruq, would you accept this in trust from me to take to Hama?"

He accepted the books and replied earnestly, "Of course, Abu Hatim. To whom should I deliver them?"

"To someone who will keep them safe, Faruq. No matter who he is."

"No transitory love is true."

——**IBN ARABI**

85

Like the apricot trees that grow everywhere in Malatya and bear fruit only in their fourth year, my life came to full fruition too in a way I loved. Imad grew up and filled the house with commotion. He was moody, cried a lot, and complained about everything. Throughout his first years his body was covered with many sores, and when he was two, we thought he would surely die because of the fevers his feeble body suffered once or twice a month. When he was four, though, he spoke for the first time—in a mixture of the Arabic we spoke at home and the Turkmen he picked up from the neighbors.

I took part of the garden and built a room there big enough for the two boys, and Imad started to sleep in it with Sadr al-Din, who was six and had memorized half of the Qur'an and many hadiths about the Prophet. Sadr al-Din would wake before me for the dawn prayer and beat me to the mosque, even on cold mornings when his little feet would sink into the mounds of snow piled up in the streets. After Ishaq was thrown from his horse and could hardly move his left shoulder, he decided to settle in Malatya. He apologized to the Sultan and asked his permission to retire from his position. As a matter of fact, he had performed the pilgrimage with a broken shoulder and retired from government service when the Sultan's subsequent actions upset him. He saw the Sultan direct his jihads against Syria and begin to mobilize armies to fight alternatively his Muslim allies, the Ayyubids—in a total breach of etiquette—and the Byzantines or the Armenians. Ishaq could not stand being part of such conduct and decided to resign.

My course in the mosque occupied its large courtyard during the spring and summer and a suite of six rooms inside during the fall and winter. I sat on a low chair that raised me only an inch or two above the heads of my pupils. Ishaq, Badr, and Sawdakin sat to my right, and to my left was a line of my best students, who copied down any views I added to my oeuvre. As for my pupils, they hailed from all over. They included disciples who lived in khanqahs and came from Tabriz, Khoy, Ardabil, Mosul, Erzurum, Nusaybin, Edessa, Aleppo, and Antalya. Some came to us knowing no Arabic beyond the short surahs they recited with their prayers, and they would attend classes for the blessing, which might illumine their hearts. I provided these students with tutors to teach them Arabic, with lessons before and after my class. I offered two different courses: one for typical students with whom I read the principles of the path, foundations of the sacred law, and exegesis of the Qur'an. The other was for elite students and my companions. Together we read to each other about higher secrets, sacred matters, and divine lights derived from unveiling, states, attraction, effusion, and ecstasy. During this session, we would attract adult Sufis with charismatic gifts, the so-called "people of blame"—the *malamatiya*—who had achieved renunciation and blessings, and even deranged individuals whose intellects had been disoriented by divine attraction. When they rushed into the special class, we would read their hearts, since we were unable to comprehend their intellects.

On a day that could easily have been ordinary had God not willed otherwise—glory to Him who said: "Every day He is splendid"[42]—someone knocked firmly on the door. I opened it to find a tall Arab man who wore a large turban over his shoulder-length hair. He was physically strong, and his handshake was rough. Even so, his expression was cautious and somewhat hopeful. Every aspiring disciple and spiritual wayfarer knocked on my door, either looking for accommodations in one of the Sufi hostels in Malatya or work in one of its monasteries. I had grown accustomed to browsing people's faces and complexions to judge whether they came from farther east or farther west, but this man made me apprehensive. I sensed that something about his face that wasn't typical of a would-be disciple.

"Are you Muhyi al-Din Ibn Arabi?"

"Yes, I am. Who are you, my guest?"

His eyes strayed into the house because he was tall enough to see over me. He seemed to be searching for something he thought might be present. Imad approached the door and stood between my legs, gazing up at the man, who no doubt seemed a giant to him. In return, the man gazed at Imad and scrutinized him for a long time. I didn't repeat my question for fear of upsetting this visitor. Perhaps he was a guest who did not wish to identify himself. As both a Hatimi and a Ta'i, I had no right to insist on learning his identity until he had been my guest for three days. That's why, after he said nothing for a long time, I opened the door wide and was about to ask him to enter. But he suddenly shuddered, as if awaking from a dream. He waved a finger in my face and said, "Listen, Man. I know you're married to Yunus' daughter."

"Yes. She is my wife and the mother of this son of mine."

His face turned white and looked furious. He shouted at me: "Depravity! Debauchery! Sin! You have married my wife!"

At that moment I heard Fatima gasp behind me and then begin to wail. The man and I both looked inside and stared at Fatima, who had approached the door. Then she threw herself on the floor and started to howl like a mother whose child has died. She suddenly ripped her bodice and bared her cleavage. Imad wept to see her in such a state. Without thinking about it, I stretched out my hand to close the door and hide her from view, but the man's grip stopped me. He knelt and released an earsplitting wail he seemed to have kept bottled up for countless years. I stood between this couple: Fatima on her knees like a slaughtered calf to my right and her first husband squatting to my left as if his back were broken.

God submits his friends to trials to examine their hearts so they will fear God. He tried me by bringing to me my wife's husband, whom I thought had died! I helped him to a seat in my parlor. He was trembling; so I gave him something to drink and wrapped a cloak around him. His eyes looked dazed as they glanced around every which way, and his face was so pale all the blood seemed to have drained from it. What happened next was that Ishaq knocked on the door by prior arrangement with me. We had been meeting like this for a couple of weeks while we concentrated on drafting an epistle about Sufi technical terms. I brought him inside and sat him down. Then I introduced him to my guest. His expression froze and remained rigid for some minutes before he bowed his head and sank into silence.

I lit a fire in the brazier, and brought the man apricots, milk, and rose water. Then I baked him some bread. He ate a little but didn't calm down. He kept repeating that my marriage to Fatima was null and void, and I didn't argue about that with him. I simply alluded to the fact that God would do as He willed and that nothing had happened in this house contrary to the will of God or His Shariah. Two hours elapsed while the man remained furious with us and hostile. Then his soul calmed down a little after he ate and drank, and his expression grew calmer. We talked about other matters, like the road from Mardin to Malatya. Caravans. The weather. People. Ishaq tried everything he could think of to distract the poor man and calm his nerves. All this had some effect on him, and he started to express his opinion to us. He smiled occasionally but then quickly concealed that smile.

I finally asked him where he had been.

"I was a prisoner in Byzantium."

"How were you all taken prisoner?"

"We left Aleppo: two hundred infantrymen and thirty cavalrymen. Our goal was to expel the Franks from the provinces of Tarsus after they had entered them and run amok there. But we all fell into an ambush between two hills on which the Franks had positioned archers overnight."

I asked him, "How many of you survived?"

"Twenty or thirty at the most. They marched us survivors to Tarsus before any reinforcements could arrive. The next day they offered us for sale in the slave market. The ruler was in a hurry to sell us to Venetian traders who were in the city. Then they shipped us immediately to Sicily."

"That was vile," Ishaq commented angrily. "Prisoners should be offered for ransom first before they become slaves."

The man didn't comment on Ishaq's statement. He nodded his head sadly and then bowed it silently. Ishaq urged him to continue his story.

"In Sicily I went from one slave merchant to another until I became the property of a vintner who used me for viticulture."

His voice shook as he recalled this. Then Ishaq asked him, as if trying to divert him from those memories, "How did you escape from captivity?"

"I didn't. I worked in the vineyard for three years till some Muslim merchants came to Sicily from Andalusia. They bundled their alms money to purchase Muslim prisoners and emancipated us."

Ishaq smiled, glanced at me, and said to the man, "What admirable fellows these Andalusians are!"

I ignored his compliment and bowed my head in silence for a long time while I reflected. Then I looked up and addressed the man directly, "Listen, Imad. . . ."

The man regarded me askance, as if worried about what I might say. Then I told him, "I will go with you to the qadi and, with my brother Ishaq as my witness, I swear I will be content with whatever the judge rules to be God's decree."

"A gift you must request is not worth having."

—**IBN ARABI**

86

Fatima wept all night long, and her eyes became red and swollen as a result. Her entire face resembled a piece of leather worn by the rain. She slept in the boy's room, hugging Imad, while I trained my eyes on the ceiling and brooded, searching for a solution to this dilemma. Could I really renounce Fatima? If I did, I could quickly marry any woman I wanted. I would also be able to keep Imad if I wished. I would be able to swear off women altogether and focus instead on my teaching and books and spending more days alone with God. If I didn't, and instead retained Fatima, I assumed nothing would change. She would continue to be as proper, obedient, and dutiful as ever, scarcely ever saying anything. *She doesn't talk to me or flirt with me. She doesn't offer me anything more than any wife would to any husband in any region of the world: just food, service, and sex.* I wasn't impressed by her learning the way I had been by that of Maryam bin Abdun. I didn't crave to hear what she would say as I had Nizam bint Zaher. She was a woman who would be easy to replace.

As I was entertaining such ideas, she opened the door and entered. It was obvious that she, like me, had found it impossible to sleep. She told me without beating around the bush, "I want you to know, Muhyi, that I wish to stay with you."

"I doubt you really mean that, Fatima."

"Whether I'm telling the truth or lying is irrelevant. I want to stay with my boy in my house."

"Why did you wail when you saw him? Why did you rip your blouse and weep all night?"

She remained silent and didn't respond. She glanced around the room to avoid looking at my face, and the darkness helped her with that. Then she burst out: "You didn't ask me, but here I am answering you. If you want me to stay, I will, and I will be content. If the judge questions me, this is what I will tell him."

Her last phrase revealed her goal, which was to turn the decision over to me, to submit to her fate like a woman who did not want to become involved in any battles. She had no doubt avoided telling me candidly what was scaring her: that I would take her young boy away from her. But I also could not bear to be parted from my son and wasn't strong enough to travel to see him.

The next day was Friday, and Ishaq spoke to the judge after the prayer service, arranging an appointment with him at court the following day, with the understanding that Fatima would accompany me. That Friday passed normally, like any other day, except for its silence. Even Imad was unusually calm and seemed to sense that a significant matter had arisen in the household, as he could tell from his mother's puffy eyelids. Sadr al-Din's father Ishaq had taken him that night, to lighten the burden on Fatima after the shock to which she had been exposed, and he had remained with his parents.

On Saturday morning, I left with Fatima for the court. We found Ishaq there together with the other man, who appeared to be ready to battle. His expression was grim and suggested a deep-seated anger. We entered the building and sat down together in the courtyard, where plaintiffs and defendants awaited their turn before the judge. Everyone was silent. Fatima was as still as a stone, and that man glared impatiently at the door to the judge's chambers. Ishaq chatted with me from time to time about matters of general interest, as if wanting to divert my attention from the separation looming for me and my wife, the mother of my son.

Finally, when we were in the courtroom, God revealed to me what I would do. I told the man: "Listen, Brother Imad."

He turned toward me, and at the same time Fatima moved her legs as if startled I was addressing her former husband in her presence. I told him, "If you desire Fatima and she wants you, then I have no objection to divorcing her, but on one condition."

"What's your condition?"

"That you both remain in Malatya, in a house near mine, till Imad al-Din reaches puberty."

The man's frown turned to an anxious look, and he started looking back and forth between me, Ishaq, and the ground. Then he said, "But I don't know anyone here, don't own any land, and have no craft."

Ishaq intervened: "This is easy. I'll quickly find work for you if you want."

Fatima made a little sound as if she wished to say something. I drew my ear closer to her, and she said to me: "My son."

"Your son stays with you."

The attendant called us to enter the judge's presence. I looked at the man, waiting for his answer. He stood up and said, "I agree."

I looked toward Fatima and told her, "If you agree, speak up."

"I agree."

We entered the judge's presence and told him what we had agreed on. The qadi looked toward me and asked me in a low voice, "Are you certain of your decision?"

"Yes."

"Then may God compensate you fully. And you, Imad, I am a witness to your oath to remain in Malatya until the boy reaches puberty. If you travel somewhere, you must not take your wife and son with you."

"I so swear."

"And you, Fatima, are you content with this?"

"I am."

"Are you in a state of ritual purity?"

"Yes."

Turning to me, he asked, "Have you had conjugal relations with her in this state?"

"No."

"Then declare that you divorce her, if that is your decision."

"I have divorced Fatima bint Yunus."

The judge turned toward Fatima and instructed her, "Your legal waiting period is three menstrual cycles, unless you are pregnant in which case it is till you give birth. Then you can marry again after that. May God preserve all of you. Depart."

As we left the courtroom, Ishaq was talking to the man and advising him to wait for news. The man nodded that he understood and went off about his business. Ishaq rushed to me and said, "The Sultan has sent for me. What would you think about accompanying me and diverting yourself in Konya for a time?"

"Fine."

"Anyone who seeks to rule over people will find that God has burdened his heart."

—**IBN ARABI**

87

Only hours after we arrived in Konya, a messenger came to us from the Sultan and invited us both to appear at court. We quickly bathed and put on new clothes and set off enveloped in wool cloaks. The rocky roads were coated with ice, and Ishaq warned me futilely not to slip on it. The two times I lost my footing I escaped without breaking my bones or smashing my cranium. Then Ishaq held my arm the rest of the way.

He smiled and said, "I don't want the Sultan to say I've brought him a broken guest."

We entered the Sultan's assembly and waited a long time. We were surrounded by other men who worked at the court, and Ishaq chatted with them while I kept my silence. Ishaq repeatedly asked the official in charge of the assembly when the Sultan would arrive. Then this official clarified that although it had not been announced, the Sultan was ill. Most of those who had come to the assembly left then—thinking the Sultan would not appear—but Ishaq, the official, and I stayed until the Sultan finally stumbled in. He walked very slowly and was followed by the food taster, who was ready to take his arm, should he lose his balance. He clearly seemed ill and coughed incessantly. He had trouble sitting down and was wheezing. We took turns greeting him.

The reigning silence was interrupted only by the Sultan's coughing and his light groans whenever he tried to adjust his seated position. Everyone remained silent, head bowed, until the Sultan finally spoke: "Ishaq, I don't think the project of jihadi volunteers is a success."

Ishaq remained silent, waiting for additional clarification, which was supplied by the official in charge of the assembly. "We dispatched six hundred young jihadis to Syria," he said, "and returned with only a hundred."

"What happened to the others?"

"They are safe, but each of them went off to do his own thing."

"But I know that most of them were from Anatolia. I selected volunteers from Sivas, Malatya, and Kayseri. Where have they gone?"

The Sultan answered this time: "This is the question for you: Where are they going?"

"Your Excellency, all I know is what you have told me."

The assembly official said, "Our spies say they have become mercenaries in any army that will have them."

The Sultan said furiously but in a tired voice, "We taught them how to fight. Now they are fighting against us."

Ishaq looked very upset—as if he thought he was being blamed for all these treasonous acts. He bowed his head and offered no response. It seemed, though, that the Sultan did not wish to continue blaming him. Instead, he said, "I don't know why you left them and went off to Malatya. I was counting on you to supervise these jihadis, and now there's not even one left."

I decided to speak. I cleared my throat, turned toward the court official. He didn't look my way, but the Sultan seemed to have heard my voice. So I said, "Please allow me, Your Majesty the Sultan, to say something."

"Speak, Muhyi."

"Anyone who is willing to sell you his sword, will sell it to anyone else. Anyone who sells his soul to God, won't."

"What are you trying to say, Muhyi?"

"I want to say that the Sultan's power and sovereignty were not founded and will not be founded on anything but a jihad against the tyranny of malefactors when he is aided by men who keep their promise and vow to serve God."

"Muhyi, you still haven't made it clear what you want to say."

"I am saying, Your Majesty, that your effort to combat the Ayyubids does not please God. In this effort you have rented a sword and unsheathed it to strike your brother's face. But it's not your sword, and your brother isn't your enemy. How can you hope for victory when you use such a sword for such a cause?"

The Sultan appeared to be too exhausted to become enraged. He shook his head no, as if he hadn't liked anything I said. Then he observed, "You know nothing about this war, Muhyi. They're the ones who started fighting us."

"Then defend yourself with what is better, Your Excellency."

"We did defend ourselves, but that wasn't successful. Aleppo was once ruled by my forefathers—before the Ayyubids. Its citizens solicited my military assistance after their kings harmed them substantially."

The court official interrupted our discussion to keep me from angering the Sultan and tried to change the subject: "If you would like, Your Majesty, we will reorganize the jihadis and place them under the command of the army. Then each man will draw a soldier's pay instead of being tempted by the allure of plunder."

The Sultan fidgeted and objected, "Booty will remain the true incentive, not military pay, even if we double the latter."

Silence reigned in the assembly, and we all bowed our heads, not knowing what to say. The Sultan began to scratch his forehead to relieve the pain and succumbed to another bout of coughing. The food taster quickly brought him a bucket in case he vomited, but the Sultan didn't. His coughing ceased, and he took some deep breaths while we remained silent. Many minutes elapsed before he turned toward Ishaq and said, "Come closer."

Ishaq approached him till he was in arm's reach. Then the Sultan told him, "I want you to go to my brother Kayqubad."

"In prison?"

"Yes. But go with as few men as possible and don't reveal your goal to anyone."

"I hear and obey."

"Tell him: 'Your brother offers to make you his heir apparent.' If he agrees, have him swear that he will not harm my sons, my aides, and my slaves. Then record that vow in writing. If he refuses, return the way you went."

"I hear and obey."

The Sultan held out his hand, and the court official hastened to place in it two folded letters. "This is my letter to my brother," the Sultan said. "The other document is a list of the princes you will visit, each in his own city, to obtain their acceptance of my brother as my heir apparent. Share with them his guarantee for the safety of my sons, aides, and slaves."

"I hear and obey."

Then the Sultan turned toward me and remarked, "Muhyi, if you want, you will accompany Ishaq and assist him with his mission."

"God willing, Your Majesty, I will."

The two of us quit the Sultan. Ishaq was sunk deep in thought as he silently grasped the two letters. We reached the house closest to the Sultan's palace and entered.

The moment we sat down by a glowing brazier, Ishaq spoke for the first time since we had left the palace. "Did you hear what he said? He is promising the sultanate to his brother, who contested it with him and previously fought against him. He wants to release him from prison and make him the next sultan!"

"God grants sovereignty to whom He wants!"

Ishaq bowed his head again and remained silent as he thought deeply while gazing at the burning coals in the brazier. Then he suddenly looked startled, as if he had just remembered something. He told me, "Muhyi, what you said to the Sultan today was extremely dangerous."

"I just said what I think."

"Yes, but you gloated over his recent defeat. Do you know what he did to the princes who betrayed him in this war?"

"What?"

"He had them burned alive!"

"My God! I take refuge with God from the tyranny of tyrants. By God, I won't ever enter his assembly again."

"Yes, that's safest for you."

"After my life with you, there will be nothing but annihilation."

— **IBN ARABI**

88

It did not prove difficult to keep my oath, because the Sultan died before the end of winter that year. His brother Kayqubad went straight from prison to the throne. I returned to Malatya by myself after Ishaq and I toured the Seljuq emirates to receive those rulers' oath of fealty to Kayqubad. On my return, I found that Fatima's legal waiting period prior to our divorce had ended. She had remarried her previous husband and was living very near what had once been my house. So I occasionally saw her husband at prayers. I brought Sawdakin and Badr back to live with me now that Fatima had moved out, and the three of us were reunited. The nanny goat had died over the winter during a freezing cold night. That dawn she lay inert, and her saliva and nose had frozen.

Even though Badr stayed at home all day long and Sawdakin looked after both of us, I found the house had become unbearably quiet. Imad wasn't there to cry at night whenever the rustling of the trees or a thunderclap frightened him. In the morning, Sadr al-Din wasn't there to recite and review Qur'an surahs and Hadith accounts he had memorized. Nor was Fatima there in her cooking area to make a clamor with her quern, a clatter with her kettles, or a thumping with her mortar and pestle. I complained about this to Ishaq at the beginning of spring. Then he procured two horses for us and we set off for Sivas together to lift my spirits.

The caravanseray we chose was at the entrance to the market, which was the most crowded *suq* I had seen in Anatolia. It was jampacked with people, merchandise, and shops. No matter which lane I wandered down, I found merchants of every ethnicity: Arabs, Kipchaks, Georgians, Armenians, and Turkmen. Each would speak to the other nationality in his own language—assisted by translators a merchant would hire for the length of his stay in this city. We deposited our luggage in the khan, handed our two horses to the owner, and headed to the public bath. We removed our clothes and immersed ourselves in the pool together with everyone else. Then the bath attendant started to scrub Ishaq while I washed my beard in the warm bath water. Although I didn't pay attention to it at that time, I heard the bath attendant say something to Ishaq about a growth on his neck: "How long have you had this?"

"I don't know. Perhaps a few months."

"Does it hurt?"

"No."

"Has it increased in size or stayed the same?"

"It began small and then grew to this size and stopped."

If I had paid attention to that conversation, God might have disclosed to me then what I didn't grasp, but He hid it from me. That tumor was consuming my friend and brought him to his grave in two months, leaving me alone. My God, how many people have I known only to have them pass! How many people have I loved only to have them vanish! How many people have I accompanied only to have them depart! Al-Khayyat, al-Hassar, al-Uraybi, al-Sabti, al-Ghawth, Zaher, and now Ishaq, who was a purer spirit than any other person I had known. A forbearing, generous person who fell asleep smiling and woke up smiling. His lips were pursed one final time when the shroud hid his face from us. When he stopped smiling, my lungs almost stopped breathing. My heart had welcomed him in the best place on Earth, Mecca, and I buried him quickly in Malatya. I cared deeply about him during the journey between those two cities, whether through deserts and forests or over mountains and plains. May God be compassionate to you, my friend, you who were both truthful and true to me.

The governor of Malatya erected a condolence pavilion for Ishaq's wake, as if he were a Seljuq prince. Rich and poor men, relatives and strangers, all gathered there to remember him. The governor himself received our condolences. The news was carried by messenger to Sultan Kayqubad, who was mobilizing his forces to wage a jihad against Qalqilya. His preoccupation with this jihad did not prevent him from extending his royal condolences to the man who had brought him the glad tidings that he was the new sultan—when he was in prison. He ordered a distribution of clothing and food to the poor, as the deceased would have wanted.

I sat grieving, my head bowed, near the governor, thinking about Sadr al-Din, who was now a young orphan. He sat beside me, and I could see both grief and astonishment in his eyes. He would be distracted in the large pavilion by all the people, who differed in their style of dress, language, and appearance, only to remember that they had all come to mourn his father. Then he would bow his head as his astonished expression became one of fear of the unknown and a feeling that the roof, which had sheltered him, had collapsed.

I returned home wrapped in the last present that Ishaq gave me when we were in Sivas: a beaver skin he had purchased from Russian merchants. He had draped it over my shoulders to shield my neck against Anatolia's bitter cold and to remind me of him. Afterwards, whenever someone mentioned Sivas, his image came to mind as I remembered the happiness of the months we had spent together there when we toured its mosques, Sufi houses, palaces, outskirts, and woods. Its people had welcomed us and entertained us, either for my sake, that of my path, or on account of Ishaq—his status at the court of the Sultanate, and his wide circle of acquaintances drawn from merchants from lands he had often visited as a messenger. We read and discussed books, welcomed pupils, traded cloaks with other Sufis, and asked God to accept our actions from us, to guide us on the path of His comprehensive love, and to raise us to the station of His affection and satisfaction.

One of the mourners at Ishaq's wake said to me, "May this be your last funeral, Master." What a silly thing to say! It's neither a wish to be fulfilled nor a prayer that might be answered. Whenever one of them said this, people understood it as: "May this be the end of your sorrows." I understood it as saying, "I hope you die soon so you won't need to attend another funeral." Who are we when stripped of our griefs? How can we safeguard our souls without them? Don't we come to death like sheep lost in valleys of neglect? Sorrow is dear to the soul of the Sufi and hated by the soul of the ignoramus distracted by the physical world. God show me, on my path, one sorrow after another. After I had entrusted my dear friend Ishaq to the soil and was sitting in my house trying to remember what we had experienced, in order to relive it, while contemplating life from the perspective of his loss and absence, Badr's other foot turned black, like the amputated one, and he was totally incapable of moving it.

Sawdakin carried him from one place to another. He stood him up, sat him down. He bathed him, even though he could not stand being moved. When he wished to move from one place to another, he would crawl on his elbows or roll from his back to his belly until he reached his destination. He endured this patiently with a pure heart and a clear mind. I brought him a physician who examined him thoroughly and then left without telling us anything about Badr's condition—as if he despaired of helping him in any way. I realized that I would soon lose my closest friend, my companion who had traveled with me from the west of the world to its east. How many times had he fed me! How many times had he bathed me! In how many ways had he served me! How many places had he followed me and held my arm! How much had he learned from me and me from him! I decided to spend the remainder of the life that God allotted Badr with him and curtailed my lessons in the mosque. I started to pass my entire day in his room. I would write while he copied. Whenever he had a question about a word, he would ask me, and I would reply in a way that disclosed the secret of my love for him and his extraordinary status in my heart.

One day I woke to find that Badr was up before me and seated, writing. When I went to him, he smiled and showed me the book he was composing. I took it from him and found that it was beautifully written and carefully bound. On the cover was a title I did not remember ever having written: *Awakening on God's Path*.

"What is this, Badr?" I asked.

"Effusions and existents that I heard from you over the course of the years but did not find mentioned in your books. Fearing they would be lost, I collected them in a book."

"You've written a book about me?"

Badr laughed and replied, "The erudition is yours, and the handwriting is mine, Master."

"I will read and edit it."

"True patience is what you display at first blush. No subsequent patience is genuine."

—IBN ARABI

89

A scribe from the Governor's Residence knocked on our door, accompanied by a soldier. They didn't enter; instead, they stood staring coldly at Sawdakin, who was trying to grasp what they wanted, because they would only say they had been ordered to escort the leper to the leper colony. Sawdakin tried to explain to them that there was no leper in the house and that they must have the wrong address. But they insisted they did not and stood steadfastly by the door. Sawdakin called me, and when I heard them say what they had told him, I pressed for more information: "Who directed you to him?"

"The physician at the hospital."

"What did he say?"

"He said that he, himself, had seen a leper in this house."

I turned toward Sawdakin, who still thought they had the wrong address. When I tried to explain that they were standing in front of the right door, I found that my tongue would not utter those words. Warm tears rolled down my cheeks, which were chapped by the approach of autumn. I went to my room—unable to look at Badr, who was languishing in the other one, unaware of what was expected of him. I lay down on my pallet, which was heaped at the side of the room, and buried my face in a sea of wool. I wept but attempted to stifle the sound. I grieved for every day I had spent with Badr, whether sleeping under the same ceiling or out in the open. Walking and riding. Settled or on the move. Well-fed or starving. In the neighborhoods of Fez, the alleys of Cairo, the lanes of Mecca, the quarters of Aleppo, and the districts of Baghdad. In every house where we had lived in so many cities and every khanqah in which we had created precious memories, every hostelry where we had stayed on routes used by travelers, in every desert we had crossed as the sun scorched our heads, on every mountain we had scaled while the cold froze our limbs, every meal we had shared as he awarded the choicest morsel to me, every drink with which we had wet our gullets, when he insisted on drinking after me.

I quit my room and found Sawdakin seated outside my door, not knowing what to do. I delegated the chore of informing Badr to him and left the house, walking aimlessly, heading nowhere in particular.

I returned to the house that night and found Sawdakin. He communicated to me with a gesture that he had told Badr about the situation. I went to him and found him busy copying something as though nothing had happened—encompassed by the serenity God grants true believers.

He looked at me and said, "I have made a copy of *Kitab al-Azma* and *Kitab al-Qurba*. I'll take sheets of paper with me to the leper colony so I can finish copying *Kitab al-Mim*!"

Tears flowed down my cheek as I smiled. Then Badr smiled, too, sensing what I was feeling. "Don't grieve, Master," he said, "I grieve only at parting from you."

"I hate for you to end up living in the leper colony, Badr!"

"It's a cherished place, Master. It's a colony for patient believers whose bad deeds are diminished daily by God and whose good deeds are multiplied."

"I will visit you as often as I can, Brother."

"No, visit me once a month and stay less than an hour, because I would never forgive myself if you contracted the disease."

I leaned over him and began kissing his head while he turned away from me shyly and modestly, trying to kiss mine. I took his hand, which was covered with spots of black and red ink, and kissed it. Then he took my hand and started to kiss it, too. I hugged him to my breast, and he let me. I began to weep, but he was calm. He patted my shoulder and rubbed my back as if calming the terror of a lost child. I finally wiped my tears away, sat up straight, and gazed at him, allowing my eyes to bid farewell to his fine face and diminish the catastrophe of his departure, which was approaching.

Silence reigned over our house while Badr arranged the papers before him, carefully closed his inkwell, and busied himself with the things around him while I remained silent and did nothing more than gaze at him. Sawdakin entered while we were in this state and chose a corner of the room for himself. He sat there, hugging his legs and hiding the lower half of his face behind his knees.

Finally, Badr, who was still looking at his paper and arranging them, said, "Know what, Master?"

"What, Darling?"

"One day when I was a child in Cairo, before I became the property of Abu al-Fattuh, a man returned me to the slaver only two days after he bought me, because I wasn't sleeping, and he thought I was ill. The slave trader immediately placed me among some other Ethiopians who had just arrived in an Arab caravan. One of them was a woman diviner who used a shell to tell fortunes. She would tell one man he was fated to end up in Baghdad. Another she said would go to Kerak. Another to Damietta. Those sad folk circled around her, each wanting to learn where the winds would blow him. Once she had finished with all of them, she turned toward me asked, 'You, kid, how about you? Don't you want to know who your master will be?' I replied, 'No, but I do want to know where my mother is.'"

Badr was silent for a time, brushed aside what he was holding, fixed his eyes on the wall as if a window on the distant past he was recounting had just opened there. Then he continued: "She struck the shell once, twice, three times, but each time shook her head in bewilderment, as if the shell were hiding its secrets from her. Finally, she sighed and threw me a compassionate look I'll never forget and said, 'Little boy, you don't have a mother. She died.' I asked her, 'How did she die?' She struck the shell a final time and then said, 'Of leprosy.'"

"Glory to God!"

"Master, I think I am only a year or two less than seventy. Whenever I remember her blow to that shell, I have remembered only her first statement: 'you don't have a mother.' I didn't remember the second part. Since I no longer had a mother, it didn't matter how she had died. Just today, I remembered this second phrase when Sawdakin revealed my destiny to me."

"May God cure you, my dear companion. May God aid you."

"I'm not upset, Master. I'm going to the Leper Colony. . . ." He sighed and his smile grew even wider as he said dreamily, "I'm going to my mother."

> *"Because I love you, I love all Ethiopians.*
> *Because I cherish your name, Badr, 'Full Moon,'*
> *I cherish your namesake, the resplendent moon."*
>
> ——**IBN ARABI**

90

The Leper Colony was located outside of Malatya—so that the wind currents would carry vapors from the lepers away from the city. Their water supply also drained from the city to them. The colony consisted of a few dozen tents, in which they lived, and a small mosque and bath house a benefactor had built for them. Lepers there were cared for by other lepers, who were compensated by visiting relatives. Some relatives would stand at a distance, look at their kinsmen, and call back and forth in a loud voice. A few would enter their relative's tent and even spend the night there. No law prevented one behavior or another—unlike the strict laws governing leper colonies in the Maghrib. Everyone conducted himself here according to the strength of his belief in God's decree and ordained destiny.

Sawdakin helped me erect a tent for Badr near the bath house and the mosque. We leveled the ground between them and cleared away the pebbles and rocks so he could crawl there whenever he wanted without injury. We instructed the servants to pay special attention to him and paid them extra to help him bathe and bring him food and drink every day. All that Badr requested were his writing implements and paper so he could occupy himself with copying books. We said goodbye to him after he urged us to leave before we contracted anything. So we left. No sooner had we departed from the colony and were approaching Malatya than Sawdakin started sobbing bitterly. His warm tears kept flowing till we entered the house, where we were alone. Both of us slept in Badr's room, while wind buffeted the house, which had once been home to a woman, children, a nanny-goat, and disciples, but today was empty, except for two men whose hearts were filled with sorrow.

Every morning I would pass by Safiya's house and find Sadr al-Din waiting for me at its doorway. We would go to class, and he would sit beside me while I read to the pupils whatever I was reading. When they left, I sat alone with him to review what he had heard and for him to have a chance to ask me about any matter that puzzled him. When we left the mosque after the sunset prayer, I would accompany him myself to his mother's house, not wanting him to walk down dark alleys alone. Then he would cling to his mother, and I would depart. Ishaq had left them enough money that I didn't fear they would suffer from poverty. I did fear they might travel somewhere else. His mother was still a young woman, and some man might seek to marry her and take both mother and son far away. This idea tormented me day after day and increased whenever I noticed Sadr al-Din's genius and his obvious dedication to seeking knowledge and following the path. I could tell from his broad forehead and clear eyes that God would grant him a mystic's taste and states if Sadr al-Din accustomed himself to ascetic training and spiritual struggle. He might be denied all of this if another man raised him as something other than the Sufi I wanted him to be. Sadr al-Din might grow up to be a soldier, government clerk, a merchant, or anything else. I consulted God for a long time about this boy until I reached a decision one morning. Then I quit my lesson in the middle, deputizing Sawdakin to finish reading the book to the pupils and left Sadr al-Din with him. Then I headed to Safiya's house, where I knew I would find her alone. I knocked on the door. I first heard her respond in Turkmen from the far side. When I didn't respond, she repeated her question in Arabic: "Who's there?"

"It's me, Muhyi."

She opened the door quickly and said, "Welcome, Master. Is Sadr al-Din all right?"

"He's fine—at the mosque. I've come to ask you a question I don't want him to hear."

"What's on your mind, Master?"

"I have come to ask you to marry me, Safiya."

She remained silent—just as I had expected—and moved the door slightly to hide her face behind it.

As I started to leave, I told her, "I'll let you think the matter over. There's no hurry. You know everything about me, and your son is like my son. I will raise both boys together. Give me your answer whenever you are ready."

I started to leave, but she called me back and said, "Master. . . ."

"Yes."

"I accept, Master."

"Don't you need to think it over, Safiya?"

"This matter was decided a long time ago. I was just waiting for you—that's all."

"Decided? Who decided it?"

"Ishaq."

"How?"

"Before he died, he told me I would marry you next. He counseled me to do this."

I left her and returned to the mosque. Her words had calmed my soul, and I felt hope return to me. My life, which had grown desiccated during the last two years, flourished again like a garden after it had lost its water supply and become parched by a drought. In only a few weeks Safiya and Sadr al-Din had moved to my house, and Sawdakin had returned to a room at the mosque. We bought two nanny-goats to replace the one that had died, and I gave a private lesson daily in my house to Sadr al-Din and Imad al-Din after the dawn prayer. I read to just the two of them. Each day, Sadr al-Din rose like a resplendent sun. Imad al-Din, though, was lazy and moody. He had trouble focusing on any subject and would only obey my orders when he saw a bamboo staff in my hands. Then he would fear its bite and obey.

My life settled down again, and God chose to grant me a series of intellectual ascensions, spiritual stations, and high ranks. From Him flowed unveilings, existents, and states, and from them various books and epistles originated. Whenever I had written a treatise or a book, I always took a copy to Badr in his tent, and he would be delighted. On the following visit, he would always have made one or two copies and would ask me one or two questions about it. I dedicated even greater attention to Sawdakin once God unveiled to me that his spirit had been lifted and elevated, becoming purely that of a Sufi, and a subtle element of the heavenly consort like a white cloud.

Everything in Malatya was calm and settled, but this was not true elsewhere. The Mongols razed Samarqand and Bukhara. They conquered many lands and approached within a stone's throw of the headquarters of the Caliphate in Baghdad. The echoes of these barbaric armies resounded in all areas of the world until people, regardless of their complexion, ethnicity, or religion, were united by fear and trepidation as they passed on stories about these people, who had become habituated to manslaughter and entertained themselves by slaying others. They would not leave a village until no breath of life or heartbeat remained there. For this reason, the Caliph in Baghdad sought assistance from the Sultan in Konya, and we heard a herald in the markets call for any rider willing to take up arms to support the Caliph. Each volunteer would be given a horse, a sword, and armor, and receive a salary until he returned. Then cavalrymen from Malatya joined men from other regions of the Sultanate, and the Sultan sent them off toward Baghdad.

During this time, I received letters—from Aleppo—asking me to settle there to teach, less than a decade after I was expelled from that city and fled to Cairo. Glory to Him Who brings changes without changing. Al-Malik al-Zahir had died and been succeeded by his son al-Malik al-Aziz, who was a child in the custody of the atabeg Toghril; matters had changed.

I was sure these letters would amuse Badr, so I took them with me on my next visit and read them to him. They did make him laugh, and he asked, "What's changed, Teacher?"

"I believe the Egyptians now control what happens in Aleppo, after the death of al-Malik al-Zahir."

"How so?"

"Al-Malik al-Adil in Egypt is the grandfather of al-Malik al-Aziz. He arranged for the oath of fealty to be given to the child's mother. The grandfather is the boy's guardian and the force keeping the child on his throne and protecting him. Without Adil's protection, the hands of the Ayyubid princes would have seized the child."

"Aleppo, then, will soon fall entirely under Egypt's control."

"Yes, Badr, and its Sufi khanqahs and zawiyas will shortly fill with disciples. They want me to teach in them."

"Will you go?"

"Not yet, Badr. Not yet."

Badr gave me a knowing look, smiled, and said, "Master. If you are hesitating for my sake, I beg you not to. I know you love Syria, and I will be fine."

"It will surely break my heart to leave you, Badr, but there are other matters that keep me from going. I haven't received God's command yet."

Then an order from God reached Malatya to seize the spirit of one of His worshippers. Badr finally died, after I realized that he would soon pass. The blackness reached his thighs, and it was impossible to amputate them without killing him. His body became bloated and very tender. His forearms and hands resembled waterskins. He lay supine during his final days and did not move. Next he refused to eat. Then patches of his skin came off, and blood flowed from those wounds. His spirit ascended to his Creator one moonless night. Sawdakin and I carried him to the cemetery, but when we set him in his grave, I began to shake like someone bitten by a scorpion. I was unable to continue. Sawdakin finished burying him alone while I watched from a distance. When he finished, he came to me, panting from exhaustion, and asked if I was okay.

With tears flowing nonstop, I replied, "How could I be 'okay' after my resplendent full moon has set? Who am I to bury someone like Badr?"

"Truth is concealed only by its clarity."

———**IBN ARABI**

91

Safiya was so serene that she rarely made a sound. When she finished her household chores, she busied herself with the garden, in which she planted every type of flower and fruit until it became a mass of leaves, branches, and fragrant sprouts all year long. She served me as if she had been born for that. Whenever I woke or returned home, I would find she had set out my wash basin, my food, and my clean clothes. She filled the house with carpets, which she spread on the floors and used to cover the walls. The house became warmer and more inviting than it had ever been. She would not go to bed before I did for fear I might need something and not find it. Her hair was thick and brown, her eyebrows were broad, and her nose was delicate. Her face was lightly freckled. She was taller than most women, and compared to other women seemed larger and stronger, and that made sense because she had grown up in a farming family—till Ishaq married her, when he was an outcast in Syria, thanks to his criticism of the Sultan, the father of Kaykhusraw, who later reconciled with Ishaq, asking him to return and apologizing to him.

I learned that only from her, and she had kept the Sultan's letter asking Ishaq to return to Anatolia with full immunity. He had written—in Turkmen—a poem that Safiya read to me and translated into Arabic:

You with the pure celestial self,
You who are the crown of fraternal assemblies,
My heart was filled with sorrow like Shah Jamshid's,

And I have become a homeless wayfarer, like a tiger in the desert

Or a whale in the sea,

Bereft of companionship. So, come!

It's time for you to return to us

And for you to seek a place here.

She was too bashful to continue, apparently fearful I would become jealous of Ishaq. Tempted to tease her, I asked, "Which of us do you love the most?"

But my attempt at humor failed, and tears suddenly came to her eyes, as if her worst fear had been realized. Then I embraced her, even as I laughed and told her, "You are the wife I love the most, and he is the friend I love the most."

"You are our Master, our Mawla, and our Teacher."

Eventually she became pregnant and in due time bore a son, who seemed to us a manifestation of God's mercy that had arrived in a time of dire need. I named him Sa'd al-Din—"Happiness of Religion"—because I was so happy with him. When I held him in my hands and contemplated his features, I found traces of Safiya's broad forehead and her thick eyebrows. I kissed him between his eyes and praised God for His blessings. I decided to take a spiritual retreat in a khanqah outside of Malatya in order to thank God. I informed Sawdakin that we were going there together, and he was delighted. We left the city with a single mule that we took turns riding till we reached the Sufi retreat a day later. We spent several weeks there with our brethren, dividing our time between vigils, fasting, and dhikr. There we encountered shaykhs from Balkh, disciples from Samarqand, and dervishes from Hamadan and Mosul. We fraternized with everyone staying at this khanqah all that time, and they included wayfarers who traveled from one Sufi house to the next, without any destination or plan. They carried with them only the wooden containers in which they collected alms. I read two books to them but ceased doing so, because they spoke so many languages that translation became a problem. We plunged into communal dhikr led by a trainer from Khoy. We did not know which Sufi order he belonged to or who his shaykh was, because each time we asked him where he was from, he replied, "From God." Whenever we asked where he was heading, he said, "To God." I asked him this question again when the two of us were alone, thinking he might be more forthcoming, but then he said, "God is the beginning. God is the path. God is the destination."

His statement amazed me, and I started spending time with him, but he didn't share any other statements. He spent most of the day by himself—by a lone apricot tree that grew against the wall of the khanqah—and spoke to no one. He would lower the edge of his tall cap over his face, cover his limbs with his thawb, leaving no part of his body exposed—till he looked like a long black tunic leaning against a tree.

Even though I longed to hear what he would say, I was repulsed by his extreme social distancing. I went to him one day when he was in that pose and asked, "If you want to be in spiritual retreat and isolate yourself, why do you stay in the khanqah?"

He raised his *qalansuwa* from his eyes and looked at me through strands of his shaggy hair, which was scattered over his face and forehead, smiled broadly, and replied, "Do you want a truthful answer?"

"Yes."

"For the food! It's delicious and wholesome."

A few days later, he disappeared. When we assembled for our morning gathering, he was missing. We saw no trace of him all day long. Then we learned that he had taken his belongings and continued his peregrinations. We wished him the best and prayed he would have a safe trip toward God. Then we returned to our affairs. Like any other fools, we assumed he was just an eccentric fellow. In the world of dervishes, it's not unusual to meet such people. There have long been fellow travelers who aren't real Sufis and men who lodge in khanqahs without belonging there. God continues to discipline and teach me, making me increasingly pious and conscious of my ignorance and lack of knowledge. *Bravo, bravo, Great Shaykh, Red Sulphur, the one to whom God grants unveilings and shows a vision of higher secrets! Your fourth pillar passed before you, and you didn't know it!*

92

I returned to Malatya a month later, accompanied by Sawdakin and four dervishes who had decided to follow me from the khanqah to Malatya to study with me. When we reached the city, I found waiting for me something I had not expected. I found my son Imad was living in my house.

Safiya finally said regretfully, "Fatima brought him and left. She said her husband insisted on leaving Malatya and could no longer bear to live here."

"Where have they gone?"

"To Mardin."

"How could she leave her child and depart? What kind of insanity is this?"

"Never mind, Master. I will raise him like my two sons."

Our household, which now consisted of me, Safiya, three boys, and two nanny-goats, was noisy. Should a guest arrive, I would not know where to seat him. If he asked to spend the night, I would not know where he could sleep. So I asked Sawdakin to find me another house with at least three private rooms. He toured Malatya's neighborhoods for several days in search of such a house without finding one. But he did find something else.

"The dervish who visited us in the khanqah, Master—do you remember him?"

"Yes. What about him?"

"He's sitting in the market and reading palms in exchange for food."

I nodded my head disinterestedly and returned to my reading. But Sawdakin interrupted again, asking, "Master, what's our view of chiromancy?"

"It is one of these three: gnosis, physiognomy, or trickery."

"Which heading do you think this dervish falls under?"

"Why do you ask, Sawdakin?"

"My soul tells me I should go have him read my palm—but I wanted to ask your advice first—to avoid causing any offense."

"Let's both go and see what sort of man he is. Where is he sitting?"

"Near the onion vendors, by the mosque."

"With God's permission, we'll go tomorrow."

Following the afternoon prayer, Sawdakin showed me where the dervish was. He was just the same as in the khanqah but looked thinner to me. He sat leaning against a wall of the mosque with his legs set before him like two poles that held up his wide, heavy, wool tunic. We approached to speak to him, but another man, who was closer, went to the dervish first and held out his palm.

The dervish pressed on the man's palm with a thin finger that ended with a rather long fingernail. Then he said, "You're not sick."

"But I'm in so much pain I can't sleep."

"Those are labor pains."

"How can it be labor when I'm a man? Are you mocking me?"

"It's not you who is going into labor. You're the site of the labor."

"Who is giving birth?"

"Your spirit."

"By God, you're mocking me, Satan!"

The furious man left the smiling dervish without paying him. As for me, I was touched then by what touches me when I experience an unveiling. Without any reflection, I turned to Sawdakin and said, "Leave us alone, Sawdakin."

Sawdakin was astonished but obeyed my request and moved away. I approached the dervish, and our eyes met as he continued to smile. The earth moved beneath me for some moments, and I sensed that I was taken by a state that had not been perfected yet but that I would soon land in. The moment Sawdakin reached the end of the alley and disappeared I said to the dervish, "How about this man who turned away, angry, because he does not know that it takes a kiln to fire clay?"

"Similarly, love is only consummated through pain."

"He assumes he's only born once."

"Whereas God creates him afresh every day."

"And he called you a devil."

"He assumes the devil is outside of him, not inside."

"What do we do with the devil within us?"

"He stays with us as long as we live. It's pointless to evict him. He's a part of us."

"How can we cleanse ourselves of his influence?"

"Fasting purifies your body; renunciation purifies your spirit."

"How do I purify my heart?"

"With love."

"You haven't read my palm yet, but you already know what's in my heart?"

"There is nothing in your heart but God, Muhyi."

Then he placed his hand on my shoulder and said, "I am your fourth pillar."

I threw myself on him and started kissing his head and beard while he patted my shoulder and pressed me to his chest fondly. My cascading tears wet his clothing. When I lifted my head, I saw that his tears were flowing with amazing serenity and that the smile on his face resembled dawn's first glow.

"What do I do now?"

"Do whatever you want and be whatever you are. God has fortified your heart with four pillars, and it will never sway after this."

"But I don't feel the steadfastness you mention, Master."

"That's because you persist in living in life. I tell you: allow life to live in you."

"I still feel perplexed about countless matters."

"Journey somewhere whenever you feel perplexed."

"I will, Master."

"Stay safe, Muhyi."

I kissed his hand, and he kissed mine. I walked to where Sawdakin had been waiting for me and leaned on him while experiencing a momentary vertigo. Then I remained where he had been standing while he went to have his palm read. Some minutes later he returned. We walked a few paces and turned down an alley. Then I felt an overwhelming desire to return to the dervish. I left Sawdakin standing there and raced back to where he was and found he had stood up and was preparing to walk away. Tall, lean, proceeding at a deliberate pace, he could have been a towering palm tree in motion. I followed him, calling after him, "Master! Master!"

With that same calm smile, he turned toward me and said, "Here I am, Dear Muhyi. What do you want?"

"I spent some time with each of my three former pillars, hearing from them while they heard from me—except for you. How can this be?"

"You have received from me something better than you received from them."

"What is it?"

"Love. It fills your heart like a sweet-water ocean where you will live peacefully despite all its breakers."

"But I long for your company and desire to see you."

"I will be with you wherever you settle and wherever you travel, because you are a Believer. Our religion is a religion of love, and all people are bound by a chain of hearts. When one link is broken, another link takes its place elsewhere."

"Will you remain here or travel?"

"I am an emissary to someone else, Muhyi, just as al-Hassar was an emissary to you. Do you remember al-Hassar?"

"Will I see you again?"

His eyes shone with happy satisfaction as he pressed both his hands against his chest and said, "Muhyi, I am your pillar. You will remain in my heart forever."

I imitated his gesture exactly, pressing both my hands against my chest, and asked him, "What is your name?"

He smiled the purest smile in the whole world and said, "I am Shams. Shams al-Tabrizi!"

93 HAMA 1982 CE/1402 AH

The city has burned to the ground. I can give no more precise description than this. Its houses, streets, mosques, squares, and markets. As well as our hearts, spirits, chests, corpses, and our breath itself. Everything went up in flames during the twenty-seven days that those demons descended on our city. They seemed to have accumulated a million years of rancor—since Iblis refused to bow down to Adam. These are modern demons with names unlike those of earlier devils. They are defense brigades, tank regiment 47, mechanical regiment 21, and battalion 21, airborne forces. Special Forces. They are all devils clad in different shades of khaki. Others were in civilian attire. They entered the city with a single mission: to kill. Nothing but to kill.

The curfew was finally lifted, and people went out to gauge the extent of their calamity. They walked down streets they didn't recognize. They passed neighborhoods they no longer knew. The sidewalk offered no clues. The mosque no longer welcomed worshippers. The market no longer sold to customers. Each pair of lungs had only a set number of breaths it could take in one day. Each heart had its own prescribed method of agonizing and could not borrow another heart's template. Every woman who had lost her child had two tears. Each widow had two griefs. Each orphan shuddered twice. These emotional reactions were rationed because there weren't enough to go around. Since no one in the outside world knew what had happened to us on account of the severe news embargo, it was impossible to import consolation from abroad. We had to console ourselves by ourselves or quit living—the way eighty minarets had quit offering the call to prayer.

People emerged from their tombs and wandered through the city. Live corpses mourning dead corpses. At no point during my trip from the Jarajimeh Neighborhood to that of Shaykh Anbar to visit my aunt did I see a single tear or hear even one moan. A downcast silence shaded the passing faces of people who seemed to fear their grief would be interpreted as sympathy for the victims—to their own detriment. For this reason, residents of the city had decided to grieve in an unemotional way and to coat their faces with a cosmetic plaster of Paris. This method had been devised to preserve sorrows in a stable physiological condition till the day came when weeping would be allowed. Then the plaster would dissolve, and we would weep. Even now, no one knows when that will happen. Even now, no one knows whether the incidents have ended or whether this is merely an armistice. A rumor is circulating among people that the ultimate goal is to liquidate the city and that convoys of bulldozers surround the city in preparation for its total eradication.

I reached my aunt's house armed with two possibilities: the possibility supported by my right arm that she was still alive and the possibility supported by my left that she had died. The possibility that she was alive was divided into two parts: either that she was fine or that she wasn't. Her death came with two other possibilities: her corpse was there—or—her corpse had disintegrated beneath the rubble of the building or had been buried in a mass grave. The possibility that physically she was healthy provided no guarantee that she was sane. The chance that she was ill opened a stream of other possibilities. What had I been able to do during those twenty-seven days besides cultivate those possibilities in the dry soil of despair and fear? The first four years of my life I had spent in the care of this aunt while my mother worked as a schoolteacher in Saudi Arabia. Whenever my mother returned on a holiday, she would tear me away from my aunt's care with no regard for my feelings.

Armed with all these possibilities, I entered the street where her building was located. I knocked on the door. It opened. I found her and embraced her. She buried her pale face in my breast and started to weep silently. I pressed my lips to her forehead and began to kiss her—just as silently. We moved into the apartment without letting go of one another so she could close the door. We passed the next ten minutes inhaling, unable to safeguard our exhalations. Finally the sound track was added to this silent film, and she asked me, "Where have you been, Auntie?"[43]

"Al-Jaramijeh has been locked down, Aunt. It was forbidden to enter or leave it."

"I told you to sleep here with me the night the events started, Son. Why didn't you? My heart was shredded worrying about you. I haven't slept for a month."

"Who could have seen this coming, Aunt? Not even Tamerlane did this to Hama."

Her thin hand reached out to close my mouth, and I smelt the fragrance of soap that always accompanies her hand now that she has succumbed to concerns about cleanliness as she ages.

She said, "Hush, son. Hush. We're defenseless! The walls have ears."

"There are no longer any walls, Aunt. How can they have ears?"

She pointed toward the heavens with her index finger and muttered an inaudible prayer. She was even afraid that augurs' ears would hear her pray. I gazed around at her apartment and found that everything there was just as I had seen it during my last visit before the events. Boxes of canned goods. Water bottles from which she had drunk half and left the remainder. All her belongings were packed in bags—ready for a quick escape. There were multiple images of the Virgin Mary scattered throughout the apartment so people would think she was Christian. She had made the huge cross herself from two intersecting boards and placed it at the center of the living room to fool any soldiers who stormed into the flat. Beside the large cross was a portrait of President Hafez al-Assad in military uniform, waving a hand that clutched artificial flowers.

"Where are my books, Auntie?"

She rose and headed to the corner, where she had hidden my bag the last time, and pulled it out from the other luggage to draw it toward me. I had told her last month, "This is the most valuable possession of the Nur al-Din Mosque's library!"

"The most important of the Muslim Brotherhood's books there, or what?"

"Not a single Brotherhood book. These are all Sufi."

"Does the Army know the difference?"

"I doubt it, but they definitely have lists of forbidden books."

I opened the valise and flipped through the books by Ibn Arabi inside it: *al-Futuhat*, *al-Fusus*, and *al-Rasa'il*. Manuscripts and copies. Those with commentaries and others that were summaries. I checked that they were all there and reassured myself. I closed the suitcase and returned to stretch out on the sofa, which was covered with tricot. I shut my eyes and tried to fall asleep but couldn't. Intermittent bursts of machine-gun fire were audible in the apartment. Hama's birds were also divided into warring factions. Crows cawed over the mounds of corpses they found in the streets while the doves that had cooed their laments for the people of Hama throughout the hostilities continued to do so.

It was some weeks later before the siege was lifted and people were permitted to leave the city. I left for Damascus with my suitcase. I wore a crucifix on a chain, since Muslims in Hama had begun to adopt crosses as a sign of innocence and neutrality. I had selected from my library dozens of books to establish my loyalty to the Baath Party and placed them in my suitcase to camouflage the rest of the books. I passed through twenty-nine checkpoints, where I had to remove all my clothes— except for my briefs that hid my loins—and stand naked before tired soldiers. They searched my bag book by book and didn't find any on their list. They took dozens of bribes from me in exchange for not sending the books to Intelligence for further scrutiny. I finally entered Damascus, for the first time in my life.

I stopped at a used book seller in al-Halbouni to rid myself of the camouflage books. I headed then to the Suleimaniya Tekkiye, where I filled my lungs with its cool air as soon as I entered its spacious courtyard. I walked to the eastern building, which I had never seen before, as if I went there every day. I knocked on several doors and walked down several corridors before I finally found myself before the Director of the War Museum. He looked up at me, through a gap between his glasses and his forehead without rising. I placed nine books on the surface of his desk and told him: "Since you are the director of a museum located in a Sufi Tekkiye, you alone will recognize the value of these books."

I picked up my empty suitcase and left his office as he began examining the books. He called after me, but I did not turn. I left the place swiftly and walked to the south bank of the Barada River. I sat there alone, opened my little notebook, and wrote these words. Then I opened the valise and ripped open its inner lining. I removed the small revolver and placed its barrel in my mouth.

TOME ELEVEN

"Every man is a minor scholar. A scholar is a major man."

——**IBN ARABI**

94

A year passed during which no one saw me but the Azeri herdsman who brought me food and water. I spent a spiritual retreat with God through all four seasons and found Him to be in each of them greater than any praise that escaped from my lips and nearer than my quavering heartbeats. I realized that He is the Companion on the Path that leads to Him. Had it not been for what I knew intuitively, I would have remained in His presence until He chose to draw me to Him. But while I may want something, He does what He wills. God chose me as a *qutb* for some mission, and now I would return to people to fulfill that mission.

I entered Malatya with all my possessions bundled together in a mat on my back. I noticed faces I recognized. They looked at me but could not place my features, because my hair had grown long, my torso had become lean, and my complexion had darkened. I went to my house and knocked on the door. Sadr al-Din opened it and yelled out my name loudly with a voice that had grown hoarser as he matured. Then he stepped forward and hugged me. Imad al-Din followed him, but Sa'd al-Din peeked fearfully between them, not knowing who was being so warmly embraced by his two brothers. I entered the house, and Safiya rushed to me with her hands coated with dough. She clasped my hand, kissed it, and wept.

That night, once the boys fell asleep, I sat on the edge of the tub, and Safiya washed my body, one part at a time.

She asked me, "How was your spiritual retreat, Master?"

"More delightful than anything I have experienced throughout my entire life."

"Are women also allowed to take a spiritual retreat?"

"Of course, Safiya. God's presence doesn't discriminate between male and female."

"But I would long for my children."

"They will grow up, and then you'll have more time."

"Do you know that Sadr al-Din has memorized all of the Qur'an?"

"That's the easy part. Now he must heed it."

"Imad al-Din won't memorize it. I don't know what to do with this boy. Has Sawdakin told you that he ran away from the mosque and returned home by himself?"

"Let's not find fault with a boy whose mother deserted him. He hasn't seen her for a long time."

"You're right. I wish she would visit him, so he could see her."

"We'll pass by her on our way and see her."

"Our way? Are we traveling somewhere?"

"Yes. To Damascus."

"Why Damascus?"

"Because Jesus, peace on him, will descend there on Judgment Day. My penitence, Safiya, has been linked to Jesus. So I want to die where he will first descend."

"How long will we stay there?"

"I told you: I want my death to occur at his place of descent."

We left on six mules in a caravan that traveled through the most beautiful spring I had ever witnessed. Anatolia seemed to be bidding us farewell while cloaked in the most beautiful garment from Nature's wardrobe. Once we left its borders, heads no longer sported the conical Seljuq hats and bore instead the graceful turbans of the Syrians. We spent a few days in Mardin but didn't find Fatima or her husband. People in the mosque told us that her father had gone on pilgrimage years earlier, had become an imam, and had not returned since. It seemed to me that Fatima had decided to sever her tie to us once she departed, leaving behind no trace or even a letter. She must have lied to Safiya that she would be in Mardin. That meant she had wanted to be free of Imad al-Din for good. May God help you, my little boy.

We reached Damascus, where we were met at its gates by leasing agents, each offering his property and describing it in the best possible fashion. We reached an agreement with one for a house with three private rooms so that I would never have to separate from Sawdakin. But he's the one who left me a few months later when he married and moved with his wife to a room attached to the neighborhood mosque. When we finally reached the house we had chosen, the three boys were exhausted. It was a structure that lacked a garden. Safiya soon obtained pots from the market and planted her shrubs in every corner of the house. Sawdakin bought some plaster and filled the obvious cracks in the house and created a doorstep for it. Everything found its place there. The three boys were in one room. Safiya and I were in another room. All my books, sheets of paper, and writing implements were stored with Sawdakin in his room. We received visitors in the central chamber around which the three rooms were arranged. We cooked in a corner of this living room.

Only a few weeks after my arrival, the Chief Justice Zaki ibn al-Zaki reserved for me a spacious corner of the Sumaysat Khanqah and dedicated to me a daily sum of thirty dirhems, which was more than I needed and less than he wanted to allot me. He escorted me to the assembly of King al-Mu'azzam Isa, who seemed to have got wind of my arrival in Damascus. He rose when I entered his assembly. Then he kissed his palm before pressing it to mine and said, "Welcome to our Shaykh! Welcome, welcome, welcome!"

He added nothing more to these repeated greetings, which I heard him use many times for other people entering his assembly. I didn't know whether he realized what his father had done to me in Cairo or whether his memory simply wasn't expansive enough to retain all the names of those his father had once imprisoned. It no longer mattered to me whether he had imprisoned me or not. When the entire world was represented in my heart, what difference was there between houses and prison cells? But at any rate, I didn't sense that I had any harm to fear from al-Malik al-Mu'azzam. In Damascus there was room for differences of opinion and disposition. In every neighborhood there was a school for this juridical doctrine or that. I myself visited all the schools of every doctrine whenever some issue perplexed me, I would visit the Shafi'is in the Atabeg School, the Hanafis in the Balkhiya School, the Malikis in the Grand Mosque, and the Hanbalis in the Umariya School. Over and above this, I taught a weekly lesson in the small Sufi khanqahs of Damascus and led dhikr sessions in outlying mausoleums.

Sawdakin married the daughter of the man who swept the mosque where we prayed. He encountered her father weeping near that mosque's mihrab one day, once people had left following the evening prayer, and inquired what had happened and tried to comfort him. The man said his wife had died, that he was elderly, and that he feared for his daughter's future. Sawdakin immediately asked to marry her, and the man agreed. I celebrated their marriage myself and gave him a dowry of two hundred dirhems for her—from surplus funds Ibn Zaki had given me. I also gave Safiya two hundred more dirhems, and she went to the market and bought the bride finery, clothing, pomades, and perfumes and fitted her out with these. I gave Sadr al-Din, who was an adolescent at the time, a hundred dirhems to buy furnishings, carpets, and kitchen equipment for their house. Then Sawdakin went to his bride after a bachelor party at the Sufi house. We wished him every success in life, and some of the dervishes danced for him. At this party they gave him colognes and herbs. He acknowledged their winks with enigmatic smiles.

Sawdakin's room in my house didn't remain empty long once he moved out. Only a few weeks after Sawdakin's marriage, Awhad al-Din Kirmani arrived from Malatya with his disciple Ayyub al-Muqri'. They knocked on my door, and I was delighted to welcome them, recalling the beautiful days I had spent with Kirmani in Malatya. I asked them about conditions in that land, and Kirmani replied with the enormous modesty and fond affection I had come to expect from him: "There was a drought, and the crops died."

"Really? What happened?"

"Its blessing was effaced, and its goodness was ripped out."

"I take refuge with God from His wrath. What happened, man?"

"The only thing that happened was that our Supreme Shaykh left that land."

I pinched his knee while I laughed, but his smile remained plastered on his face as if he really meant what he had said. Then he added, "Ayyub and I ask your permission, Master, to join you in Damascus."

"You are most welcome."

"You can achieve more by leniency than you can by force
but cannot achieve by force what you can by leniency."

—IBN ARABI

95

News came from Baghdad that Caliph al-Nasir had died. The Damascenes were astonished by his death, as if someone who had been caliph for forty-six years would not die. Baghdadis we knew in the tekkiyes and markets were anxious about their prospects, and some of them had known no other caliph since their birth. They were caught off guard and started discussing the matter as if something significant might occur in Baghdad following the demise of their long-lived caliph. People's intentions and motives differed. Many Baghdadis traveled home after residing for years in Damascus to avoid the Caliph's taxes, severity, tyranny, and other harms he had done them. As if to balance the scales, other people came to Damascus from Baghdad, fearful of the changing circumstances, the city's turmoil, the approach of the Mongols toward their borders, and the territorial ambitions of the survivors of the Khwarazmian Dynasty to their north.

Al-Malik al-Mu'azzam presided at a funeral service for Caliph al-Nasir and held a wake at which he received condolences from people who had not known the Caliph, who had not recognized him as their sovereign, and to whom he had been of no significance. I attended that wake, greeted the King, who welcomed me with his customary multiple salutations. His tongue loved to repeat "*Marhaban!*" automatically. All the same, he still remembered my name and patronymic. I sat beside the Qadi al-Qudat, the Chief Justice, who made room for me and, as usual, began to ask me how I was and what I needed or wanted. I thanked him and praised him. Then after a short silence, he turned to me and whispered, "I would like to offer you some advice, Master. Do you see the man who is greeting the King now?"

I looked at the massive, cleanshaven man, who was leaning on his son's shoulder and walking with difficulty, and replied, "Yes, I've seen him before but don't know who he is."

The Judge laughed and said, "I think you must be the only resident of Damascus who doesn't know who he is. This is Hibat Allah ibn Rawaha, the chief merchant of Damascus."

I smiled and said, "We're in different trades, and deal in different markets."

The Qadi laughed and commented, "There's no doubt about that. No doubt, Master. The important thing is that he visited me some days ago, wanting to fund the building of a madrasa dedicated to Shafi'i jurisprudence."

"Another Shafi'i madrasa? There are already nineteen of them in Damascus. Isn't that a bit much?"

"This is his legal sect. We shouldn't blame him. I agreed to his request and the decision has been made to build this madrasa near Bab al-Faradis. But what I wish to ask you concerns Taqi al-Din al-Shahrzuri."

"What about him?"

"Ibn Rawaha wants to put him in charge of this madrasa."

I nodded my head disinterestedly and replied, "That's his religious trust. He can select any principal for it he wants."

"But I need to grant my approval for directors of these schools. What do you think?"

"I have no opinion about this, Judge. You know there is some animosity between Sufis and the jurists. I fear that if I make a recommendation to you, I will be judging a man based on my animus toward him. So spare me this, and may God spare you."

Shortly thereafter I left the wake to return to my teaching, brooding about this new madrasa. I did not care whether it was affiliated with the Shafi'is or the Hanifis. What concerned me was the preponderance of schools teaching their students to hate Sufis, to denigrate the Sufis' importance, and to cast doubt on Sufis' beliefs. Every day, someone came to our khanqah to curse us and disparage what we say or claiming to be one of us in order to spy on us and report back to the madrasas what we say. Such a person might try to preach to us, grasping our hands, as if we were sinners. Glory to God! What they begrudged us was our love for God. Their intellects could not comprehend the esoteric; so they brought us the exoteric. How could I convince one of them in a few words truths that had taken me many years of spiritual retreats, solitude, reflection, and travel before God revealed them in an effusion? How could they grasp that God-given learning is not provided by instruction and not comprehensible via logic? Instead God reveals it to people who experience a taste, or *dhawq*, which their hearts imbibe before their intellects do, and their spirits before their eyes.

I entered the khanqah after the lesson had begun. Kirmani yielded back to my place as teacher after I had asked him to substitute for me while I attended the wake. I gestured to al-Muqri' to continue reading, which he did. But I was too preoccupied to pay attention to what he was reading. I was a *qutb*, a pillar, now. I had to adopt a stance and specify for Sufis what their states are, one protecting their honor and dignity. Taqi al-Din al-Shahzuri did not seem a bitter enemy; indeed, he was the least hostile to me of the lot. I decided that once the lesson ended, I would visit the Chief Justice and share with him the fears I harbored about feeding the anti-Sufi hostility perpetuated by schools of the four branches of Islamic jurisprudence.

I prayed with the Judge in his mosque, and he invited me to his house after prayers. In keeping with his longstanding practice, he had his children greet me, one by one. Even his daughters, who looked to me like young women of approximately the same age, came to welcome me, wearing long, light veils, while their father instructed them, "Greet our master. Benefit from his blessing and his beneficence."

Once all his children departed, I seized the opportunity to share with the Judge my reason for seeking him out. He contracted his eyebrows as he reflected deeply and tapped his lips with his fingers as he typically did when he was thinking. While still sunk in thought, he whispered, "You're right, Master. You are right."

"What can you do about the situation?"

He inhaled deeply, leaned back, and said, "Less than you think, Master. I cannot stipulate what they teach in their madrasas."

He remained silent for a time but eventually added shyly, "But you, Master, might not blame the jurists if you learned what some Sufis do in their khanqahs."

"What do they do?"

"I hope you will not construe my words as criticism—but dancing all night long and dhikr accompanied by tambourines and drumming make some jurisprudents dismiss the seriousness of instruction in Sufi houses."

"What else, Judge?"

He completed his statement while avoiding my eyes: "What some Sufis say, Master, is also hard for the populace to digest. How can ordinary people grasp that Pharaoh was a Believer? How can they comprehend that God and existence constitute a unity? How can they understand that divinity inheres in all religious icons, even idols?"

"I myself say all these things; me and no one else. If you harbor blame for me, tell me directly and don't generalize your comments."

"Excuse me, Master. I do not doubt the scope of your learning and the purity of your intent. But occasionally, I find no way to rebut people who complain to me about you. It is only fair—if we wish to defend Sufis against the harm done them by the jurists—for the Sufis to moderate their claims and to cease provoking the masses."

When he ended his statement, he looked up at me graciously, trying to discern my reaction. I took a few breaths to calm myself before answering. Then I decided not to reply. I rose and said, "You're right, Judge. I will reflect on what you have said."

"When I grew serious about inquiry and verification, they left me no friend among men."

——**IBN ARABI**

96

Sawdakin knocked on the door in a far more urgent way than normal. When Imad al-Din opened the door, Sawdakin kissed his forehead and shouted at him, "Where's our master?"

Soon we were both rushing toward his house. The moment we entered, he took his newborn son from the midwife's hands and placed him in mine as his eye flowed with tears. I whispered the call to prayer in the baby's ears.

Then Sawdakin suggested, "Pray that God will make him one of those who follow our path, Master."

"No, Sawdakin. The path to reality takes as many forms as there are travelers."

"Pray that God will make him one of the people of heaven, Master."

"No, Sawdakin. God created him on this earth, not above it. It is our mother."

"Pray to God to truly show him the Real and to shelter him from doubts."

"No, Sawdakin. Existence is all one big doubt. You yourself are all you know of it."

"Pray to God to bestow knowledge on him."

"No, Sawdakin. Knowledge dispels ignorance but doesn't bring happiness."

Sawdakin was at a loss then, but his happiness trumped his anxiety. Taking the newborn from me, he said, "Pray for him however you see fit, Master."

"I will ask God to make his heart resemble Mecca, where the fruits of everything are collected."

"Amen. May God never deprive us of your beautiful prayer, Master."

"What have you named him?"

"I named him: Tahir."

"That's not a family name for you. Why did you choose it?"

"He's named for a Cairo merchant I worked for when I first started on the path. He lent me money I could not repay. He forgave me that debt."

"Everyone named for him will possess a share."

I left the jubilant Sawdakin at his house. I was headed home but, when I entered the lane, caught sight of the Judge, who was waiting for me. I left him and retraced my steps. I began to prowl through the alleyways till I reached the covered market where I could spend time till the Judge departed. During the previous days I had received a series of his messages, which I had not answered. No doubt he was entertaining doubts about me, but I would not reply to him, no matter what, until we brought to justice the man who had fouled the door of the khanqah with cattle dung. I had submitted a complaint to the Judge but then saw that man walk past the khanqah daily, none the worse for his deed.

A messenger came to me from al-Malik al-Muʿazzam some days later summoning me to appear in his assembly. I learned that Qadi ibn al-Zaki was responsible for this invitation. I went to the assembly at the time specified. When I entered, I found the only people present were the King's courtiers and secretaries. He stood up when he saw me and kissed his own hand, with which he then seized mine as he greeted me. Then he gestured for me to sit down beside him and immediately said, "The Chief Justice has complained about you to us, Master."

"When the Judge lodges a complaint against you, who can adjudicate the claim!"

The King pretended to laugh and told me, "Perhaps you realize, then, the difficulty the King faces when forced to judge between the Supreme Shaykh and the Chief Justice. What a dilemma!"

I smiled but made no comment on his statement. Then he immediately said, "Listen, Master. The Qadi informed me that you lodged a complaint with him against the man who tossed excrement at the khanqah. That was no doubt a vile act, which we do not condone."

Then the King changed his tone and said in a low voice, "But, Master, neither the Judge nor I think it useful to punish the man. The cleft is too wide for any punishment to repair."

"Which cleft do you mean, Your Majesty?"

"You know what I mean, Master."

"If you would mention it yourself, doubt and uncertainty would be dispelled and removed."

"I am referring to *Fusus al-Hikam*, your latest book, which is currently being copied in the Stationers Market."

"What about it?"

"I will show you now 'what about it.'"

Then he shouted in a loud voice: "Scribe!"

A man carrying the King's inkstand rushed toward him from the edge of the chamber but stopped halfway and retraced his steps after the King said, "Bring the letters."

He was absent briefly and then returned with a stack of papers he placed in my hands. The King said to me, "Read them, Master, and judge for yourself."

Opening one letter after the other, I found that each contained a complaint to the King from some jurist about one, two, or three phrases in *Fusus al-Hikam* and a warning about how dangerous and misguided this book is. After the fifth letter, I stopped reading and looked up to find the King resting his chin on one hand and gazing at me with keen interest.

He finally said, "Do you see now, Master, that the matter goes far beyond an idiot tossing filth on the door?"

"What does Your Majesty the King think?"

"Master, you know best what you wrote. My learning does not come close to what God has given and disclosed to you. But I am responsible for political affairs. This book is upsetting the populace and riling people."

I remained silent. Then the King added in a more accommodating tone: "Master, this isn't Malatya, and the citizens aren't Turks."

Looking him straight in the eye, I responded, "You're right. And the rulers are Seljuqs!"

The King recoiled, surprised by my answer. He shouted at me, "What is this, Master! I show you favor. I consult you. Then you insult me in my own assembly!"

"This isn't intended as an insult, Your Majesty. It's a political fact. The Seljuqs have granted refuge to the Sufis out of love and conviction. The Ayyubids granted Sufis refuge to provide them defense against the Shi'ah."

The King shouted again, defensively: "This is an unjust suspicion, Master! You will find no *madhhab* that doesn't have a madrasa, a shaykh, and pupils in Damascus. You won't find another city in the Islamic World where every seeker of wisdom can attain his goal. So, be fair, Master, and look with the eye of truth!"

"This is exactly what I have tried to do, Your Majesty. All the schools of jurisprudence are to be found here. All of them for political reasons."

I stood up, preparing to depart, before he granted me permission. The King's eyes widened as he heard me say, before I departed, "King al-Mu'azzam, you should know that I am here in Damascus not for your sake or to shelter in your shade, for God's earth is vast, and God's shadow is even vaster. But I have grown old, have achieved my goal, and wish to die here, where Jesus—may God grant him peace—will descend and where his noble feet will alight first. If you restrict me, I will depart from constriction to roam free until God exchanges one for the other."

97

I turned sixty-three today—an important and serious milestone
—but no one around realized I was this old. My beard was no
whiter, nor was my back more bent. Safiya would set out for me
the same clothes she did every morning, and Sadr al-Din would
accompany me to the lesson and back, like every other day. I
would say some words, accomplish some things, eat, and breathe
the air like all those human beings treading this earth around
me. But I knew, better than anyone else, that reaching this age
was more significant for me than turning sixty-two or sixty-one.
This is the age by which an individual's conditions, words, and
deeds must change. It is the age at which my beloved Prophet—
may God bless him and grant him peace—died after delivering
his message and guiding his people. God did not grant to him
even one more year but did to me, a worthless miscreant. No
doubt the years God has granted me and denied to his beloved
friend will cost me dearly. *Woe to you, Muhyi, if you squander them*
on projects that aren't beneficial. Rise from your bed. Go teach. Proclaim
what you hold within you. Record the learning, discourse, and gnostic
insight God has unveiled to you.

Throughout the day a succession of thoughts came to my
mind—so many clusters of ideas, existents, and descents that I
could scarcely sort them out before the next wave flooded over
me. They were just like the swarms of locusts that had blanketed
the sky of Damascus days earlier and that still covered its alleys,
streets, walls, and roofs. These were large, powerful locusts that

wouldn't die even after you stepped on them twice. They scaled the trees, gnawed on leaves, copulated on the walls, slipped inside people's garments and turbans, and penetrated women's long veils so that you would find a woman twitching in public like a slaughtered goat, as she tried to dislodge the locust before she hastened on her way, even as small boys laughed at her. Every place in Damascus was filled with them, except for the khanqah where I taught. The locusts seemed to be avoiding it as if it were invisible. People said, "Even the locusts avoid the filth of the Sufis." Others remarked instead, "Even locusts won't harm Sufis, who are God's guests on this earth." Each person explained what he observed according to his predilections and frame of reference.

Even al-Malik al-Mu'azzam and the Chief Justice wished to observe this phenomenon for themselves. I was shocked when I was teaching to see them enter the Sufi house together, without any bodyguards or courtiers. From the distance the Judge waved to me, and the King merely smiled. Then they sat down modestly at the edge of the assembly. I finished my lesson as usual and, whenever I glanced in their direction, found them listening carefully and respectfully. I guessed they were there to reassure me after what had happened my last time in the King's assembly. When the lesson concluded, I greeted them and thanked them for coming. Then I escorted them to the khanqah's courtyard where we shared a meal. The dervishes brought us our customary fare of bread, milk, and grapes.

King al-Mu'azzam ate some and then commented, "What excellent food you have! I thought you were abstemious and austere?"

I was about to reply when the King's loud chortles stopped me. He patted my shoulder and said, "Just kidding, Master. Don't criticize me anymore; you've already criticized me enough recently."

Qadi Ibn al-Zaki spoke for the first time, remarking: "Al-Malik al-Mu'azzam and I have come to ask a question the jurisprudents were unable to answer."

I responded calmly, pretending that the question wasn't one that troubled or upset him and that he simply wanted to provide some pretext for their visit: "Please, King."

The King smiled courteously and said, "I wanted to ask you about those who say that Ali had more right to the Caliphate than Abu Bakr."

The Judge completed the King's question by adding, pointlessly, "You know, Master, Shi'is think Ali had more right to be the Caliph of the Prophet Muhammad, may God bless him and grant him peace, than anyone else, whereas the Sunnis think Abu Bakr did. And each group clings to their view. What do Sufis say about this matter?"

Everyone fell silent, and heads turned toward me, waiting for my response. I said, "As you know, King al-Mu'azzam, God's will supersedes any other will and His knowledge is superior to any other knowledge."

The King replied humbly, "You're right. Glory to God."

I continued, "Since God knew Abu Bakr would predecease Umar, Umar would predecease Uthman, and Uthman would predecease Ali, God chose a collective caliphate, and that is what happened."

The King nodded and looked genuinely interested. So I continued, "Our Exalted God knew in advance how long each of these four men would live. Then His volition gave each precedence according to the length of their life. Just that."

I turned to look at the Judge as I continued, "If both these groups would respect the will of our Exalted God and submit to it, there would be no problem. Then those who currently disagree would have nothing to disagree about and those who fight one another would have nothing to fight about."

The King, who clearly was reflecting on what I had said, proclaimed, "May God unveil the truth to you, Master."

Everyone said "Amen" to the King's prayer, and he rose and prepared to leave. I accompanied him to the door of the khanqah, where he kissed his palm and pressed mine with it. He left with the Qadi, surrounded by swarms of locusts, which leapt to flee from their steps and clung to their tunics. I waited till they vanished from sight at the end of the lane and then returned to my class, pondering deeply the significance of today's visit from the King and the fact that he had sat in on one of my classes. I feared that something was happening at the court and that the Chief Justice was part of it. As I looked at the faces of my students, who sat in a circle around me, and at the dervishes distributed through the khanqah, I wondered: even assuming I have enough clout and status to shield myself against the machinations of sultans and kings, what will become of these poor fellows?

This troubling thought haunted me for days and nights while I occupied myself with teaching and writing. I reflected on the fragility of the Sufi houses and the weakness of Eastern Sufis, who were totally dependent on religious trusts and the beneficence and approval of the ruler. Things were different in the West. My mind was preoccupied by political considerations for a long time. Then as I performed my prayers one night, I asked God to grant me some relief, and His intervention arrived rapidly when politics took care of itself. In a few months, strife drove a wedge between al-Malik al-Muʿazzam in Damascus and his brother al-Malik al-Kamil in Egypt. The Frankish Emperor Frederick landed his forces in Acre with the goal of taking Jerusalem while the Khwarazm Shah mobilized his forces in northern Iraq, intent on taking Baghdad. Al-Malik al-Muʿazzam found himself between three hostile, alien armies, any one of which might end his reign. He lost interest in the madrasas and khanqahs, the rumors spread by jurists, and the plots of fools. When I visited him to offer my condolences on the death of one of his ministers, he scarcely recognized me. His eyes were wandering, and the blood had drained from his face. I left his assembly feeling sad, and that was the last time I saw him. He succumbed to dysentery and died. We walked in his funeral procession to a spot in the desert, since he had instructed that he should be buried among paupers with no mausoleum or monument.

I forgot to ask him for a photo or what he looks like. I would have been calmer while I waited for him in the café, instead of constantly turning around to look the way I'm doing, making me seem as though I have a neck that doesn't support my head. Is this what happens before lovers meet—while they wait for each other in Corniche cafés? Do they gaze at everyone going or coming, waiting for the person who wrote those letters—like in the movies? What a life I've led till fifty-three—knowing nothing about such stories. I spent the first, Catholic, half of my life in a nuns' school and the Muslim half as a wife. Neither one faith nor the other allowed me to wait in a café for a lover. The pleasure of looking around, examining faces, and pondering possibilities while dreams rolled across a table with a tablecloth that was kept billowing by a sea breeze. I know these things don't necessarily lead to a happy marriage, as almost all my girlfriends have assured me, while envying me my affectionate husband and wonderful children. But something a woman never forgives herself is denying love a chance to set the edges of her heart ablaze one day and make it seem as noble and venerable as the pages of ancient manuscripts.

My heart, on the contrary, is still as fresh as if it were wrapped in plastic. Things happen around it, and situations pass by it, without it reacting. The only reason for this icy composure is that I am a very frank woman. Love requires imagination, and the imagination is a mosaic of little lies, that's all. Since I was a child, I was born with an intellect that could not invent a lie or program one. That's why I've never imagined anything, dreamt or hoped for anything. Instead, in exchange, I worked and applied myself, and lived up to expectations. A little machine in a feminine guise. Yes, this is the best way of describing how I was formed and the most appropriate justification for a loveless life. It is also what made me the happiest student in the nuns' school. Everything that happened in its porticoes totally agreed with me. I never once complained about the strict regimen guiding our school days. What I did complain about was the end of the school year when controls lessened a little and the nuns grew a little slack. Girls were let out early. They joked around. They threw acorns at each other. Before they reached their homes, they would have exchanged epithets on the way with a boy or two.

The waiter noticed my coffee cup was empty, picked it up, and departed. I looked at my watch. My appointment with him was for five p.m. From now on I would be able to blame him for being late or curse him if he did not come. But what would keep him from coming? Two thousand dollars was more than a Syrian refugee— who could scarcely find a bite to eat in Beirut, which is far more expensive than any Syrian city—would dream of. I carry all the bills in my handbag, in cash, ready to place them in his hand, when he gives me the manuscript. The autobiography of al-Shaykh al-Akbar Muhyi al-Din Ibn Arabi, the subject of the dissertation for which I was awarded my doctorate eighteen years ago.

I remember clearly the morning I defended my dissertation at the Sorbonne. It was in autumn and colder than I had expected. I spoke for four hours straight before a panel of seven French examiners about the symbolism and nihilist tendency in the thought of Ibn Arabi. A student who had no imagination and had never experienced love spoke for four hours about the Master of Love and the Professor of the Imagination in Islamic Sufism! That really was astonishing for me. Yes. I astonished myself in front of all of them. Then I astonished all of them when I revealed my big surprise to them right after my dissertation: I announced that I had converted to Islam!

At that time, I had to write a document that was much more difficult to write than my dissertation. This was a letter to my father responding to his letter in which he had accused me of abandoning Jesus the Savior. In several pages I wrote in a café like this one, where I'm waiting for the Syrian refugee today—but in Paris—I explained to him how Ibn Arabi had brought me to Jesus by another path. Didn't he always repeat that he was guided by Jesus? This had first attracted me to him when I read:

There are four bodies: the body of Adam, the body of Eve, the body of the offspring of Adam and Eve, and the body of Jesus. God created Adam without a male or a female. He created Eve from a male but without a female. He created their offspring from a male and a female. He created Jesus from a female without a male.

I felt very connected to Ibn Arabi that day. After spending years with Ibn Arabi, I no longer knew which had led me to the other: Jesus or Ibn Arabi? I wasted no time trying to answer this chicken-egg question. I was certain that they united to form a unitary belief that suited me perfectly. I believed in both and became a Muslim woman guided by Jesus on the path of al-Shaykh al-Akbar.

Because no one could live with such a complex creedal identity in a country like Lebanon, I remained in France and married Raimond, who was one of the seven adjudicators I surprised by announcing my conversion to Islam at my dissertation defense. In the course of nine years we had three children—Roger, Manu, and André—and traveled to Murcia, Seville, Fez, Tunis, Cairo, Damascus, Aleppo, Konya, and Malatya in an attempt to follow the spiritual voyage of Ibn Arabi; but this attempt failed. Raimond said we failed on account of the chain's missing link: we couldn't visit Mecca, because he was Christian. Mecca thus was the essential spiritual hub for Ibn Arabi. Our excursion, however, was the basis for our first joint research paper on the spiritual geography of the life of the Master Shaykh. We wrote another paper on chemistry and theurgy in the incarnational philosophy of Ibn Arabi. We wrote yet another paper on his symbolic passage between the Sufi stations. There was another on his phenomenological states. One on the finite and infinite in his cosmic view. Writing about him contributed both to our intellectual development and to our ascent of the academic ladder. Even lovemaking was more satisfactory after a dinner table discussion of Ibn Arabi.

He finally arrived. Extremely thin, hollow cheeks, wearing black trousers and a denim jacket. Curly hair, a soft voice. He greeted me very courteously and sat down. I fixed my eyes on the cloth bag that he hung from the side of his chair before he took a seat. I wanted to reach inside that bag and touch the manuscript that had brought me all the way to Beirut from Paris. He ordered coffee. Then, observing how curious I was, he finally put his hand in the bag, brought out the manuscript, and placed it before me.

"Here it is, Madame."

"How do I know it's authentic?"

He laughed nonchalantly and shrugged his shoulders. "I don't know! I personally do not know whether it is authentic or not."

"Where did you get it?"

"I found it in my late brother's room. It was in the box in which he placed his valuables."

"Have you shown it to an expert on manuscripts to authenticate it?"

He smiled slightly and made a short deprecatory sound to express his indifference. He asked, "Madame, where in Damascus would I find an expert who would give me the time of day? And if it clearly was genuine, how would I know he would return it to me?"

"How can I be sure you're not selling me a forged manuscript?"

He shrugged his shoulders and raised his eyebrows but said nothing. I knew I would have no trouble authenticating the manuscript in Paris. My colleagues in the manuscript department could easily run the necessary carbon-dating tests. I would also have no problem asking an expert to compare the handwriting to that of authentic manuscripts in the handwriting of Ibn Arabi. But I also didn't want to seem an idiot who would travel from Paris to Beirut on account of a manuscript offered for sale on the internet and pay the vendor two thousand dollars for a forgery!

"I'm sorry, Madame. You have a right to question the genuineness of the manuscript, but, frankly and truthfully, I know nothing about manuscripts. All I know is that my brother purchased quite a few and spent a long time examining and copying them. I think he would not have preserved this manuscript in a locked box if it weren't quite valuable."

Then he shrugged his shoulders again and continued, "I am, by contrast, a brass connoisseur. Show me a piece of brass, and I'll tell you which artisan struck it out of all those in al-Hamidiya Souk!"

"Fine. Fine."

I brought the bills out of my handbag and placed them on the table. He took them, thanked me, said goodbye, and departed. Before he was out the door of the café, he came back and returned to where I still sat. He asked to borrow a pen from the waiter and wrote his telephone number on the napkin that came with his coffee and handed it to me.

He said, "This is my number in Beirut. If you find the manuscript is a fake, I will try to return the money to you."

There was a tear in his eye when he added, "I don't want to do anything that would stain the honor of my late brother."

"Sufism devoid of morality is worthless."

——IBN ARABI

99

Sadr al-Din became an adolescent, and his zeal to pursue learning grew so intense that I no longer felt I could satisfy it. I split responsibility for instructing him with Kirmani after I gave Sadr al-Din some advice I think he will never forget. I secluded myself with him in the khanqah, drew him close to me, grasped his earlobe, and pinched it so forcefully that he winced with pain. Then I told him, "Shaykh Kirmani was one of your father's companions and is one of the best people who follow the Sufi path. What he knows will be useful to you, and he possesses the type of taste called *dhawq*, but. . ."

Squeezing his ear tighter to make him pay attention to me with every one of his senses, I continued, "But he is smitten with the beauty of young men!"

Sadr al-Din's eyes grew wide with astonishment at what I said after he had closed them because the pain was so intense. His mouth fell open as if he had heard something shocking and unpleasant. "What?"

"You heard what I said. Don't make me spell it out for you and criticize my companion. Learn from him but draw a line there. Only sit with him at the khanqah. No place else. And be on guard!"

"Yes, Master."

I let go of his ear, and its lobe turned red. The boy's head remained bowed as he tried to digest what I had told him. I harbored no doubts about Kirmani's piety and merit but realized that he was no more protected against God's cunning than I was.

I hoped Sadr al-Din would soon be able to grow a beard so I could stop worrying about him whenever he was out of sight.[44]

Imad al-Din, on the other hand, would only come if I shouted. He would not obey an order until I had spoken harshly to him. He would only stop doing something when I slapped his thigh or pinched his arm. He had become a boy whose only interest was in playing ball or backgammon in our neighborhood's alleys. I took him to the khanqah repeatedly, but the moment my eye left him, he rushed outside, trading barbs with the holy fools gathered at the doorway. He would taunt and tease them; then they would chase him to the end of the lane. At that point they would turn back, and he would as well. One day a simpleton named Ya'qub grabbed his occiput and dragged him into the middle of the courtyard where the lesson was in progress. I was reading to my pupils when Ya'qub shouted, "Keep this son of yours away from us! If you don't, I'll crush his bones!"

Some of my students rose to thrash the fool for his bad behavior and others rose to protect him from the first group. Imad al-Din escaped from Ya'qub's hands and fled, as if he hadn't been responsible for turning the khanqah head over heels. When I returned home, I didn't find him there. He roamed the neighborhood till I fell asleep. Then he slipped into the house, entered his room, and slept between his two brothers as if he hadn't done anything. When we rose in the morning, he popped out of bed and headed to the mosque before I did so I would forgive him. I forgave him, since there was little else that I could do. But he wasn't deterred.

He returned home one day weeping bitterly, even though he hadn't cried for the past two years. Safiya was the only one at home, and she was alarmed when he returned home earlier than usual, weeping unexpectedly. She questioned him till she grew tired of it but couldn't get him to explain what was wrong. He filled a jug with water and propped it against the door to the boys' room so she wouldn't enter. He stayed in his room all day long, and all Safiya heard was his moaning. When I returned, she told me. I asked him what had upset him, but he didn't reply. Then I delegated the task to Sadr al-Din, who informed me before I went to sleep that the holy fools had knocked him down that day and poured hot pepper between his buttocks. Imad al-Din left the mendicant fools alone after that; if he even saw one at the end of the lane, he would stop and retreat or head down some other alley.

The pepper must have stung terribly to impact my son Imad this way, but in a few weeks the inhabitants of Damascus suffered a far greater pain. Even if the sky had poured down torrents of rain and high winds had filled their noses, eyes, throats, hearts, and spirits with hot pepper, people would not have suffered so bitterly. You could not walk along a lane without hearing wails and laments. You could not enter the mosque without hearing people repeating: "All power and strength are God's alone" and moaning. You could not walk through the market without observing people's griefs and pains. The king, al-Kamil, had ceded Jerusalem to the Frankish Emperor in a peace treaty. Had the Franks taken that city by force, in a war, through combat, that would have been easier and lighter for the souls of the Muslims to bear—especially older men like me who had witnessed the day Salah al-Din had recovered Jerusalem. Now they witnessed the day one of his grandsons returned Jerusalem to the Franks voluntarily!

Al-Malik al-Nasir Dawud, who had ascended the throne of Damascus, announced a period of mourning. At that time the weeping grew more intense and the wailing more prevalent, as funeral rites were held. Pupils and dervishes in our khanqah were as inflamed as anyone outside it. They repeatedly interrupted my lesson with questions unrelated to the book we were reading or to the topic we were studying. They kept asking about Jerusalem, jihad, obedience, and things their souls were experiencing, making their blood boil. Even Sawdakin, who was still preoccupied by his baby who was learning to crawl and walk, bought a sword, armor, and a helmet, on the assumption that al-Nasir Dawud would soon launch a jihad to take back Jerusalem.

But no one was able to leave Damascus, whether for jihad or any other reason, because al-Nasir Dawud did not proclaim a jihad or mobilize an army. Instead he organized a festival in the courtyard of the Grand Mosque. In it, preachers and poets competed to create panegyrics for his uncle al-Kamil and elegies for the Sacred City of Jerusalem. Then authentic sorrow became mixed with political mischief. Al-Kamil, for his part, as soon as he had relinquished Jerusalem to the Franks, headed toward Damascus to wrest it from his nephew. He laid siege to us for a year, during which members of the elite were harmed by the disruption of the flow of river water into the canals, the plunder of produce from estates in the Ghouta, and the exorbitant increase in prices. Sufis, who consumed bread and milk at all times, did not feel the pinch. They laid siege to themselves constantly and therefore did not feel the external siege during hard times. Unlike the sorrows and griefs, the political earthquakes that shook Damascus brought security and tranquility for me and my students. The more that people were preoccupied by who was living in the palace, the less they muttered about those living in Sufi retreats.

"Subsistence not followed by annihilation should not be trusted."

—IBN ARABI

100

The seventy years that had descended heavily on my back had sharp claws. I first decried my memory. I would walk down a lane on some errand, go halfway, and then not remember where I had come from or where I was heading. Then I decried my joints, because I could not stand or sit down without them cracking loudly, as if I were in a blacksmith's shop. Safiya rubbed my knees with a mixture of meadow saffron and camphor oil every night, but that didn't help. I had begun to sway as I walked and to stretch out my legs while I sat, to avoid bending my knees. Death had sent me so many messages and heralds that I would have no reason to be surprised by its sudden arrival, day or night. My hair had turned white, my back had become bent, my pains had increased, my vision had weakened, I had lost much of my hearing, and my memory was fading. As if that were not bad enough, my companions and associates had left me for the company of the Exalted, Forgiving God. I had exhausted myself by walking in their funeral processions when they died in Damascus or hearing the news when they died elsewhere. My companion Abd Allah the Armenian, who was known for his charisms, Bayram al-Mardini who was known for his spiritual retreats, al-Suhrawardi who was distinguished by his manly virtues, and Ibn al-Farid, author of *al-Ta'iyyat*, had all passed. The only one left waiting to join them was Muhyi al-Din Ibn Arabi, who was known for his offenses, sins, and regrets!

I could no longer even sit through an entire class. I would deputize a student to read the book while other students listened until he had finished. Then they asked questions. If a question came up more than once, I deputized Sawdakin or an outstanding student to answer for me. Sawdakin was my only remaining companion. Kirmani had left for Cairo, taking Sadr al-Din with him, and I had encouraged them to do that, because there was nothing further for either of them to learn in Damascus, no book they had not both read, and no shaykh they had not questioned. Sa'd al-Din had grown up and started to accompany me to the khanqah, where he would sit listening calmly and silently. But he would not make any comments or ask any questions. As for his older brother, days passed without my seeing him, except by chance before I went to bed or just as I woke up. He had purchased a large cage in which he raised various types of birds, some of which he sold in the souk. He and his mates played with the others. When Damascus was struck by a heavy downpour, which destroyed houses and hostelries, and the water level rose head high in some neighborhoods, water filled the cage and his birds perished. Then he grieved for them dramatically—as if the entire religion of Islam had collapsed and become alien.

Members of the Ayyubid family ruled Damascus in succession. One would follow his brother and another his father until I could no longer remember at times who ruled us. I would remember only when a preacher offered a prayer at the mosque for the current king. The moment I left the mosque I would have forgotten. My students told me one day that al-Nasir Dawud had moved his army from Kerak and retaken Jerusalem from the Franks, and I wept with happiness. Then the next day I concluded my class with the familiar prayer for God to return Jerusalem to us. At the time I didn't realize why students looked at me so compassionately then. But from the concatenation of all these phenomena I realized that I had reached an age when life was more stressful than death.

This suffering at the loss of my health and the death of my companions soon stretched even to my pocketbook as poverty struck me. Ibn al-Zaki and his brothers had stopped bankrolling me—to pressure me—after complaints against me multiplied. The religious trust fund, the waqf, that had supported the khanqah was destroyed by the flood. One day I found I didn't have enough money to pay our household expenses. Safiya tolerated this matter for a time but then complained that she didn't have enough to buy food for our supper. We fed Sa'd al-Din the last loaf of bread, and the only thing left in the basket was a few dates. So we went to bed hungry that night. The next morning my empty belly reminded me of the state of my pocketbook. I left the house and walked in the opposite direction, not to the khanqah but to the Ghouta. I stood there with men waiting for someone to hire them to work in the fields. Most of the men standing with me were picked, except for me. People were put off by my white hair and bent back; they also passed on hiring a cripple and an unusually short fellow. We three sat down, waiting for fortune to find its way to us until the sun was in the zenith of the sky. Then a man came and hired all of us. He sent the two other men to the field and took me with him to a small orchard near his house. I continued pruning trees, gathering leaves, picking fruit, and watering the plants till evening. His wife fed me, and he gave me a couple of dirhems to buy supper for Safiya and Sa'd al-Din.

I did this for eight months or perhaps nine. I no longer remember. I began at the end of last winter and here I am at the doorstep of another winter. Students came to my house when they missed me at the khanqah, and I told them I would not be going there anymore. I named those I trusted to teach my books, and they left. Sawdakin assumed I was sequestering myself and sequestered himself outside of Damascus. My path going to and coming from the orchard became my daily routine. My knees would occasionally groan with pain, and I would sit down repeatedly before I finally reached the orchard. There I started with the easy tasks, fearing that the more challenging ones would leave me exhausted before I finished. I would scatter grain for the chickens and clean their coop. I would collect the eggs in a basket and place it at the couple's door. Then I would rake the leaves that had fallen and start the water flowing in the canals. None of this hurt my back. By the time I finished sweeping up the dirt, the broom would feel heavy. I opened the irrigation canals with my hands after I was unable to carry the hoe. My arms failed me and wouldn't reach fruit that was slightly too high.

This work became increasingly taxing till I spent an entire day doing what I had previously finished in half a day. But I could think of no easier job than this while hiding from people's eyes. I had learned that if I apologized for my books and retracted everything I had said, money would flow again, and my life would be easy. But we reach an age when retracting statements is far more bitter than senility and physical pain. I would never return to Ibn Zaki or to the principal of the khanqah to ask for a dinar or two. I would work in this orchard as long as I could stand on my feet, eating from the labor of my hand until God chose to draw me beside him and seat me in His house, where there is no labor or fatigue.

By the middle of winter, it was increasingly cold and frigid. The wind traversing the narrow alleys almost swept me off my feet if I were walking into it. I left my house with the end of my turban wrapped around me, wearing a thick wool cloak, and found the streets in tumult. Waves of people were shouting in the alleys, reciting the call to prayer, and repeating "Allahu Akbar." Boys knocked on doors, asking men to join them. I avoided the crowds, in which people were packed together as in in a war, and hugged the walls, trying to reach the orchard on time. But the lane I entered became increasingly crowded, and people grew ever rowdier. Whiplashes fell on old men, boys, and youths—individuals who were rioting and those just passing by—like me. A whip struck me on the shoulder and cheek, and I fell to the ground. The feet of the crowd trod on me, and my head banged against the wall of a house. I stood up with difficulty—my joints groaning with pain. I felt very dizzy and close to fainting. I pressed against the wall to keep from falling and sheltered my body on the doorstep of a house. A crowd of people was running down the alley, their backs stung by the whips. Their shouts grew increasingly louder as they started to hurl rocks at the soldiers. I stood up when I felt I had regained enough strength and walked a little until someone's hand caught my *thawb* and I fell again. I choked on the dust that was kicked up by fleeing feet and horses' hooves. A rock ricocheted off a soldier's armor and hit my jaw, knocking me to the ground once more. I knew I wouldn't be able to stand up. I covered my head with my hands and shouted to God: "Your grace, Gracious God!" I think I lost consciousness for a time; I'm not sure.

When I came to, I found myself covered with dirt and my turban untied. A line of blood ran from my mouth, which contained a loose tooth. The alley was less crowded—most of the people had fled and dispersed. I could hear their chants in the distance, and youngsters passing by me repeated them. One boy saw me stretched out on the ground, unable to rise unassisted. He rushed to me, reached out his hand, and said, "May God repay you, Shaykh. May God reward your suffering for the truth."

Then he turned to a companion and said, "What excuse do we have if we don't free al-Izz ibn Abd al-Salam from prison, when we are men with sound bodies, when this elderly man has turned out to support him and been severely injured?"

The youth took my arm and helped me stand up, and the pain I felt in my ribs was excruciating. I touched my chest and observed a painful projection that suggested that one or two ribs had been broken. I stood there considering what to do. If I continued walking to the orchard, I wouldn't be able to perform any work. If I had broken a rib, I wouldn't be able to do any chores. If I returned home, I would go to bed without any supper. I decided to continue to the orchard. If my rib was broken, the pain would persist for many days. Why should I add the pain of hunger to the pain of my rib?

I finally reached the orchard. I pressed my left arm over my broken rib and started doing my chores. I dropped an egg, and it broke. When I let the water into the irrigation channels, I sat down to rest. I collected the leaves and picked some fruit before stopping, gasping for breath. I felt blood rushing to my head, as if I were standing on it and not on my feet. I sat down to catch my breath. When I tried to stand up once more, the earth rocked before me, and I fell flat on my face. The chickens scattered around me in alarm. My eyes fixed on a yellow leaf I hadn't swept up, and I died.

Life in the *barzakh*, in the liminal state before and after life, is easy. You con-template life bereft of volition. You don't act; you don't react. A man and a woman carry you into an unfamiliar house. They feel your pulse, repeat that all power and strength are God's alone. Then they hide the world from you with your cloak. The litter bears you to a familiar house. I hear their voices and detect their scents. If my eyelids move, I notice their weeping faces. Safiya weeps at being widowed a second time. Sawdakin is clutching my feet as if he might not bury them with me. Sa'd al-Din is trembling like a sparrow on a rainy night. Ibn al-Zaki is delivering his instructions to the washer, whose hand explores my chest, belly and limbs. Imad al-Din pours water over my head. As the camphor water pours over my head, he blocks my nostrils, so I won't smell it. The fabric of the shroud envelops me, blocking my view. My body sways on the shoulders of the men bearing me. It finally lies by the mihrab of the mosque. The call to prayer resounds. The imam leads the prayer. He does not recite the Qur'an surah called "Ya Sin." People pick me up, wails ring out. I make out the voices of my students. I hear the clatter of their sandals. The voices dwindle and seem farther away as the dirt heaps up. The last sound I hear is a fiery scream Sawdakin released involuntarily.

MOHAMMED HASAN ALWAN

Toronto 2016

TRANSLATOR'S NOTE

Since this novel contains technical terms from works by Ibn Arabi, I have consulted some relevant works of scholarship on this major figure in Islamic thought—including especially Claude Addas, *Quest for the Red Sulphur*, and William C. Chittick, *Ibn al-'Arabi's Metaphysics of the Imagination*. Barbara Teresi lists in her Italian translation of this novel sources for its epigraphs, on page 541, without identifying pages individually.

The plot of this novel involves Ibn Arabi's attempt to contact his four pillars and thus become a pole. Understanding these roles is important for the reader of *Ibn Arabi's Small Death*, and Addas, on page 65 of her book, provides a succinct explanation: "At the summit of the pyramid [of initiation] are the four Pillars (*awtad*), with first of all the Pole (*qutb*), followed by [the other three]. . . . The true holders of these functions are the four prophets, who are considered by Islamic tradition to be always living: Idris, Jesus, Elijah, and Khadir. . . . Each of these prophets . . . has a substitute (*na'ib*) in the world below: a man who fulfills the function in question."

ENDNOTES

1   Qur'an, Hud, 11:67 and Al-Ahqaf (Winding Sands) 46:24

2   Qur'an, Al-Nasr (The Victory) 110:1

3   Qur'an, Ya Sin 36:12

4   Qur'an, Ya Sin 36:43

5   Qur'an, Ya Sin 36:65

6   Qur'an, Ya Sin 36:65

7   Qur'an, Ya Sin 36:76

8   Qur'an, Ya Sin 36:59

9   Qur'an, Ya Sin 36:1-3

10 Qur'an, Ya Sin 36:4-6

11 See al-Ghazali's complete text in *Averroes' Tahafut al-Tahafut (The Incoherence of the Incoherence)* translated by Simon Van Den Bergh (Cambridge: E.J.W. Gibb Memorial Trust, 1987).

12 Part of a poem attributed to Muhammad ibn Muqla.

13 Qur'an, Al-Nisa'a (The Women) 4:43.

14 Qur'an, Al-Kawthar (Kawthar) 108:1.

15 Qur'an, Al-Rahman (The Merciful) 55:64.

16 Cf. Qur'an, Tahrim (Sanctification) 66:12 and Al Imran (The Family of Imran) 3:37 and 3: 42-43.

17 *al-Musta'in*, a pharmaceutical book that the Andalusian physician Yusuf al-Baklarish al-Isra'ili dedicated to al-Musta'in-billah, the emir of Zaragoza.

18 See William C. Chittick, *The Sufi Path of Knowledge*, pp. 229-230.

19 Qur'an, Al-Nisa'a (The Women) 4:157.

20 Claude Addas in *Quest for Red Sulphur*, p. 116, tells a slightly different version of this story, and identifies the miracle-worker walking on the sea as Khadir aka Khidr, Khezr,

etc., who is frequently identified as the mysterious sage who instructs Moses in the Qur'an.

21 Algiers

22 See Claude Addas, p. 19.

23 Ahmad Abu al-Abbas al-Sabti was a Sufi saint who died in Marrakech in 1205 CE.

24 Qur'an, Al-Naml (The Ants) 27:37

25 Qur'an, Ta Ha 20:55

26 Qur'an, Al-Duha, (Morning Light) 93:3

27 For an alternative version of this dream vision see Claude Addas, *Quest for Red Sulphur*, p. 178.

28 Yemma Gouraya

29 Qur'an, Ya Sin (Ya Sin) 36:1-2

30 Aqaba

31 Qur'an, 57: 23 Al-Hadid (Iron)

32 Claude Addas in *Quest for Red Sulphur* provides an alternative account of the incident at the Ka'aba, pp. 208-211.

33 Qur'an 95: 3, Al-Tin, (The Fig)

34 See: Qur'an, 18: 9 ff Al-Kahf (The Cave)

35 Qur'an: Ahl al-Kahf (The People of the Cave) 18:103-104

36 Qur'an 27:7 Al-Naml (The Ants)

37 Qur'an 93: 3 Al-Duha (Morning Light)

38 *Bahalil* (plural of *bahlul*); see Claude Addas, *Quest for Red Sulphur*, page 88, for Ibn Arabi's three categories of demented, holy people.

39 This chapter is attributed to the Algerian resistance and spiritual leader Abdelkader ibn Muhieddine, who died in Damascus in 1883 CE.

40 Translator's Note: I have chosen to follow Claude Addas for the names of these two shaykhs: Abu al-Abbas al-Uraybi and Abu Imran Musa ibn Imran al-Mirtuli. See: Addas, Claude. *Quest for the Red Sulphur: The Life of Ibn 'Arabi*, trans. Peter Kingsley (Cambridge, [UK]: The Islamic Texts Society, 1993) pp. 68-69.

41 Ibn Arabi, *Al-Futuhat al-Makkiy*

42 Qur'an, 55:29 Al-Rahman

43 Translator's note: This reversal ("Aunt" for "Nephew") is a Levantine custom.

44 See Claude Addas, *Quest for Red Sulphur*, pp. 228-229.

TRANSLATOR'S BRIEF BIBLIOGRAPHY

Addas, Claude. *Quest for the Red Sulphur: The Life of Ibn 'Arabi*. Translated by Peter Kingsley. Cambridge, [UK]: The Islamic Texts Society, 1993.

Alwan, Mohamed Hasan. *Una Piccola Morte*. Translated to Italian by Barbara Teresi. Roma: edizioni e/o, 2019.

Badr al-Habashi, Abdallah. *Inbah 'Ala Tariq Allah min Kalam al-Shaykh*. Damascus: as-Siddiq lil-'Ulum, 2016.

Bolens, Lucie. *L'Andalousie Du Quotidien Au Sacré (XIe-XIIIe Siècles)*. Collected Studies Series CS337. Brookfield, VT: Variorum, 1990.

Chittick, William C. *Ibn al-'Arabi's Metaphysics of the Imagination: The Sufi Path of Knowledge*. Albany: State University of New York Press, 1989.

Hava, J.G., *Al-Faraid Arabic-English Dictionary*. Beirut: Catholic Press, 1964.

Hopkins, J.F. P. *Medieval Muslim Government in Barbary until the Sixth Century of the Hijra*. London: Luzac & Company, Ltd., 1958.

Ibn Razīn al-Tujībī. *Faḍālat al-khiwān fī ṭayyibāt al-ṭa 'ām wa-al-alwān: Ṣurat min fann al-ṭabkh fī al-Andalus wa-al-Maghrib fī bidāyat 'aṣr Banī Marīn*. Edited by Muhammad B.A. Benchekroun. Beirut, Lebanon: Dar al-Gharb al-Islami, 1984.

Zaouali, Lilia. *Medieval Cuisine of the Islamic World: A Concise History with 174 Recipes*. American ed. California Studies in Food and Culture 18. Berkeley: University of California Press, 2007. *https://adamahmed.blogspot.com/2010/06/would-that-i-could-tell-if-they-had.html* accessed January 14, 2020

ABOUT THE AUTHOR

Mohammed Hasan Alwan, a Saudi Arabian novelist, was born in Riyadh, Saudi Arabia, in 1979. He earned a B.A. from King Saud University in 2002, an MBA from Portland State in 2008, and a Ph.D. from the University of Carleton in Ottawa, Canada. He currently lives in Canada. He won the 10th International Prize for Arabic Fiction (IPAF) in 2017, for *Mawtun Saghirun* (A Small Death).

Alwan commented on this occasion:

> It might seem odd to choose to write a novel about Ibn 'Arabi with all those extreme Eastern concepts, whilst residing in this distant cold corner of the world in Canada. I often think about this. So, at first, I directly linked it to me feeling nostalgic. Then I realized that being exposed to what is seemingly foreign or different is what drives me to reconnect with myself, as well as with my heritage and old culture.

Alwan has published four other novels: *Saqf al-Kifaya* (The Ceiling of Sufficiency, 2002), *Sophia* (2004), *Tawq al-Tahara* (The Collar of Purity, 2007), *al-Qundus* (The Beaver, 2011) and *Jirma al-Turjuman* (Germa the Interpreter, 2020). His scholarly work, *Migration: Theories and Key Factors* was published in 2014.

In 2009-10, Alwan was chosen as one of the 39 best Arab authors under the age of 40 by the Beirut39 project and his selection was published in *Beirut39*, an anthology. He also participated in an International Prize for Arabic Fiction Nadwa (writers' workshop) in 2009 and served as a mentor for its Nadwa in 2016. In 2013, his novel *al-Qundus* was shortlisted for the International Prize for Arabic Fiction and in 2015 its French translation won the Prix de la Littérature Arabe for the best Arabic novel translated into French that year.